ELISABETH
Passage of Promise

ELISABETH

Passage of Promise

a novel

TOM ROULSTONE

Covenant Communications, Inc.

Published by Covenant Communications, Inc.
American Fork, Utah

Printed in Canada
First Printing: July 2004

11 10 09 08 07 06 05 04   10 9 8 7 6 5 4 3 2

ISBN 1-59156-531-6

Acknowledgments

My thanks go out to all of you who have read my previous novels *One Against the Wilderness* and *Fleeing Babylon*. If it had not been for your support and encouragement, I would not have had the motivation to write *Passage of Promise*. Special thanks to Bill and Kathy Nilsson, Dr. Kathie Black, Maria Szijj, Valerie Holladay, Charlene Hirschi, and the evaluators at Covenant Communications, who read various drafts of the manuscript and offered valuable feedback. I can say, without exaggeration, that had it not been for their guidance, this novel would never have been published. While I gratefully acknowledge all the help I received in preparing the manuscript, I alone am responsible for any errors in the final product.

I express appreciation to all those at my alma mater, Brigham Young University, and specifically at the Harold B. Lee Library, who have kindly assisted me over the years. Finally, let me thank Shauna Humphreys and Angela Colvin of Covenant Communications, who have shepherded this novel through to publication.

Dedicated to the memory of
Soren and Mary Hoyrup

CHAPTER 1

Elisabeth Ashcroft sat on a four-poster bed and stared at the door. Although the fire in the hearth glowed cheerily, its warmth did not reach her. Filled with anticipation, uncertainty, and fear, she felt completely unprepared for her wedding night. Her mother and her nanny, the two women who could have tutored her, had gone out of her life many years before. Her widowed father had been absolutely no help at all. True, her maid, Maggie Stowell, had given her some advice; but what did a single girl like Maggie know about the protocol of the marriage night?

Elisabeth shivered. The silk peignoir, a gift from her husband, was no protection against the cold of this high-ceilinged room in her new husband's ancient manor house. *It must be after midnight. Where can he be?*

Her mind flashed back to the wedding ceremony. It had been all she'd hoped for. Resplendent in a white, flounced gown of Indian muslin, she had glided down the aisle of the sixteenth-century church on her father's arm to stand before the bishop of Somerset. Her mind was awhirl as she, the twenty-seven-year-old daughter of a lowly vicar, entered English high society. Thoroughly caught up in the pageantry, the display of wealth and power, and the admiration of the wedding guests, Elisabeth could hardly believe her good fortune. Beside her stood the powerfully built Eustas, ninth Earl of Claverley, dressed in an elegant, albeit dated, gray frock coat from Savile Row. Though twice her age, the master of Claverley Hall was, in Elisabeth's eyes, the most gracious and gentlemanly man she had ever known.

Yes, all had gone well at the wedding and the subsequent marriage feast. Even the weather, which had been threatening rain all day, held off until the guests had made their way from the church to Claverley Hall. The only "fly in the ointment," as Maggie would have said, was her new husband's drinking. As the evening had worn on, Elisabeth had worried at the liquor he so freely consumed. Having grown up in a home where temperance was the rule and having "signed the pledge" as a young girl, she drank no liquor herself.

Elisabeth went over to the fire and warmed herself, then went back to sit on the bed. She was soon cold again. Walking briskly to an adjoining dressing room, she put on an old, quilted robe she had brought from home. Loosely tying the braided rope around her slim waist, she again sat on the bed. Once more her eyes were drawn to the door. Suddenly it flew open.

"My bride . . . my bride . . . I've come." Lord Claverley slurred the words as he clung to the doorjamb for support. Cravat askew, waistcoat buttons undone, and graying hair hanging in his eyes, he no longer resembled the elegant nobleman of a few hours earlier.

Elisabeth leapt to her feet. Heart beating against her ribcage, she stared in horror as her husband of only eight hours staggered toward her. His rheumy eyes narrowed, focusing on Elisabeth's unfashionable robe. "Take it off. Off with that monstrosity!"

Disgusted at his tone, Elisabeth stood erect. "I will not, sir!" She tightened the knot in the braided rope. "Please leave me, and do not return until you are sober."

"Off with it, woman, or—"

Claverley lunged at his young wife. Grabbing her shoulder with one hand, he attempted to rip the robe off with the other. Elisabeth cried out as his fingers dug into her shoulder. She tried in vain to squirm out of his viselike grip. Frustrated that he could not tear off the heavy robe, he threw her onto the bed and tried to rip apart the tie rope. Elisabeth fought back, her screams echoing around the cavernous room.

Suddenly, Maggie Stowell exploded into the room. The stocky girl of eighteen pounced on Claverley like a tigress protecting her young. Fastening her hands around his arm, she pulled with all her might. He swatted her away like a fly. Again she grabbed him, and again he swatted her away. A third time she yanked his arm. He turned in fury and lashed out, his heavy fist striking the girl's cheek, sending her sprawling onto the floor.

Elisabeth leapt from the bed, darted around the big man, and helped Maggie to her feet. Roaring like a wounded bull, Claverley charged the two women. He didn't reach them. Tripping on the carpet, he plunged to the floor. On the way down, his head hit the edge of a heavy mahogany dresser. He lay still. Blood trickled from a gash on his forehead. Horror-struck, Elisabeth and Maggie stared at the inert figure.

"Is he . . . dead?" Elisabeth asked in a hushed, shaky voice.

After a moment's hesitation, Maggie knelt beside him and tentatively put her hand on his chest. She shook her head and scrambled to her feet. "He's breathing, but just barely."

Elisabeth's hand covered her mouth. "Oh, Maggie, how could I have been so wrong? What are we to do?"

"No use crying over spilt milk, Miss Elisabeth. Come. We must away from this place." Elisabeth allowed Maggie to pull her into the dressing room, where the maid threw a cape around her mistress's shoulders and led her down the back stairs and out into the wet night.

On a good day, the path through the wood and over the fields to the vicarage was a pleasant twenty-minute walk from Claverley Hall. This moonless night, it was an obstacle course of muddy puddles, grabbing briers, whipping branches, and protruding roots. But Elisabeth's physical discomfort was no match for the torment in her mind.

What have I done? How could I have been so foolish? How could a man, seemingly so kind and considerate, turn into a monster? Surely it was not just the wine. Surely he must not really love me . . .

A pang of conscience shot through Elisabeth, for she knew that indeed, she did not love Eustas Claverley. Was this her punishment for seeking social status and marrying a man she didn't love? Was this her just reward for coveting Claverley Hall?

She cried out in pain as a brier raked her ankle and fastened onto her silken nightdress. Shivering in her sodden slippers, she tried to be patient while Maggie freed her from the brier. "Don't fret, miss, we'll soon be out the wood and into the fields. Follow me."

They were no sooner on their way again than a night bird's cry paralyzed Elisabeth. Slivers of fear coursed through her body. She gasped for breath.

Maggie was again at her side. "Not much farther, Miss Elisabeth. We'll soon be home."

At the edge of the first field, Elisabeth paused to wipe the tears and rain from her face. Then she plunged on after Maggie. Crossing the fields was easier than going through the wood, freeing Elisabeth's mind. Thoughts of her impossible situation tripped one over the other. *How could such a perfect day turn into such a disastrous night? What will Father think of me deserting my husband and running home after the marriage's first challenge? Will he demand I return to Claverley? I will not return! Never will I give myself to a man who cannot control himself.*

By the time they had waded through the wet fields and reached the lane to the vicarage, Elisabeth's silken nightdress was ruined and she had lost all sensation in her feet. The heavy door of the house Elisabeth had lived in all her life was bolted. Maggie worked the doorbell vigorously, and soon Elisabeth's father, Reverend Philip Ashcroft, tall and gaunt, stood in the doorway in nightshirt and cap, a lit candle in his hand. Speechless, he stared at the disheveled young women as if they were strangers. The ever-practical Maggie grabbed Elisabeth's arm and pulled her into the doorway. The vicar instinctively moved aside to let them through.

Later, after Elisabeth and Maggie had changed into dry clothes and seen to their scratches and abrasions, they met with Elisabeth's father in the parlor and related all that had happened. The vicar gazed on his only child. He shook his head in disbelief. "I don't know what to say, daughter. I thought I was doing right by persuading you to wed Lord Claverley and rise above your station. Now I stand condemned for having done so."

Elisabeth looked on her father with compassion. "You didn't force me, Papa. Not really. I'm of age. I have no one to blame but myself. I coveted Claverley Hall. Now I must pay the consequences."

In similar circumstances another man and daughter might have taken comfort in an embrace. But Philip Ashcroft had no tactile tendencies; they had disappeared with his wife's death when Elisabeth was four years old. Elisabeth knew from the older members of the parish that her father had never been the same after her mother died. Although always reserved in his manner, he had once fought for the rights of others, especially for the abolition of slavery—the ruling passion of his early years. Now he sat across from his daughter in an ineffectual stupor, unable to comfort her and unable to suggest a solution to her problem. His Sunday sermons were brilliant, but he had lost the human touch. Consequently, over the years his parishioners had come to look to Elisabeth for comfort and advice.

Reverend Ashcroft shook his head. "There's nothing I can do, daughter. Lord Claverley is my superior, and as advowson for the parish, he controls my benefice. Defy him and my career is forfeit." All this was said with his head bowed. Now he looked up. "'Tis gone three, daughter, and you are done in. Sleep is what you need. Perhaps in the light of day an answer will come."

But sleep would not come. Again, her mind teemed with unanswered questions. *Was I wrong to flee? Should I have seen to his wound? Is he dead? Will Maggie and I be tried for murder and hanged or transported? Will the scandal ruin Papa? What life is there for me here if I'm estranged from Claverley?* Fingers of light were stealing into the room by the time her body succumbed to so many exhausting hours, and she fell into a troubled sleep.

* * *

A bluebottle fly droned in the bay window. Elisabeth's eyes blinked open and immediately closed against the bright sunlight. She felt sick as the events of her wedding night crowded her consciousness. The rattle of a carriage on the cobblestones in front of the vicarage snapped her out of her stupor. Slipping out of bed, she hurried to the window and pushed aside the white lace curtain. A relieved sigh escaped her lips. It was her husband, looking none the worse for his overindulgence and clout on the head.

Minutes later, Maggie slipped into the room. "'Tis himself, Miss Elisabeth, and he's acting as if butter wouldn't melt in his mouth. He saw the bruise on my cheek and gave me this." She held up a small gold coin.

Elisabeth's eyebrows arched. "And you took it? It's conscience money, surely."

"Spends just as good as any other money," Maggie said with a toss of her black curls.

Later, Elisabeth sat in the parlor with her father and her husband. Expressionless, she listened to her husband's words of apology.

"Reverend Ashcroft, I abjectly apologize for my outrageous conduct toward your daughter. In the excitement of the day I overindulged. As you well know, a man is not himself when he's full of wine. I've always admired your attitude about temperance, and I'd do well to follow your excellent example." Turning to his wife, he gently took her hand. "Elisabeth, if you will only come back, I will forgo the marriage bed until I have proven my love and esteem for you. Please give our union, sanctified by God, another chance."

Once again he was the suave aristocrat who had wooed and won her. Elisabeth weakened. She was relieved at his promise to forgo intimate relations until she had time to accustom herself to him. Business in London would keep him away for the next fortnight, he said, giving her time to familiarize herself with her duties at Claverley Hall. With an expansive gesture, he offered her the keys to his office and strongbox so that she could have money for her personal needs and for the household accounts. Not even the housekeeper, Mrs. Blackmore, he said, had a key to the strongbox. When Elisabeth didn't protest, he placed a chain holding the keys around her neck, warning her to always keep them on her person.

Her husband's seeming sincerity laid Elisabeth's fears to rest. She agreed to return to him and give the marriage a chance. Before leaving, Lord Claverley asked to see the Reverend Ashcroft in private. The minister, who had also been won over by the aristocrat's cajolery, nodded, and the two men left Elisabeth and went into the vicar's study and closed the door.

* * *

During her husband's absence in London, Elisabeth assumed her duties at Claverley Hall. On her first day, she summoned Mrs. Blackmore to the small business office. When the tall, severe-faced housekeeper entered the room, Elisabeth was sitting at a desk with the account books spread out before her. Mrs. Blackmore drew herself up, folded her arms, and stared down at her new mistress.

"Thank you for coming, Mrs. Blackmore," Elisabeth said. "I—"

With an audible sigh the housekeeper cut Elisabeth off. "There's no need to bother your head about the accounts, miss. I've looked after them these many years."

"Thank you, Mrs. Blackmore, but I will look after the accounts from now on. And I am not a 'miss.' Kindly refer to me by my proper title. Now, I see that the accounts have only recently been paid, having been overdue for many months. Why is that?"

The housekeeper shifted from one foot to the other and grimaced. "The master had no money till now."

"But this huge estate and—"

"Mortgaged to the hilt, don't ye know."

"And now? From whence has come the money to pay off the accounts?"

Mrs. Blackmore looked at Elisabeth smugly. "From your ladyship, of course."

At her maternal grandfather's death, Elisabeth had inherited a sizable fortune, payable when she married. But how had Claverley gotten his hands on her money so soon? Elisabeth looked to the housekeeper for an answer.

"The master borrowed the money against your fortune, your ladyship. Till he married you, he hadn't two farthings to rub together."

Elisabeth felt heartsick. She closed the books. "That will be all, Mrs. Blackmore."

Over the next several days, silent war waged between the housekeeper and the new lady of the house. Fortunately, most of the servants hated Mrs. Blackmore, so Elisabeth was not without allies. Her chief support was Maggie, who became her eyes and ears at Claverley Hall.

About a week after Elisabeth had taken up her duties, she was in her bedroom when Maggie entered.

"Whatever is the matter, Maggie? You look like you've seen a ghost."

"'Tis the master—"

"Has something happened to him?"

Maggie slowly shook her head. "He's in London with his mistress gambling away your money."

Elisabeth's hand went to her mouth and she sank to the bed. "How . . . how do you know this, Maggie?"

"I heard 'em talking in the kitchen, Miss Elisabeth . . . your ladyship. Cook says it's a crying shame what he's doing. She says . . . she says he only married you for your money."

Elisabeth's face first drained of color and then, when the initial shock had worn off, it crimsoned. Anger welled up within her, both at her own naïveté and her husband's perfidy. After a while she calmed down and tried to think. *At least, according to Mrs. Blackmore, he's spending borrowed money. I must hurry home and put a stop to his getting my inheritance.*

She confronted her father in the vicarage parlor. "Papa, by no means let Claverley get his hands on my inheritance. He's not only a drunkard but a wastrel and an adulterer." Reverend Ashcroft swallowed hard and slowly sat down on a sofa. He appeared as a man completely defeated by life. Elisabeth gasped. "Oh no. Don't tell me he has already gotten it?"

He slowly nodded. "I'm afraid so, daughter. That's what Claverley wanted to see me about in my office the day after the wedding."

Elisabeth sat across from her father. "Couldn't you have done something?"

He shook his head forlornly. "I had no choice in the matter. As soon as your vows were spoken, Claverley became the owner of all you had. I assumed you knew. Ironically, that is why you ended up with the inheritance rather than your mother. Your grandfather didn't want me to have it. He never approved of me."

Suddenly, Claverley's conciliatory attitude on the morning after the wedding became clear to Elisabeth. Desperate for money, he had flattered Elisabeth and her father into believing that he was truly repentant in a ploy to get her inheritance immediately rather than going through a protracted court battle.

Though reluctant to return to Claverley Hall, Elisabeth could see no alternative. She returned to the manor house and waited impatiently for her husband to return from London. On the day he returned she confronted him in the front hall.

"Sir, you will give up your mistress forthwith," she said coldly, "and cease squandering my money. If you do so, I will be a dutiful wife in all ways."

He threw his greatcoat on a bench and laughed. "You have no idea how to be a wife, you sanctimonious little prig. Jenny Jacobs is more suited to my nature. She knows how to please a man. I shall not throw her over. Grow up and be satisfied with your lot, a lot many women would kill for. As for me squandering *your* money, you don't have any money. And I'll do whatever I want with *my* money. Now step aside. It's been a long journey, and I need a drink."

Though her face was flushed and she was shaking all over, Elisabeth stood her ground. "Sir, I demand an annulment of this sham marriage."

Claverley grew serious. He stuck his face close to Elisabeth's. His words were clear and brutal. "You shall not have an annulment—not now, not ever. Is that plain enough? If you and that insipid father of yours conspire to get one, I'll ruin you both."

Pushing past her, he stalked off.

Elisabeth's trembling hands covered her face. Slowly she turned and on leaden feet went to her bedroom. Maggie joined her there. Gathering up Elisabeth's few personal belongings and shoving them into a small carpetbag, they once more fled Claverley Hall, this time for good.

After putting away her belongings in her old room at the vicarage, Elisabeth sat on her bed and pondered her fate. Inadvertently, her hand went to the chain around her neck. Claverley's chain. In a burst of passion she ripped it off, hurling it and the keys across the room. They hit the hardwood floor with a metallic clank and disappeared under her five-drawer dresser. For a long moment she stared at where they had gone. *Would that the chain that binds me to Claverley could be so easily broken.*

CHAPTER TWO

That same day, Elisabeth met with her father in his study. He sat behind his desk, and she sat in a wing chair across from him.

"Are you sure that there is no hope for this marriage?" he asked.

Elisabeth sat straight in the chair and looked directly at him. "Absolutely none. I will not surrender myself to such a man, nor will I live with an adulterer."

He nodded. "Then we shall proceed with the annulment petition and let Claverley do his worst. I have reviewed the grounds for an annulment. Sadly, we do not have a strong case—hardly any case at all. You gave your consent to the marriage, you are of age, of sound mind, and you are not closely related by blood to him. All we have in our favor is that the marriage was not consummated and that he assaulted you and Maggie. I've had her take the pony and trap down to Ainsley to testify to the bailiff that Claverley struck her. Unfortunately, the bruise is all but gone, but perhaps it will serve. Is there anything else I might add to the petition?"

Elisabeth stared at him, surprised at the question. "There's the theft of my inheritance for one thing. And there's his blatant adultery for another. Surely those things are relevant."

The vicar sighed. "Not as relevant as they should be—hardly relevant at all in this world of unjust laws and double standards. However, I will include them."

As Reverend Ashcroft sealed the completed petition, Elisabeth asked him a question that had long been on her mind.

"Papa, many years ago I asked you about my inheritance and you said that you would tell me about it in the future. You've explained that Grandfather left the money in my name rather than Mama's because he didn't accept you as a son-in-law. What elicited his antagonism? And how did he amass his fortune in the first place?"

Her father finished what he was doing, looked up at her, and pursed his lips. "I imagine it's time for you to know the truth. I have kept this unpleasantness from you because it reflects poorly on your dear mother's family. Although she was personally blameless, I did not want to dishonor her memory. But I suppose you have a right to know about your ancestors." He paused, seemingly unsure of how to proceed. Elisabeth's expectant face prompted him to go on. "You know, of course, that I have long advocated the abolition of slavery. I was only sixteen when parliament abolished the Atlantic slave trade, but it took another twenty-six years before it was abolished throughout the empire. During that time, I worked with William Wilberforce in the abolition movement. It was then that I first met and fell in love with your mother. With that preface, let me now answer your two questions, which are intimately connected—your grandfather didn't approve of me because I was an abolitionist, and his fortune had come from the slave trade."

Elisabeth gasped. "You mean my inheritance came from the suffering of those poor Africans?"

He nodded. "I'm afraid so, my dear. Your grandfather and I were on opposite sides of one of the most divisive social issues. When your mother accepted my proposal of marriage, her father disowned her. We eloped, and your mother never saw your grandfather again. The loss of his only daughter broke the old man's heart. When she died so young, he was conscience-stricken and willed some of his fortune to you. He made sure that the money would not get into my hands by adding the codicil that you would not receive it until you were married. Of course, I never wanted his blood money."

Tears stung Elisabeth's eyes. "Thank you for telling me all this, Papa. If nothing else, it has assuaged the sting of losing my inheritance to Claverley. Like you, I would not have been comfortable spending money gained through human suffering."

That evening, Elisabeth sat on her bed and pondered her fate. For some reason her eyes were drawn to the five-drawer dresser, and she thought about Claverley's keys. Fishing them out from under the dresser, she hurled them out the window and into the rhododendron bushes. *If he demands them, I'll simply tell him that I threw them away.*

After this brief distraction, she returned to sit on the bed and ponder her predicament. How could she, a seemingly intelligent person, have made such an error in judgment on such an important decision as marriage? How could she have waited so long to wed and then made such a botch of it? True, she had had little experience with men and was getting desperate as she advanced into spinsterhood; but still, she should have known better. She thought of the boys and men who had taken an interest in her over the years. Although few in number, any one of them would have been preferable to Claverley, she concluded.

Elisabeth's mind went back to a conversation she'd had with Maggie a year before.

"Maggie, why do you think men shy away from me? Am I that unattractive?"

Maggie had grinned at her mistress. "You know you're not unattractive, Miss Elisabeth. I'd give my right arm for a slim figure like yours, for your smooth skin and your honey-colored hair. Did you know that local lads go to great lengths to get a glimpse of you as you ride by in the trap?"

Elisabeth treated Maggie's question as rhetorical as she'd gazed into a hand mirror. "I hate my freckles and turned-up nose," she said. "And my lips are too thin."

Maggie shook her head. "Come now, Miss Elisabeth, you know it's not your looks what scares men away. It's just that you're too smart for 'em. Men like pretty women with no brains. You've always got your nose in a book or are scouring the parish for sicklings. Being a vicar's daughter, you come across as a bit of a prig. A man likes a little slap and tickle behind the bushes."

"Maggie!" said Elisabeth, turning red. "You do go on."

"Sorry, miss, but you did ask. The fact of the matter is you int . . . you intimate men."

Elisabeth smiled. "'Intimidate,' I think you mean. Perhaps you're right. Maybe I should try harder to develop my feminine wiles. But I find most men boring and self-absorbed. Is it too much to ask for an intelligent, confident man who loves the things of the Spirit?"

"Probably," Maggie said with a mischievous grin as she left the room.

Ironically, one of the things that had attracted Elisabeth to Claverley was that she did not intimidate him. He was so suave and sophisticated, so self-assured. As she thought about their courtship, she could think of nothing to indicate his true nature. He truly had been a gentleman.

Again her mind traveled back, this time to the annual May fete, wherein the inhabitants of the whole parish had gathered on the grounds of Claverley Hall for a day of games, contests, and feasting. Following through on her resolve to increase her "feminine wiles," Elisabeth, with Maggie's help, had arranged her hair in ringlets, had bought a new frock and bonnet for the occasion, and had even applied a minuscule film of lip rouge. It was there that the courtship of Elisabeth and Lord Claverley had begun. Impeccably dressed in a tweed hunting suit, the lord of the manor had astonished Elisabeth by complimenting her on her appearance and then asking, "Would it be permissible to call on you, Miss Ashcroft? I have already obtained your father's consent."

Elisabeth had stammered a reply, and throughout the summer Lord Claverley had escorted her to church socials, whist drives, and boating on the River Barle.

But what about the pre-courtship years? Had there been signs indicating his true character, signs that she should have recognized, signs that should have prevented her from rushing into an ill-starred marriage? In retrospect, she thought that there had been.

She and Claverley had both lived in the parish all their lives, but Claverley, at past social gatherings, had hardly noticed her at all. In fact, at one annual fete, she recalled, he had walked right past her with a long face, seemingly resentful of her presence on the estate grounds. That was the real Claverley, she now concluded. *Why could I not have seen that his changed attitude was merely superficial? I am intelligent enough. I should have seen it.*

Troubled that she had not, Elisabeth thought on her education, seeking for some cranny through which the skill of discernment might have slipped. As a child, she had been introduced to the domestic arts. But when her Nanny Craig had immigrated to

America, needlepoint and knitting had ceased to be part of her world. From the beginning, her father had given his daughter a son's education. Her fertile mind soaked up languages and literature like a blotter. Nothing could diminish her love of learning, both temporal and spiritual. She had even become dissatisfied with the sterile creeds of Christendom, especially her own church, the Church of England, and had read every book and pamphlet she could find on dissenting views. She especially enjoyed the writings of Erasmus and Martin Luther.

Perhaps she'd spent too much time *reading* about people and ideas when she should have been gaining firsthand knowledge. Could she resume her old life of looking after her father, ministering to the medical needs of the parish poor, and studying? Could she give up all hope of ever having a loving husband and children? What if the council denied the annulment? Would she be forced to spend the rest of her life married to a man who didn't love her—a man who made it clear that he had only married her for her money? The prospect brought tears to her eyes and, burying her face in a pillow, she wept bitterly.

CHAPTER THREE

"You'd visitors from America when you was away," Maggie said weeks later as she helped Elisabeth unload the small, pony-drawn trap. Elisabeth and her father had been to town for supplies, and Reverend Ashcroft had already gone into the house.

"America?" Elisabeth asked, surprised.

Maggie nodded. "Mormon missionaries. They's looking for a place to preach."

"Well I hope you sent them packing."

"Heavens, no. One of 'em is young—about your age—and handsome!"

"Handsome is as handsome does, and from what I've read in the newspapers, Mormons do strange things."

"Like what?"

"Like having more than one wife."

Maggie took this information in stride. "Be that as it may, Miss Elisabeth, they's coming back this evening to see the master."

To Elisabeth's surprise, her father cordially welcomed the American missionaries when they returned that evening. Maggie was right. The younger of the two, an Elder Jonathan Kimball, was handsome. He did most of the talking. The older missionary, Elder Cyril White, appeared to be rather awed to be in a vicar's home. Elisabeth excused herself shortly after the missionaries arrived.

Later, her father said that he had given permission for the Americans to give a series of lectures in the church hall every night from Monday to Friday. The first lecture was scheduled for the following Monday evening. Despite her interest in religion, Elisabeth had no desire to attend.

"Change your mind and come with me, Miss Elisabeth," Maggie urged on Monday afternoon. "It'll be a lark. Besides, you've always got your nose in books about America. Now's your chance to listen to real Americans."

Elisabeth finally gave in to Maggie's badgering, and that evening found them both sitting in a hall full of curious parishioners. After the vicar's prayer, Elder White stumbled through a few preliminary remarks, and then Elder Kimball, full of confidence, began to speak. The handsome young American, who spoke of a new dispensation of the gospel of Jesus Christ, enraptured Elisabeth despite her misgivings. His countenance shone as he testified of angels visiting the earth, restoring ancient authority lost through apostasy.

While Elisabeth was thrilled with the message, she could see that her father was not. He apparently did not take well the implication that he had no authority "to preach the Gospel and administer in the ordinances thereof." After the meeting, he coldly shook hands with the missionaries. It was plain that he wanted to have nothing more to do with them but felt bound by his promise.

The next evening, Elder Kimball again delivered the bulk of the lecture. This time it was on the need for modern prophets. He talked of a man called Joseph Smith and claimed that Smith was a prophet. A book called the Doctrine and Covenants, recently published in England, purported to contain revelations Smith had received from God. Elisabeth could not wait to get a copy. After the lecture, people young and old crowded around the missionaries. Elisabeth waited patiently until Elder Kimball was free.

"Please take this copy, Miss Ashcroft," Elder Kimball said. "We have more in our room in the village."

"Thank you, Elder Kimball. May I ask a question?"

"Of course, Miss Ashcroft."

She hesitated. "Do Mormons . . . do Mormons practice polygamy?"

He looked her straight in the eye. "Yes, Miss Ashcroft. Like the patriarchs of the Old Testament, some of our leaders have been called upon to practice this ancient principle. However, as missionaries we are not authorized to preach this principle at this time. You will have to judge the truth of the restored gospel by what we are authorized to preach."

At that moment another person claimed the missionary's attention, and Elisabeth was left to ponder his words. Despite this admission, by Wednesday evening she had read the whole of the Doctrine and Covenants and was thrilled with its message. Finding the "Lecture on Marriage," which did not mention polygamy, especially intriguing, she read it several times. Wednesday's lecture was on the Book of Mormon. She also secured a copy of this book. By Thursday evening she had read most of it. After Friday's lecture, several people applied for baptism. This was too much for Reverend Ashcroft. With the missionaries still in the hall, the vicar stood up and publicly denounced them and their teachings.

Elisabeth was embarrassed for the missionaries. She didn't know what to think. She loved her father, but the teachings of the elders had sunk into her soul, filling it with light. It seemed to her that she had been waiting for their message all her life. Never had the Spirit of God permeated her body with such power. After each meeting she'd return home to her room eager to read the new scriptures and pray about what she had read. Having applied the test of the prophet Moroni in the Book of Mormon, she'd gained a firm testimony of the book's divine origins.

As she lay awake in her bed on Friday night, she pondered the challenge before her. *If I'm baptized into The Church of Jesus Christ of Latter-day Saints, it will devastate Papa. If I'm not, I will be denying the inspiration of the Holy Ghost, for surely He has testified to my soul that the restored gospel is true. What am I to do?*

A familiar passage from St. Matthew entered her mind and she opened her Bible and read it aloud: "For I am come to set a man at variance against his father, and the daughter against her mother, and the daughter-in-law against her mother-in-law. And a man's foes shall be they of his own household. He that loveth father or mother more than me is not worthy of me . . . And he that taketh not his cross, and followeth after me, is not worthy of me."

Elisabeth had often read these words, but she had never supposed that they could apply to her. For a long time she debated within herself the advantages and disadvantages of joining the Mormon church. *How will it change my life? Will Papa turn me out?* By the time she finally drifted off to sleep, her problem was still unresolved.

The following Sunday, Elisabeth's father took for his text St. Matthew 7:15, "Beware of false prophets, which come to you in sheep's clothing, but inwardly they are ravening wolves." He never once mentioned the missionaries by name, but the implication was obvious, especially to Elisabeth. Nevertheless, at supper that evening she decided to test the waters. "I'm thinking about being baptized by the Mormon missionaries, Papa."

He did not flare up in anger. That was not his way. Rather, he glared at her coldly for several seconds before saying, "You are of age, daughter, but be assured that if you join the Mormons you will no longer be welcome under my roof." Having said this, he rose from the table and stalked off to his study. Elisabeth sat at the table wondering what she should do. Not yet ready to break with her father, she decided not to force the issue.

* * *

"Did you hear the Mormon missionaries are leaving?" Maggie asked a week later.

Panic seized Elisabeth. "When?"

"Day after tomorrow. They's having one more dunking tomorrow, then they's off. They want to see you before they go, but they didn't want to upset the master by coming here. Would you like to meet them at my folks' place?"

"Please don't refer to a baptismal service as a dunking, Maggie. Yes, I do want to see them."

"Yes, Miss. I won't. I figured you'd want to meet them, so I set things up for seven."

As she drove the pony and trap to the Stowells' that evening, Elisabeth wondered if she were rushing toward baptism the way she had rushed into marriage. Perhaps she should back away from Mormonism. Perhaps her interest was a reaction to the loneliness and self-loathing she felt after her marriage breakup. Perhaps she should turn around and go home.

But she didn't turn around, and when she saw Elder Kimball's brown eyes light up upon seeing her, she knew that she would be baptized. For the next two hours, the Mormon elders instructed Elisabeth further in the principles of the new faith. During the closing prayer she experienced an epiphany, and she knew without doubt that her decision to be baptized was correct. Only one niggling problem spoiled her complete joy. The elders knew her as Miss Elisabeth Ashcroft. Should she confess that she was married?

"Did you mean what you said about me having to leave home if I joined the Mormon church, Father?" Elisabeth asked at breakfast next morning.

"I did."

"Then, regretfully, I will be gone by this evening."

The vicar looked up, eyes round and mouth half open. "Where will you go?"

"To Maggie's parents' in the village. They have graciously offered me Maggie's old room. Maggie will stay here, of course. You couldn't get along without her."

Her father didn't challenge this last statement. During the brief period Maggie was at Claverley Hall, the domestic routine at the vicarage had broken down. The Ashcroft home had several servants, but Maggie was the glue that held the household together.

That afternoon, Elisabeth was among those on the banks of the Barle River who had presented themselves for baptism. She was so sure that the annulment would be granted that she had decided not to reveal her marriage. It was a lovely day in the early autumn of 1850. Elisabeth's senses drank in the greens and yellows and browns of the foliage, the intense blue of the sky, and the many shades of color on the dappled water. Filled with the Spirit, she saw everything with new eyes.

Before the ordinance took place, Elder Kimball spoke of the commandment for the Saints to gather to Zion. He testified that God had led His people to the valley of the Great Salt Lake and that it was His will that people from every nation, kindred, tongue, and people should gather there. Elisabeth thrilled to the missionary's words. But how could she ever take part in the gathering?

Trembling all over, Elisabeth took Elder Kimball's hand as he led her into the river. She smiled up at him. "Ready?" he asked. She nodded and bowed her head. She hardly heard the brief prayer. As if in a dream, she sank under the water and felt it closing over her. Then the elder's strong arms drew her up out of the water, and together they waded to the shore, where an elderly woman wrapped her in a blanket.

Elder White confirmed Elisabeth a member of The Church of Jesus Christ of Latter-day Saints on the banks of the river. Her elation soon turned to sadness when the elders confirmed that they would be leaving the area the next morning. As she shook hands with Elder Kimball before they parted, Elisabeth somehow knew that they would meet again. Over the brief period of their acquaintance, she had come to respect and admire him, and appreciated his kindness and devotion to the cause of the restored gospel. She had become attached to him in a way she couldn't understand. Although she would not admit it even to herself, her feelings for this servant of God exceeded friendship.

Elisabeth's face was still aglow when she entered her new home later that day. Maggie's parents greeted her warmly and invited her into a small parlor where the three of them sat down.

"And how is your leg?" Elisabeth asked Maggie's father.

Amos Stowell slapped his thigh. "As fit as a fiddle, thanks to you, Miss Ashcroft. You've the gift of healing, you have, lass. All the common folks in the parish is beholden to you. The higher-ups have their doctors, but we have you. The missus and me also 'preciate you learning Maggie her letters."

Elisabeth blushed at the compliment.

"Wasn't the river awful cold, dear?" Mrs. Stowell asked.

Elisabeth nodded. "I suppose so, but I was so filled with the Spirit I hardly noticed it. Of course I was shaking all over, but I don't think it was just because of the water temperature."

Elisabeth had been at the Stowells' for only a few days when her father showed up and pleaded with her to return home. She was happy to do so, and over the next month neither of them spoke of her baptism. Before leaving the area, the elders had organized a small branch of the Church in Ainsley, the closest village to the vicarage. Meetings were held on Sunday evenings, and Reverend Ashcroft did not complain when Elisabeth borrowed the pony and trap to attend the Mormon meetings. Maggie would sometimes accompany

Elisabeth, although the maid had lost interest in the new church after the first missionary meeting.

As autumn progressed, Elisabeth continued to enjoy her new faith, but she felt increasingly unsettled and unsatisfied with life at the vicarage. Although she studiously avoided the topic of religion, she felt that a wedge had been driven between father and daughter. Also, constant talk at Church meetings of "gathering to Zion" left her disconcerted. How could she go to America while she was still bound to Claverley? Each day she fervently prayed that the annulment request would be approved.

After checking the mail for many weeks and finding nothing, she was surprised one day to receive two letters, one from the ecclesiastical council and the other from Elder Kimball. She rushed home to her room and sat at her writing desk. Placing both letters on the desk, she stared at them, not knowing which to open first.

Reasoning that the council's letter was the one most likely to contain bad news, she decided to open it first and get it over with. Her hands trembled as she broke the official-looking wax seal and unfolded the single page of beige paper. Scanning the contents, her eyes fastened on the words "request denied." Her heart sank and tears leapt to her eyes. The hope she had lived on for so many months dissipated. Thrusting aside the council's letter, she dabbed her eyes and looked at the other letter. The joy she had felt in receiving it was gone. Nevertheless, she slowly opened it and read:

Liverpool, October 15th, 1850

Dear Sister Ashcroft,

Tomorrow I leave for Zion. I am sad to leave England and all of the wonderful people I've met here, not the least you, dear sister. Many of the English Saints are gathering to Zion. A widow of my acquaintance, Sister Jean Brenton of London, has booked passage on the George W. Bourne *out of Liverpool. It leaves for New Orleans in early January. She has four children and has asked if I know anyone that could help her with the youngest, Charlie, and be a companion to her fifteen-year-old daughter Glynis during the long voyage and subsequent overland haul. I immediately thought of you. Sister Brenton has considerable means and would be willing to pay most of your expenses. All you need to provide would be your transportation to Liverpool and passage to New Orleans—about fifty pounds would more than cover it. As I am leaving tomorrow, you will have to make arrangements directly with Sister B if you are interested. Enclosed is her London address. If you come to Great Salt Lake City, I will arrange a place for you to stay. Please give this your prayerful consideration. I will anxiously read immigrant lists in the new year. They are published in the newspaper long before the wagon trains arrive in the valley. Please remember me to your father. Although he withdrew his support from us, he is an honorable man and I bear him no ill will. May the Lord be with you always.*

Yours in Christ,
Jonathan Kimball

Hope flowed into Elisabeth as she reread the letter. Cervantes' words came into her mind, *"Fortune leaves always some door open to come to a remedy."* The council had closed a door on her, but a new one had been opened. Here was a chance for a new life, far away from her sterile existence in the shadow of Claverley Hall. She slowly folded the letter, and on a whim took up her pen and wrote on the envelope, "Elisabeth Kimball." She gazed on the name for a moment. *It has a nice ring to it,* she concluded. Immediately she repented her impulsive act: *Until an annulment is final, I have no right to think such thoughts.*

Elisabeth shared the council's letter with her father. "I'll appeal the decision," was all Reverend Ashcroft said. She read both letters to Maggie.

"Sorry, Miss Elisabeth. I know how much you wants to be free of Claverley. Maybe you'll find a way to nobble the committee." Maggie picked up the other letter. "Do you think you'll go to America? I think Jonathan fancies you!"

"Don't be a silly goose, Maggie," Elisabeth said, her cheeks coloring. "We are only friends in the gospel. Besides, I'm a married woman."

"More's the pity. Are you really married if you've never conjugated it?"

Elisabeth laughed. "That's close, but I think you mean 'consummated.' Yes, I'm afraid so. I'm going to write to Mrs. Brenton and tell her my situation. If she doesn't mind that I'm married, I'll think more seriously about emigrating." She paused for a moment, lost in thought. "Poor Papa would be devastated."

"Don't worry. I'll look after him."

* * *

Widow Brenton replied to Elisabeth's letter by return post. She empathized with Elisabeth and said that she didn't mind that she was married. She suggested that perhaps in the New World such a marriage would not be recognized.

With Sister Brenton's letter still in her hand, Elisabeth knelt down beside her bed and prayed for guidance. Over the next week, she continued to pray. Finally, she made the momentous decision: she was going to America. She immediately sat down at her desk and wrote two letters. The first was to her former nanny, telling her that she was going to America and would possibly be able to visit her before heading west. Nanny Craig, now Mrs. Mary Kenny, had married an American late in life and had moved to Philadelphia ten years earlier. Elisabeth had last heard from her former nanny when the latter's husband had died two years before. It would be wonderful to see her old nanny again. The second letter was to Sister Brenton. Elisabeth gave Maggie the letters to post.

"You're really going?" Maggie asked. "Out there to a land of wild animals and savages?"

"We have savages here too," Elisabeth said, thinking of her wedding night. "Yes, I'm really going. I've asked Mrs. Brenton to book passage for me. I'll pay her back in Liverpool. What with, I still haven't determined."

"You've no money?"

Elisabeth shook her head. "Not a penny. Papa looks after the money. If I need anything from the shops in Ainsley or Glastonbury, I just put it on an account and at the end of each month Papa gives me the money to pay the accounts. I've never really had any need for money."

"I wish I could help you, Miss Elisabeth, but I'm skint. Even the money I got from Claverley's gone."

"Thanks, Maggie. I know that if you had any money you'd share it. But money is the lesser of my two problems. I'm dreading telling Papa about America."

Maggie put a comforting hand on Elisabeth's shoulder. "Despite the way he is, he really does love you. Maybe he'll give you the money."

Reverend Ashcroft did not offer to finance Elisabeth's voyage to America. The confrontation took place in the parlor two days after Elisabeth's discussion with Maggie. "Going to America, daughter? Have you lost your senses?" It was the first time Elisabeth had ever seen her father lose his temper. "You say God has called you to America. Surely you know that's utter foolishness. More like that young man has captured your fancy. A woman of twenty-seven years should know better." After a pause he calmed down and tried reasoning with her. "At least stay until we learn the council's decision. Wait a year, and then if you still want to go, I'll give you my blessing."

Elisabeth slowly shook her head, her eyes beseeching his understanding, if not his support. "I'm sorry, Papa. Such a chance as I have might not come again. Please understand."

He sighed in fervent frustration. "Oh, why did I let those Americans under my roof?" With that he left the room, without accepting another word from her.

Elisabeth ran to her room and cried her eyes out. Hoping that her father would change his mind, she did not bring up the subject again. But as the year drew to a close, she became desperate. *How am I to get fifty pounds sterling?*

Lying on her bed one evening just before Christmas, Elisabeth racked her brain for ways of raising the money. She thought of selling some of her clothes. But that would take time, and she had no idea how she would go about it. Then she thought about borrowing the money from Sister Brenton. Elder Kimball had said she was well off. Perhaps she would allow Elisabeth to pay the fare when they got to Zion and she had time to earn it. Elisabeth rejected this idea. It would not do to begin their relationship in this manner.

As Elisabeth's eyes wandered around the room, they fell on the five-drawer dresser. She recalled fishing Claverley's keys out from under it and throwing them out the window. A bold idea leapt into her mind.

Maggie laughed out loud when Elisabeth told her the idea and asked for her help in executing it. "You amaze me, Miss Elisabeth, you surely do. If you don't mind me saying so, when we fled Claverley Hall that night you seemed weak as water. But now you're bold as brass. You seem a new woman. Of course I'll help you. It'll be a lark."

Elisabeth was pleased with Maggie's words, but she didn't comment on them. Instead, she continued outlining her plan. "We'll have to do it when he's not at the hall. Time is short. Find out if he's going to be away over Christmas. If he is, we'll do it then. Boxing Day would probably be best. The servants will be distracted with their presents."

Maggie nodded enthusiastically and then asked, "Where did you say you threw the keys?"

* * *

And so it was that on Boxing Day, December 26, Elisabeth and Maggie went to Claverley Hall. Maggie walked around to the servants' entrance, and Elisabeth marched up to the front door and rang the bell. The butler's jaw dropped when he saw her. Nevertheless, he stepped aside as she boldly entered. She had almost gotten to the office when Mrs. Blackmore stepped in her way. "What are you doing here?"

Fear shot through Elisabeth, but she knew that she couldn't show it. She spoke in a haughty tone. "I've warned you before, Mrs. Blackmore, to address me by my proper title. If you continue with this intransigent behavior, you will be dismissed. Is that perfectly clear?"

The two women glared at each other for a long moment until the housekeeper dropped her eyes to the floor. "Yes, your ladyship."

"Now, Mrs. Blackmore, go to the kitchen and ask cook what's for supper. That will be all." The housekeeper left and Elisabeth exhaled mightily. Just then Maggie arrived and Elisabeth said, "I've sent Mrs. Blackmore to the kitchen. Go after her and make sure she doesn't come near the office. I'll leave when I get the money and meet you as planned."

Praying that the lock had not been changed, Elisabeth inserted the key into the office door keyhole. It clicked and the door opened. Once inside, she locked the door behind her and went to the cupboard containing the strongbox. In seconds she had the box open and fifty pounds in her hands. Relocking the box, she was about to close the cupboard when a thought occurred to her. Sitting down at the desk, she took pen and paper and wrote the following note:

To Whom It May Concern:

I have withdrawn fifty pounds for my personal use.

Lady Elisabeth Claverley

Placing the note in the strongbox, she relocked it, closed the cupboard, and exited the office.

Maggie was waiting for her just inside the wood on the path to the vicarage. "You get it?" she asked.

Elisabeth opened her purse and triumphantly held up the money. Maggie, face flushed, let out an excited squeal. "Bold as brass you are, Miss Elisabeth, bold as brass!"

Pleased at Maggie's admiration and at the success of their venture, Elisabeth smiled. Taking the keys and broken chain from her purse, she said, "We won't need these again." She handed one of the keys to Maggie, and together they pitched them far into the bushes.

Elisabeth was about to send the chain after them when Maggie stopped her. "That's gold, Miss Elisabeth. It'd be a terrible shame to throw it away."

Elisabeth looked at the chain in her hand and nodded. "You're certainly right, Maggie. For your help in our successful venture, you can have it. Just don't wear it around anyone from Claverley Hall."

"Wear it? I'll have it sold before you can say Jack Robinson."

Over the next two days, Elisabeth's heart skipped a beat whenever she heard the doorbell clang. But she had no reason to worry. Claverley was in London and wouldn't be back until the New Year. If all went according to her plans, Elisabeth would be on her way to America by the time he returned.

CHAPTER FOUR

When Elisabeth was ten years old, she had accompanied her father to a football game between the Glastonbury Gladiators and the Ainsley Argonauts. It wasn't supposed to be much of a match. The Gladiators were undefeated and had challenged all the towns and villages in southwestern England to raise a team to play them. Responding to the challenge, the boys of Ainsley village threw together the Argonauts. Almost everyone in the parish had attended the game. Incredibly, when there were only five minutes left in the match, the Argonauts scored the only goal. Elisabeth, who had been bored through most of the game, caught the enthusiasm of the crowd. If the Ainsley boys could hold out for only five more minutes, they would do the impossible. The Argonauts had held out, and the crowd had gone wild.

Now, as she stood at the rail of the sailing ship *George W. Bourne,* surrounded by the Brenton family and almost three hundred other Latter-day Saints, Elisabeth felt the same sensation she had during those last five minutes on Ainsley Common. Over to her right the first mate was supervising the removal of the gangplank. In a few minutes the ship would be ready to sail. Her heart pounded in her chest. It was nearly impossible for her to believe that it might be so simple. Might she really be allowed to leave England without hindrance? Or would some hand reach out to pull her back to the life that had become intolerable to her?

Grabbing the ship's rail with trembling fingers, she nervously eyed the entrance to the Liverpool dock as a black chaise-and-four rattled unexpectedly onto the quay. A ripple of fear coursed through her.

Letting go the rail, she took a deep breath and poised herself to merge into invisibility amongst the crowd. A tall, gaunt man emerged from the carriage. It was her father. Relieved that it was not Claverley, Elisabeth exhaled. But why had her father come? *Will he force me to stay? He must know I cannot.*

After a moment's hesitation, Elisabeth made her way to the first mate. "Please, may I go ashore? My father's come all the way from Somerset to see me off."

The first mate gave her a speculative glance, as if to determine whether or not she was worth the bother. Seeing that she was well dressed and pretty, he looked up at the captain on the bridge. The captain nodded.

As fast as her petticoated skirt and winter coat would allow her, Elisabeth hurried down the gangplank and through a knot of well-wishers. As she approached her father, she slowed, still uncertain of what his presence at the dock might mean. "So you've come, Papa," she said, stopping a few feet in front of him. "You've come to say good-bye and Godspeed, I hope."

He nodded. "Aye, daughter, I couldn't bear that my angry words would be the last you'd ever hear. I can't understand this . . . this folly. But I love you, lass, and I wish you well."

"And I love you," she said through her tears. She wanted to throw her arms around his neck but forced herself to stand motionless, knowing that such impulsive behavior would embarrass him and that he would pull away. So she said only, "Folly it may be, but I must go. God has called me to gather with the Saints in America."

"Can I not persuade you to stay?" Elisabeth heard the pleading in his voice. "I so wanted to attend the London World Exposition with you this summer. I suppose I'll have to go alone." This appeal tugged at her heartstrings. She too had looked forward to attending the exposition and seeing the marvelous Crystal Palace, but her mind was set and she was silent. He tried another tack. "You cannot run away from your problems, you know. They will follow you across the Atlantic. The annulment appeal may yet be successful. The council may still set you free."

She slowly shook her head. "Claverley has the council in his pocket. The die is cast. I've been called to Zion and I must go."

He nodded gravely and thrust a leather pouch into her hand. "Here's twenty guineas to help you on your way."

Fresh tears watered her eyes. "Thank you so much, Papa." She knew the sacrifice to his pride behind this gesture. "And thank you so much for seeing me off. Regretfully, I must go now. The ship is ready to sail."

He nodded and stiffly embraced her. "Give my best to Nanny Craig . . . that is, Mrs. Kenny, when you see her, and my condolences on her loss." He turned to leave, then paused. Elisabeth saw the effort it cost his reserve to turn back. He took a small pair of scissors from his pocket. "May I have a lock of your hair to remember you by?"

She nodded soberly and pulled a curl from under her bonnet. Her father, his hands trembling as hers had earlier, clipped it off and put it into his pocket. Not looking at her, he turned away. She watched him climb into the chaise, and then she hurried back to the ship.

Despite the hollowness she felt at the realization that she was indeed leaving her home and father, possibly forever, her heart lifted at the expressions of goodwill from her fellow Latter-day Saints as she again took a place at the rail. Her father's hired coach was still on the dock, and that comforted her a little. He did love her, she thought, as she wiped her eyes, even though he may not have always shown it. He would fight for her with the council in recompense for his role in the unhappy life she was leaving behind. But she feared he would not win.

With the anchor weighed and the hawsers cast off, a tugboat shepherded the *George W. Bourne* out into the Mersey River to await a fair wind. Elisabeth again wiped her eyes and waved good-bye to her father and to England.

* * *

Thirty-seven days after the ship had cleared the Irish coast, Elisabeth was reading on deck when the cry of "Land ho!" rang throughout the ship. Heart beating fast, she jumped to her feet and went to the rail.

"The Bahamas, miss," said a sailor. She squinted to make out the tiny islands on the horizon. *Not quite America, but getting closer every day. What will it feel like to step onto American soil? How many more months before I'm in Zion and face-to-face with Jonathan Kimball?* Elisabeth sighed, knowing that her journey was far from over.

Three days later the ship sailed into the Gulf of Mexico, and several days after that a cheer went up from the crowded deck as the ship entered the mouth of the Mississippi River. There, a New Orleans–bound steamboat took the *George W. Bourne* in tow.

Over the next days, Elisabeth spent as much time on deck as she could, barely able to contain herself as the wonders of this new land passed before her. One sunny morning she studied the sugar and cotton plantations lining the river, each plantation dominated by an invariable white mansion, with its broad verandah covered with jasmine and honeysuckle. Lush gardens surrounded each house, and beyond these, orange, plum, and peach groves all in bloom. Elisabeth inhaled the blossom-scented air and delighted in the gift of such an early spring. *It will be two more months before the blossoms are out at home.*

Glynis and little Charlie Brenton joined her at the rail. Over the weeks at sea, Elisabeth had almost become part of the Brenton family of four children: George, nineteen, Edward, seventeen, Glynis, fifteen, and Charles, eight. Edward, Glynis, and Charlie had accepted Elisabeth as a sister, but George had fallen in love with her. Despite her protestations that she was married and that she could never think of him as other than a friend, George persisted in his advances, obviously agreeing with his mother that, under the circumstances, Elisabeth's marriage would perhaps not be recognized in the New World. Now, Glynis mirrored Elisabeth's fascination with the sights and smells of the New World. Charlie was more taken with the wildlife. "Look, Sister Elisabeth, look!" he cried as a flock of storks took wing along the shore.

Gliding up the "Father of Waters," as the Mississippi River was known, the ship passed hundreds of black slaves laboring in the sun. It was the only sour note in this symphony of the senses. *How can it be? How can the inhabitants of such a blessed land countenance slavery? When will America follow the example of England and free the slaves?* Elisabeth thought in frustration.

Later, Sister Brenton joined her children and Elisabeth on deck. "Do you think that members of the Church have slaves, Sister Brenton?" Elisabeth asked.

"I don't think so, dear," Sister Brenton said. "The Book of Mormon speaks out against slavery."

Elisabeth nodded. "That's right. Ammon said that it was against the law of his people. Hopefully, it will be against the law in America someday."

* * *

After three days in New Orleans, Elisabeth and the Brentons, along with the majority of the immigrant Saints from the *George W. Bourne,* boarded the three-hundred-by-sixty-foot steamer *Concordia* and continued upriver to St. Louis. It was still too early for the Saints to begin their overland journey, so many of them took work in St. Louis to earn extra funds for the next leg of their journey. Sister Brenton rented a house for a month and located a suitable short-term governess. Elisabeth would use the time to travel to Philadelphia and visit her former nanny. The whole Brenton clan saw her off at the ferry, which would take her across the Mississippi River to Alton, Illinois, where she would catch a series of steam trains to Philadelphia.

"It's still not too late for you to change your mind and let me go with you," George said as he placed Elisabeth's portmanteau among the ferry baggage. "I'll . . . we'll worry about you traveling all alone."

"Thanks so much, George, but I'll be fine. As Mr. Charles Dickens observed after his trip to the New World, a woman can travel alone anywhere in the eastern states in complete safety." George nodded at her words, his expression mixed. He was continually delighted at her intelligence and education, but was obviously chagrined that she'd used it this time to divert his advances. She hugged each of the Brentons in turn and then boarded the ferry. "In less than a month we'll all be together again," she called as she waved good-bye from the ferry deck.

CHAPTER FIVE

A week later, a weary Elisabeth descended from a horse-drawn omnibus before a mansion in the fashionable Spring Garden section of Philadelphia. "It's magnificent!" she said to the driver. She had no idea that her old nanny lived in such a neighborhood or in such a house.

"One of the finest in the city," the driver said as he hoisted Elisabeth's portmanteau onto his shoulder. After depositing it on the porch, he hesitated awkwardly for a moment while Elisabeth's eyes drank in the building and grounds. With a discreet cough he said, "I must be off now, miss . . . the other passengers . . ."

"Of course," Elisabeth said, prying her eyes from the monumental Corinthian columns flanking the ornate front door. "Thank you for your kindness." She opened her purse. "I'm afraid I have only English money."

"That's fine, miss. Gold spends just the same here."

The driver's words reminded Elisabeth of what Maggie had said about Claverley's gold coin. The remembrance brought on a sudden pang of homesickness. How she missed Maggie, her father, and England. But she didn't fret long. The front door of the mansion suddenly opened, revealing a liveried servant. He was a small, wiry man. Elisabeth figured that he was in his late forties or early fifties. As he came toward her, she noticed that he had a slight limp.

"Miss Ashcroft?" he asked, his voice hinting at his surprise. "How did you find us?"

"The omnibus driver was very helpful. He said that everyone knows the Kenny mansion."

The servant nodded. "Ah, of course. I am John, Mrs. Kenny's factotum. Please come in. You may leave your baggage there." Ushering Elisabeth into the foyer, he instructed her to take a seat while he went in search of his employer.

Elisabeth gazed around the large, ornate room. *Nanny Craig has surely done well for herself. I wonder if wealth has changed her?*

"Bless my soul, Lizzie. Is that really you?" Mrs. Kenny's voice quivered with both advanced years and pleasure.

Giving a start at the sound of her name, Elisabeth turned toward the elderly woman, who slowly made her way toward her.

"Nanny Craig! Dear Nanny!" Elisabeth cried, running to the woman and embracing her tenderly. Oh, it was so good to see her old nanny again! How she had missed her!

"Well, now, miss," the old woman said with a trace of an Irish brogue. "We've been expecting you these many weeks. How my old heart sang when I got your letter." She stepped back to examine Elisabeth. "Sure, and you've grown into a beautiful woman. Why has no man captured your heart?" Elisabeth smiled but did not answer. "Well, come into the drawing room, dear, and tell me all about your life." Mrs. Kenny took Elisabeth's hand and led her into the next room. "Rose'll bring us some tea."

"Nanny—I mean, oh dear. I mean—Mrs. Kenny . . ." Elisabeth frowned in confusion. "You're not Nanny Craig anymore and Mrs. Kenny sounds so formal . . ."

"Now you're a grown woman, dear, you may call me Mary if you wish, and I'll no more call you Lizzie. From now on you're Elisabeth." The old woman smiled at her former charge.

"Mary," said Elisabeth, trying out the name and remembering what she was going to say before she got sidetracked. "May I have milk rather than tea?"

After a black maid had brought the refreshments, Mrs. Kenny said, "You didn't say much in your letter—only that you'd joined the . . . the Mormons and were coming to America."

Elisabeth noted her friend's hesitation. *I hope I can make her understand.* She lowered her eyes. "Perhaps I should have told you the whole story. But I thought it best to wait until I saw you and could explain everything in person."

Mrs. Kenny nodded, her expression sympathetic. She waited for Elisabeth to go on.

Elisabeth was silent, remembering. During the long ocean voyage she had tried to forget her life in England and the problems she had left unresolved. How could she have any hope of happiness otherwise? But she could no longer ignore the reality. Though she had tried to leave them behind, her trials were always with her. She thought of her father. Certainly his advice to marry Claverley had changed her life. But she could not blame him. It had been her decision.

"Elisabeth, are you unwell?" Mrs. Kenny's face showed deep concern as she leaned toward Elisabeth and reached for her hand. "You seem of a sudden quite pale."

Elisabeth swallowed and forced herself to take a deep breath. Surely her friend would understand and not judge her. Nevertheless, it was with no little courage that she said, "I left behind a husband in England, Mary. Lord Claverley. No doubt you know of him."

Mrs. Kenny's jaw dropped, and she stared openmouthed. "Eustas Claverley? Why, he's twice your age and a notorious rake. How on earth did you ever come to be married to him?"

How indeed? Elisabeth sighed, looking off into space. Then she turned to Mrs. Kenny and told her story.

When Elisabeth had finished, Mrs. Kenny nodded sympathetically. "You poor dear. What a predicament to be in! I can't understand why the council would not release you from that brute. Oh well, you're here now and far away from his grasp. I'm sure in America you'll find happiness."

"I'm sure I will," she said. "I have found the source of true happiness. Shortly after fleeing Claverley Hall, I had the good fortune to be introduced to the restored gospel of Jesus Christ."

Elisabeth went on to tell of her conversion. When she had finished, she paused and looked down at the handkerchief in her hands, which she had twisted into an unrecognizable mass. Breathing deeply, she lifted her eyes to those of her friend, fearful of the scorn she might well see in them.

But Mrs. Kenny merely looked concerned. "I hope you haven't jumped from the frying pan into the fire, dear. The papers are full of stories about the Mormons, none of them flattering."

Elisabeth shook her head and sighed. "Persecution always follows the true Church." She paused before adding, "It's you I must thank, for preparing me to receive the truth."

"Me?" the older woman nearly choked with surprise. "How could a lifelong Presbyterian prepare you to become a Mormon?"

Elisabeth smiled. "You taught me to love the scriptures. How well I remember your sitting on my bed each evening reading to me from the Bible."

A wistful expression crept over Mrs. Kenny's face. "Those were wonderful times right enough. Helping raise you, especially after your mother passed, is the closest I ever came to motherhood. How I missed you when I removed to America!"

"And I you. Was Mr. Kenny a kind husband?"

"He was, surely. I so wished we'd met earlier in life. I would have been proud to bear his children. But it was not to be. Now, tell me more about this Kimball fellow. You've not said so, but your eyes glowed when you mentioned his name. Has he asked for your hand?"

Elisabeth blushed. "Of course not. I'm a married woman. We are only friends in the gospel. That's why he invited me to Utah Territory."

"Mmnn," Mrs. Kenny said, obviously unconvinced. Then she changed the subject. "How did you leave your father? He must have felt terrible after all that you've been through."

Elisabeth felt unexpected tears well up in her eyes. At length, she brushed them away. "He all but disowned me when I said I was going to America. But he had a change of heart and came to the quay to see me off, and we parted kindly. I feel for him, all alone in the vicarage. Thankfully, he has Maggie Stowell to look after him. Leaving him . . . leaving England . . . I never thought I'd be able to make such a difficult choice."

The two women were silent, both thinking of England. At length Mrs. Kenny appeared to make a difficult decision. "As I mentioned, I've read a great deal about the Mormons in the newspapers. I find much of it disturbing. I must say, dear, it seems queer that you'd be part of such a sect. You've always been such a proper girl."

Elisabeth was at first taken aback, and then she smiled tolerantly at her friend's apprehensions. "Don't believe all you read in the newspapers, Mary. Our persecutors have got up many wild stories. Don't worry, Nanny Craig, your little girl will not end up in a seraglio in Utah Territory!"

"I'm glad of that." She gave a sigh of relief. "It's a lifetime ago since I was 'Nanny Craig.' I am quite happy here now, but coming to America and getting married at my age was almost too much for me—does this Jonathan Kimball know you're married?"

Involuntarily, Elisabeth closed her eyes at the question, one that she had steadfastly refused to ask herself. "No," she whispered.

"Do you plan on telling him?"

"Of course, but I think everything will be different here in America. I have faith that things will work out. Either the annulment appeal will be successful or my sham of a marriage will not be regarded here." She shifted uncomfortably in her chair and looked around the room. "Mr. Kenny certainly left you well provided for," she said, eager to take their conversation in a new direction. "How did he obtain his fortune?"

Gazing around the tastefully appointed drawing room, Mrs. Kenny gave a rueful sigh. "He left me with more money than I can ever use, but I'd give it all up to have him with me again. Still, I'm thankful for the few years we had together. He made his fortune through dint of hard work and a measure of luck. He started out as a printer, and when he succeeded in that he got into real estate, and then importing and exporting with England. That's how I met him, you'll recall. He was in England on business and visited his cousin, who happened to be a nanny like me. She introduced him to me and the rest, as they say, is history—ancient history to you, no doubt."

Elisabeth smiled. "All I can remember was that a rich American came and stole my nanny away. I don't think I was very polite to him the one time we met." She paused before adding, "I'm glad that your fortune is not from a dishonorable source. Learning that my inheritance came from the slave trade shocked me. But the knowledge took the sting out of losing it to Claverley."

When she learned that her young visitor could only stay a week, Mrs. Kenny was sad but not surprised. Elisabeth had indicated in her letter that she could not stay long. "At least we'll have time for me to show you around the city. It's an exciting place. I think you'll be interested to know that we have a women's medical college here, the first in the country."

"For women to become doctresses? How wonderful."

Elisabeth, like many others in England, had been thrilled when the English woman Elizabeth Blackwell became the first woman medical doctor in America. Although Miss Blackwell had emigrated from England when she was young, the British were still proud to claim her. In fact, when the news of her success reached England, the popular magazine *Punch* celebrated by publishing a humorous poem. Elisabeth, who had an excellent memory for such things, was pleased to be able to quote the first stanza for her friend:

> *"'Young ladies all, of every clime,*
> *Especially of Britain,*
> *Who wholly occupy their time*
> *In novels or in knitting,*
> *Whose highest skill is but to play,*
> *Sing, dance, or French to clackwell,*
> *Reflect on the example, pray,*
> *Of excellent Miss Blackwell!'"*

Mrs. Kenny laughed. "When you were a little girl you were always bringing home and tending to sick birds and small animals. Has your interest in healing grown?"

"It has. Over the past few years I've had the opportunity of being of some help to those in the parish who couldn't afford a doctor."

Mrs. Kenny looked pleased. "Would you consider postponing your journey west and attending the college, dear?"

Elisabeth considered the suggestion for a moment. She wondered if it was prompted by Mrs. Kenny's desire to save her from the Mormons, but she didn't voice the thought. It was true that she had enjoyed her work with the sick of the parish, and if an opportunity for such an education had presented itself in England when she was younger, she would have snatched it. For now, however, her only goal was to get to Zion. "I expect that medical practitioners are at a premium in Utah Territory or Deseret as we call it. Perhaps one day . . ."

Mrs. Kenny nodded at Elisabeth's noncommittal tone. "Well, dear, it's getting late. Let's get you settled in your room. Rose has it all made up for you."

As Elisabeth unpacked her bag, she found the small, corked bottle Maggie had given her as a going-away present. Maggie's note was still attached to it:

Lemin juse for frekkles. I heerd the sun is awful hot out ther.

A tear came to Elisabeth's eye as she recalled her long struggle to teach Maggie to read and write. *Oh, Maggie, how I miss you!*

Later, lying in bed, Elisabeth's thoughts turned to Deseret and Jonathan Kimball. She imagined his face when he would look at her. She pictured how his eyes would light up as they so often had when they discussed the scriptures. Would he take her hands in his when they met again? Would he press his lips against them?

I've got to stop thinking about him. It's not right. I have no claim on him. I'm going to Deseret because of the gospel, she chided herself.

For a long time her thoughts would not let her fall asleep. She finally decided to go to the kitchen and fix herself a mug of warm milk. Easing out of bed and slipping on a robe, she quietly made her way downstairs. No sooner had she gotten to the kitchen than plaintive sobs, amplified in the stillness of the sleeping house, emanated from somewhere close by. Elisabeth followed the sound into a hallway and stopped at a door. She knocked tentatively. The sobbing instantly stopped.

Elisabeth waited for the door to open, but there was only silence. She knocked again, a little harder this time. After a brief pause, the door opened slightly. Rose, the black servant she had met earlier, peered from behind the door, her eyes round and swollen.

"I's sorry fo' wakin' ye', Miss 'Lis'bet," the woman said in a low voice. "I's gwyne to shet up drekly."

Elisabeth could only imagine what sorrow had caused the mournful cries that had led her to this room. "That's all right, Rose," Elisabeth said. "May I be of service to you?"

Rose opened the door wider and stepped aside. Elisabeth entered the room and the women sat across from each other.

"Hain't nufin' t'be done," Rose said, shaking her head. "Hain't nufin' t'all."

"Are you not happy here?"

"Yass'm, Miss 'Lis'bet. I's mos' happy heah. D'missus treat me fine. It's jest I miss my Thomas 'n' little Freddie sumfin' fierce. I hain't seen 'em fo' three year." She hung her head and the tears flowed unabated.

Alternately soothing and probing, Elisabeth soon learned the cause of Rose's inconsolable sorrow. She had trouble understanding all of Rose's words, but she got the gist of her story. Rose had grown up a slave on a Mississippi plantation. Her mother was a household servant, and when Rose came of age, she too served in the big house. At eighteen, Rose married the footman, Thomas, and they had a son, Frederick. Their master, "Mars Coombs," was a kindly man, and the little family had as good a life as possible under slavery. Then Rose's world fell apart when Mr. Coombs was thrown from his horse and died.

The planter's widow sold the plantation and moved to South Carolina to live with her sister. The new owner, "Mars Brown," brought about many changes, which included selling off "excess" slaves. Thomas pleaded in vain that his family be allowed to stay together, but Rose ended up on a plantation in Georgia. She did not know what had happened to Thomas and Freddie.

Rose had come to be with Mrs. Kenny through a series of peculiar events. Not long after moving to Georgia, she had accompanied her new owner and his wife on a visit to Philadelphia. There, Brown got into a card game and lost all his cash. Afraid to tell his wife that they did not have money for the fare back to Georgia, he decided to sell Rose. But this was not a simple matter. Traffic in slaves was illegal in Pennsylvania.

Somehow, Brown learned that Mrs. Kenny was looking for a maid. He offered her the opportunity of redeeming Rose. Taking pity on the frightened woman, Mrs. Kenny asked Rose if she would like to stay in Philadelphia as a free woman and work for her. Rose readily agreed. So Rose gained her freedom, Mrs. Kenny gained a maid, and the Georgia planter gained the money for him and his wife to get back home. Elisabeth silently wondered how the planter had explained to his wife the loss of their slave.

"That's quite a tale," said Elisabeth, squeezing the callused brown hand that she now held in her own two hands. "I do understand how it feels to be in an unfamiliar place, away from family, and you not even knowing where Thomas and Freddie are. But don't despair. I'll talk to Mrs. Kenny and see what she suggests about finding your loved ones."

"Oh, de missus, she's got a man lookin'. Trouble be, de black folk affeared to talk to 'im, and de white folk doan trus' No'thners."

Before returning to her room, Elisabeth promised that she would add her prayers to Rose's, and that she would ask Mrs. Kenny for a report on the detective who was searching for Rose's husband and child.

Awaking early next morning, Elisabeth's thoughts turned to her family. She hardly remembered her mother; a flood of gratitude for her father and Nanny Craig flowed over her. *I don't believe I've shown enough appreciation for them. When I write to Papa, I'll tell him how grateful I am for all he has done for me. Although I felt deserted when Nanny Craig went to America, I'll be ever thankful that she taught me to pray, to read, and even to dream. I wonder how Papa fares without me? How I miss him and England. At least I know were he is. How I pity Rose, not even knowing where her husband and child are.*

At the sound of a tap on the door, Elisabeth called, "Come," and smiled when Rose entered carrying a covered breakfast tray. "Please put it on the table. How are you feeling this morning? A little better, I hope."

"Mos' considerable, Miss 'Lis'bet. Thank ye fo' yo' kindness las' night."

Later when Mrs. Kenny came upon Elisabeth, the younger woman said, "I spoke with Rose last night, Mary. I think it's wonderful that you've hired a man to look for her husband and little boy."

"'Tis nothing, dear. What's the use of money if I don't do some good with it?"

"Indeed." Elisabeth said aloud. *What good is anything the Lord blesses us with,* she continued to herself, *unless we use it for the betterment of those who are less fortunate.*

* * *

Over the next five days, John toured Elisabeth and Mrs. Kenny around Philadelphia in an elegant town carriage. Elisabeth learned that the college for women doctors was as yet only a few rented rooms in a house on Arch Street, but Mrs. Kenny assured her that on Elisabeth's next visit, she would find a real college.

Too soon the week was over, with many of the sights unseen. "I'm sad to see you go, love," Mrs. Kenny said on the evening before Elisabeth's departure. "Your visit's done me a power of good. I hope you've enjoyed yourself."

Elisabeth touched the old woman's arm. "Oh, I have so very much, Mary. But there are several places I wish I'd visited."

"That's good," Mrs. Kenny said with a smile. "Now you'll have to come back again."

Elisabeth nodded. "For example, Benjamin Franklin's grave. Papa and I so enjoyed reading his maxims. Like Papa, Mr. Franklin believed in education for women and in freeing the slaves. Speaking of Papa, I must write him a long letter tonight."

Mrs. Kenny looked lovingly at Elisabeth, and it was obvious that she wanted to say something but was unsure how to say it. She finally got it out. "One last thing, dear. Do you have enough money for your journey? I'd be happy to—"

Elisabeth nodded. "With what Papa gave me at the dock and what's left from Claverley's money, I'll have enough. Thank you so much for asking."

"Claverley's money," Mrs. Kenny said with disgust. "Your money, don't you mean? Had it been me, I'd have taken a whole lot more than fifty pounds!"

After a tearful departure, Elisabeth retraced her route back to St. Louis, where she rejoined the Brentons. In preparations for their journey west, Sister Brenton had purchased eight yoke of oxen and four wagons. In mid-April, Elisabeth and the Brentons boarded the steamer *Financier,* bound for Alexandria, Missouri, where they would begin their overland journey. Barges lashed to either side of the *Financier* transported Sister Brenton's oxen and wagons. Their first night on the river, Elisabeth and Glynis slept for the first time in a wagon. Sister Brenton occupied a wagon by herself, and the boys used the other two wagons. Though not the most comfortable of beds, Elisabeth could not help feeling as though she traveled at the height of opulence, as all her comforts were provided by the pure love and generosity of her friends. A niggling doubt told her she was not pulling her share, but she pushed it aside with the sure knowledge that she too would come upon opportunities to give her bit of good to the world.

CHAPTER SIX

Aboard the *Financier,* Sister Brenton had arranged for a young Mormon lad, Jeremy Pitt, to drive one of her wagons. And so the four Brenton wagons moved off the Alexandria dock with George driving the lead wagon, Edward the second, Sister Brenton the third, and Jeremy bringing up the rear. Elisabeth and Glynis rode in Sister Brenton's wagon, and Charlie rode with Jeremy. West of Alexandria the wagons halted in an open area next to a small stream. There, the English pioneers set up camp. It would be the first time any of them had camped out.

George set up a sheet-iron stove his mother had purchased in St. Louis for fourteen dollars, and with Glynis' help, Sister Brenton soon had supper ready.

"What a delicious meal, Sister Brenton," Elisabeth said. "I didn't think eating in the outdoors could be such fun. Please allow me to do up the dishes. I must become more domestic."

"Of course, dear," Sister Brenton said, "Glynis will help you."

That evening Sister Brenton called her little group together for prayer. She asked George to be voice. He thanked Heavenly Father for His protecting care over sea and land. That night, Elisabeth slept in the same wagon as Sister Brenton and Glynis. They had no sooner settled down for the night than a long, plaintive howl sent shivers through Elisabeth.

"Don't worry, girls," Sister Brenton said. "It's only coyotes, a kind of big, gray fox. The man who sold me the wagons told me about them. They won't harm us."

The coyote chorus kept Elisabeth awake for over an hour. When they finally stopped their howling, Elisabeth soon fell asleep.

Next morning under a sunny sky, the wagons moved west, and before noon they rendezvoused with other Mormon wagons at a staging area.

The auspicious beginning was not to last, and for the next two months the wagons inexorably crawled westward in a haze of rain, thunder and lightning, mud, quagmires, and swollen rivers. The impossible trails resulted in broken wheels, broken harness, and broken tongue pins. But occasionally the rain would abate, and the travelers would get some relief. During these brief moments, the prairie revealed its hidden beauty in carpets of violets, primroses, daisies, bluebells, lilies of the valley, and wild roses. On one such day, as she and Glynis sat amid the flowers some distance from the camp, Elisabeth decided that life was much like their journey to Zion. The path of life was fraught with obstacles as one struggled forward each day, footsore and weary, and one might wonder if the effort was worth the goal. Then suddenly something wonderful happened that made life worthwhile again, like her finding the restored gospel amid her despair. She expressed these thoughts to Glynis.

Glynis nodded as she added another link to a daisy chain. "So I guess we should be grateful for a day like today."

Elisabeth looked up at the cerulean sky and took a deep breath of the flower-scented air. "We certainly should. Tomorrow the rain could well return."

* * *

It was an evening in late September when Elisabeth first set eyes on the Great Salt Lake Valley. Eight and a half months earlier she had boarded the *George W. Bourne* in Liverpool. And now she was here at last. Many thoughts coursed through her mind as she stood looking down into the valley, bathed in gold by the last rays of the sun. *Zion, Zion at last.*

That night Elisabeth could not sleep. Her racing mind, full of questions, would not let her. *What will I do when I get there? How will Elder Kimball react when I tell him that I'm married? Will he be angry that I did not tell him before I was baptized? What will he think of my brown face and trail-worn clothing, my gritty hair devoid of curls? How*

will he know I've arrived? Will I have to seek him out or will he find me?
Should I arise early in the morning and spend longer than usual working
on my hair? Should I wear my best dress tomorrow?

Before falling asleep, Elisabeth decided to get up early in the
morning, but despite her good intentions, she awoke as usual to the
trumpeting call of the camp bugle. A second blast followed the first,
then a third and a fourth.

Sister Brenton clambered from her bed and pulled back the
wagon cover. "What's all the racket?" She stared out into the
morning. "Why, people are coming to greet us, coming from the
valley!"

Elisabeth and Glynis scrambled from their beds and peeked over
Sister Brenton's shoulder. People on horseback, in buggies, and in
wagons were pouring into the camp. Glynis clapped her hands. "How
wonderful!"

Elisabeth stared out at the gathering throng. *Is Jonathan among them?*

The three women competed for space as they prepared to meet
their guests. Elisabeth quickly braided Glynis's hair and Glynis recip-
rocated. Elisabeth put on her good dress, the one she'd been saving
just for this moment. When she finally stepped out of the wagon, her
heart sang with anticipation. But all she saw were strangers.

Sister Brenton was soon engrossed in conversation with people
she and her husband had known in England, and Glynis found
herself the center of attention of several young men and women.
Elisabeth shyly hung back near the wagon.

"Sister Ashcroft!" a masculine voice called. "There you are."

Elisabeth grew faint at the sound of the familiar voice. He had
come for her! She must be strong. She forced herself to breathe deeply
and smile naturally at Jonathan Kimball, who came rushing up to her,
his faced flushed with happiness. He took both of her hands in his.

"Sister Ashcroft, how wonderful to see you. I saw your name on
the list of immigrants in the newspaper and have been watching for
you. How well you look."

Elisabeth forced a calm to her voice that she did not feel. She was
certain that Jonathan must hear the thumping of her heart. "I do
thank you, Elder Kimball," she said, lowering her eyes. "You are very
kind. But I truly must look a sight."

Jonathan shook his head. "No indeed, you've survived the journey remarkably well. When I learned you were coming, I took the liberty of speaking with an elderly Swedish couple in the ward, Brother and Sister Nilsson. Their house is small, but they have a spare room they'd be happy to offer you."

"Thank you very much. It will be wonderful to live in a house again and sleep in a real bed."

"You're more than welcome. I was hoping you'd get here in time, and here you are."

"In time?" Elisabeth ventured, not understanding.

He nodded, the blush coming back into his cheeks. "I'm to wed this Saturday. I so want you to meet my bride-to-be, Becky Sanderson."

His words, said so casually, sent Elisabeth into shock. A sick feeling lodged in the pit of her stomach. She suddenly felt cold. Surely, she had misunderstood him. Surely, the intimations of his feelings for her could not have been wrong. She slowly withdrew her hands from his, not wanting him to feel how cold they had become.

"Yes, I'm to be wed this Saturday," he continued. "I've told Becky all about you. I know you'll love her as I do, and—" Jonathan stopped in midsentence. Concern creased his brow. "Are you not well, Sister Ashcroft? Please forgive me for rambling on. You've had a long journey and must be worn out."

Elisabeth listened to his words as if they came from far away. She nodded courteously, as if to a stranger she had just met on the street. She pressed her cold hands against her cheeks and was surprised at how warm her face was when her entire body was cold.

"It's all the excitement," she finally managed to say. "I must lie down. Thank you for speaking with the . . . the Swedish couple. For now I . . ." Speech failed her. She turned quickly and sought refuge in the wagon.

She lowered herself to the bed and buried her face in a pillow. "What a fool I've been," she groaned as the tears gushed out of her.

Later, she started at a light touch on her arm. It was Glynis. "Elisabeth, Brother Kimball is inquiring about you. What shall I tell him?"

Elisabeth sat up and dabbed her eyes. "Tell him I'm indisposed. Thank him for his concern."

Glynis nodded. Soon after, she returned. The fresh tears on Elisabeth's face were silent evidence of her pain. "I wish I knew how to help you, Elisabeth."

"A fool like me is past help. My father was right. A woman of my age should know better." She wondered if her father were right about other things, too. If she could be wrong about Jonathan Kimball, could she also be wrong about the inspiration that led her to Utah or, for that matter, the inspiration that had led her to join the Church? These thoughts flitted through her mind, but she did not voice them.

Glynis sat beside Elisabeth and stroked her hair as a mother would stroke that of her child. With wisdom beyond her years, she said, "You're not a fool, Elisabeth. Fools cannot truly love."

These words, so unexpected, touched Elisabeth's heart and brought fresh tears to her eyes. She reached out and embraced her friend. "Thank you, Glynis. With your help and the Lord's, I'll get through this."

Somehow Elisabeth did get through the next two days, and soon she and her fellow immigrants entered the city of the Saints to an overwhelming welcome. That same day, Elisabeth got another disappointment. The Brenton family had decided to continue on to Ogden, north of the city, where they had English friends. Elisabeth was invited to go with them. What should she do, move into the accommodations Jonathan had arranged for her, or go to Ogden? She decided that it was only common courtesy to visit the Nilssons before making a final decision. The elderly Swedish couple were so happy to see her, and so proud of how they had fixed up her room, Elisabeth didn't have the heart to disappoint them.

George helped Elisabeth move her few belongings from the wagon to her room. "May I call on you once we're settled?" George asked as they stood outside the Nilsson cabin afterwards.

Elisabeth smiled. "Of course, George—as a friend. I want you to know how thankful I am for all you've done for me over the past months. You've been a perfect gentleman." George's face fell, but then he nodded and squeezed her hands in farewell.

Glynis was the last one to say good-bye. She hugged Elisabeth for a long time. "Ogden's not that far away, Elisabeth. If you need me, I'll come visit you."

"Thank you, Glynis. I'm sure I'll be fine."

Full of emotion, Elisabeth waved good-bye to the Brentons as the wagons headed north. Deep in her heart, she knew that meeting them was not accidental. For some reason God wanted her in Zion and had arranged for the Brentons to come into her life. Ironically, it was Jonathan Kimball, the source of her great disappointment, who had introduced her to the gospel, to the Brentons, and to the Nilssons. *God truly does move in mysterious ways,* she thought.

When the wagons were out of sight, Elisabeth went inside her new home, and Soren and Sigrid Nilsson welcomed her with smiles, gestures, and a few words in broken English.

A master carpenter, Brother Nilsson had fashioned the cabin with his own hands. Elisabeth's room was neat and clean with calico curtains on the single window. A multicolored, hooked rug next to the bed covered the planed floorboards. The lumpy horsehair mattress left much to be desired, but it was a step above a straw mattress, upon which many of the Saints slept.

All in all, Elisabeth was pleased with her new lodgings, but she was perplexed about her life. That first day, she retired early and lay on the bed in semidarkness, pondering her future. Should she have gone with the Brentons? What lay ahead for her in Great Salt Lake City? Her fantasy that somehow Jonathan Kimball would solve all her problems had turned to dust, and she could not find the energy to think of what she should do next. Although she was well educated, she had no practical skills that she could think of to support herself in such a pioneer community. *What is to become of me?* Fortunately, the money her father had given her at the Liverpool dock and what was left of Claverley's fifty pounds provided her with some security. For the time being, she could at least pay her own way.

As much as she tried to block him out of her mind, her thoughts kept returning to Jonathan Kimball. For the hundredth time she asked herself how she could have made such an error in judgment about his intentions. *Why am I so foolish about men? Have I absolutely no discernment regarding them?* A knock at her bedroom door interrupted her thoughts. "Come," she said, sitting up and turning up the oil-lamp wick.

"Peoples here," Sister Nilsson said.

"Thank you, Sister Nilsson." Elisabeth followed her landlady into the kitchen. There stood Jonathan Kimball and a pretty young woman. Sister Nilsson shuffled off, leaving Elisabeth staring awkwardly.

"Becky Sanderson," said Jonathan, pointing to his companion.

A sick feeling invaded Elisabeth's stomach as she shook Becky's small hand. "I'm pleased to meet you. Please be seated."

Becky sat at the kitchen table, but Jonathan remained standing. "I'm sorry, but I must leave you ladies. I have a priesthood meeting tonight. Should I pick you up later, Becky?"

Becky shook her head. "I'll walk home. Have a good meeting." When Jonathan had left, Becky turned to Elisabeth. "I'm so glad to finally meet you, Sister Ashcroft. Jonathan has told me so much about you. He is in awe of your learning and sophistication." Elisabeth felt anything but sophisticated. Not able to come up with a proper response, she merely smiled and waited for Becky to continue. After another awkward pause, Becky said, "I've come for two reasons, Sister Ashcroft—or may I call you Elisabeth?"

"Of course you may." Elisabeth desperately tried to appear calm when her insides were in turmoil.

Becky smiled gratefully. "First of all, Jonny and I want to invite you to the wedding feast on Saturday. We're having it at the hall in Warm Springs. That's north of the city. There'll be dancing and entertainment as well. Will you come?"

Elisabeth hesitated. "I'm not sure how I would get there."

"Oh, Brother and Sister Nilsson are coming. You can go with them. They'll be staying with their daughter in Ogden, but we'll arrange a ride home for you. Please say you'll come."

Elisabeth didn't want to go, but she couldn't think of a graceful way of getting out of it. "I'll certainly try to be there."

Ignoring Elisabeth's noncommittal answer, Becky smiled and said, "Then it's settled. Jonny'll be as pleased as I. Now to the second reason for my visit. I teach at the Fifth Ward school, and the sister who was to take my place has taken ill. Jonny suggested that this might be a good opportunity for you, to help keep you occupied until you're more fully settled. We're planning a wedding journey to visit family in Provo—probably about two weeks. We realize that it's a great imposition, but I'd be relieved to know that the children are in good hands. Will you do it, please?"

Elisabeth paused before answering. Then she nodded. "I've been wondering what to do with myself. And I do love children. Yes . . . yes, I'll be glad to do it."

Becky clapped her hands in delight. "Perfect! And you will love these ones." Then she grew serious. "I would like to be your friend, Elisabeth. I can only imagine how difficult it must be for you, a proper English lady, coming here to the semiwilderness. Please let me help you in any way I can."

For a long time after Becky had left, Elisabeth lay on the bed and rehearsed her conversation with Becky. *"Proper English lady,"* indeed. *She must think I'm ancient. She is very young—not more than twenty, I would guess. And she is very pretty and sweet. I can see why Jonathan has fallen for her.*

Elisabeth wished she could find something wrong with Becky, but she couldn't. It was clear to her that Becky would make Jonathan a wonderful wife. The invitation to teach for a fortnight was an unexpected blessing. It would give Elisabeth something to do while she contemplated her future.

Before falling asleep that first night in Zion, Elisabeth was feeling a little better about her situation. But she felt that it would take a long time to get over Jonathan Kimball. She wondered why God had made life so difficult for her when it seemed so easy for girls like Becky. After pondering the question, her sterner side took voice. *Face reality, Elisabeth. Give up the search for a husband. Like it or not, you're married and have no right to think about another man until you are free. Deep down you knew that you had no right to fantasize about Jonathan Kimball. Deep down you knew that Jonathan Kimball was not for you.*

CHAPTER SEVEN

Against her better judgment, Elisabeth decided to go to the wedding feast. Now, as she stood with Brother and Sister Nilsson just inside the doorway of the Warm Springs Hall, she wished she hadn't come. The pain of her disappointment was still too raw. During the long, uncomfortable journey—the dust and oppressive heat were almost unendurable—from the city to Warm Springs, she had gotten progressively out of sorts, and once again had questioned her decision to come to Utah.

"Good," Sister Nilsson said, nodding her head at the decorated hall.

Elisabeth ran her eyes over the garlanded walls with new candles in each of the wall brackets, the tables topped with white linen, the flowered centerpieces, and the blue-and-white bunting bedecking a makeshift stage. She grudgingly admitted to herself that, given what they had to work with, the decorators had done a good job. But it was not what she was used to, and she wondered if she would ever feel at home in the "semiwilderness," as Becky had called Utah. Would she ever truly feel that she was "no more a stranger and foreigner but a fellowcitizen with the saints, and of the household of God"?

"Not good," Brother Nilsson said with professional disdain, nodding at the split log benches with legs bored into the rounded side. He shook his head, looking for all the world as if he wanted to rush home for his tools.

Elisabeth agreed with Brother Nilsson that the benches were eyesores, but Sister Nilsson, attempting to put a good face on things, said diplomatically, "Won't see when sit down. They do well enough."

"Unless we get slivers," said a female voice from behind them.

Elisabeth turned. "Glynis! I'm so glad to see you." The friends embraced warmly. "Is your family all here?"

"Just me and George—he's tending to the horse and buggy."

Her friends' presence raised Elisabeth's spirit, but when the bride and groom, who had been married that afternoon in President Brigham Young's office, entered the hall, Elisabeth again wished she hadn't come. *Why am I putting myself through this torture?*

After supper, which Elisabeth picked her way through, the Nilssons left for Ogden. Elisabeth felt stranded and even more out of place. Glynis was preoccupied with several young men, and although George's attentions were a safe harbor from her storm of emotions, she was reluctant to use them. She liked him too much to encourage his devotion in order to use him as an emotional crutch.

While the men moved the tables to the walls and placed the benches row on row in preparation for the evening's entertainment, the band of two violins, one piano, and one accordion played a medley of popular tunes from the makeshift stage. Elisabeth found a seat near the center of the hall, and George was soon by her side.

When all was ready, the master of ceremonies, a Brother Joseph Matlin, mounted the stage. He was tall and thin with a long white beard and the mournful expression of an undertaker, which made everything he said tragicomic. For the next hour, musical numbers, recitations, and jokes entertained the guests. Despite herself, Elisabeth got caught up in the fun, and for at least a little while forgot her own tragedy. She even smiled wryly when the master of ceremonies, tongue in cheek, admonished the bride that it was the duty of a wife to stand by her husband through the troubles of life, which the groom wouldn't have if he hadn't gotten married in the first place!

The entertainment ended with a young boy reciting "A Boy Stood on the Burning Deck."

When the benches had been placed against the walls and candle shavings spread on the wooden floor, Brother Matlin announced that the bride and groom would lead the Grand March. Jonathan and Becky glided onto the floor, followed by most of the guests, including Elisabeth on George Brenton's arm.

With the Grand March over, George returned Elisabeth to her seat. "Are you not well, Elisabeth?" he asked. "You look like you've lost a shilling and found a sixpence."

The English saying made her smile. "I'll be fine, George. I just feel out of place here. It's not what I'm used to."

"I know what you mean. Let me get you a glass of lemonade."

Arising once again, the master of ceremonies suggested that a waltz by the bride and groom would perhaps not be untoward, despite some prejudice toward the popular new dance.

On cue, Jonathan again swept Becky onto the floor.

"What a handsome couple," said a woman sitting next to Elisabeth. "They seem meant for each other."

Elisabeth gazed on the happy couple, and a knot tightened in the pit of her stomach. She turned her head to face the lady beside her, who was introducing herself as Sister Brady. Although she was in no mood for introductions, Elisabeth's natural politeness caused her to acknowledge the woman and give her own name. Loud voices at the entrance of the building interrupted them. Both women turned to see that the bride and groom had suddenly left off dancing and that Jonathan was embracing and slapping the back of a newly arrived guest. The stranger was disheveled, and his ragged clothing, scraggly beard, and unkempt hair were at odds with the appearance of the other guests. Even by candlelight, Elisabeth could see the dust rising from the stranger's tattered coat as the groom thumped his back.

He looks like a tramp. And yet Jonathan and Becky appear most happy to see him. I wonder who he is? At that moment, both Jonathan and the stranger turned in Elisabeth's direction. She instantly averted her eyes.

When she looked up again, George Brenton was standing in front of her. She drank the proffered lemonade and then took George's arm for another dance. Afterwards, George escorted Elisabeth back to her bench beside Sister Brady, bowed, and went off to get more refreshments.

"Handsome young man," Sister Brady said, nodding toward George. "A friend?" Elisabeth nodded, explaining that they had met on the ship to America. "Just a friend?"

Elisabeth smiled wryly. "He's only nineteen, much younger than I."

The woman looked surprised. "Oh, I wouldn't have thought you were much more than that."

Elisabeth acknowledged the compliment with a tight smile. "I'm closer to eight and twenty."

"Really? Well, don't worry, dear. Men are pouring into the valley daily. You'll find someone sooner or later."

At that moment, Elisabeth noticed out of the corner of her eye Jonathan and the tramp coming toward her. It appeared that Jonathan was about to introduce the stranger to her. As they got closer, Elisabeth's stomach turned. Besides his tattered clothing, the tramp's face was a mass of burnt and peeling skin, his lips covered with blisters. Ordinarily, her heart would go out to one in that condition and her greatest desire would be to help heal him. Now, however, a wave of revulsion swept over her. To her troubled mind this man seemed to epitomize all the crudities of the West, all the disappointment she had felt since first entering the valley. She not only didn't want to meet him, but she wanted to flee from him and this place; she wanted to go back to England and forget she had ever come to Zion.

As Jonathan and the stranger got closer, a wedding guest engaged the groom's attention. The tramp, however, kept coming and was soon standing in front of her.

"Good evening, Miss Ashcroft," he said politely. "My name is Gren Sanderson, Becky's brother. I apologize for my appearance—"

A wave of nausea swept over Elisabeth. Staggering to her feet, she whispered hoarsely, "I'm sorry, Brother Sanderson, but I am not well." At that moment George returned. She grabbed his arm. "George, please help me outside."

Elisabeth clung desperately to her young admirer as she filled her lungs with the cool night air. George had never seen her like this. On the boat she had been the one unfailingly administering to the needs of those overcome with seasickness. Now, *she* clung to him, weak and dependent.

Gradually the nausea passed and she was able to whisper, "Please take me away from this place. Please take me home."

George nodded. "Of course, Elisabeth."

He led her to a buggy and helped her into it. Removing a blanket from under the seat, he wrapped her in it. "Will you be all right for a minute while I tell Glynis?"

"Yes," she whispered. "I'm sorry to ruin your evening."

"Think nothing of it. I'll be right back."

After a moment, Becky and Jonathan were at her side. "Oh, Elisabeth, I'm so sorry you've taken ill," Becky said. "Let Jonny and me take you back to the city."

Elisabeth vigorously shook her head. "Certainly not! It's your wedding night. Please go back to your guests. I'm feeling better now. George Brenton has agreed to take me home."

Becky looked unconvinced. "Are you sure? If it was I who had almost fainted—"

"I'm very sure. The spell has passed. I'm fine now. I'm sorry for all the fuss."

Becky squeezed Elisabeth's hand. "All right, dear, if you're sure. Take care of yourself. I'll see you in two weeks. If you have any problems at the school, please see my friend Sister Eliza Snow and she'll help you. We'll wait with you until your George returns."

After a seemingly interminable journey from Warm Springs to the city, the buggy finally pulled up in front of the Nilssons' cabin. George, who had kept a comforting arm around Elisabeth for most of the journey, now shyly withdrew it and helped her out of the buggy.

"How can I ever thank you, George?" Elisabeth said. "Please come in and have something to eat before you go back. I'm sure I can find you something."

George accepted the invitation and was soon sitting at the kitchen table eating bread and cheese, washing it down with milk. When he was finished, he said that he had best be going, as he was supposed to have the buggy back in two days. Elisabeth waved to him from the doorway and hoped that he had not read too much into her letting him hold her during the journey. With George gone, a vast loneliness engulfed her. Feeling isolated and vulnerable, she shuddered as she reentered the empty cabin and closed the door behind her. The door had no lock, adding to her vulnerability. Gazing around the room for something to prop against the door, her eyes fell on Brother Nilsson's old muzzle-loader over the mantelpiece. She took it down, and for some inexplicable reason noted that it was much heavier than her father's rook rifle.

In her room she leaned the gun against the wall near her bed, propped a chair under the door handle and, without saying her prayers or removing her best frock, crawled under the covers. She was exhausted. Almost every night after saying her prayers she would usually lie awake thinking about the events of the day before falling asleep. This night was the exception. Lost in an alien world and feeling abandoned by all, even God, she had never felt so miserable. But she didn't want to think about it. She sought only oblivion, trusting Shakespeare that sleep would "knit up the ravell'd sleeve of care."

CHAPTER EIGHT

When Elisabeth awoke, the room was filled with sunlight. It was Sunday morning—at least, she assumed it was morning—and she could think of no good reason for getting up. She had planned to attend a meeting in the Bowery, but that wasn't until the evening. As ever, a night's sleep had renewed her spirit and she felt that she could think about her future more rationally. Her mind turned to the events of last evening and she smiled wryly, thinking that *for some reason* she had developed an aversion to weddings.

As she thought about her future, she decided that she could stay in Utah or return to England. Neither option appealed to her. Perhaps if her fantasy about Jonathan Kimball had become reality, she could have adjusted to this alien world; however, she didn't think she could do it alone. But could she return to England with her tail between her legs and admit to her father that she had been so foolish? Could she resume her old life, or even worse, return to her adulterous husband? No. There must be another way.

She pondered the question so hard her head ached. And then an alternative presented itself. She could accept Mrs. Kenny's invitation to stay with her in Philadelphia and attend the women's medical college. Elisabeth clutched at the thought like a drowning person might clutch at a proffered rope.

But could she face another journey over the mountains and across the plains? She didn't think she had the strength. Besides, it was late in the season. She would probably have to wait until spring to go east. She felt trapped. But there was another way to the East, she had learned. If she could get to the Pacific Coast, she could take a ship around the

Horn to Philadelphia. Had she enough money? She thought so. The idea of escape brought a measure of peace to her mind.

In the meantime, she had promised Becky that she would teach school, and she would keep that commitment. Over that fortnight she would make inquiries about how to get to California via the southern route.

Her thoughts were interrupted by a knock at the front door. Not wanting to see anyone and thinking that it was probably for the Nilssons anyway, she ignored it. But the caller would not be denied and continued knocking. With a sigh, Elisabeth finally eased out of bed. She was about to put on a robe when she realized that she was already dressed. She ran her fingers through her hair. *I must look a fright. Maybe I can ask whoever it is to come back later.* On stockinged feet, she gingerly made her way through the quiet cabin. Cautiously approaching the front door, she called out, "Who is it?"

"Sister Eliza Snow."

Elisabeth had heard of Sister Snow both from Becky and from other members of the Church. They all seemed to set great store by her. *I wonder what she wants?* Elisabeth didn't want to be rude, but equally she didn't want to greet this woman in wrinkled dress and frowsy hair. She hesitated before saying, "Brother and Sister Nilsson are not here."

"Miss Ashcroft? It's you I have come to see."

Elisabeth sighed and opened the door to a distinguished woman in a black dress with black silk edging. A bouquet of marigolds in her hands contrasted with the woman's somber clothing. Her faced seemed familiar to Elisabeth, who suddenly remembered that her visitor had been at the wedding feast. As the older woman entered the cabin, she handed Elisabeth the flowers. "These were outside the door and there's a note attached—undoubtedly from one of your admirers. Perhaps you should put them in water."

As Elisabeth did so, a small square of paper fluttered out of the flowers. It read: "Miss Elizabeth Ashcroft." She placed the bouquet and note on a sideboard and, waving her guest to a chair at the kitchen table, sat across from her.

"I see that you've recovered well, dear," Sister Snow said. "Sister Becky Sanderson . . . that is, Sister Kimball, was most distraught about you last night. She asked me to call on you."

"That was kind of her. I'm feeling much better this morning, thank you. I don't know what came over me. I'm usually a very healthy person." She brushed a strand of hair from her face. "Please excuse how I look."

"Think nothing of it. I'm at fault for coming unannounced. I'm so glad to finally meet you, Miss Ashcroft. I've known about you for a long time. As a friend of Jonathan's mother, I was privy to the news he sent from England, and in one letter he told of your conversion. He spoke of you in such glowing terms. He also told of your interest in medicine."

Elisabeth wondered what else this woman knew about her. "Yes. I am interested in the healing arts; I have been all my life."

"In that case, would you like to join our Female Council of Health? It's an organization designed to increase the knowledge and availability of medical services among the Saints. We meet every week, usually at the home of Brother and Sister Richards."

Elisabeth was noncommittal. "Thank you. If I decide to stay in the valley, I'll consider attending."

"Oh, you're thinking of leaving so soon?" Sister Snow looked concerned.

Elisabeth nodded. "I've been invited to stay with a friend in Philadelphia and attend the new women's medical college. I've given it some serious thought."

Sister Snow nodded in approval. "A worthy aspiration. We could certainly use more trained medical people here. In the meantime, do you have enough to keep you busy?"

"For the next fortnight I'll be teaching school for Becky Kimball. After that, I don't know."

Sister Snow looked thoughtful for a moment, and then explained why she had asked. "Sister Forin at the mercantile would like to get away from time to time, and she asked me if I knew of anyone who could fill in for her. Also, Sister Sessions, one of our midwives and a leading light in the Female Council of Health, is looking for a young woman to train. You immediately came to mind. If you are interested in either position, please let me know."

Elisabeth promised to consider both opportunities, and Sister Snow said that she would recommend her to Sister Forin and Sister Sessions.

As she rose to take her leave, Sister Snow shook Elisabeth's hand and asked her if she were planning to attend the meeting in the Bowery that evening. Elisabeth said that she was.

After Sister Snow had left, Elisabeth returned to sit at the kitchen table and thought about her visitor. She decided that she liked Sister Snow and would be happy to have her as a friend. Her eyes fell on the flowers, causing her to go to the sideboard and examine the note. *Whoever left them spelled my name with a "z." He obviously doesn't know me well.* Absently, she began to rearrange the marigolds. *I wonder if it is an admirer? No. More likely Becky arranged for them last night. Perhaps they're from her garden.*

That evening, Elisabeth walked over to the Bowery. As she entered the crude structure of poles and brush, her mind flitted back to England and the magnificent church buildings she had known. The stark contrast caused her once again to feel out of place and doubt the wisdom of having come to this land.

As she stood wondering whether or not to stay at the meeting, Sister Snow hailed her and waved her over. Elisabeth accepted the invitation. Reading Elisabeth's expression, Sister Snow assured her that a tabernacle, then under construction, would soon be finished and the Saints would no longer have to meet outdoors.

Elisabeth was barely seated when President Brigham Young and several leading brethren took the stand. After a hymn and prayer, Brother Orson Pratt spoke on the plan of salvation. Afterwards, President Young spoke for ninety minutes on the importance of education and the role of women in furthering it among the Saints. Elisabeth listened intently to this second president of the Church. His earthy wisdom pleased her. Despite the recent trials of her faith, she knew through the whispering of the Spirit that he truly was a prophet of God.

"How are you feeling now, dear?" Eliza Snow asked after the meeting was over.

Elisabeth appreciated the woman's concern. "Much better, thank you. Though I imagine it will be some time before I feel at home here."

Sister Snow only nodded, understanding.

* * *

Although Elisabeth enjoyed her two weeks teaching school, it was with a certain relief that she turned the students back over to Becky Kimball on the latter's return.

"How can I ever thank you?" Becky asked, as Elisabeth finished up some marking at the teacher's desk.

Elisabeth smiled. "I confess, I quite enjoyed it. I hope you will call on me again if you need me." She paused for a moment before awkwardly adding, "There's something that's been bothering me, Becky." She paused again.

"Go ahead, Elisabeth."

Elisabeth took a deep breath, considering what Becky had told her about the wedding guest who had inspired Elisabeth's sickness, and about how to apologize for her behavior. "I feel so bad about the way I treated your brother. He politely introduced himself and I . . . well, I snubbed him. I feel I behaved badly. I like to think I'm a much kinder person than that, but that evening I wasn't myself. Also, he presented a rather . . . a rather unorthodox appearance . . ."

Becky laughed. "You mean he looked as ugly as sin!"

"Well, yes." Elisabeth laughed as well. "I've been wanting to apologize to him, but I'm told he's gone off to California. If you write to him, will you extend my apology?"

Becky smiled. "Better still, why don't I give you his address and you can write him yourself? About his appearance, he's really not bad looking at all when he's cleaned up. Have you any idea why he looked so awful that evening?" Elisabeth shook her head. "He'd just gotten back from California. He was over there as a gold missionary—"

"Gold missionary?"

Becky explained that President Young had sent several men, mostly veterans of the Mormon Battalion, like her brother Gren, to mine gold for the Church. The Saints needed the gold to help them get established in the valley. When she and Jonathan had set the date of their marriage, they had sent an invitation to Gren. As luck would have it, he was planning to return home with a gold shipment and would be able to attend the wedding.

"He and four companions," Becky continued, "set out in plenty of time, but they ran into trouble on the Forty-Mile Desert—an awfully hot place between here and the mountains. Three of the mules sickened and died. The men could have saved themselves, but they refused to abandon the gold. They sent one man off on the remaining mule to get help while Gren and the others pushed and pulled the wagon under a merciless sun until their strength was gone. Imagine! As you saw, Gren's face got horribly burned during the ordeal. The man who set out to get help finally returned with fresh animals and water, and Gren was able to make it home on the very day I was married. Since he'd promised to attend, and since he's as stubborn as his mules, he headed straight for Warm Springs."

Chagrin showed on Elisabeth's face. "Oh, Becky, now I feel even worse . . . snubbing a hero."

"Don't let it bother you. He's a very forgiving person. Even though you did bruise his pride, he was still asking about you before he left. I'm sure he'd love to hear from you."

Elisabeth looked at the name and address Becky had written for her. "'Grenville.' I was wondering what Gren was short for."

Becky smiled. "Our mother's maiden name."

The following day, George Brenton came down from Ogden and took Elisabeth for a drive in a borrowed spring gig. It was a bright fall day. Despite the rough, dusty road, Elisabeth's spirit soared as they drove around the valley. Optimism filled the air as Great Salt Lake City rose before them. Many of the Saints had moved out of their original habitations in the Old Fort in the city's center and were busily improving their one-acre lots. The afternoon was filled with hammering and sawing. For a while Elisabeth forgot about her disappointing introduction to the valley and vowed to put it out of her mind and enjoy the beautiful day.

The only cloud in an otherwise glorious day was George, who surprised her completely with another declaration of devotion. "I love you, Elisabeth," he blurted out just as they halted in front of the Nilsson cabin.

Elisabeth smiled kindly at her youthful suitor, but her words were firm. "Now, George," she said, taking his hand. "We've been through all this before. You know I'm married and am much too old for you. I'm sure you'll find someone wonderful closer to your age."

"I don't want anyone younger. I want you!"

"I'm flattered. I truly am. But it can never be. Please go now. You have a long journey ahead of you." Ignoring his protestations of love, she climbed down from the carriage and gave him a steady look until he fell silent. "If you pray about it and really listen to the Spirit, you'll know that we can only be friends."

It was obvious that this was not the answer George wanted to hear. Clearly he was prepared to keep talking until he had won her over, but Elisabeth's eyes were unwavering, and at last he snapped the reins and drove off. He did not look back.

Elisabeth sighed deeply and went inside the cabin.

Sister Nilsson looked up when Elisabeth entered. "Flowers. In room."

And indeed there were, petunias this time. Their aroma filled the room, and Elisabeth hurried to them to look for a note. As before, the attached piece of paper read simply, "Miss Elizabeth Ashcroft."

Elisabeth inhaled the honeyed air. *Who could have sent them? It couldn't be George. He was with me all day. Who could it be?*

* * *

The following Monday, Elisabeth found herself behind the counter of the Livingston and Kinkead General Mercantile store. The shop belonged to a "gentile" merchant who had a good relationship with the Saints. A Sister Florence Forin was the chief clerk.

"I'll be fine," Elisabeth said to Sister Forin as the shopkeeper prepared to leave. The bell above the door tinkled as Sister Forin closed the door behind her.

Elisabeth surveyed the multitudinous merchandise and then turned to the thick price book in front of her. *At least, I think I'll be fine.* She leaned on the counter and began to study the prices. She looked up when the bell announced her first customer. A leather-clad figure, followed closely by a young Indian woman with a child strapped to her back, entered the store. To her English eyes, it was a strange family; but Elisabeth had seen similar families on her way across the plains.

The trapper harshly commanded his wife to sit on an upturned barrel, and then demanded of Elisabeth where whiskey could be found. When she wasn't helpful, he left his wife there, intending to find some. Elizabeth saw how uncomfortable the girl was and offered her a rocker.

After a while, Elisabeth directed a surreptitious glance toward the mother and child gently rocking in their chair. Suddenly looking up, the mother caught the expression on Elisabeth's face and read her longing. She struggled from the rocker and held out the baby. Elisabeth hesitated. The girl persisted, and Elisabeth came out from behind the counter and drew the baby to her.

Contentment flowed through Elisabeth as she rocked the baby. The mother, again sitting, smiled, and the eyes of the two women communicated on a level deeper than language.

The tinkling of the doorbell broke the moment. "Git out hyar." The trapper motioned his wife with one hand. His other hand clutched the neck of a gallon jug.

After they had gone, Elisabeth rocked for a long time. She could still feel the warmth of the baby in her arms.

Later that evening, Becky Kimball visited Elisabeth. The two women talked for a while, and as their friendship deepened Elisabeth shared her experience with the Indian girl and confessed her profound longing for a child. "You'll get married and have children some day," Becky said, comfortingly. "Have you written to Gren?"

Smiling at Becky's obvious matchmaking, Elisabeth shook her head. "I decided not to. He might misinterpret my writing to him. When he returns, I'll apologize in person." She then turned the conversation in another direction. "I noticed the dearth of school supplies when I was teaching, so I took the liberty of writing to my friend in Philadelphia to send some. She has lots of money and loves to do charitable work. I ordered a whole lot . . . *McGuffey's Readers, Smith's Arithmetic, Kirkham's Grammar* and so forth, plus chalk and slates."

Becky's face glowed as she looked at Elisabeth. "Thank you so much. We can surely use them. You are very kind. The man who wins your heart will be getting an angel."

If I were only free to give my heart. Will that day ever come?

That evening Elisabeth couldn't sleep. She tossed around a long time before she gave up on sleep and turned her mind to what was bothering her. Although she still did not feel fully at home among the Saints, she was having second thoughts about fleeing to Philadelphia. Doing so, she had come to feel, would be in a sense abandoning her new faith. She felt caught between two worlds, and she knew that she'd never be happy until she had chosen one or the other. "One can't run with the hares and hunt with the hounds," her father had often said. First, she decided, she needed to strengthen her testimony and become fully integrated into the gospel. Then, if Heavenly Father wanted her to get a medical degree, she would gladly go east. With this thought in mind, she climbed out of bed, knelt on the rug, and after thanking her Heavenly Father for her fledgling testimony and for His watchcare during the long journey to Zion, she pleaded for guidance.

CHAPTER NINE

One morning in late November, Elisabeth was eating breakfast with the Nilssons when a knock sounded at the door. It was Jonathan Kimball. "Can you teach school today, Elisabeth? Becky is feeling a bit under the weather."

"Of course. Tell Becky that I'll visit her on the way to the meetinghouse."

Becky was sitting at the kitchen table when Elisabeth arrived. "You look awful, Becky. Let me help you into bed."

Elisabeth took Becky's elbow and was helping her arise when Becky's eyes widened, and she pressed a hand to her mouth. Elisabeth quickly lowered her back onto the chair, snatched up a basin, and held it in front of Becky just in time for her to become violently ill. Elisabeth stayed with her friend until Becky was in bed and looking better.

She arrived at the school late to find the pupils enjoying the delay. It took a while to restore order. The rest of the day went well, and Elisabeth's thoughts often turned to Becky. What would cause her to be so ill? Food poisoning? Influenza? Cholera? She wondered how she'd find her friend that evening. To her surprise, she discovered a healthy-looking Becky chatting with Jonathan in the kitchen. "You hardly look sick at all," Elisabeth said. "Are you fully recovered?"

Becky smiled. "I'm afraid not. According to Sister Sessions, I won't recover for about eight months!"

"You're with child!" Elisabeth hugged her friend and sincerely congratulated her and Jonathan. Although tired and hungry, she took the time to listen to the young couples' plans for adding extra space to their house in preparation for the baby. She was happy for her friends, but a little envious, too.

That evening Elisabeth lay in bed contemplating Becky's happy news. *Becky is only twenty-one years old. She has a loving husband and will soon have a child. I'm twenty-eight and have neither.* Allowing herself the indulgence of self-pity, she wondered why life, at times, was unfair. Getting out of bed, she paced around the small room. Her eyes fell on her Bible, and without thinking she picked it up. Sitting on the edge of the bed, she turned up the wick on the bedside lamp and thumbed through the pages until she came to the story of Jacob, Rachel, and Leah. She smiled wryly when she read, "And when Rachel saw that she bare Jacob no children, Rachel envied her sister; and said unto Jacob, Give me children, or else I die."

When Elisabeth had read this passage in the past, she could understand Jacob being upset with Rachel. Now, all her sympathy was with Rachel. She read further of the birth of Rachel's children, Joseph and Benjamin, and Rachel's death in bearing Benjamin brought to her mind the great sacrifice mothers make in bringing children into the world. *Strange, how we're so constituted as to be willing to go through the pain of childbirth to satisfy an inner longing.* Closing the Bible, she sat for a long time and thought about her life.

Admitting to herself that she had many blessings, she knelt beside her bed and thanked her Heavenly Father for all of them. Before she got back into bed, she asked once more for the patience to endure until her matrimonial challenges were solved. The last thought she had before falling asleep was a determination not to envy Becky's good fortune.

* * *

In December George Brenton visited Elisabeth and invited her to Great Salt Lake City's major Christmas ball. Elisabeth suggested that he might take a girl closer to his age, but he insisted that she was the only partner he wanted. At last she relented with the warning, "Only if we go as friends."

Over the months, she had taken little time with her appearance. Why should she? Why should she make herself attractive to men when she had no right to encourage them? As long as her face was scrubbed, her clothes clean, and her hair pulled back into a bun, she would do. On the day of the ball, however, Becky visited Elisabeth with a different view in mind. "Elisabeth, you are a beautiful woman and I'm here to make sure it shows. I've bought you a new dress and I insist on you letting me do something with your hair." Despite Elisabeth's objections, Becky had her way.

"You . . . you're a vision of beauty," George stammered that evening when he came to collect her.

Elisabeth blushed. "And you will be the handsomest man at the ball, George. Young women will be swarming around you, and you'll forget all about a spinster such as I."

"Never!" he said.

At the ball, when George had gone to fetch refreshments for the two of them, Jonathan Kimball approached her. She was pleased with herself that she had gotten over him and that they could talk as friends. He asked how she was enjoying the festivities. Elisabeth said that she was having a good time. He then asked about George's intentions.

Elisabeth laughed. "Whatever do you mean?"

"Has he proposed?"

Elisabeth nodded. "Constantly. He is such a dear young man. He even elicited the poet Robert Herrick's poem 'Counsel to Girls,' to bolster his suit. It is about women who turn down suitors until the day comes when the unfortunate women have lost their beauty and youth. Do you think I've lost my prime, Jonathan?" she asked in mock seriousness.

"Certainly not. In fact, the reason I asked about George is that Becky is determined to get you and her brother Gren together. You saw him at his worst, but he really is presentable when dressed in clean clothes and not covered with peeling skin and blisters. He'll be back from California in the spring. If you're still free at that time . . ."

Elisabeth swallowed hard and a pang of conscience shot through her. *I should tell Jonathan that I'm not free. I should confess now what I should have confessed before my baptism. But what will he and Becky think of me? Oh, why have I carried this charade on so long?*

George's return rescued her from Jonathan. Thrusting her doubts away, she said, "Please put the refreshments on the bench, George.

They're forming a Virginia reel and I'd so like to join in." Then she waved goodbye to Jonathan as George took her arm.

* * *

Winter passed into spring, and Elisabeth continued to get gifts from her secret admirer. Every few weeks a package would show up at her front door, always with "Miss Elizabeth Ashcroft" printed on a small square of paper. When flowers were no longer available, other gifts followed: a silk handkerchief, a writing pad, and a small bottle of Lily-of-the-Valley scent. Elisabeth recognized the latter as having come from Livingston and Kinkead's. She asked Sister Forin if she knew who might have purchased the scent. "Oh, Lily of the Valley is very popular," Sister Forin had replied, and quickly turned to serve a customer who had just entered the store.

Most often her admirer—for so she had convinced herself that the gift-giver was—would plant the presents when Elisabeth was at a church meeting, causing her to wonder why he was not in church also. One Sunday afternoon she almost caught him. She was home alone with a cold. The house was very still. Lying on her bed, halfasleep, she suddenly heard a noise at the front door. Quickly going to the window, she saw a half-grown boy stealthily rounding the corner. He had deposited the bottle of scent at the front door. As she picked it up, she shook her head. *I wonder why only boys seem infatuated with me? Perhaps it's just as well. If a man should show interest, I'd only have to tell him that I'm not free.*

CHAPTER TEN

One day in late spring of 1852, nine months after her arrival in the valley, Elisabeth was clerking at the store when in walked a tall man with a black, three-piece suit hanging loosely on his gaunt frame.

"Good day," Elisabeth said from behind the counter.

"Good day, miss." He removed his hat and smiled. Despite his sallow complexion, he was handsome. He placed a black leather bag on the counter. "I need a few supplies. Would you happen to have any spirits of hartshorn, tincture of castor, or liquid laudanum?"

She shook her head. "I'm afraid not, doctor. Our apothecary supplies are limited. We do have some patent medicines such as Loxol Pain-expeller, Seven Barks Compound, and Kickapoo Worm Killer."

The young doctor gave a resigned smile. "Oh, well, perhaps I'll just look around—" A paroxysm of coughing stopped his words. Turning away, he bent forward and coughed into a handkerchief. Elisabeth left and quickly returned with a glass of water. He received it gratefully and drank slowly. The pallor of his face was even worse than before. With a wry smile he handed back the glass and said, "Physician, heal thyself."

"I'm sure you would if you could," Elisabeth said with feeling. "Can nothing be done?"

He shook his head. "Consumption. Perhaps I'll die slower in California. Let me introduce myself—Philip Osgood of Philadelphia."

She introduced herself and asked, "So you're going to California for your health?"

He nodded. "If a miracle happens, I would like to return to Philadelphia, the medical capital of America. It's a marvelous time for medicine . . . so many new developments."

Elisabeth smiled. "Such as the establishment of a female medical college?"

"Exactly. So you've heard about it?"

"I have and I think it's wonderful. I've even been contemplating going there myself."

He nodded in agreement. "It is wonderful. Unfortunately, the old guard is extremely opposed to it, as they are to all advances in medicine!" His passionate words brought a little color to his cheeks.

Elisabeth smiled inwardly and hoped that no customers would disturb them. She liked this man and longed to know more about the current state of medicine. She smiled at his ardor.

"Among other things," he continued, "unsound religion is hampering progress. Some even believe that eliminating pain with ether or chloroform is against God's will. I'm an agnostic myself. I just can't trust such nonsensical religions. Tradition is also in the way. Many doctors are resisting the research showing that proper hygiene can halt the spread of contagion. They say that they are too busy to wash their hands or clean the filth from their clothes!"

His passionate advocacy brought on another paroxysm of coughing, cutting short their discussion. When it was over, he apologized and said that he had better go. He paused at the door. "Dr. Elizabeth Blackwell, whom I'm sure you've heard of, is also a disciple of the new medicine. Perhaps as more women become physicians, the profession will change for the better." He paused before adding, "I hope I'll see you again before I head for California."

"I'll be serving in the shop for the next few days," she said evenly.

After he had gone, Elisabeth reflected on their conversation, and her mind again turned to Philadelphia and medical school. She wondered what it would be like to live in a mansion and attend the college. It seemed that fate was nudging her in that direction.

After a while, her mind turned to some news that she had heard that day. Since it would be many years before the temple would be ready, temple ordinances, which had generally ceased after the Saints were driven west, would soon be available again in the Council

House. *I wonder if Becky and Jonathan will be able to receive their endowments before the baby is born? It would be nice if their baby were born under the covenant.* The missionaries had taught Elisabeth the importance of temple ordinances. Now that these ordinances would be available again, Elisabeth resolved in her mind to settle for nothing less than celestial marriage. *If I'm ever free to marry again, I'll do it right the second time.*

Late that night, a thumping on the front door awakened Elisabeth. Brother Nilsson opened the door to find Jonathan Kimball, out of breath and clearly distraught, standing there. "Becky needs Elisabeth!" he cried.

Elisabeth quickly threw on her clothes and was soon at Becky's bedside. In the big double bed, the mother-to-be looked like a frightened little girl. "I'm all wet!" she groaned when she saw Elisabeth. "I think I'm having the baby."

"You couldn't be," Jonathan said. "It's too soon."

"Thank you, Dr. Kimball," said Elisabeth dryly. "Now make yourself useful and find Sister Sessions—no, wait, she's in Provo. Go find somebody."

Jonathan bolted from the room. Elisabeth did what she could to make Becky comfortable before going to the kitchen and putting a kettle to boil on the stove. Upon returning to the bedroom, she arranged a basin and towels on a dressing table. She returned to Becky's bedside. "Don't worry, dear, Jonathan will be back with someone soon. If worse comes to worst, I've been working with Sister Session, and I'm confident I can deliver the infant myself."

Within the hour, Jonathan returned with a midwife, a Sister Rutley, who immediately examined Becky. When the midwife was finished, she took Elisabeth and Jonathan aside. "The child wants to be born; it's in a perfect position, but there's a problem. Sister Kimball is a mite small."

"A mite small?" Jonathan repeated, looking sick.

"Perhaps you should wait outside, Brother Kimball," Sister Rutley said, not unkindly, "and let us women handle this."

For the next five hours, Becky wore herself out trying to give birth to the baby, but to no avail. Finally, Elisabeth sought out Jonathan. He leapt from a chair when he saw her.

"Jonathan, I'm afraid we are at a loss to know what to do, and the poor dear's exhausted. Something more has to be done. Since you've already given her a priesthood blessing, please try to find a Dr. Philip Osgood. He's visiting the city, probably staying at the hotel."

When Elisabeth returned to the room, she told Sister Rutley what she had done. "Dr. Osgood believes in scrupulous cleanliness, so would you please reheat the water on the stove? I'll sit with Sister Kimball for a while."

The midwife complied, and when she had finished, she approached Elisabeth suspiciously. "I've not heard of this Dr. Osgood. Who is he?"

"Let's go into the hallway," Elisabeth said, taking Sister Rutley's elbow. Elisabeth closed the door behind them. "He's a young doctor on his way to California."

"A gentile?"

"Yes."

"I don't like that," Sister Rutley said, shaking her head. "I don't like that one bit. Sister Kimball's in God's hands now."

Where her friend's welfare was at stake, Elisabeth would brook no opposition. "Well, Sister Rutley, God helps those who help themselves. If Dr. Osgood comes, he'll be in charge."

The midwife stiffened. "We'll see what Brother Kimball says about that. After all, Brother Kimball called me to his wife's confinement."

Elisabeth went one better. "True, but *Sister Kimball* called me."

Sister Rutley was not beaten. "You know President Young doesn't hold with gentile doctors," she said, as if it were the final word on the subject.

But Elisabeth would not concede. "From what I've learned about Brother Brigham, he's the soul of practicality. Under the circumstances, I feel certain that he'd approve. Now let's hear no more of this. I appreciate your help, Sister Rutley, as I'm sure Brother and Sister Kimball do. But when Dr. Osgood arrives, he will be in charge and that's all there is to it." Elisabeth opened the bedroom door and held it open for Sister Rutley. The midwife hesitated and then reentered the room.

A half hour later, Jonathan returned with the young physician. After being introduced to Sister Rutley, the doctor approached Becky, who lay trembling with fear and exhaustion.

He gave her a comforting smile. "So the child is having a problem putting in an appearance. I'm Dr. Osgood. As soon as I wash up, I'll examine you."

"Over here, doctor." Elisabeth directed him to the dressing table.

"Thank you. This is perfect," he said, nodding at the basin of water. Removing an envelope from his bag, he held it up so that Elisabeth and Sister Rutley could see it. "Chloride of lime," he said as he poured the white powder into the water.

"Mr. Kimball," Dr. Osgood said as he washed his hands, "If you plan on staying, you'd better wash up too. But I'd prefer you wait outside." Jonathan left. "Now, ladies, please change the water and wash your hands in this stuff."

Elisabeth quickly complied, but Sister Rutley folded her arms and said, "My hands are perfectly clean."

The young doctor resorted to friendly persuasion. "Now, Mrs. Rutley, let's not be difficult. Please wash your hands, or I'll have to ask you to leave."

After a moment's hesitation, the midwife pursed her lips, gave an audible sigh of protest, shook her head, and finally washed her hands.

Dr. Osgood turned to Becky. "How's our patient?"

"It's very painful, doctor. I never knew it would be like this."

The doctor nodded empathetically. "Fortunately, the remembrance of the pain will subside once you have the babe in your arms. You are a brave woman and you are doing well. I'm now going to examine you." With a modesty sheet in place, he manually examined Becky. "Mmm, a tight fit, but the baby's in a good birth position."

"That was my conclusion too," Sister Rutley said proudly.

"Excellent," Dr. Osgood said with no trace of condescension. "A second opinion is always good. Now I'm going to do a diagonal conjugate measurement." When he had finished, he was quiet for a moment. "Miss Ashcroft, in my bag you'll find a set of forceps wrapped in a white cloth."

Elisabeth withdrew the instrument and handed it to the doctor. "Here you are, doctor."

He acknowledged her assistance with a nod and said to no one in particular, "I wish we were in a hospital where I could administer anesthesia." He turned back to Becky. "Now, Mrs. Kimball, this is going to be uncomfortable but needs to be done. The head of your baby is lodged in the pelvic cavity. I'm going to use an instrument to assist in getting your baby's head free. Once the instrument is locked in place, I'll gently pull and I want you to push with all the strength you have." Becky's eyes went wide at these instructions. She nodded doubtfully. The doctor turned to Elisabeth and Sister Rutley. "Any questions, ladies?" They had no questions. "Then let's proceed." Becky gave a low groan as the instrument entered the birth canal. Once it was around the baby's head, the doctor locked it in place and said, "Now, push with all your might." Becky obeyed and screamed in pain. "There's movement . . ." the doctor began.

The doctor's body quivered. Grabbing Elisabeth's hand, he placed her fingers around the forceps handles, and, gasping, flung himself from the room. Despite her shock, Elisabeth followed through, and in minutes the baby was born. Sister Rutley immediately took over.

The infant was in her mother's arms by the time Dr. Osgood, pale and shaken, returned. "I'm sorry I bolted. Another paroxysm—"

"We understand," Elisabeth said. "All is well."

He smiled. "So I see." He looked with appreciation on Elisabeth and Sister Rutley. "I've never worked with better colleagues." Turning to Becky, he added, "Nor with a better patient."

Becky smiled at him. "Thank you so much, Dr. Osgood. You were right. The pain and suffering seem a small thing now I have my baby in my arms."

He examined the newborn. "She's small, but perfect. Birth never ceases to amaze me. This little girl's birth is . . . it's a miracle. Had she gone full term . . . well, it's a miracle."

Elisabeth gave him a teasing smile. "An agnostic believing in miracles?"

"I'm not a very devout agnostic," he said, grinning in return.

Elisabeth laughed. "Well, I must agree a miracle was involved. I don't believe it was merely happenstance that caused you to enter the shop yesterday."

"Would someone please get Jonathan?" Becky asked.

"Of course," Dr. Osgood said. "He's in the hall, frantically pacing."

"I'll get him," Sister Rutley said. "And then I must be off. My husband will be wondering what happened to me. I'll be back as soon as I attend to his needs." Elisabeth thanked the midwife as she was leaving.

With Jonathan gushing over his wife and daughter, Dr. Osgood took Elisabeth's elbow and ushered her into the hall. He looked into her eyes and then looked away. So confident during the delivery, he now stumbled over his words. "Miss Ashcroft," he began, "I'm leaving in the morning, but I wanted to say that if circumstances were different . . . that is, if I weren't dying . . .You're so lovely, so capable. Just the sort of woman . . . " his words trailed off.

Elisabeth stood in silent wonderment at this admission, but after only a moment touched his arm. "I understand," she said gently, "and I'm very flattered." She paused, not knowing what else to say. Then a thought rescued her. "Oh, we must attend to your fee."

He slowly shook his head. "No fee for miracles." Gazing into Elisabeth's hazel eyes, he sighed and then straightened his shoulders, becoming a professional again. "You really should attend medical college. You'd make an excellent physician." With a quick wave of his hand, he turned and left.

Elisabeth watched him go. "Godspeed, dear Dr. Osgood," she whispered. Turning slowly, she opened the bedroom door. Jonathan was sitting on the bed with his arm around Becky, who held the baby in her arms. Elisabeth gazed on their happiness for a moment. Then, as tears seeped from her eyes, she softly closed the door.

Several weeks later, Elisabeth watched as Jonathan took his daughter in his arms and gave her a name—Elisabeth Rebecca Kimball—and a blessing.

Elisabeth gazed on the beautiful child and slowly nodded. *Elisabeth Kimball. It does have a nice ring to it after all.*

CHAPTER ELEVEN

One sleepy summer afternoon, Elisabeth was leaning on the counter in the store, wishing she were somewhere else, when her mind turned to her secret admirer. Suddenly she had an inspiration. *Since some of the gifts were bought here*, she reasoned. *I wonder if there's a record of the purchaser? Let me see, it was in the spring when I got the bottle of scent.* She opened the account book, found the page for March, and started running her fingers down the columns. "Here's one," she said aloud, "Lily of the Valley charged to the account of . . . mmm . . . nobody I know." She kept looking. "Ah, here's another one. Charged to . . . Brother Gren Sanderson!"

For a long time she stared at the column. Then she began to look for other items. Sure enough, she found the silk handkerchief and the notepad also charged to his account. She noticed that his account balance got steadily smaller with each purchase. This led her to leaf back in the book until she found a deposit of twenty dollars in gold dust to Gren's account. *So,* she thought, *he must have made the deposit before he left for California and given his accomplice instructions to purchase the items and draw from his account. He certainly went to a lot of trouble. The young boy I saw must be his accomplice, and Sister Forin must have been in on it too.*

For a long time after her discovery, Grenville Sanderson dominated Elisabeth's thoughts. She tried to picture what he must look like without all the blisters and scraggly hair. *Becky said he's handsome. He probably is. Becky is certainly pretty.*

A sick feeling came over her and she wished she had not found out that Becky's brother had given the gifts. While his identity was unknown she could enjoy the game. But now, she could only think of how hurt he'd be when she told him that she was a married woman. He obviously was interested in her or he wouldn't have set up this elaborate scheme.

"Sister Forin," said Elisabeth when the latter came to relieve her. "Are you sure you don't know who purchased the bottle of scent I received from my secret admirer?"

Sister Forin smiled guiltily. "I don't believe I said I didn't know. I believe I said that Lily of the Valley is a popular scent. Obviously you've discovered our little scheme. I figured you would eventually. Make sure that Gren knows you figured it out for yourself. Tim and I were sworn to secrecy."

"Tim?"

"My son."

"Ah, the deliverer of gifts."

"Yes. The flowers came from my garden. Gren arranged it all before he left. How do you feel about your discovery?"

"Sad that the little game is over. Now I must face reality. Of course, I'll return the gifts when I see Brother Sanderson."

"Why would you do that? He really is a wonderful man and a great catch. If I had a marriageable daughter, I'd be proud to have him as a son-in-law."

Elisabeth wanted to unburden her soul, but she didn't. All she said was, "For personal reasons."

Two weeks later, Elisabeth was again behind the counter when a man entered the store and doffed his hat, revealing light brown hair. He was handsome and well dressed. *There's something familiar about him.* Had she seen those sparkling blue eyes before? "May . . . may I be of service?" she stumbled over her words.

"I hope so," the man said, smiling. For a long moment he gazed at her, the smile not leaving his face.

Elisabeth grew uncomfortable. "You'll have to tell me what you want if I'm to help you," she said, indicating with a wave of her hand the merchandise-laden shelves.

"Of course. I'm sorry. You'll find my request rather unusual. I'm . . . I'm looking for . . . for some female companionship. For the past year I've been working in the gold mines in California, and I need someone to recivilize me."

Elisabeth suddenly recognized him. The last time she'd seen him, his face had been grimy and covered with a scraggly beard, but there was no mistaking those clear blue eyes. "Sorry," she said lightly, trying desperately to be nonchalant, "we do not provide that service. May I interest you in something else?"

"Afraid not. That's all I came for." Again, they gazed at each other in silence. "Perhaps you would consider personally filling my order?"

Elisabeth shook her head. "That's not possible. Besides, I already have several suitors . . . and even a secret admirer."

"I've journeyed long to reach my home and you," he said, his eyes twinkling. "I'm prepared to vanquish all suitors."

"I'm afraid you must be mistaken, sir. My name is Elisabeth, not Penelope."

Elisabeth liked his laugh.

"A secret admirer, you say. Have you any idea who he is?"

"I suspect one Grenville Sanderson, but he's off in California grubbing for gold. Perhaps you met him out there? If he's the one, perhaps he'll come back as rich as Midas and seek out a more worthy companion than I."

"Oh, I doubt that he'll come back rich. I hear he's a gold missionary. The gold will go to the Church. I do know of him. He's a hard worker and an excellent fellow all around."

She smiled. "And modest, too."

He laughed again and then grew serious. "May I call on you, Sister Ashcroft?"

Elisabeth's heart fell and she dropped her eyes. She felt guilty for having engaged in light banter with a man obviously serious about her. She didn't know what to say. Finally, she looked up at him and shook her head. "I'm . . . I'm so sorry, Brother Sanderson. It's not possible. I'm not free."

"Not free? I don't understand."

Elisabeth was not prepared for this. She wanted desperately to tell him the truth, but she just couldn't do it. She just couldn't abide seeing the honest expectancy in his eyes change to pity when she told him how foolishly she'd behaved before joining the Church. She flushed miserably and couldn't look him in the face. To her relief, the bell rang and a customer entered the store.

"Please come for me at six o'clock," Elisabeth said quickly. "I'll explain everything then."

When the customer had left, Elisabeth pondered on what she would tell Gren. It was tempting to hide behind half-truths, but she knew she must tell him all. He deserved the truth. Yes, he would be hurt, but it was time for her to unburden her soul. It was time for her to face the reality that she had no right to live under the guise of eligibility. Once the decision was made, she could hardly wait for six o'clock to come. As the afternoon ground on, the minute hand on the clock in the corner seemed to lose its power of movement. At one point Elisabeth went over and tapped on the glass. But the clock was working, and at length it was six o'clock. Quickly locking the door, she turned to see Gren Sanderson waiting in an open carriage. "I thought we'd drive up to the bench. We can get a good view of the lake from there, and the wildflowers are in bloom."

Elisabeth knew that she had no right to accept his invitation. She should tell him now and get it over with. Prolonging her confession was wrong. But she wanted to see the lake. She wanted to see the flowers and breathe in their fragrance. Above all, she wanted to be with this kind, generous man who had the strength of character to overlook her spurning him when they first met.

She allowed Gren to help her into the carriage. "Would you mind if we stopped by the Nilssons' first?" she asked. "I should let them know where I am so they'll not wait supper for me."

After doing so and then reaching their destination, Gren hitched the horse to a tree, helped Elisabeth from the carriage, and walked her through a profusion of pink, blue, lavender, and yellow flowers to a small hillock. The Great Salt Lake shimmered in the distance. "How grand," Elisabeth said. "It takes my breath away,"

"I thought you'd like it." Gren gazed at the lake and then gazed at Elisabeth. His expression of wonder did not change.

They sat on the hillock and stared across the valley to the water and the blue-gray bulk of the mountains beyond. Gren waited for Elisabeth to speak. She paused, took a deep breath of the flower-scented air, and slowly turned to him. "Brother Sanderson, I have a confession to make, a confession I should have made when I first entered the valley. I'm not who you think I am. I'm . . . I'm an impostor."

He stared at her in confusion and disbelief. "That needs some explaining."

"It does," she agreed, and told him all.

He listened patiently until she was finished. Then he stood up and stared off across the lake. "You didn't tell the missionaries you were married?"

"No. I know now that I should have, but at the time I wanted them to think well of me—I didn't want them to know how foolish I'd been. Besides, I was sure that the annulment would be approved. Finding the gospel so filled me with the Spirit, I couldn't believe that anything could go wrong in my life again."

"You say your father has appealed the council's decision?"

"Yes. But like the mills of God, council decisions grind slowly. I don't expect an answer for many months. In the meantime, there is nothing I can do."

Suddenly, Elisabeth felt cold all over. Gren turned just as she shivered.

"You're cold," he said, taking off his coat and wrapping her in it. "I'll take you home."

They hardly spoke as the vehicle lumbered down the rutted trail. When they drew up in front of the cabin, Gren methodically looped the reins over the front handrail and stared straight ahead. Out of the corner of her eye, Elisabeth could see Sister Nilsson peering out the window. Elisabeth didn't know what to do. Should she climb down by herself? Should she wait to see what Gren would do? After an awkward pause, both of them spoke at once.

"I'm sorry," said Gren, "you go ahead."

"No, you please."

He nodded and turned to her. "Sister Ashcroft, I've never believed in love at first sight, but since I first saw you at the Warm Springs Hall, I haven't been able to get you out of my thoughts. Your face has filled my mind these many months. It has eased the pain of hours in water up to my waist; it has helped me endure the long, lonely nights. My sister and brother-in-law have given such a good report of you, and having confirmed their praise through our conversations this evening, I can see they did not exaggerate a thing. If anything, you are even more wonderful than they described. What you have told me has changed nothing in my feelings for you. I am considering waiting for you till you're free."

Elisabeth lowered her eyes and sadly shook her head. "The chances of my becoming free are remote. It would be cruel of me to give you any encouragement. The valley is full of eligible girls. You had best forget me and find some girl who is free to accept your love."

Gren took her hand and squeezed it. "Perhaps. But I'm twenty-eight years old. I've served in the Mormon Battalion. I've served as a gold missionary. God has kept me busy until we could meet. I'm used to waiting." He paused. "If you were free, would you allow me to court you?"

Elisabeth hesitated. "That is not a fair question, Brother Sanderson. I'm not free, and though I've racked my brain, I can't think of any way of getting free. However, let me say this. From what Becky and Sister Forin have told me about you, and from our time together this evening, I believe that any single woman would be honored to have you call on her."

He shook his head. "I'm not giving up for now."

Elisabeth gazed at him and shook her head. "Becky said that you are as stubborn as your mules."

They both fell silent.

"Where do we go from here?" Gren finally asked.

"Nowhere, I'm afraid. Please wait." Elisabeth quickly climbed down from the carriage and went into the cabin. She returned with the notepad, scent, and handkerchief and handed them to him. "I want you to know how much these and the flowers meant to me over the months. It was exciting and flattering to know that someone was interested in me. However, I must return them. Until I am free, our only connection can be our friendship and fellowship in the gospel. I hope that you can understand. And it would be a great sign of your respect for me if you do not mention our dilemma until I am free—my feelings are tender on the matter." She slipped out of his jacket and handed it to him.

He took the jacket and items and laid them on the buggy seat. "I don't understand," he said, abjectly. "I don't understand why fate has brought us together and at the same time conspired to keep us apart." He paused. "I will prayerfully consider this," he promised. "Good night, Elisabeth. Thank you for being honest with me."

Tears sprang to her eyes. *He said my name. How natural it sounded on his lips. Oh, when will this nightmare end? When will I be free?*

Full of emotions, Elisabeth went inside. Sister Nilsson gave her a questioning look. Elisabeth wished that she could explain to this good woman what had happened. But how could she? She wasn't sure herself what had happened or what it meant for the future. "Good night, Sister Nilsson. I believe I'll forgo supper."

Elisabeth threw herself onto the bed and wept. When she could cry no longer, she sat up, dried her eyes, and tried to make sense of her life. *I'm glad I told Gren the truth. A great burden has been lifted from my shoulders. Now I must tell everyone, especially Becky and Jonathan and Sister Snow. Confession truly is good for the soul. I'm suddenly free to get on with my life—freed from the delusion that somehow my married state would evaporate and that I could fall in love and marry. Now I can focus on other things. Perhaps I should go to medical school. Yes, that's what I'll do. I'll write Mary and find out how I'd go about getting registered.* Excitement crept into her as she contemplated this new adventure. Then, the vision of Gren's sad face came before her. *Perhaps there is more I can do to dissuade him from waiting for me. Do I really want to dissuade him?* The confidence she'd felt only a minute before began to wane. She pondered on what her responsibility was for Gren's state of mind. Gradually an answer came. *No, I'm not responsible for Gren's happiness or unhappiness. He is a mature man, a godly man. He will be inspired to do what's right. If we are meant to be together someday, he will wait. If we are not meant to be together, he will find someone else. Either way, my job is to get on with my life and stop living in a fantasy world. Claverley once told me to grow up. Perhaps the events of this day have moved me a few steps in that direction.*

Becky visited Elisabeth later that evening. It was evident that Elisabeth had been crying. Becky put her arms around Elisabeth's neck. "You poor dear. Gren told me everything. I had no idea that you were suffering under such a burden."

Elisabeth sat on the bed and motioned for Becky to sit on the one chair in the room. "I'm glad he told you. I want the whole world to know. Telling Gren has cleansed my soul."

"Be assured that Jonathan and I will stand by you. Gren believes he'll wait for you even though you have told him not to."

"We shall see. I think he understands, though, that we need to go our separate paths for the time being. It wouldn't do for either of us to sit around waiting for me to be free when we have no idea how long that will take." Elisabeth smiled wryly. "I guess one positive thing is that Claverley is in his mid-fifties and drinks too much. He can't last forever."

Becky's mouth fell open. "Elisabeth! I'm surprised to hear you talk so."

"It's the new Elisabeth you hear. I've decided to start calling a spade a spade and stop being so naïve. If I'm going to be a doctress, I must be more of a woman of the world."

"A doctress?"

"Yes. I've decided to take Mrs. Kenny's offer of living with her and attending medical college."

Becky stared at Elisabeth. "You have my head spinning. You're truly going to Philadelphia?"

"That's what I've decided. Do you wish me luck?"

"Of course. I'm one hundred percent behind you!"

Later, Elisabeth saw Becky to the door. Brother and Sister Nilsson were sitting across from each other at the kitchen table, she was knitting and he was reading an outdated copy of a Swedish newspaper. After saying good-bye to Becky, Elisabeth turned to her landlady. "Would it be all right if I got myself something to eat, Sister Nilsson? I'm suddenly famished."

After she had eaten, Elisabeth returned to her room and wrote three letters: one to her father, wherein she pressed him to do all in his power to get the annulment; one to her husband, saying that if he would only consent to the annulment she would not try to recover her inheritance by legal means; and one to Mrs. Kenny, asking for information on the medical college.

CHAPTER TWELVE

In August 1852, The Church of Jesus Christ of Latter-day Saints met in a special conference wherein the Church leaders announced to the world that plural marriage was officially part of its practice. Elisabeth was sitting with Sister Eliza Snow in the tabernacle when she heard the news. Like most of the Saints, Elisabeth had anticipated the announcement. Nevertheless, it still came as something of a shock to her. Sister Snow leaned over, took Elisabeth's hand, and squeezed it. "Finally," she said.

Elisabeth gave her a weak smile. She was happy for Sister Snow and the other plural wives who had been living under a cloud. But the announcement gave her a hollow feeling in the pit of her stomach. It was not only because she felt that it would bring increased persecution, but also because she'd heard from Becky that Gren had been ordained a seventy. He and others with this missionary calling were being trained to go to the principal cities in the United States and set up newspapers to explain plural marriage and other Church doctrines. *Where will he go? How long will he be gone? And what if he is called to live the principle himself?*

Gren was not sent out with the first set of missionaries, who went to Washington and established *The Seer*, although he did spend a lot of time away from home traveling to the outlying settlements on Church assignments. Meanwhile, Elisabeth was kept busy working in the store and accompanying the midwife, Sister Sessions, on her rounds. The school supplies Elisabeth had requested from Mrs. Kenny finally arrived, and Becky was ecstatic as she unpacked the books, chalk, and slates. A thick envelope addressed to Elisabeth accompanied the supplies. While Becky was busy rearranging a storage room to house the new supplies, Elisabeth sat at a desk and opened the envelope to find a note from Mrs. Kenny, a brochure on the Female Medical College of Pennsylvania, and a sealed letter, which she immediately knew was from her father. Her hands shook as she broke the wax seal. A small, folded piece of paper fell to the floor. Ignoring it, she began reading the letter:

Dearest daughter,

> *I am ruined. Claverley has destroyed me. A month since, he privily threatened me with gaol. Demanded my fortune, small as it is. I tried to expel him, but he forced me to hear him out. He claims that you not only deserted him but that you stole money from his strongbox. He charged me with complicity—aiding and abetting your escape, a felony. Claimed he had a witness who saw me at the Liverpool dock giving you money.*

Her hands were trembling so badly, that she almost dropped the letter. Steeling herself, she kept reading:

> *He threatened that if I didn't turn over 1,000 pounds instantly, he'd have the law on me. I thrust him from the house and consulted my solicitors. To my horror, they substantiated the gravity of my position. By law, Claverley had me. Going to court would have taken all my money and he would undoubtedly have won. I could not abide the scandal of having your good name dragged through the press nor of my ending my days in gaol. I acceded to his demands.*

Elisabeth felt sick inside. What kind of a daughter would leave her father to the likes of Claverley? And yet, in her impulsive flight, she had done so. *Oh, Father! Father, what have I done?* Forcing her eyes back to the letter, she read on:

> *Elisabeth, I do not blame you for this misfortune. Nay, the fault was mine. I approved the marriage. You were right to escape*

to America. Have a good life there. Worry not for me. Knowing that you are safe from Claverley's grasp is my only consolation. Do not for any reason return to England.

Your wretched but affectionate father
P.S. Annulment appeal was denied. I am sorry.

Elisabeth dropped the letter to the floor and cried out as she hunched over the desk and smothered her face in her arms.

Hearing Elisabeth's anguished cry, Becky hurried back into the room. "Elisabeth, whatever is the matter?"

Elisabeth sat up and wiped her eyes. She reached down to pick up the letter and spied the folded piece of paper that had fallen out of it. She picked both up. Handing the letter to Becky, she unfolded the paper. It was a note from Maggie Stowell. It read:

Miss Elisabeth,

The master ask me to post this letter. Hes in a bad way. Been in bed with the doctor a fortnight. Not expected to live. Somthing to do with Claverly. Hes mad for money Claverly is. Herd from the cooks helper at the Hall, ruff sorts in London is dunning him for gambling detts.

Sorry about the master your father. He is kind to me. If he passes on I will try and scrape up the money to go to America. England is no place for me.

Your obedent servent and frend,
Maggie

Elisabeth numbly handed Becky the note and took the letter from her. When Becky had finished reading the note she put a comforting hand on Elisabeth's shoulder. "Oh, Elisabeth, I'm so sorry. What will you do?"

"What can I do? If I go back to England, Claverley will have me arrested for desertion. I have no money to fight him in the courts. I'm helpless. I was so wrong to desert my father and come here. Oh, how could I have made such a mess of things?"

Again she broke into tears. For a long time Becky could find no words of solace; all she could do was rub her friend's shoulders. Finally, Elisabeth sat up and wiped her tears. Mechanically, she scanned Mrs. Kenny's note, which had no news, and then turned to the brochure.

After a moment she shook her head and looked up at Becky. "It never rains but it pours."

In response to Becky's puzzled look, Elisabeth handed her the brochure and pointed to a sentence. Becky read it aloud: "'To qualify for admission, a candidate must have studied privately for at least two years under the supervision of a respectable practitioner of medicine.'" Becky shook her head. "Oh, no, Elisabeth. I'm so sorry. I know how much you wanted to go."

Elisabeth stared blankly. "How can I ever believe in inspiration again? I was sure that I should come to Zion and I was sure that I should go to medical school. Now both decisions have proven wrong."

That evening Elisabeth wrote a long letter to Mrs. Kenny thanking her for the supplies and telling her of the double blow contained in her father's letter and in the college brochure. She ended on a philosophical note by quoting from Isaiah: "For my thoughts are not your thoughts, neither are your ways my ways, saith the Lord," but it was strictly for Mrs. Kenny's sake. Elisabeth's faith had been dealt a crushing blow, and she doubted that she could recover from it. She sealed the letter and sat staring at it for a long time.

Despite her disappointment, Elisabeth carried on. What else could she do? She found comfort in her association with the sisters in the Female Council of Health, many of whom had suffered much more than she had in accepting the gospel. She also took satisfaction in the knowledge that the gospel and medicine could work together for the benefit of the Saints. The more she studied, the more she was convinced that Dr. Osgood was right: the world was on the cusp of a new era in medicine. It was time for a gentler approach, time to abandon such procedures as indiscriminate bleeding and cupping and such poisons as arsenic and the mercury-based calomel. She may not be able to go to medical school, but there was no reason she should not become a good nurse and midwife.

* * *

On February 14, 1853, President Young spoke at the ground-breaking ceremony for the temple as Elisabeth, the Nilssons, and thousands of other Saints looked on. Jonathan's uncle, Elder Heber C. Kimball, offered the prayer. It was a beautiful, sunny day, and the assembled Saints were treated to the music of several bands.

Elisabeth was in a happy mood. As she gazed on the crowd, her eyes fell on Jonathan, then Becky with Elisabeth Rebecca in her arms, and, close by, Gren. Suddenly, a chill shot through her. Beside Gren stood a pretty young woman with her arm through his. Elisabeth quickly pulled her eyes away. She could feel the blood draining from her face. A dull pain settled in the pit of her stomach. She wanted to run from the place, but she forced herself to stay. *Stop it, Elisabeth! You've been doing fine. Don't let this vex you. Gren is only following your instructions. You told him to find another, and he has.* Involuntarily, her eyes were again drawn to Gren, who was bending down talking to the woman. The woman laughed and tapped him affectionately on the arm. Elisabeth could stand no more. Mumbling a quick excuse to the Nilssons, she turned and threaded her way to the edge of the crowd. As she numbly started for home, she again remonstrated with herself. *Stop longing for something you can't have. Concentrate on life as it is, not as you would like it to be.*

When she got home, the cabin was chilly. She stirred up the embers and put several logs on the fire. Then she went to her room, wrapped herself in a comforter, and lay down on her bed. *My father's dying, the annulment was denied, I can't go to medical school, and now Gren has found another. Is there anything else that can go wrong in my life? Is this the nadir?* Bitter tears began to flow, and she made no effort to stop them. After a long time she cried herself to sleep. It was almost dark when a noise awakened her. She listened. It was a knock at the front door. She had no desire to see anyone. After a while she could hear the visitor walk away and she could hear voices. Curious, she went to the window. In the semidarkness she recognized Gren. Was that Becky on the wagon seat? No. It was the woman from the groundbreaking ceremony. Devoid of hope, Elisabeth watched them drive off. *Now I truly have reached bottom,* she thought.

For a long time she lay on the bed feeling sorry for herself. Another knock at the front door roused her. Could Gren have returned? Her heart raced as she swung her legs off the bed and felt her way in the darkness.

"Elisabeth? Are you home, Elisabeth?" Becky poked her head in the front door.

"I'm coming, Becky. Let me get some light."

Elisabeth poked a taper into the dying embers of the fire and lit a candle. Then she lit an oil lamp.

"We ran into the Nilssons at the temple site and they said you'd left early," Becky said. "They met some friends at the ceremony and are visiting with them. I told them that I'd look in on you. I brought you some soup."

"Thanks, Becky. I'm feeling better. The soup smells wonderful. Let me heat it up. Will you join me?"

While the soup was heating, they talked about the ceremony and other general topics. After a pause in their conversation, Elisabeth asked, "How is Gren?"

Becky looked puzzled. "Wasn't he just here? He said he was going to visit you."

"He did come, but I missed him. Perhaps he'll come again tomorrow."

"I'm afraid not, Elisabeth. He's gone!"

"Gone?"

Becky nodded. "Yes. He left for Provo, and then he's off to San Bernardino with dispatches from President Young to Elders Lyman and Rich. It was all very sudden."

Elisabeth tried to appear calm. "When will he be back?"

"He didn't know. It's a long way. Maybe not until late spring or early summer."

Elisabeth slowly nodded. "You'll miss him."

"I guess we all will," Becky said perceptively before changing the subject.

* * *

Summer came and Gren had still not returned. One evening in July, Elisabeth and Sister Sessions were visiting at the home of Willard and Susannah Richards when news came that the Ute Indian chief,

Walkara, had declared war on the Saints. Although the fact that Gren was safely in California pleased her, Elisabeth returned home full of misgivings. When she got home the Nilssons had retired. Lighting a candle, she quietly went to her bedroom. As the room filled with light, she saw a letter on her pillow. Her heart fluttered when she realized it was from Gren. She read:

Dear Elisabeth,

I'm sorry I missed you before I left for California. I'm back in Utah, but the militia has been called out and I'm to stay down here to help garrison the southern settlements. Hopefully the war will not last long and I can see you again soon. Tell Becky and family my whereabouts. Please write me at General Delivery, Fillmore.

In haste,
Gren

The brief note filled her with hope. *He hasn't completely gone off me!* she thought. But then concern for his safety also filled her, as well as confusion about why he hadn't mentioned his lady friend or the possibly changed nature of his feelings for her. He had, after all, brought the woman to visit her before leaving for California. But she had no choice but to shrug off her concerns, as she was the one who'd requested his silence on the matter.

Gren was mistaken in his hopes for the Indian war to end quickly; it dragged on for months. Fortunately, President Brigham Young's handling of what became known as the Walker War resulted in the Saints taking a defensive stance, thus greatly reducing the number of casualties. Small communities were literally hauled to bigger settlements, log by log. Once fortified, the Saints lived in relative security. Ironically, during the months of Gren's absence Elisabeth fared better than when he was near. Mormon men were so often away from home on missions and other Church assignments that Mormon women had become inured to life without them. In the meantime, life went on.

It was May 1854 when Gren finally did return. His first stop was the Nilssons. Elisabeth wanted to throw her arms around his neck, but she contented herself with a handshake. As they sat across from each other in the front room of the cabin, they talked about many things, including Gren's nephew, Jonathan Grenville Kimball, born two months earlier. Having exhausted all the news, Gren suddenly seemed uncomfortable, as if he wanted to say something. Then he apparently changed his mind and began telling her about his experiences in the southern settlements. The evening passed with such chatter, leaving Elisabeth—throughout a sleepless night—to mull over what he might have wanted to say.

CHAPTER THIRTEEN

Elisabeth had rejoiced with Becky and Jonathan over the birth of their second baby, but it had only made her more conscious of her own lonely state. A frequent visitor at the Kimball home, Elisabeth was almost a member of the family. Two-year-old Elizabeth Rebecca made no secret of her affection for her "Aunt Elisabeth," although when she tried to say it, it sounded more like "An Lickabess." Despite the love that accompanied it, the title was growing increasingly painful to Elisabeth. The thought plagued her that she would be only "Aunt Elisabeth" forever.

She found some comfort in her continued work with Sister Sessions. But it was a double-edged sword. Each time she saw new life come into the world, she rejoiced; but it also made her feel inadequate. Often a thoughtless word, invariably said without malice, would cut her to the quick. She became moody and at times testy with those around her. On one of those occasions Brother Nilsson said, "Elisabeth, it time we learn about your childs."

"My childs?" she asked, bewildered.

"Ja. It time we ask Lord." He pulled out a kitchen chair and motioned for her to sit on it. She obeyed. Sister Nilsson looked on with interest.

His rough hands cupped the crown of her head, and she listened intently to his broken words of blessing. "You marry an' bear healthy childs in Lord's good time. Be of good cheer. Promise certain . . ."

Elisabeth's heart was so full she didn't hear the rest of his words. Filled with confidence that the promise was sure, she basked in a warm glow as the tears wet her face. Her faith was sufficient that she

now knew she would have children someday. But would they be with
Gren? Would his patience endure? Even after the assurance of Brother
Nilsson's blessing, the thoughtless comments of others still afflicted
her. From time to time she sought out Sister Eliza Snow, in whom she
had already confided about her married state.

"Becky's Elisabeth and I had the baby out in the pram the other
day," Elisabeth said to Sister Snow one day in the late summer of
1854, "and Sister Hollinger stopped to see us. She fussed over the
baby for several minutes and then said to me, 'And when are you
going to have a husband and babe of your own, dear?' I could have
strangled her!"

Sister Snow laughed. "I'm sure she didn't mean any harm. Didn't
you say that Brother Nilsson had promised you children in a priesthood blessing?" When Elisabeth nodded, Sister Snow smiled at her
encouragingly. "Well, then, all that's required of you is patience."

Elisabeth sighed. "Abraham's wife Sarah was also promised a child.
It took years for that promise to be fulfilled. I hope that I'm not 'old
and well stricken in age' before my promise is fulfilled."

Sister Snow nodded. "It's hard to know why things happen the
way they do. All I can suggest is to keep busy with worthwhile
projects until you are able to marry and find yourself in the family
way. Your teaching, for example, is a great boon to the children. Also,
your work with Sister Sessions is greatly appreciated. Perhaps there are
other things the Lord would have you do while you are not encum-
bered with a family. Are you still interested in attending medical
college?"

Elisabeth nodded. "I was, but I found out I didn't qualify for
admission."

"Oh well, dear. Don't despair. The Lord is well aware of you, and
I have no doubt that he will guide you in the path you should go."

Sister Snow's words were prophetic. A week later, Elisabeth
returned home from her rounds with Sister Sessions to find a letter
from Mrs. Kenny. She quickly broke the seal and read:

My Dear Elisabeth,

I take pen in hand to inquire why I haven't heard from you in such a long while. When I wrote you that you could go to the college as a listener, I was expecting to hear that you were coming to Philadelphia hastily. I can only assume that you did not get my letter. This being the case, let me repeat what I said. The college admits two kinds of scholars, 'candidates for graduation' and 'listeners.' It is only the first group that needs to have studied with a doctor. The listeners need only a character recommendation. I, of course, can provide that. In the college's first year, 1850–51, there were only eight candidates for graduation; the other thirty-two students were listeners. So, my dear, if you would like to attend as a listener, hurry along. The new school term begins on the first Monday in October . . .

The paper rustled in Elisabeth's hand and her heart pounded. She could go to college after all! She skimmed the rest of the letter, which told of life at the mansion: Rose's husband and child had still not been found, the gardener had quit and a new one had been hired, and John was still as faithful as ever.

Elisabeth rushed out to the kitchen and told Brother and Sister Nilsson the news. Then she threw on her shawl and headed over to tell Becky. She wanted to tell Sister Snow too, but it was too far to walk.

"We'll take you to Sister Snow's in the buggy, Elisabeth," Becky said after Elisabeth had told her the news. "We were going to take the children for a ride anyway. We'll drop you off and pick you up later."

Sister Snow was almost as excited as Elisabeth. "So you can attend as a listener?"

"Yes. I wouldn't be able to get a degree, but I could attend any classes I wished to. As I think I mentioned, I even have a place to stay. My former nanny has invited me to stay with her. My only challenge now is to find a way to get to Philadelphia. The new term begins in about six weeks."

Sister Snow smiled. "It's strange how blessings so long denied sometimes seem to pour out all at once. I've just heard that President Young is sending a new batch of missionaries to the East. Elder John Taylor will lead them. I believe they will be leaving very soon. Would you like me to see if you can go along?"

When Elisabeth returned home, she was surprised to find Brother and Sister Nilsson chatting with Dr. Philip Osgood at the kitchen table. Both men arose when she entered the room.

"Dr. Osgood!" she exclaimed. "I'm surprised to see you—"

"Alive?" he interjected with a grin.

Elisabeth smiled. "How long has it been?"

"Over two years. Two long, dull years."

Dr. Osgood consented to dine with them, and as they sat down to supper, Elisabeth asked how he had found California.

"An interesting place. But not for me. Not for me to sit around waiting for death. Of course, I was able to practice my profession—doctors are in great demand out there—but I loathed being out of the mainstream."

"California seems to have agreed with you, though. You're looking much better," Elisabeth said.

"Thank you. But this respite may not last. In the meantime, Dr. Oliver Wendell Holmes of Boston has asked me to collaborate on the reissue of his article 'The Contagiousness of Puerperal Fever.' We are bringing in additional research, especially that of Dr. Philipp Semmelweis of Vienna, Austria." Turning to the Nilssons, he said, "Childbed fever causes the death of many mothers during labor and lying in. Dr. Holmes' article explains how to avoid this through proper hygiene. I jumped at the chance to go to Boston and work with this renowned physician."

"Good," Brother Nilsson said. "Elisabeth say, old doctors need to change to new way."

Elisabeth nodded her agreement. She turned to Dr. Osgood. "I have been continuing my interest in medicine. I study regularly and accompany a midwife on her rounds. I've also been attending a local health council. It's unfortunate that the meetings have been suspended for the summer, or I'd arrange for you to speak there. In the meantime, after we eat, would you mind summarizing the evidence Dr. Semmelweis has gathered? I'd like to leave it for the sisters in the council."

"Leave it? Are you going somewhere?"

Elisabeth smiled broadly. "You'll be happy to know that I've decided to attend the women's college in Philadelphia. I hope to leave as soon as I can find a way to get there."

The young doctor got so excited, Elisabeth was afraid he'd jump up and kiss her. "I couldn't be happier for you, Miss Ashcroft. You'll make a wonderful doctress, a wonderful doctress. And I have a way for you to get there. Come with my party and me. When do you have to be there?"

"In a little over a month."

"Wonderful! We are traveling by horseback with two light wagons, one for the wife and child of one of our party. You could travel with them in the wagon or ride as you wish. We'll be traveling swiftly, so you should make it to a railhead in time for you to get to Philadelphia. Please say you'll come."

Elisabeth took a deep breath. She looked at Brother and Sister Nilsson, who gave her encouraging smiles, and then back at Dr. Osgood. Taking a deep breath, she said, "May I think about it?"

"Of course. However, we are leaving tomorrow."

After supper, Dr. Osgood took a sheaf of paper out of his black bag and began to list the information Elisabeth had requested. For the next hour he told the fascinating story of Dr. Philipp Semmelweis' research at an obstetric clinic in Vienna.

Elisabeth and Dr. Osgood, sitting close together at the kitchen table, were so engrossed in their study they failed to hear Sister Nilsson open the door to another visitor. Face flushed with excitement, Elisabeth turned to see Gren, confusion clouding his face. Elisabeth leapt to her feet. "Oh, Gren, I have the most wonderful news. I can go to college in Philadelphia after all, and I can travel with Dr. Osgood's party and be in Philadelphia in a month!"

It was clear from Gren's expression that this was not wonderful news to him; nevertheless, he forced a smile and congratulated her. After a brief, awkward pause, Elisabeth said, "Oh, I'm sorry, Gren. This is Dr. Philip Osgood, who delivered Elisabeth Rebecca."

Gren shook his hand. "I'm honored to meet you, Dr. Osgood. My sister has sung your praises. Thank you for all you did for her."

Dr. Osgood smiled and nodded. "It was my pleasure."

"Well, I see you are busy," Gren said after another awkward pause. "When would you be leaving, Elisabeth?"

"Tomorrow, I'm afraid. Please don't go yet. Dr. Osgood and I are almost finished."

"Brother Sanderson," Brother Nilsson said diplomatically, "I show you cabinet I make in back shed."

Dr. Osgood soon left after getting Elisabeth's promise that she would let him know that evening if she were going with him. After he was gone, Gren returned from viewing Brother Nilsson's handiwork.

"I'm sorry, Gren," Elisabeth said as she and Gren sat alone in the front room. "This is all so sudden. Despite my excitement about going, I'll miss everyone terribly. In fact . . ." She hesitated. "In fact, if you don't think I should go with Dr. Osgood, I'll not."

Gren smiled sadly. "Of course you should go. It appears that he could get you there in time, and going to college has been your dream for ages. It's just that . . . never mind. Though I'll . . . we'll miss you too, it's too good an opportunity to miss. Would you like me to give you a ride over to the hotel so you can tell the doctor that you'll be ready tomorrow?"

Elisabeth hesitated. She felt suddenly confused and hurt. She wanted him to promise her he'd wait, or ask her not to go, or at least explain what he was feeling and if his heart were possibly with another. Through a mist of tears, she said, "I . . . I don't know what to do. Please, tell me what to do." Gren took her hand and squeezed it. Then she took his proffered handkerchief and dabbed her eyes. She sighed deeply and smiled sadly. "I haven't even asked why you came to see me," she said, fearing his answer.

Gren shrugged. "It's not important now."

"It's important to me," she said firmly.

He bowed his head and then looked at her sheepishly. "I've been called on a mission to New York City."

Elisabeth's eyes went wide, and her mouth fell open. She was shocked and somehow relieved. "Not important? Why, it's more important than my going to Philadelphia!"

Gren smiled. "Well, let's just say they're equally important."

"When do you leave?"

"September fourth. It will be a large party, and we'll be traveling rather slowly— should take about two months to get there. Elder John Taylor will be in charge. We'll be setting up a newspaper. Elder Taylor's son George will be my companion. George and I have been friends for years."

Elisabeth was thoughtful. "That's two weeks away."

"Yes." He paused for a moment. "There's more. Sister Snow actually told me that you could qualify for the college. She said that Elder Taylor has consented to your going along with the missionary party if you wish. A Sister Caroline Gilliam will be traveling with us—she wants to visit relatives in the South—and would like a female companion to accompany her on the journey, at least as far as the Mississippi."

Elisabeth's face lit up. "Then I'll go with you. Dr. Osgood will understand."

"But Sister Snow told me that you had to be there in six weeks. Like I said, it will take us about two months and we're not leaving for two weeks. Dr. Osgood could get you there on time."

For a moment neither of them spoke. Then Elisabeth brightened. "I know what I'll do. I'll write to Mrs. Kenny and ask her to let the college know that I'll be late. I believe that listeners have much more flexibility than graduates.

The thought of traveling with Elisabeth brought a smile to Gren's face. Then he pursed his lips and thought for a moment. "Perhaps Dr. Osgood would take the letter. He could mail it at Kanesville. It would be faster than the regular post."

Elisabeth nodded. "Then that's what we'll do!" Gren's obvious pleasure at the idea of her joining him was all she needed for now. Perhaps he would explain on their journey where his heart lay.

Later, Elisabeth visited Dr. Osgood while Gren waited for her in the buggy. The doctor was calm, and accepting of Elisabeth's decision not to go with him. He promised to post her letter. "Are you in love with Mr. Sanderson?" he asked as she was leaving. She smiled bravely, but didn't answer, afraid of what she might give away. "It's plain he's in love with you!" he finished good-naturedly. This proclamation troubled Elisabeth almost more than it pleased her. If such were the case, why was she unable to detect it?

Later still, Elisabeth and Gren visited Jonathan and Becky to tell them the news. Gren confided that he had some reservations about his abilities to work on a newspaper. "Elder Taylor will have to be patient with me."

"Just another example of challenges helping toward perfection," Becky said. "Will you be expected to write articles, too?"

"Maybe a little. Elder Taylor is a brilliant writer. I'm sure he'll be doing most of it although with his help I think I could put together a fairly good article. In our seventies meetings we've gone over, point by point, arguments supporting our right to practice plural marriage. I've learned a great deal. I'm sure we'll be called upon to proselyte as well as publish the paper."

The next two weeks sped by, and on the evening of September third, Becky and Jonathan were at the Nilssons' to help Elisabeth load the wagon with her belongings. George Taylor had driven over the wagon that Elisabeth and Sister Gilliam would be traveling in. Becky pulled back the wagon cover and looked in. "Lots of room."

"Yes," Elisabeth said, "Sister Gilliam and I should be comfortable."

"Will you be bunking with Gren, George?" Becky asked.

George nodded. "We're already packed."

"What will you do with the wagon and horses when you get to the East?" Becky asked.

George smiled. "You're just full of questions, Sister Kimball. We'll sell them when we get to the Missouri and use the money to pay for the rest of the trip."

"Excited about your classes, Elisabeth?" Jonathan asked.

Elisabeth nodded. "It's been a long time since I've been in school—at least on that side of the desk. As a listener I can pick and choose the lectures and demonstrations I want. I'll take all the classes I can in obstetrics and diseases of women and children. I'm rather pleased the way things turned out—my only being a listener. I really don't think I'm cut out to do dissections."

They all laughed at the inadvertent pun. "I'm sure you'll do marvelously," Becky said. "We'll miss you so much!"

Elisabeth hugged her friend. "And I you. I'll live for your letters."

Next morning, Elisabeth was breakfasting with the Nilssons when Becky, Jonathan, Elisabeth Rebecca, and baby Jonathan arrived. "We're here to accompany you to Little Mountain," Becky said.

"Wonderful," Elisabeth said. "Brother and Sister Nilsson and the Brentons are also seeing us off. I understand that lots of people will be going with us to the first night's campground."

Besides the missionaries' party of ten wagons, twenty-seven missionaries, three women—Caroline Gilliam, a Sister Cobb, and

Elisabeth—and Sister Cobb's three children, dozens of well-wishers in all sorts of conveyances accompanied the party out of Great Salt Lake City on a sunny September morning. It looked as if the Saints were abandoning the valley and returning to the East.

Elisabeth and the Brentons had a wonderful reunion. Elisabeth was particularly delighted to meet George Brenton's fiancée, Eloise Packer. "You are so fortunate, Eloise," Elisabeth said when they first met. "George is a wonderful man. He'll make you very happy."

After supper that evening at the bottom of Little Mountain, the whole party assembled around a bonfire and sang the songs of Zion. Then Elder John Taylor arose and announced the names of those officers who had been chosen to manage the wagon train. A good-natured groan went up when it was announced that Brother James Craig had been appointed trumpeter. No one took more delight in waking everyone up in the morning than Brother Craig.

Elder Taylor then bore his testimony and invited others to do so. Elisabeth's heart swelled within her as Gren rose and thanked his Heavenly Father for the great privilege of representing the Church to the people of New York City. He then bore a strong witness of the restored gospel.

CHAPTER FOURTEEN

The next morning, the eastbound missionaries and westbound friends and family parted. George Taylor drove Elisabeth and Sister Gilliam's wagon. Sister Gilliam sat up front with George while Elisabeth rode in the back holding the wagon cover open with one hand and waving with the other. She continued to wave until the knot of friends had disappeared. Then, gingerly picking her way to the front of the wagon, she sat on a box behind Sister Gilliam, who turned and smiled at her. "Are you all right back there, dear?"

Elisabeth nodded. "I'm at sixes and sevens—excited to be starting a new adventure, but sad to be leaving home."

Sister Gilliam nodded in sympathy. "I feel the same. It's a long way to the East and the South." Then she smiled knowingly and added, "At least you and Elder Sanderson will not need to say good-bye for a while."

Elisabeth raised her eyebrows. "Why do you say that, Sister Gilliam?"

A look of chagrin came over the older woman's face. "I'm sorry if I offended you, dear. It's just that Elder Sanderson has made no secret of his . . . his esteem for you. I assumed the feeling was mutual."

Elisabeth's face softened. "I'm not offended, Sister Gilliam. And I do hold him in great esteem. However, I have no claim on him."

Three days later, the missionaries learned from a group of California-bound travelers that fighting had broken out near Fort Laramie between the Sioux and the U.S. cavalry. On the cavalry's side, only the interpreter survived the ensuing battle. Despite this report, the missionaries continued on, confident that they were on God's errand and would reach their destination safely.

Over the next weeks, Gren took every opportunity to show his concern for Elisabeth by making sure that she and Sister Gilliam ate well. One day it would be a rabbit, the next a string of fish or a brace of grouse. When Elisabeth would finish a letter to Becky or the Brentons, Gren would make sure that it was sent with a westbound wagon train. Elisabeth tried hard to remain aloof and not encourage him. But she wouldn't have been human if she had not been influenced by his devotion. Each day she found it harder to maintain the fiction that she did not adore him.

Their journey along the Mormon Trail proceeded uneventfully, notwithstanding the usual hardships of the trail—especially the harsh wind and the never-ending dust in their hair, eyes, mouths, and clothes. As they neared the halfway point of Fort Laramie, extra sentries were posted. But to their relief the nights passed peacefully.

After a one-day stopover at Fort Laramie, the missionary train was on its way again. In mid-October, forty-three days after leaving the Great Salt Lake Valley, the travelers reached the Missouri River at Old Fort Kearney. Two days later, the wagon train divided, with some— including Elder Taylor—going north to Council Bluffs, and the remainder—including Elisabeth, Gren, George, and Sister Gilliam— going south to St. Joseph. At this city the latter four boarded the *Polar Star*, a steamboat bound for St. Louis, while the rest of the party remained behind to sell the horses and wagons.

* * *

On their second afternoon aboard the *Polar Star*, Elisabeth took a stroll on deck while Sister Gilliam napped. She found Gren leaning on the rail watching the Missouri shore go by. She joined him at the rail. "How refreshing the breeze is! Where is George?"

"In the cabin, drawing. He's quite the artist. I thought I'd get some fresh air."

"Sister Gilliam and I were talking this morning about how strange it will be being in the East again," Elisabeth said after a long silence. "Although it's only been three years, it seems like a lifetime ago."

"Has it only been three years since we met?"

Elisabeth nodded. "I'm still embarrassed about how I treated you."

Elisabeth stepped away and inspected him from head to toe. "You're a little better looking now, I must admit. You certainly clean up nicely."

Gren doffed his brown felt hat and said, "I'm glad you approve, m'lady."

Elisabeth laughed. Shoulders almost touching, they again leaned on the rail. "Here comes a northbound steamboat," Gren said, pointing downstream.

Elisabeth squinted. "What's in that large wooden cage on the lower deck?"

Gren squinted too. "Can't quite make it out, but they're animals of some kind."

"Cats," said a voice from behind them.

"Cats?" Elisabeth turned and took the offered spyglass from the first mate. "You're right! Look, Gren."

Gren took the spyglass, and after taking a look, he and Elisabeth turned to the mate for an explanation.

"They're bound for one of the frontier forts, no doubt," the man said. "The forts are overrun with vermin. An army officer from New Fort Kearney told me the mice and rats eat more horse feed than the horses. It's costing the government a fortune. Cats help keep down the costs. In New York or Philadelphia, a stray cat's a nuisance. On the frontier, it's a prized possession."

The mate had just concluded his explanation when a violent shock jarred the boat from the pointed prow to the rounded stern. Elisabeth and Gren clung to the railing.

"Never fear," said the mate, picking himself up off the deck, "sounds like we hit a sawyer." He scurried off to see to the problem.

The boat's engines ground to a halt, although the huge vessel continued downstream in the current. Within minutes the engines reengaged, and the giant paddle wheels began to turn again with a swoosh.

"Your hat!" Elisabeth said. "It's gone."

Gren's hand went to his head. "It must have gone over the rail when we hit the sawyer."

They both leaned over the rail and looked up the river. The hat was nowhere in sight. "Perhaps it was blown onto the lower deck," Elisabeth suggested.

"Could be. Let's take a look."

At the stern, they found a set of stairs leading downward. The lower deck was loaded with livestock, hogsheads, coiled rope, and crates. Amid the cargo sat roughly clad men and women. Two black slaves, a man and a woman, sat on the deck, shackled to one of the pillars supporting the upper deck. The man had Gren's hat perched on his head at a rakish angle.

"Thank you for looking after my hat," Gren said, smiling and reaching out his hand. A fearful look clouded the man's ebony face as he grabbed the hat from his head and held it out to Gren. "Is there anything I can do to repay you?"

The man appeared relieved at Gren's politeness. "Watta, suh." The man nodded toward a barrel with a dipper hooked on the side.

"Water? Certainly." Gren unhooked the dipper, raised the lid, and filled the dipper. He was in the act of passing the water to the slave when a whip cracked. Gren cried out as the leather thong slashed into his hand. The dipper clattered to the deck, and the water pooled at the feet of the man and woman, who greedily scooped up the precious liquid with their hands. The whip cracked again, slicing into the black man's leg above his ankle. The slave screamed in pain.

The man with the whip cursed Gren. "Ye see what ye've made me do! Ah hates t' return damaged goods. Now, git back upstairs whar ye belong an' leave other folk's property be."

"How dare you!" Elisabeth said as she tied her handkerchief around Gren's wound.

The slaver surveyed Elisabeth. His lips twisted into a mock smile, revealing uneven, tobacco-stained teeth. Touching the whip handle to the brim of his hat, he gave a slight bow. His demeanor changed in a flash, however, when Elisabeth leapt forward, scooped up the dipper, and made for the water barrel. He raised the whip as if to strike her. Leaping forward, Gren wrenched the whip from the man's hand and threw it overboard.

"Ye'll pay fer that, nigger-lover," the slaver growled, pulling a horse pistol from under his coat.

"Put it away, Talbot." The accent was English and the speaker, emerging from the gathering crowd, held a derringer leveled at the slaver.

Talbot turned to face the Englishman. "Mind yer business, limey. They wuz messin' wi' the runaways."

"Be off," the Englishman ordered.

"Ye gonna make me wi' thet pea-shooter?" Talbot said. "Yo's bluffin.'"

"Try me," said the Englishman coolly.

Elisabeth held her breath as the two men glowered at each other over their weapons. Talbot's hand began to shake slightly under the weight of the pistol. With a curse, he stuck the gun into his belt and slunk away. Elisabeth slowly exhaled.

The Englishman turned to Gren and Elisabeth. "My manservant will see to that wound."

"Thank you, but it's only broken the skin. This man needs the help," Gren said nodding at the chained man, who was intently watching Elisabeth as she refilled the dipper and took it to his female companion.

"Anthony Brideswell," the Englishman said, extending his hand.

"Gren Sanderson." They shook hands. "And this is Miss Elisabeth Ashcroft."

Elisabeth again filled the dipper and handed it to the male slave before she stood and shook hands with the stranger.

"From England's southwest, no doubt," the stranger said.

"Yes, Somerset," she said, surprised.

"I heard it in your voice when you reproved Talbot." Anthony Brideswell smiled. "The man's a thoroughly disagreeable fellow. And a poor hand at poker."

"Sir Anthony." A small, round man panted as he pushed his way through the crowd.

"See to his wound, Blodgett," Sir Anthony said, nodding toward the chained man.

Soon the captain and his two mates dispersed the crowd. At Sir Anthony's invitation, Elisabeth and Gren followed him to his cabin, where they were introduced to Lady Brideswell. Soon after, Blodgett joined them, and without comment he skillfully bound up Gren's wound.

Elisabeth inspected the bandage. "Very well done, Mr. Blodgett. I have an interest in medicine. I'm on my way to train at a medical college in Philadelphia."

"Is that so?" Sir Anthony said. "Maybe you should take Blodgett along with you. He could do with some more training."

"You didn't think so in India, sir," Blodgett said evenly.

Inclining his head toward his manservant, Sir Anthony smiled. "He'll never let me forget that he saved my life in India. Now, may Blodgett get you some wine? Oh, that's right, Mormons don't drink spirits."

"How did you know our religion?" Gren asked.

"Oh, little escapes me. Actually, I didn't know. But I observed you refusing tea, coffee, and wine at the dining table last night and deduced that you were Mormons. My wife and I spent some time in Great Salt Lake City on our way from San Francisco. I'm fascinated by any and all religions . . . have studied them around the world— Parsee, Hindu, Islam. Yours is especially intriguing since it's the only American religion I know, apart from the aboriginal ones, that espouses polygamy. I wonder . . ." He paused, thinking. "Mr. Sanderson," he said at last, "would you care to answer some questions about your religion?"

"I'd love to, sir. It will be my first opportunity to do so since I was called as a missionary. I must confess I'm a little nervous. I've been afraid that people might scorn me."

Sir Anthony nodded sympathetically. "I understand your concern. No doubt you will have your detractors. The trick is to be bold and shrug off spiteful comments. After the Napoleonic Wars, the Duke of Wellington attended a reception which included his former enemies. When he entered the room, the French marshals made some derogatory comments and turned their backs on him. The duke merely shrugged and said, 'I have seen their backs before.'"

Elisabeth and Gren laughed. Soon Gren and Sir Anthony were lost in conversation and Lady Brideswell took the opportunity to converse with Elisabeth. At one point in their conversation, Lady Brideswell paused and studied Elisabeth for a moment. Then she said, "May I ask you a personal question, Miss Ashcroft?" Elisabeth nodded her assent. "Why are you and Mr. Sanderson not married? You are obviously very much in love."

Elisabeth blushed. "Is it that obvious? I have tried to hide my feelings for him."

Lady Brideswell smiled. "A woman in love has as much of a chance of hiding her feelings as this boat has of going upstream without the paddles turning."

Elisabeth took a deep breath and sighed. "I have no right to encourage his love because . . . because I'm not free, and the reason I'm not free is . . . well, it's a long story."

Lady Brideswell looked past Elisabeth to where her husband and Gren were deep in conversation. Then, she took Elisabeth's arm. "Come, dear, let's take a stroll on deck and you can tell me."

After Elisabeth had told her story as fully as she could, Lady Brideswell shook her head and sighed. "It is a tragic tale, my dear, but not an uncommon one. The plight of the married woman in England is shocking. Last year in *The Times,* Mrs. Caroline Norton compared the status of married women in England to Negro slavery in the United States. Neither slaves nor married English women can make contracts or have monies of their own without consent of their 'masters.' As Blackstone put it, 'When a man and woman marry they become one, and that one is the husband.' Of course, if that husband is like my Tony or your young man, who, I dare say, is excellent marriage material, there would be no difficulty. But the rub is when one finds herself bound to a Eustas Claverley." She paused before asking: "You say that your father launched an annulment appeal on your behalf?"

"Yes, but it was denied."

Lady Brideswell smiled sadly. "I'm not surprised, dear. Church synods rarely if ever reverse decisions. In your case the council members no doubt reasoned that you are the guilty one, having 'deserted' your husband."

"What I can't understand is why Claverley opposes the annulment. He's already got my money and has probably gambled it away by now."

"That's the very reason. If an annulment were granted, it would be as if the marriage had never taken place. He would have to pay back your money. I'm sure it was he who pressured the council to reject the appeal." Seeing Elisabeth's crestfallen expression, Lady Brideswell quickly added, "Don't fret, my dear. Times are changing. Mrs. Norton and others are supporting a bill in the British Parliament, which, if passed, will correct some of the flagrant injustices to married women. For example, it will take jurisdiction in marriage cases from the Church of England and place it in secular courts. The bill is a great stride forward, though it is far from perfect. Unfortunately, it perpetuates a double standard by stating that a husband need only show proof of his wife's infidelity to gain a divorce, but a wife must prove her husband's infidelity plus another cause, such as extreme cruelty, desertion, or bigamy."

Elisabeth sighed. "A divorce in my case would not answer. It must be an annulment. As I'm sure you know, the Church of England does not recognize civil divorce. It would kill my father if I were to get a civil divorce and remarry. I have hurt him enough already."

Lady Brideswell nodded sympathetically and thought for a moment. "I suppose an annulment is not completely out of the question. As mentioned, the times are changing for the married woman—the threat of the new parliamentary bill decreasing church power is causing the ecclesiastical councils to be a little more reasonable. With enough money and a good barrister-at-law, you might be able to force the issue, especially since the marriage was never consummated. Besides the expense, it would also require your going home to England." She patted Elisabeth's arm. "If you do decide to pursue it, dear, Tony and I will do all we can to help you. We are not without influence in England." She took a card from her purse and gave it to Elisabeth.

Tears pooled in Elisabeth's eyes at the generosity of this woman whom she'd barely met. "Thank you, Lady Brideswell. Thank you for all your kindness. If I do decide to further pursue an annulment, I'll certainly get in touch with you."

CHAPTER FIFTEEN

The rest of the journey proceeded without incident. When the *Polar Star* reached St. Louis, there were more paddle wheelers than the dock could hold. A forest of smokestacks protruded from the boats anchored five deep. "How are we ever to get ashore?'" Elisabeth asked as she and Sister Gilliam approached Gren and George at the rail.

"I don't know," Gren said. "Wait here and I'll try to find out." Gren returned quickly. "We're to leave our things in the cabins. They'll be brought ashore later. In the meantime, we can go ashore from boat to boat."

Elisabeth and Sister Gilliam gave him dubious glances as he and George took their arms and guided them to a line of people forming at the stern. A broad gangplank with wooden sides had been fastened from the *Polar Star* deck to the deck of the *Edinburgh*. When it was their turn, the two women clung to the men as they crossed over to the *Edinburgh*. From that boat they crossed to the *Susquehanna* and so on until they got to the dock. "How will they know where to take our luggage?" Elisabeth asked as they stepped onto the dock.

"The first mate recommended the American Hotel," Gren said, "so I'm having it all sent there. After those weeks on the trail and nights on the noisy steamboat, it will be wonderful to stay in a hotel, even for one night."

Gren kindly refused Elisabeth's offer to pay for the hotel rooms. The next morning the travelers were off again. A steam ferry took them across the Mississippi River to Alton, Illinois, and several steam trains took them all the way to Philadelphia via Cincinnati and Pittsburgh.

Elisabeth was completely exhausted by the time the train arrived at the Philadelphia station. "This trip wasn't any easier the second time," she said. She wanted so much for Gren to escort her to the mansion to meet Mrs. Kenny, but he and George had a connection to New York in only twenty minutes. Sister Gilliam had a connection to Virginia and several points south in one hour. So they made their farewells in the depot, which was not at all a pleasant setting for good-byes. Indeed, it was a noisy, dirty place. A locomotive with five passenger cars puffed officiously beside the platform, steam blustering out of its side in periodic blasts. Men's shouts mingled with the rumbling of carts as baggage was loaded and passengers sought favorable seats as far away as possible from the soot-belching engine.

As they stood in the station, Gren took Elisabeth's arm and drew her away from the others.

"I guess this is our last moment," he said, his voice tender and regretful. "I hate to leave you in this awful place."

Elisabeth shook her head, trying to hold back the tears. "Don't worry about me. I've been here before. Just take care of yourself." They gazed at each other for a few seconds and Elisabeth felt the love welling up inside her, love that she'd suppressed for so long. *I can't break my resolve now.* Abruptly breaking the mood, she asked, "Is there a branch of the Church in Philadelphia?"

Gren shook his head. "Not anymore, I'm afraid. But I'm sure missionaries will be visiting periodically—I know this one will whenever he gets a chance!"

There had been a large branch of the Church in Philadelphia at one time with over three hundred members, Gren explained, but it had broken up in the early '40s when the Saints had gathered to Nauvoo, Illinois. Later, the Philadelphian Saints moved west with the body of the Church.

"Colonel Thomas Kane lives here and is a good friend of the Church," Gren continued. "I'm sure that any of the brethren who travel east will pay him a visit and undoubtedly stay to hold public meetings."

"I'll miss going to Sunday meetings," Elisabeth said. "I so enjoyed them. I will have to depend on prayer and scripture reading to feed my spirit, but it won't be the same."

"Perhaps my letters will help. Will you write to me?"

"Of course."

The thought of getting Gren's letters was small comfort to Elisabeth. She decided to again change the subject before her emotions betrayed her. "How will you know where to go when you get to New York? It's such a large city."

"If all goes well, Brother Taylor will be there ahead of George and me. He said he'd leave a message for us—*poste restante,* I believe he called it—at the main post office."

Elisabeth nodded. "That's right—Poste restante. It means 'to remain until called for.'"

Gren nodded in interest, then took Elisabeth's hands in his and looked at her earnestly. "Would you . . . that is, would it be permissible for me to give you a farewell embrace?"

Elisabeth smiled. "Permissible and desirable." As they embraced, she managed to slip a coin into his empty watch pocket. "Do take care of yourself, Gren. I wonder when we'll meet again?"

"Philadelphia is only four hours from New York by train, and now with the telegraph it's only minutes away. I'm sure Elder Taylor will allow me a few days to come and visit."

Elisabeth fervently hoped so.

CHAPTER SIXTEEN

On the way to Mrs. Kenny's, Elisabeth no longer tried to restrain her tears. How lonely she felt, cut off from Gren and her friends and family! What was she thinking of, she wondered tearfully, attending college at her age? But her need for more medical knowledge and the need for that knowledge among the Saints stiffened her resolve. She would carry out her task, as she knew Gren would carry out his.

It was almost six o'clock by the time she arrived at the mansion. The monumental Corinthian columns flanking the ornate front door were as impressive as ever, but as she surveyed the grounds it was obvious that the new gardener had not been doing his job. Elisabeth rang the bell while the omnibus driver deposited her baggage on the porch.

"Ah, Miss Elisabeth," said John warmly, coming out onto the porch in answer to the bell. "We've been expecting you. It's wonderful to see you again. Come in, come in. I'll go find Mrs. Kenny."

"Elisabeth!" Mrs. Kenny said as she came toward her. Elisabeth ran to the old woman's open arms. For a long time they held each other, their tears mingling as Elisabeth pressed her cheek against the older woman's.

Mrs. Kenny wiped her eyes with a handkerchief. "Sure, I haven't cast eyes on your lovely face these three years. You're as welcome as the flowers in May. Every day since I got your letter, you haven't left my mind."

"Well, I'm finally here," said Elisabeth, brushing away a tear. "It's good to hear your voice again."

Mrs. Kenny took Elisabeth's hand and led her into the drawing room. "Rose'll bring us some refreshment. You must be famished after your long train ride."

Elisabeth nodded. "Yes, I am famished and absolutely worn out, but my journey was lightened by three most agreeable companions."

"Well, sit down, dear, and tell me all about the people you met along the way and the adventures you had."

"Miss 'Lis'bet'!" Rose said as she entered with a tray of sandwiches and a jug of lemonade. "Yo' do look fine."

Elisabeth complimented Rose on her apparent good health and appearance. After the maid had gone, Elisabeth asked, "How is she doing? Still no word of Thomas and Freddie?"

The older woman shook her head. "I'm afraid not, but under the circumstances Rose is doing well enough. I don't know what I'd do without her."

Elisabeth gazed around the beautiful drawing room. "I so appreciate your letting me stay with you. If I were all alone in lodgings, I don't know how I'd be."

"You're more than welcome, dear. This place is too big for just me. It's a lot to keep up."

"I noticed that the grounds have . . . are . . . somewhat . . ." Elisabeth realized how impolite her comment would sound.

But Mrs. Kenny smiled understandingly. "Our new gardener has been . . . been indisposed," she said after searching for the right word. "His back's been tormenting him something fierce, he says. But to be honest, I think he's malingering."

"Shouldn't you let him go and hire someone who will do the job?"

"Oh, I couldn't do that," said Mrs. Kenny, surprised at the suggestion. "He hasn't two ha'pennies to rub together." Mrs. Kenny suddenly remembered that she had a letter for Elisabeth and sent her to fetch it from the table in the foyer.

Elisabeth retrieved the letter and quickly returned to the drawing room. Her face glowed. "It's from Maggie. Do you mind if I read it now?"

"Of course not, dear." Mrs. Kenny excused herself so that her young friend could read the letter in private.

Elisabeth sat on the sofa and, with eager hands, broke the wax seal.

Miss Elisabeth,

On the last day of awgust your father past from this world. His last words was Im glad Elisabeth is save in America. He had a good send off. Church people come all the way from London. One of them was a bishop. The new minister is a yung maried man with children. His wive asked me to stay on. I will for awile. I still want to go to America. Claverly hasnt changed. Word is hes deep in dett. Hope you ar well. Sorry to give you bad news.

Your obedent servent and frend,
Maggie

Elisabeth methodically refolded the letter and sat holding it for a long time. She felt numb and sick to her stomach. She couldn't shake the feeling that she had contributed to her father's death. For what she had done to her father, Elisabeth felt suddenly unworthy of Gren and began to convince herself that they would never marry.

"Bad news?" Mrs. Kenny asked as she entered the room. Elisabeth nodded, as she shared the tidings and the tears began to flow. As in days past, Mrs. Kenny took Elisabeth in her arms and comforted her. There was nothing she could say.

After a while, Elisabeth wiped her eyes and stood. "Thank you, Mary. I'll go to my room now." Mechanically, she climbed the stairs. In her room she knelt by her bed and prayed. Miraculously, the painful self-recriminations eventually gave way to a quiet inward peace as her mind settled on the glorious reunion of her father and mother. *Mama and Papa are together again and that's all that matters,* she assured herself at the end of the prayer.

The next morning Elisabeth wrote a letter to Maggie. She then went downstairs and found Mrs. Kenny in the kitchen.

"Are you feeling better this morning, dear?" Mrs. Kenny asked.

Elisabeth shook her head. "Not much. How can I? My only consolation is that Mama and Papa are together again. He was never the same after she died."

The two women were silent, and then Mrs. Kenny spoke. "You'll be wanting to know about the college. Will you be up to starting in a day or so?"

Elisabeth nodded, remembering why she had come to Philadelphia. Maggie's letter and her response to it had occupied her thoughts completely. "Yes. I will start as soon as possible. But the joy has gone out of this new adventure."

"I've sent a note to Dr. Longshore, the college president, and let him know you've arrived," Mrs. Kenny said. "When I talked to him last, he told me he's planning a meeting of all the students—an assembly, I think he called it. He said to let him know when you arrived and he'd call the meeting."

"You know him personally?"

"Yes, dear. He's a neighbor and a fine Quaker gentleman. You'll find it quaint that he uses "thee" when he's talking to one person and "you" when he's talking to more than one. He left you some papers about the college. They're in the drawing room."

Numbly, Elisabeth followed Mrs. Kenny into the drawing room. Their talk drifted from the college to other things. They spent the afternoon and evening together. Elisabeth was glad of the company. She didn't want to be alone. When she finally did get to bed, she couldn't sleep. After a while she raised the wick in the oil lamp by her bed and began to pore over the college papers. She learned that Dr. Longshore, besides being the college president, was also professor of obstetrics and diseases of women and children. *I'll certainly attend his lectures.* She studied the curriculum and decided to immerse herself in medicine by attending lectures on anatomy, physiology and hygiene, theory and practice of medicine, materia medica and therapeutics, and chemistry—the whole curriculum except for surgery.

She gazed at the papers scattered over the bed and spilling onto the floor. *I should clean up this mess and try again to sleep.* Suddenly she was glad that she had the college to occupy her time and her mind. She would lose herself in her work and stop thinking about the past and the future. *I can't do anything about the past, and the future is in God's hands. All I have is the present.*

CHAPTER SEVENTEEN

Elisabeth awoke long before daylight next morning. Despite her late-night resolve, her thoughts immediately turned to her father, bringing a return of the sick feeling in the pit of her stomach. *Why did I leave him? Why was I so selfish and headstrong? How I wish I could make amends.* For a long time her mind churned with self-recrimination. She tried to stop thinking altogether, and when that didn't work she turned her thoughts to Gren. *I'm glad he's in New York serving the Lord. Oh, how thankful I am for his friendship.* Hour after hour her mind raced on, until mental exhaustion again brought sleep. The room was filled with sunlight when she awoke for the second time. She heard a gentle knock at the door. "Come."

"Breakfas'," Rose said, entering with a covered tray.

"Thank you, Rose." Elisabeth got out of bed. "Please, put it on the table. Thanks for being such a good friend to Mrs. Kenny. She told me how much you mean to her."

"Thank yo', Miss 'Lis'bet. An' thank yo' fo' yo' kindness las' time yo' was heh."

"Think nothing of it." After Rose had left, Elisabeth put the tray on the bed and tried to eat, but she had no appetite.

It was noon before Elisabeth went downstairs. "So your friend Mr. Sanderson will be working on a Mormon newspaper," Mrs. Kenny said at lunch. "I hope it does some good." She shook her head. "It's beyond me how . . . never mind. We'll not talk of it. Are you looking forward to being a scholar again?"

"Yes. Hard work will keep me from dwelling on Papa's death. Have you heard from Dr. Longshore yet?"

"A message came a few minutes since. The meeting will be the day after tomorrow at ten. I've already enrolled you as a listening student, as you asked in your letter. I hope you're not disappointed with the college. It's still in the rented rooms over on Arch Street. Someday, I'm sure, it'll have more impressive buildings."

"I'm sure I'll enjoy the lectures. Thank you so much for all your help. In the papers you gave me, it says that over a thousand dollars was spent in renovating the rooms. I also noted that fees have to be paid before one begins study."

"Don't worry your head about the fees, dear. You're all paid up to take as many lectures as you wish. Also, in the library are copies of each of the books you'll need."

"The library at the college?"

"No, the library here. I had Miss Morris from the college send them over. The library's just off the small parlor. John will show you later. As for me, I'll have to put my feet up. Pass me that footstool, there's a dear. My bunions are torturing me."

Elisabeth put a pillow under Mrs. Kenny's raised feet. "I'm sorry to hear that there have been no developments in the search for Rose's husband and boy."

"Yes, it is a pity. The South's a different world from here. But we haven't given up hope."

In the afternoon, Elisabeth followed John into a tastefully appointed small parlor, decorated in light pastels of beige, pink, and cream. On the west wall a set of French doors opened onto a garden. Elisabeth surveyed the room and paused to examine an exquisitely framed copy of Sir Thomas Lawrence's *Pinkie* hanging over the marble fireplace. She gazed with admiration on the lovely young English girl in flowing white dress and pink sash. *I can see why it has caught the imagination of the world and become so popular.*

"In here, miss," John said as he slid open a set of carved pocket doors in the center of the east wall, then stood aside as Elisabeth entered the library.

Impressed, Elisabeth gazed around the book-lined room. She finally sat beside a stack of books on a polished oak table. Picking up one of the books, she read the title aloud, "*Anatomy,*" and began leafing through it. One by one she perused the books. Closing the last one, she shook her head. *There's so much to learn. How will I ever do it?*

The next morning at breakfast, Elisabeth announced that she wanted to take a walking tour of historic sites. Mrs. Kenny insisted that she take the carriage, but Elisabeth insisted on walking. They compromised: once downtown, Elisabeth would walk and John would follow in the carriage at a discreet distance. It was ten o'clock before Elisabeth finally got away.

"Where'd you like to start, Miss Elisabeth?" John asked as Elisabeth climbed into the carriage. "Independence Hall and the Liberty Bell, I suppose?"

"No, John. I think I'd like to visit Benjamin Franklin's grave. It suits my mood of late."

"Right you are. Over to Fifth and Arch at the Christ Church cemetery."

The morning sun warmed her face as Elisabeth climbed down from the carriage in front of the burial ground. She quickly found the six-by-four-foot flat marble slab with its simple inscription: "Benjamin and Deborah Franklin, 1790."

After studying the inscription for a moment, she took a seat on a nearby stone bench. Almost at once, though, she arose and went back to the carriage. "I'd like to stay here for a while, John. I don't wish to have you wait. Is there something you need to do?"

"As a matter of fact, there is. Why don't I fetch you in a half hour or so?"

"Splendid."

Returning to the graveyard, she wandered among the gravestones, thinking about her parents and brooding upon the tenuous nature of life. Eventually she found her way back to the stone bench beside the Franklins' grave. Sitting down, she closed her eyes, and one of Franklin's maxims from *Poor Richard's Almanac* came into her mind: *'At twenty years of age, the will reigns; at thirty the wit; and at forty, the judgment.'* I'm now thirty. I guess it's time that my wit reigned. As she thought about other aphorisms, it occurred to her how much Benjamin Franklin and President Brigham Young were alike in their practical approach to life. *Perhaps I must become more practical and less prone to let my emotions govern my actions.*

Without warning, a shadow blocked the sun and a shiver went through her. Opening her eyes, she gasped and her hand went to her mouth. Before her stood an ancient man with a long white beard.

His lips formed a toothless grin. "Sorry I startled ye, miss." He pointed to the gravestone with his cane. "I saw ye looking at Ben 'n' Deborah's grave and thought ye might have some questions. I've studied Ben all my life—ever since I attended his funeral when a lad of ten."

"It's quite all right," Elisabeth said, recovering. "When I opened my eyes and saw you standing there, I thought you were Father Time himself!"

The old man laughed and introduced himself. "Obadiah Warren. Sexton of this burial ground."

"Thank you, Mr. Warren." Sliding over on the stone bench, she added, "Would you like to sit down, sir?"

"Thank ye, I would." The sexton eased his old bones onto the bench.

For the next half hour, the old man was in his glory, having an eager student to listen to his tales of Ben Franklin. Elisabeth was especially interested in Mr. Warren's recitation of Franklin's battle with the minister of the Presbyterian Church over the legalistic teachings of John Calvin embodied in the *Westminster Confession of Faith.*

"The upshot of the whole affair," the sexton concluded, "was that Ben left the Presbyterians and never returned. He eventually rented pew number seventy in Christ Church and, as you see, is buried here beside his wife, who died twenty-five years before him."

After a pause, the old man said that although Ben Franklin had unorthodox views, he did believe in the resurrection. To prove this point, he quoted Franklin's epitaph, which had not made it onto the gravestone:

> "*The body of Benjamin Franklin, printer,*
> *(Like the cover of an old book,*
> *Its contents worn out,*
> *And stript of its lettering and gilding)*
> *Lies here, food for worms!*
> *Yet the work itself shall not be lost,*

For it will, as he believed, appear once more
In a new
And more beautiful edition,
Corrected and amended
By its Author!'"

For some reason a tear came to Elisabeth's eye. She surreptitiously wiped it away. "Thank you very much, Mr. Warren. Although I have read it before, your rendition makes it mean much more to me. It certainly does testify of his belief in the Resurrection."

Elisabeth thanked the sexton. "My father and I have always found Mr. Franklin and his writings fascinating."

Rising carefully, the old man leaned on his cane. "I'll no doubt be seeing Ben soon," he said with a twinkle in his eye. "I'll tell him that a beautiful young woman finds him fascinating. He'll like that." Nodding his head in farewell, the old sexton turned away and was soon lost among the headstones.

When John returned, he found Elisabeth on the stone bench, deep in thought. "For you," he said, handing her a cut-glass bowl of ice cream, a silver spoon protruding from the side.

"How did you know I love ice cream, John?"

"Who doesn't love ice cream?"

Elisabeth tried a dainty taste. "This is delicious! Where did you ever get it?"

"Over to Parkinson's on Chestnut Street—the best ice cream in the city."

When Elisabeth had eaten the last spoonful, she announced that she had decided to forgo her walking tour. Rather, she would like a carriage tour of all the historic places in the city within walking distance of Independence Hall.

"I'll plan out a walking tour for my . . . my friend if he comes to visit. I'll be sure to include Parkinson's Ice Cream Parlor, of course. If there's a jeweler's shop on the way, I'd like to make a purchase."

That night Elisabeth was reading in the library when Mrs. Kenny interrupted her concentration to ask if she would like some warm milk to help her sleep.

"Yes, thank you. I'll be along directly."

"What are you reading, dear?"

"*The Westminster Confession of Faith*," Elisabeth said, handing the book to Mrs. Kenny. "The sexton at Christ Church burial ground mentioned it to me. It's what you believe."

"What I believe?" The old woman took the book, opened it, adjusted her spectacles, and slowly read a random passage out loud: "'God from all eternity, did, by the most wise and holy counsel of His own will, freely, and unchangeably ordain whatsoever comes to pass: yet so, as thereby neither is God the author of sin, nor is violence offered to the will of the creatures; nor is the liberty or contingency of second causes taken away, but rather established.'"

Mrs. Kenny looked puzzled. Closing the book, she handed it back to Elisabeth. "I believe that?"

Elisabeth nodded. "Your church does."

Mrs. Kenny slowly shook her head. "I believe the Bible, dear. It would take a Philadelphia lawyer to understand that stuff. Let's get your milk."

CHAPTER EIGHTEEN

At precisely 9:45 the next morning, John dropped Elisabeth off at 229 Arch Street. She walked up a short flight of stone steps to the front door, over which a newly lettered sign declared: "Female Medical College of Pennsylvania." Entering the building, she continued up a flight of stairs to a long corridor running to the back of the building. An elderly woman sat at a desk at the far end of the corridor. When Elisabeth got close enough, she recognized Miss Morris from Mrs. Kenny's description. A few feet away from the desk a door stood ajar. Female voices spilled into the hallway from the room.

"Good morning," said Elisabeth to Miss Morris, "I'm just starting."

"Name, please?"

"Elisabeth Ashcroft."

The elderly woman ran a bony finger down a column. "Ah, here it is." Withdrawing a pencil from the mountain of white hair piled on her head, she checked off the name. "Miss Elisabeth Ashcroft of Somerset, England. Welcome to America."

Hearing this description of her brought a pang of conscience, causing Elisabeth to feel like an impostor. *This is no way to begin,* she thought. "Actually, Miss Morris, I'm from Utah Territory and I'm . . . I'm not single, I'm married."

"Utah Territory? Married?" the older woman looked startled. "I'm sure that Mrs. Kenny called you Miss Ashcroft and said that you are here from England."

"I am from England, originally. But more recently I'm from the West—"

"Never mind, dear." Miss Morris pointed to the open door with her pencil. "Go on in. We'll sort this out later. Dr. Longshore's a stickler for punctuality."

Elisabeth entered a sparsely furnished room, which contained about three dozen mismatched chairs in rows, most of which were occupied by women of various ages. At the front of the room was a table with a lectern on it. Behind the table was another row of chairs; the wall held a large blackboard. Elisabeth felt a rush of gratitude when some of the women acknowledged her entry with polite smiles. She took a chair near the end of a row and sat down.

A few minutes later Miss Morris scurried in and placed a sheaf of papers on the lectern. Then she took a seat behind a small desk in the corner near the door. Shortly thereafter, six men and one woman entered the room. Five of the men and the woman sat on the chairs behind the lectern. The sixth man remained standing. He was tall and distinguished looking, with muttonchop side whiskers. His attire testified to his Quaker background.

"Welcome to our first assembly," said the man behind the lectern. "We will have such meetings throughout the term as need arises. Today we wish to introduce two new students and review the rules of the institution. As most of you know, I am Dr. Joseph Longshore—" He paused as all eyes turned to the door. A pretty young woman with flushed cheeks dashed in and took the seat next to Elisabeth. She flashed Elisabeth a smile as she took a deep breath and composed herself.

Dr. Longshore paused long enough to let the newcomer get settled. "Behind me are seated the other members of the faculty. We note with pride that this year for the first time we are honored to have a female faculty member, Dr. Ann Preston, who was among those of our first graduating class only three years ago. Now she is our professor of physiology and hygiene, and an example for all of us."

The new professor smiled, and Elisabeth noted a resemblance to Sister Eliza Snow. Both were outwardly sedate, but one glance at their faces confirmed their iron wills.

Next, Dr. Longshore introduced the other faculty members. The last to be introduced was the youngest and most handsome, Dr. Sidney Lester, professor of anatomy. Of slight build, he wore no facial hair except for his side whiskers and a small, neatly trimmed mustache. His clothes were of the most fashionable cut. A titter swept the room when Dr. Longshore mentioned that the young doctor was the only bachelor on the faculty. Dr. Lester smiled benignly on the appreciative students. His smiled rested on Elisabeth and lingered there longer than Elisabeth found comfortable. The girl beside her turned and gave Elisabeth a knowing smile. Elisabeth's cheeks burned, but she willed herself to sit quietly and without expression.

"Three years ago," Dr. Longshore continued, "when Dr. Preston graduated, we held the commencement at the Musical Fund Hall. Outside that hall were fifty policemen for our protection. Why? Because so many people then and now will not accept the fact that women have a right to practice medicine. Permit me to quote from my commencement address given that day: "'We have all been engaged in a new but momentous enterprise. We have met alike the frowns and prejudice of the community, and labored hand in hand to sustain our institution against powerful opposing forces. The community will expect as much—nay, more—of you than of your professional brethren. And the question now to be settled to put the opposers of female medical education forever to rest, is whether woman can here sustain herself or not. Are you prepared to make the effort?'"

Here the doctor paused before concluding solemnly, "'Your friends are all looking to you and to your future conduct and success with feelings of most intense interest. Do not, because you are women, regard yourselves as inferior!'"

The rest of the meeting was taken up with housekeeping concerns. When the president stressed punctuality, his gaze fell on the young woman next to Elisabeth. She moved uncomfortably in her chair, and Elisabeth gave her an encouraging smile. Eventually, Dr. Longshore introduced the two new students, asking them to stand when their names were called.

"Miss Elisabeth Ashcroft of Somerset, England." Elisabeth wanted to declare that she was from Utah Territory. She was not ashamed of it. But not wanting to create a spectacle on her first day, she simply stood, smiled politely, and sat down again. "Abigail Smith of Pike's Point." The place name caused a titter from the other students. The girl seated next to Elisabeth arose and lifted her chin ever so slightly.

When the meeting was over, Elisabeth turned to her seatmate. "Abigail? I'm Elisabeth. I guess we're starting together."

"Call me Abby," the pretty girl said. "I do believe Dr. Lester is taken with you, Elisabeth."

Elisabeth raised her eyebrows. "To quote my friend Mrs. Kenny, Dr. Lester is a little too full of himself!"

Abby laughed. "So you're from England?"

"Originally, and it's clear that you're not from here. You have a distinctive accent. Where is Pike's Point?"

"Actually—" Abby was cut short by the arrival of Dr. Lester, who had escaped a coterie of younger students.

"I'm sorry to interrupt you, ladies. I just wanted to welcome you to the college. Hopefully, you will both be attending my anatomy lectures."

Elisabeth found herself annoyed by the man's attentions. "Perhaps," she said, coolly.

In contrast, Abby was clearly pleased with his interest. Her cheeks flushed with color and she could only nod her head in response.

Dr. Lester soon bade them good day and left them. "Isn't he so handsome and refined?" Abby said to Elisabeth.

"And he knows it," Elisabeth said dryly. "Now tell me, Abby, where is Pike's Point?"

"Here in Pennsylvania, northwest of Harrisburg . . . in the hills. But my accent comes from Boston." She smiled at Elisabeth's confusion.

Abby explained that up to the age of fourteen, she had talked like other hill folk in western Pennsylvania. Then she began to do housework for a Dr. Waldie, and he had opened up a whole new world to her.

"He encouraged me to read books from his library, and he corrected my diction. Soon I began helping him with his patients. Three years ago, he got sick and sent for his sister, Miss Emmeline Waldie of Boston. When Dr. Waldie died, he left everything to his sister. She was going to sell the house and return to Boston, but when she learned that Pike's Point had a schoolhouse but no teacher, she decided to stay and reopen the school."

Miss Waldie had taken Abby under her wing. When no doctor was found to replace Dr. Waldie, Abby had moved in with Miss

Waldie and begun doctoring the people of Pike's Point. Miss Waldie had continued Abby's education, tutoring her in diction and all aspects of deportment.

Abby flashed her pretty smile again. "Miss Waldie will be pleased to know that you commented on my Bostonian accent!"

"Miss Waldie should be congratulated. What made you decide to come to the college?"

Once again, Elizabeth discovered, it was Miss Waldie's doing. The doctor's sister had read about the college and encouraged Abby to enroll. Both knew that it was unlikely that Pike's Point would attract another doctor. It had been a labor of love for old Dr. Waldie to practice there. If it hadn't been for his family's money, he could not have done so. Similarly, Miss Waldie's personal funds had allowed her to teach school for a mere pittance.

"She is financing your education?"

"Not fully. She convinced the community that supporting me at college would benefit all if I promised to return and practice in Pike's Point. I promised, so here I am." Abby paused for a moment. "With Miss Waldie and the community supporting me, I feel a great weight of responsibility. I must do well."

Elisabeth smiled encouragingly. "I'm sure you will. In a way, I'm here under similar circumstances. Back in Utah Territory there is a great need for doctors."

"Utah Territory! Not England?"

"Well, both, actually," Elisabeth said with a smile, and for the next twenty minutes Elisabeth told Abby her story.

"It must be strange living away out there among people who practice polygamy."

"Not so strange. It's a wonderful place and the people are very kind. I miss them all, especially my friend Becky. You remind me of her."

"I miss my family and friends too." Abby sighed. "Especially Jerry . . . Jeremiah Potts. He's my beau, though I doubt if we will ever marry."

"Why not?"

"Well he's . . . he's rather uncultured," Abby's pretty face clouded with chagrin. "You'll probably think poorly of me, but I agree with

Miss Waldie that Jerry would be a poor choice for me once I become a doctress. He's handsome, honest, and a good worker—he has a green thumb, as they say. And he does love me, but he has little education and speaks like a . . . well, like a Pike's Pointer."

Elisabeth was trying to think of an appropriate response to Abby's admission when Dr. Longshore approached them. "Ladies," he said, shaking their hands, "welcome to the college. I'm sorry to interrupt your discussion. Miss Morris tells me there's a problem with thy registration, Miss Ashcroft. May I see thee in my office?"

"Certainly, sir. I'll be right along."

He nodded. "Miss Morris will show thee the way."

Elisabeth smiled at Abby. "Dr. Longshore's speech—the 'thees' and 'thys'—will take some getting used to. Before I go, would you do me a favor?"

"If I can."

Elisabeth asked Abby if she would take a message to John that she would be a little longer. When she learned that Abby lived thirteen blocks away on Market Street, near the gasworks and river (which was the reason for her tardiness that morning), Elisabeth offered Abby the use of the carriage. She wrote a note to John to that effect. Elisabeth was pleased that she'd found a friend on her very first day. It would ease her loneliness.

Abby went off to find John, and Elisabeth proceeded to Dr. Longshore's office.

"So, Miss Ashcroft," Dr. Longshore said, motioning for Elisabeth to take a seat. "I understand there's an irregularity with thy registration."

"Yes, sir. Mrs. Kenny . . . I believe you know her?"

"I do, an excellent woman and a great friend and benefactor of our institution."

"She's my oldest friend and I love her dearly. But she was not entirely truthful when she enrolled me." The doctor raised his eyebrows and motioned for her to go on. "I was registered as Elisabeth Ashcroft of England. In reality I'm from Utah Territory."

"Why, I wonder, did she do that?"

"I can only surmise that she wished to protect me and the college. You see, I am a member of The Church of Jesus Christ of Latter-day Saints. Some people call us Mormons. I imagine that with all the negative stories in the newspapers about polygamy, Mrs. Kenny thought it prudent to enroll me by my former place of residence."

Dr. Longshore stroked his chin whiskers. "Perhaps Mrs. Kenny did the right thing. Our enemies will use any excuse to cast shadows on our fledgling institution. On the other hand, I commend thee for thy forthrightness. I must confess I know little about the Mormons, and what I do know comes from the newspapers and is no doubt slanted." He smiled gently at her. "As I'm sure thee knows from my speech and dress, I myself am a Quaker. We try not to judge unfairly."

Elisabeth nodded. "There's more, Dr. Longshore. I am enrolled under my maiden name, which is the way I wanted it, but I don't wish to be under false pretenses. Several years ago I was wed in England to Lord Claverley of Somerset . . ."

Elisabeth held nothing back, feeling that she owed Dr. Longshore nothing less than the truth. He listened patiently, and when she was finished, he said, "I sympathize with thee wholeheartedly, Miss Ashcroft. The plight of the married woman in England is shocking. The English Quakers are doing their part in helping to bring about reform, just as we here in America are trying to free the slaves."

Elisabeth nodded. "As much as I desire a medical education, if my presence will cause embarrassment for the college, I will withdraw."

Dr. Longshore placed both hands together, rested his chin on them, and closed his eyes. After ruminating for several seconds, he opened his eyes. "While I know little about the Mormons, a member of one of the college's founding families, the Kanes, knows a great deal. Permit me to consult with Friend Thomas Kane before I make a decision. I'll send a message immediately to his office in Independence Hall. If he is not available for sixth day, I'll let thee know."

"Sixth day?"

Dr. Longshore smiled. "We Friends don't use the days of the week or the months because they are mostly the names of pagan gods. Rather, we use numbers. For example, today is what thee would call the fourth of November. We call it fourth day, eleventh month. I assume that thee is staying at Mrs. Kenny's over at Broad and Brown Streets?"

Elisabeth nodded.

Dr. Longshore stood and rang a small bell on his desk. "Miss Morris will see thee out."

"Thank you, doctor," Elisabeth said as she arose. "I was pleasantly surprised to find a female clerk at the college. Most institutions have males."

He nodded. "True. But we feel that women should not only enter the man's world of medicine but other areas as well. I'm convinced that no male secretary in Philadelphia could take dictation as quickly and as accurately as Miss Morris. She is an amanuensis *par excellence.* Has thee heard of the new Pitman method of shorthand?"

"Oh yes. Sir Isaac Pitman's phonetic shorthand was very popular in England."

"It has now crossed the ocean and Miss Morris has already mastered it. Ah, here she is. Our amanuensis, registrar, student counselor, purchasing clerk, bursar—a woman of many hats. Not much goes on in this institution without her knowing about it."

The white-haired woman smiled at the compliments as she piloted Elisabeth out of the office. A few minutes later, Elisabeth emerged onto Arch Street, where she found John waiting for her. She learned that he had just returned from taking Abby home.

"Miss Smith is a most pleasant and attractive young woman, if you don't mind me saying so, Miss Elisabeth. If I were twenty years younger . . ."

Elisabeth smiled. "Why have you never married, John? If you don't mind my asking?"

"I don't mind. I was betrothed once but never married. She wed another while I was off in Mexico."

"Mexico?"

John smiled at Elisabeth's surprise. "I probably don't look much like a soldier, but I was with General Scott when we took Mexico City back in '47." He slapped his thigh. "That's where I got this game leg." His smile faded. "When I finally got home she'd . . . well, it's all water under the bridge."

"I'm sorry, John. Sorry for dragging up a painful memory."

He shook his head. "No harm done, miss. We have to play the cards we're dealt." He smiled mischievously and added. "Besides, I read somewhere that marriage is not a word, but a sentence!"

Elisabeth smiled as John helped her into the carriage. He was about to close the door when she asked him another question. "I had an interview with Dr. Longshore and he mentioned Colonel Thomas Kane, but he didn't use Colonel Kane's military title when referring to him. Do you know why?"

John nodded that he knew. "Quakers believe that all people are equal. They don't acknowledge titles and so forth. They usually refer to people by their first name, or precede it with 'Friend.' Their belief in equality is one reason that they are leaders in the abolition movement and in the education of women."

"Why do they use 'thee' rather than 'you'?" was Elisabeth's next question.

John knew the answer to that as well. "For the same reason. When George Fox started Quakerism in the seventeenth century, the word 'you' as a singular pronoun was used only for upper-class people and 'thee' was used for common people. They didn't feel that the distinction was moral. They continued to use 'you' only as a plural pronoun."

As she rode home, Elisabeth decided that she liked Dr. Longshore and his philosophies, and Miss Morris and Abby Smith, but that there was something repellent about Dr. Sidney Lester. She hoped that he was not going to be a problem.

The next morning, Elisabeth kept busy going through her belongings and arranging her clothing. In the afternoon, she and Mrs. Kenny toured the city in the carriage. They dropped by Abby's place—a shabby brownstone on the wrong side of town. Abby apologized for her poor accommodations and for the unfriendly landlady, Mrs. Steinke, but she averred that the rent of $1.50 per week was all she could afford on her allowance. Her gratitude was evident as she accepted Elisabeth's offer to join her and Mrs. Kenny on their carriage ride, and she was quick to accept Mrs. Kenny's invitation to dine with them. By the time Elisabeth accompanied Abby home in the carriage, Elisabeth felt as if she had always known her new friend.

"I'm meeting with Dr. Longshore again on Friday," Elisabeth said as Abby descended from the carriage. "In the meantime, please don't mention to anyone that I'm married or that I'm from Utah Territory."

Abby promised. As the carriage drove away, Elisabeth noticed someone peering through a slit in the curtains at a window of the shabby brownstone.

CHAPTER NINETEEN

On Friday at two o'clock sharp, John dropped Elisabeth off at the college for her meeting with Dr. Longshore and Colonel Kane. Miss Morris showed her into the office. The two men rose to greet her. Miss Morris took a seat in the corner, pen poised. When they were all seated, Colonel Kane turned to Elisabeth. "And how fare my friends in the Great Basin, Lady Claverley?"

"Very well, sir. But please . . . call me by my maiden name."

"Of course, Miss Ashcroft. And President Young?"

"As far as I know, he's doing well. Before I left Utah Territory I listened to him preach, and he was in fine form."

"Friend Thomas and I have been having a most interesting discussion, Miss Ashcroft," Dr. Longshore said. "He has given me much insight into the Mormon people. Although he doesn't countenance polygamy—and has written to Brigham Young saying so—he nevertheless has great admiration for thy people. Furthermore, he sees a great deal of hypocrisy in those who fulminate against plural marriage while at the same time winking at immorality in American society. We were just discussing Martin Luther, who, Friend Thomas informs me, suggested to one of his supporters, the German nobleman Philip of Hesse, that taking a second wife was preferable to having a mistress, the usual custom of upper-class Europeans. But I'm sure that a young woman such as thee is not interested in such matters and in dry history."

Elisabeth smiled. "Actually, sir," she said. "I enjoy studying the past, although I find some merit in Miss Jane Austen's assertion that in history 'the men are all good for nothing, and hardly any women at all.'"

Miss Morris suppressed a laugh, and the men smiled.

"Based on Friend Thomas's recommendation," Dr. Longshore continued, "my decision is that we make no effort to cover up the fact that thee is married. As for thy religious beliefs, there is no law—Friend Thomas informs me—in Utah Territory forbidding plural marriage. And, if Martin Luther was right, there is no divine law against it either. So, Miss Ashcroft, we welcome thee to the college. In good conscience, however, I must add that my decision is not solely altruistic. As Martin Luther needed the support of Philip of Hesse, we need the support of generous patrons such as Mrs. Kenny. Thee has been introduced to the college as 'Miss Ashcroft,' and I see no reason why we should not continue to address thee as such."

Colonel Kane spoke up. "I would like to commend you, Miss Ashcroft, for your honesty in bringing this whole matter to our attention. I wish you all the best in your studies."

That afternoon, Elisabeth confronted Mrs. Kenny about registering her as coming from England rather than Utah Territory. "How could you, a God-fearing woman, countenance such subterfuge?" she asked, but her eyes sparkled and her tone was impish.

"I know 'twas a white lie," said Mrs. Kenny, chagrin clouding her face, "but I felt 'twas for the best. Do you not mind the Bible stories of Abraham in Egypt and in Gerar? He told white lies, saying Sarah was his sister."

"That's true," Elisabeth responded, "but as I recall, the Egyptian pharaoh and the king of Gerar censured him for doing so."

"Well, dear," said Mrs. Kenny, a little peeved at being caught in her white lie, "you do what you must. But before you go broadcasting that you countenance polygamy, you'd better talk to Dr. Longshore about it."

Elisabeth put her arms around her friend. "I'm not upset with you, Nanny Craig. I know you had my welfare at heart, and I love you for it. I've already talked to Dr. Longshore, and we've decided to leave things as they are. I'll continue to go under my single name, but if the subject comes up we will freely acknowledge that I'm married and from Utah Territory."

CHAPTER TWENTY

On the following Monday morning, Elisabeth presented herself before the desk of the "woman of many hats."

"I understand that Mrs. Kenny has paid for my lectures and demonstrations, Miss Morris."

"She certainly has, dear. Which ones would you like to take?"

"All except surgery. I don't think I'm ready for that yet. Also, is anatomy taught by anyone other than Dr. Lester?"

Miss Morris gazed up at Elisabeth. "No, dear. Unfortunately, the college is still so small we have only one faculty member for each subject. Has Dr. Lester . . . offended you in any way?"

"Not at all, but I think I'll forgo his classes."

"As you wish."

Elisabeth was the first to class that morning for Dr. Longshore's lecture on diseases of women. As she sat in the empty room, she was both elated and fearful. *Can I do this after all these years?* Fortunately, she was not long in thinking such thoughts, for the room began to fill. Just seconds before Dr. Longshore's entry, Abby squeezed into the seat beside her.

"We should have gone by your place and picked you up this morning, Abby," Elisabeth said after the lecture was over. "I was so excited about starting, I didn't even think of it."

Abby gave her usual broad smile. "No harm done, Elisabeth. Of course, if you want to pick me up tomorrow, I'll not refuse."

"We will for certain. Perhaps we can give you a ride home today as well. What time do you finish?"

"Six o'clock, after Dr. Lester's class."

"Oh, I finish much earlier."

"You're not attending his lecture?"

Elisabeth shook her head. "No, I'm not." She gave no explanation, and Abby did not pry.

After Dr. Longshore's lecture, Elisabeth and Abby both attended a lecture on hygiene given by Dr. Ann Preston.

At the conclusion of the lecture, Elisabeth went up to the front of the room and thanked the teacher. "I once spoke with a Dr. Osgood," Elisabeth said, "and he agrees completely with your beliefs. I even took notes from our discussion for our local health society."

"Philip Osgood?"

"Yes, do you know him?"

"Not personally, but I'm familiar with the work he's doing with Dr. Holmes in Boston. Much of my lecture material comes from Dr. Holmes' essay, 'The Contagiousness of Puerperal Fever.'"

"I believe that Dr. Osgood is working with Dr. Holmes on a reissue of that essay."

Dr. Preston nodded and looked at Elisabeth appraisingly. "I must be off, Miss Ashcroft, but I'd like to speak with you more about this." She then surprised Elisabeth by asking her if she would summarize her notes and give a class presentation.

While she waited for Abby in a small study room, Elisabeth used her time to review her class notes. The time passed quickly, and she was surprised when Abby joined her.

"There you are, Elisabeth." Abby gave an exaggerated sigh and plopped down in a seat across the table from her new friend. "I'm doomed!"

Elisabeth smiled. "It couldn't be that bad."

Abby nodded her head vigorously. "It *is* that bad! Dr. Lester speaks a different language—and I'm going to have to learn it if I ever hope to graduate. Why can't doctors call a spade a spade, or in this case a clavicle a collarbone, a scapula a shoulder blade, or a sternum a breastbone? Why do they have to surround medicine with so much mystery?"

Elisabeth gave a wry smile as she answered. "A doctor can charge more for curing *acute gastroenteritis* than for curing it by its usual name—stomachache!"

"Old Dr. Waldie never bothered with Latin terms. Oh, Elisabeth, you must take Dr. Lester's anatomy class with me, otherwise . . ."

" . . . otherwise you're doomed." Elisabeth laughed. "All right, my friend, I'll do it."

"You will?"

Elisabeth nodded. "As I was waiting for you, I thought how silly it is of me to not take a class just because the teacher makes me uncomfortable by . . . by leering at me."

"Leering at you?"

"Well, staring at me, then."

"You are very attractive. I'd think you would be used to men staring at you."

"Not the way he does—but thank you for the compliment."

Abby smiled mischievously. "I have to keep on your good side if you're going to tutor me in anatomy and transport me in your carriage."

At this Elisabeth jumped up. "Oh, no! I forgot all about John. He was to pick me up two hours ago."

Elisabeth and Abby exited the college to find John patiently waiting in the carriage. "I'm so sorry, John. Have you been here all this time?"

John shook his head. "Oh no, miss. When you didn't come down I thought I had my times mixed up so I asked the janitor. He said the last class was over at six o'clock. So, here I am."

When Elisabeth asked if John would drive Abby home, he said that Mrs. Kenny had invited Miss Smith home for supper, if she'd like.

"I would like," Abby said. "The more time I stay away from my lodgings and Mrs. Steinke, the better I like it!"

As the carriage turned into the lane leading to the mansion, Elisabeth once again noted the poor state of the landscaping. The stalks of dead flowers, piles of autumn leaves, and broken branches strewn about all testified of the gardener's dereliction of duty. "Something has to be done about the landscaping," said Elisabeth as she and Abby climbed out of the carriage. "If you had only seen how lovely it was when I visited three years ago, you'd know what I mean."

Abby looked around. "Then let's do something about it. We can work on it in our spare time."

"Begging your pardon, Miss Abby," John said. "Mrs. Kenny would never let you ladies do such work. Besides, we have a gardener."

"Then let's offer to help him do it," Elisabeth said, catching Abby's enthusiasm. "Let's go right now." Abby nodded her agreement.

John smiled at the girls' naïveté. "All right, but I must warn you, you'll find Murphy a hard man to pin down. He could talk the hind leg off a goat."

The three of them found Mr. Murphy sitting in front of the cottage, a Donegal cap on his head, his feet on a stool, his pipe in his mouth, and a newspaper spread across his knees. Clearly surprised by this delegation from the big house, he struggled to his feet. As he did so, he made a great show of rubbing his lower back. Removing his cap, he spoke in a heavy Irish brogue, "Good evening to ye, Master John, and who are these visions o' beauty?"

"None of your blarney, Murphy," John said. "We're here to see why the gardening isn't getting done."

"Well now," said Murphy, easing back onto his chair, "without a word o' a lie, me back's been tormenting me something fierce, so it has. But I'm better now than I was before, but not as well as I was before I was as bad as I am now. It'd destroy me altogether if I tried to get down on me benders. Another few days o' rest, an' I'll be right as rain. Rest'll do me a power o' good, so it will. Sure, an' I'm glad ye showed up. Such educated folks as ye can answer me a question. Can ye tell me what brings on the lum-bay-go?" He drew out this last word and accompanied it by rubbing his lower back.

Elisabeth started to respond, but John raised his finger. "I'll tell you what brings on lumbago, Murphy. It comes from drinking cheap whiskey, carousing with low people, and sleeping in a ditch because a body can't make it home. It comes from leading a lazy, dissolute life among the dregs of society. That's what brings on lumbago!"

"Thank ye, Master John," said Murphy, politely, "I only ast 'cause it says here in the *Evening Bulletin* the Episcopal bishop o' Philadelphia has come down with the lum-bay-go!"

Abby squealed with laughter. John threw up his hands in disgust. Elisabeth, suppressing a smile, said with complete seriousness, "Mr. Murphy, let's return to the subject at hand. Have you been malingering?"

"Ma-lin-ger-ing?" Mr. Murphy said, pronouncing the word carefully.

"Faking your backache!" John said, none too gently.

Murphy took on a pained expression. "Fakin' it? Why I swear on me mother's grave, me back's bin murdering me, so it has. If there's a word of a lie in it, may God set me on the hottest hob in purgatory, and may I spout steam till Good Friday falls on a Saturday!"

John again threw up his hands, and this time he stalked off.

"John was right when he told us that you could talk the leg off a goat," said Elisabeth with a sigh, "but the fact remains the gardening needs to be attended to. Either you must do it, or Mrs. Kenny will have to find someone else. However, Miss Smith and I are willing to help you until you get back on your feet. Do you accept our offer?"

Murphy's eyes brightened. "Ye ladies would atchelly help?"

"Yes," said Elisabeth. Turning to Abby, she asked, "Would the mornings be better?"

Abby nodded. "Lectures don't begin until ten o'clock."

"All right," Elisabeth said, turning back to Mr. Murphy. "We'll be here at seven o'clock sharp tomorrow morning. Be ready to show us what to do and what tools we will need to do it."

"Seven o'clock? Why it's barely light at tha' hour."

"Sharp," Elisabeth said. Taking Abby by the arm, she turned on her heel, and they marched back to the house.

CHAPTER TWENTY-ONE

After arranging with Miss Morris to attend Dr. Lester's lectures, Elisabeth awaited with some trepidation for her first anatomy class to begin.

"It'll be fine," Abby said, seeing Elisabeth's tenseness.

And it was fine. Except for politely welcoming her to the class, the young doctor treated her the same as all the other students.

"Didn't I tell you?" Abby said after class, "Dr. Lester isn't the monster you seem to think he is."

Elisabeth wasn't convinced. "That remains to be seen."

On Saturday, Elisabeth and Abby joined other students at the Lying-in Asylum in the same building as the college. They observed the various doctors as they examined a steady stream of indigent women, mostly pregnant, who used the clinic's free services. At two o'clock, the clinic closed, ending the week for the students.

As Elisabeth and Abby prepared to leave the clinic, Dr. Lester stopped them. "And how was your first week, ladies?"

"It went well," Elisabeth said, trying to show proper deference to her professor, while at the same time trying not to encourage him.

Abby blushed and nodded. Dr. Lester's presence left her tongue-tied.

"May I speak with you a moment, Miss Ashcroft?"

"I'll wait outside," Abby said and quickly left the room.

Dr. Lester turned on his considerable charm. "I understand that you're staying at the old Kenny mansion."

"Yes," Elisabeth said in a formal, even tone. "I am fortunate. Many of the students live in rather spartan lodgings."

"Such as Miss Smith?"

Elisabeth stiffened. "You seem to know a lot about your students, Dr. Lester."

He smiled. "Only the pretty ones. Would it be acceptable to call on you this weekend?"

"To what purpose?" Despite her sheltered upbringing, Elisabeth knew very well his purpose.

"Well, you're a single woman and I'm a single man. I'd think that the purpose would be obvious."

Elisabeth wanted to tell him that she was not a single woman, but she felt it was none of his business. Besides, she took perverse pleasure in turning him down. She smiled sweetly. "I'm afraid I must refuse your kind offer, Dr. Lester." She turned to leave.

"Perhaps another time," he called after her.

She stopped at the door and turned to face him. "No. Not another time."

"May I ask why?"

"A woman need not explain why she refuses a man's offer to call. However, an obvious reason is that you are a professor and I am a student. It seems to me that the college must have some rule against such liaisons."

He shook his head. "As a matter of fact, it doesn't."

"It's a new institution. Give it time." With that, Elisabeth continued out the door.

"Tell me everything," Abby demanded when Elisabeth joined her.

"Not much to tell. He asked to call on me, and I refused him."

"You told him you're married?"

"No. I confess this is a complication I didn't foresee in going by my maiden name. But I made it clear to him that I would not change my mind. I think he understood and will not bother me again."

Abby looked doubtful. "I wouldn't be so sure. He's very charming. I'd think that any woman would be pleased at his interest."

"Not I!"

* * *

That evening, Abby again dined at the mansion. Over the week she had almost become a fixture. Elisabeth appreciated her new friend's optimistic outlook and cheery personality. Abby's company helped ease Elisabeth's longing for Gren and her worry over her father's death. Returning from accompanying Abby home, Elisabeth immediately sat down at the writing desk in the library and penned another page in a long letter to Gren. She wondered how many pages her letter would be by the time she finally got his address. *I suppose I could send it to General Delivery, New York City,* she thought. But she decided to wait a few more days.

When she had finished writing the page, she copied most of it and added it to the letter she was assembling for Becky. As her eyes glanced around the ornate room, a feeling of thankfulness filled her. She wondered what accommodations Gren had found and whether he was getting enough to eat. *How blessed I am since joining the Church! If only I could be free of Claverley, life would be perfect.*

The next week passed quickly. Schoolwork, gardening, letter writing, walking, homework with Abby, and even knitting lessons from Rose filled her days. The only dark spot in her second week at the college came toward the end when Dr. Lester again asked to call on her. Once more she refused, not giving him any reason.

"I can't understand your reluctance," Dr. Lester said as he and Elisabeth stood in the lecture room after class. Abby had gone ahead to the study room to wait for Elisabeth. "I'm not exactly hideous, I come from a respectable family, and I'm engaged in a noble profession. What could possibly keep you from allowing me to court you?"

Elisabeth took a deep breath. "Dr. Lester, if I have in any way encouraged your advances, I apologize. However, I thought I had made it crystal clear that I am not interested in you other than as my instructor. Please do not broach this subject again. Good day." She quickly left the room.

He followed her into the hallway, but upon seeing Miss Morris at her desk, he retreated back into the lecture room.

Elisabeth leaned against the wall and took a deep breath. When she had gained her composure, she made her way toward the study room. "So, he's at it again?" Miss Morris said as Elisabeth passed her desk.

"Pardon?" Elisabeth said, halting in some surprise.

Miss Morris smiled wearily. "Do you have a few minutes, dear?"

Elisabeth glanced toward the study room. "Yes . . . yes, of course, Miss Morris."

The elderly woman motioned Elisabeth into Dr. Longshore's office and closed the door behind them. When they were both seated, she said, "We'll have privacy here. Dr. Longshore will not be back today. As I believe Dr. Longshore mentioned on your first day here, there isn't much that goes on around here that I'm not aware of. I'm not one to gossip, but I feel that there's something you must know about our Dr. Lester. He comes from good stock and acts as if butter wouldn't melt in his mouth, but as you may have realized, he is not what he seems."

Miss Morris went on to say that halfway through the previous college year, a sweet young woman, Emily Pendergast, had left Philadelphia to return home. Ostensibly, she had left because of illness, but Miss Morris feared that the young woman was in the family way.

Elisabeth was not surprised at what she heard. Although she couldn't quite put her finger on it, from the very beginning she'd also had her suspicions about Dr. Lester. "Certainly an investigation was held?"

The older woman shook her head. "Not a formal one. I did write to Miss Pendergast but received no reply. Without evidence, there was nothing we could do. Being a new institution, and one with tremendous opposition, a scandal could ruin us."

"I appreciate your telling me this, Miss Morris. Please be assured that I've made it clear to Dr. Lester that I have absolutely no interest in him."

Miss Morris looked at her in astonishment. "Oh, Miss Ashcroft, you misapprehend me. I have no fear of your falling under his spell. Oh, good heavens, no. My concern is for your young friend."

Puzzlement spread across Elisabeth's face. "Abby? Why, as far as I know, Dr. Lester has never even approached her."

"That's probably true, dear. At present he appears to be quite taken with you. But I fear that once he sees that he has no chance with you, he'll turn his predatory eyes elsewhere. I've seen how Miss Smith looks at him. I fear she would be more susceptible to him."

Elisabeth nodded. "I see. Well, I'll certainly do all I can to see that Miss Smith doesn't get hurt."

Miss Morris smiled gratefully. "I've never had children of my own, and I must admit I'm a bit of a mother hen to the students."

Elisabeth left Dr. Longshore's office deep in thought. She walked down the hall to rejoin Abby. Suddenly, Dr. Lester emerged from the study room. He smiled at Elisabeth and headed for his lecture room.

Abby looked up when Elisabeth entered the room, and Elisabeth could see that her friend's eyes were bright and that her face was flushed. Abby quickly dropped her eyes to the book in front of her. "You were a long time," she said.

"Sorry. Miss Morris wanted to see me. What was Dr. Lester doing here?"

Abby didn't look up. "He wasn't looking for you, if that's what you mean."

Elisabeth sat down across from Abby. "All right, Abby, out with it—what's going on?"

Abby finally raised her eyes from her book and smiled with satisfaction. "Dr. Lester asked me to go to the Chestnut Street Theater with him on Saturday."

"And you accepted?" Elisabeth couldn't keep the disapproval out of her voice.

"Of course I accepted. I'm not a married woman like you."

Abby lowered her eyes and said nothing more. Elisabeth was sure that she was only pretending to study her book. Neither spoke for a long time, then Elisabeth said, "I guess it wouldn't do any good for me to ask you not to go?"

"Why shouldn't I go?" Abby demanded, looking up with flashing eyes. "He's a doctor, he's handsome, he speaks well . . . in fact, he's just the kind of man Miss Waldie wants me to marry."

"Marry? Miss Waldie doesn't know him. Nor do you, I might add."

"And you do?"

"Well, I believe I've had a little more experience with men than you. I've just come from talking with Miss Morris, and she has warned me about Dr. Lester. She said that a young woman who had spent time with Dr. Lester left the college midterm, perhaps in the family way."

"Perhaps? I'm surprised at you, Elisabeth, listening to gossip. I know you've never liked him. I don't know the source of your prejudice, and I don't think you know either. Nothing you can do or say will stop me from seeing him!"

Breathing heavily, Abby returned her eyes to her book, and Elisabeth tried another tack. "Miss Morris has known him a lot longer than you or I, and to be forewarned is to be forearmed."

"Thank you, Benjamin Franklin." Abby's tone was acerbic.

Elisabeth's heart sank. She sighed deeply. "Abby, over these past weeks we've become friends. I wouldn't want anything to interfere with our friendship. I'm only thinking of your welfare."

Abby looked up. "If you're truly my friend, you won't interfere. I'm not a child. I can take care of myself." Her face softened and she reached across the table and took Elisabeth's hand. "Your friendship is important to me, Elisabeth, and I appreciate so much all you've done for me. I'm sorry I was rude to you. It's just that . . . it's just that I want you to share in my happiness." She withdrew her hand and slid the book across to Elisabeth. "Now, friend, will you please help me memorize all these muscles that start with 'sterno'?"

Elisabeth gave a resigned sigh and looked down at the book. "Sternochondroscapular."

"An occasional muscle arising from the . . . manubrian of the sternum and first costal cartilage and passing . . . and passing . . ."

". . . lateralward."

". . . lateralward and backward to be inserted into the upper border of the scapula." Abby gave a deep sigh. "I'll never learn this stuff."

"Of course you will. Tonight we'll study hard for our examination on Friday."

CHAPTER TWENTY-TWO

Over the next two days, Elisabeth and Abby avoided the subject of Dr. Lester. The two friends worked in the garden, attended classes together, and studied long into the night. Despite Abby's misgivings, she did well on her anatomy quiz. Elisabeth got the highest mark in the class. After school was out for the day, John picked them up from the college and drove to the mansion. A letter from Gren awaited Elisabeth.

With a quick thanks, she snatched it from Mrs. Kenny and took the stairs to her room two at a time. Her hands shook as she lit the gaslight, hastily broke the wax seal, and read:

Dear Sister Ashcroft,

> *We've finally met up with the Brethren. When we got to N.Y. we went to the post office but there was no note from Elder Taylor. What a huge city! We didn't know what to do. We wandered around asking people if they knew any Mormons. They looked at us as if we were crazy. All we could do was take lodgings. We got the cheapest we could find at 25 cents a night each. Meals go for about half that. Before the week was out, our money was gone and still no note from Bro. T. As I sat wondering what to do I put a finger into my pocket and pulled out a gold ~~ginia~~ ~~guine~~ coin. I thought it was a miracle! You wouldn't know how it got there would you?*

Elisabeth smiled and continued reading:

I thought about using it to buy tickets to Philadelphia. But we decided to wait a few more days. After going to the post office twice a day for over a week, a letter was finally there. Bro. T and the others took longer to get to N.Y. than planned as they spread out and sold subscriptions to the newspaper on the way. Bro. T has rented rooms on the third floor of Mrs. Englebrecht's boarding house, at 256 Hicks St. in Brooklyn, as a mission office. You can write to me here. George and I share a room. It has two single beds, a table, washstand, grate, three chairs and a sofa. The windows are loose and Jack Frost comes in when he pleases. The other day, George was working at the table on the masthead for "The Mormon"—that's what our newspaper will be called—when he said the room was cold enough to freeze the head off a nail. Despite all, it's good to have something to do. We have been going around trying to find any members and selling subscriptions. Also Bro. T has been helping immigrants from England to go west. Of course they'll have to wait for the spring now. Meanwhile, a member called Bro. Ebeneezer Young of Westport, Connecticut has hired some emigrants at his cotton mill so they can earn money for the trip west in the spring. All in all, things are tolerable. If there is any chance to come visit you, I'll take it.

As ever,
Elder Gren Sanderson

Elisabeth wiped her eyes and began rereading the letter. She found the salutation and complimentary close rather formal, but she allowed that Gren was playing by her rules in their relationship. A sound at the door caused her to look up. Abby stood there.

Elisabeth motioned for Abby to sit beside her. "Would you like to hear what Gren has to say?" Abby nodded, and Elisabeth read the letter out loud.

"Strange," Abby said. "Here you're living in luxury, and Gren's living like a pauper only four hours away."

"Yes, but he's doing what he has been called to do. Ironically, I'm happy that we're apart in the sense that we are both busily engaged in activities that keep us from worrying about the fact that we can't be together. Does that make sense?"

Abby grinned. "If you say so!"

Later that evening Elisabeth accompanied Abby home in the carriage. "Do you want us to pick you up for the clinic in the morning?" Elisabeth asked as Abby was getting out of the carriage.

Abby hesitated. "No, thank you, Elisabeth. I'm not going." With that, she started toward her lodgings, then suddenly turned back. "I wasn't going to tell you because I knew you wouldn't approve. Dr. Lester is sending me to get fitted for a dress appropriate for the theater. When I told him I didn't have anything to wear, he offered to buy me a dress. Despite what you think, he's a kind, generous man."

Before Elisabeth could respond, Abby was gone. A sickening feeling spread through Elisabeth's stomach. She wanted to warn Abby once more, but what could she say? Abby had clearly told her not to interfere. All the way home and all through the weekend, Elisabeth worried about her friend.

On Sunday afternoon Elisabeth attended the Presbyterian Church with Mrs. Kenny. A Reverend Hasslet, visiting from Boston, gave the sermon. He spoke on Calvin's five points: the total depravity of man, unconditional election, limited atonement, irresistible calling, and the perseverance of the saints. Elisabeth disagreed with almost everything he said.

On their way home in the carriage, Mrs. Kenny asked, "What did you think of Reverend Hasslet's sermon, my dear? I invited him home for dinner. I thought you might be interested in learning about Boston."

Elisabeth smiled inwardly. *You mean you thought I could perhaps be weaned away from Mormonism by this persuasive preacher.* But she didn't speak her thoughts, knowing that Mrs. Kenny was still very much a nanny looking out for her little girl. "He gave an erudite presentation," Elisabeth said diplomatically.

Elisabeth enjoyed the reverend's visit and learned much about Boston. When he had gone, she and Mrs. Kenny retired to the small parlor.

"Thank you for being so polite to Mr. Hasslet," Mrs. Kenny said. "I admire how you can get along with those who don't believe as you do. There is too much religious intolerance in the world."

Mrs. Kenny picked up her knitting, and Elisabeth opened the Book of Mormon and began to read. For a long time they carried on their individual pursuits without speaking. After a while Mrs. Kenny laid her knitting aside, looked thoughtful, and said, "May I ask you a question, dear?"

"Certainly."

"It comes from Mr. Hasslet's sermon. Perhaps I need to go back to the beginning and tell you about when I was a wee girl in Ireland."

Elisabeth was delighted. She had always loved her nanny's stories of growing up in the north of Ireland. Putting her book down, she gave Mrs. Kenny her full attention.

"When I was a girl, I attended morning Sunday School. On Sunday evenings I stayed home whilst my parents went to church. One Sabbath I was so inspired by my Sunday School lesson, I felt a craving for more religion. That evening I followed my parents to church. I crept in the back door and found a hiding place behind the organ." She was quiet, as if remembering, and Elisabeth waited for her to continue.

The older woman's voice trembled as she described what she had heard: "The minister preached that from the top of our heads to the soles of our feet, we are rotten sinners. There's absolutely no good in us. We all deserve to be thrown into a lake of fire and burned forever. He described in awful detail the agony of the damned souls . . . the wailing and weeping and gnashing of teeth and all. It fairly made my skin crawl. I kept expecting him to say that only the bad people would suffer so, but he never did. He kept repeating that every one of us merited eternal damnation. Finally, he did say that in God's great love and mercy He had chosen some people to escape the fires of hell. Not that they deserved it; even they were depraved, but for some reason He chose some to go to heaven—'the elect,' he called them.

"I slipped out the back door and ran home, my face wet with tears. That night, I dreamt I was thrown into a lake of fire, which was particularly disturbing to me, because when I was a wee girl, I burned my hand on the grate. Ever after, I was deathly afraid of fire. After that sermon, it was a long time before I could sleep peacefully again." Mrs. Kenny stopped and looked at Elisabeth. "I guess over the years I've heard many similar sermons; however, I've learned to take them with a grain of salt. But I know I'm not long for this world. With death staring me in the face, I feel my old fears return to haunt me. I'm just a plain woman. I know I'm not of the elect. When I die, do you think I'll really be thrown into a lake of fire and burn forever?"

At the sight of her friend's honest emotions, Elisabeth felt tears well up in her own eyes. For a moment she couldn't speak. Then she dabbed at her eyes and went to sit beside her friend. Taking Mrs. Kenny's gnarled hands in hers, she said earnestly, "Mary, in all my thirty years, I have never met anyone with a better heart than yours. When you die . . ." Her voice caught on the word. "When you die, your body will go into the ground to await the Resurrection, but you—your spirit—will go back to God. He will welcome you with open arms. Let me read something to you; it is in the Book of Mormon." She looked through the pages swiftly. "Here it is.'

'Now, concerning the state of the soul between death and the resurrection—Behold, it has been made known unto me by an angel, that the spirits of all men, as soon as they are departed from this mortal body, yea, the spirits of all men, whether they be good or evil, are taken home to that God who gave them life. And then shall it come to pass, that the spirits of those who are righteous are received into a state of happiness, which is called paradise, a state of rest, a state of peace, where they shall rest from all their troubles and from all care, and sorrow.'"

Elisabeth looked up from the book. "Through the restoration of the gospel, the Lord has revealed the truth to us. It is a false teaching of men that only a few selected Christians will be saved and the rest of mankind will be cast into hell without a chance of redemption. The millions upon millions of people who have not had the opportunity of hearing and obeying the true gospel of Jesus Christ in this life will be given that opportunity after death. Whether we spent this life as a Catholic, a Protestant, a Hindu, or a Mohammedan we will have the opportunity in the afterlife of accepting Christ as our Savior. Those who accept and repent will not have to suffer for their sins, because Christ has already done that for all of us. Those who do not accept the gospel will have to suffer for their own sins, but even that suffering will be for a limited time. Because of Christ's atonement, we will all be resurrected and be placed in the kingdom our works have merited. So, Mary, let not your heart be troubled. When you pass on, a glorious future awaits you."

Mrs. Kenny's face was bright despite her tears. "Thank you for your words of comfort, my dear. I think I'll go to bed now and sleep easy. I believe what you have said. Although I've tried to ignore my feelings, I think I've known for a long time that there is more to your church than the papers make out. I'm an old woman, and I don't think I can change, but I'd like to know more about your restored gospel."

After Mrs. Kenny had left, Elisabeth sat for a long while, enveloped in the warm glow of the Spirit. *If only Gren were here to share this moment. I hope that he's having success in his missionary work.* She thought back to her own conversion. *Yes, the way I feel now is the way I felt when I first heard the gospel. There's a special spirit in missionary work.* She sighed with contentment, then readied herself for bed.

CHAPTER TWENTY-THREE

On Monday morning Abby could not say enough about the exquisite gown she had worn and her thrilling evening at the theater. "After the play he took me to a little café where we had coffee and cakes. He was a perfect gentleman—didn't even try to kiss me or anything."

Elisabeth smiled at her friend. "I'm happy for you. I imagine you can take care of yourself."

"Of course I can. I may be a country girl, but I wasn't born yesterday."

Over the next weeks, Elisabeth saw less and less of Abby. They no longer studied together in the evenings and only occasionally at school. One day Mrs. Kenny asked Elisabeth why Abby wasn't coming around anymore.

Elisabeth sighed. "She spends a lot of her time with Dr. Lester. He's been tutoring her in anatomy."

During the weeks that followed, Elisabeth came to believe that although Dr. Lester had turned his attentions to Abby, he still coveted her. Several times she caught him staring at her when he thought she wasn't looking. Although this bothered her, she decided to ignore him and not make an issue of it.

In mid-December, Gren wrote to say that he was coming to Philadelphia to meet with Colonel Thomas Kane and would be able to spend Christmas in Philadelphia. Elisabeth could hardly contain herself as the days counted down.

To celebrate Gren's visit, Mrs. Kenny was planning an elaborate Christmas dinner. She hired the cook and kitchen staff of a neighboring mansion whose owners were in Europe. Abby accepted an invitation for herself and Sidney Lester.

A week before Christmas, Elisabeth entered the college just before ten o'clock as usual. Miss Morris smiled at her. "No classes today, Miss Ashcroft. We're to have a special treat. Dr. Elizabeth Blackwell is paying us a visit."

Elisabeth's heart skipped a beat. *Dr. Elizabeth Blackwell, here? How wonderful!*

A sense of anticipation filled the lecture room as the whole student body awaited the arrival of the first woman doctor in the United States and the inspiration for most of the women in the room. When she finally arrived, accompanied by Dr. Ann Preston, the students gave her a standing ovation. Dr. Blackwell's cheeks reddened as she motioned for the students to sit. Although she was not a Quaker, she wore a plain gray poplin frock and a little Quaker bonnet.

After a brief introduction by Dr. Preston, Dr. Blackwell took the podium. Her face glowed as she launched into her presentation.

Enthralled, Elisabeth, with pencil poised, could hardly wait to hear how this unassuming woman had accomplished the prodigious task of breaking down the barriers preventing women from becoming medical practitioners.

"It all began," Dr. Blackwell said, "when a dying female friend suggested that I study medicine." Dr. Blackwell's eyes grew wide as she described her reaction to this suggestion. "I was utterly shocked. It was all I could do to visit my friend, as I couldn't bear the sight of medical paraphernalia and especially medical books. My interest was in history and metaphysics. I explained to her that I was interested in the moral and spiritual side of life, not the body, and that the very thought of dwelling on the physical structure of the body and its various ailments filled me with disgust."

Elisabeth was sitting on the edge of her seat, furiously scribbling notes, so eager was she to learn what could possibly have changed Miss Blackwell's mind. She desperately wished that she, like Miss Morris, knew shorthand.

Dr. Blackwell said that it had taken a long time for her to be reconciled to the idea of becoming a doctress but that once the idea was planted in her mind it wouldn't go away. She eventually came to believe that God had called her to break the barrier keeping women from medicine. Convinced of her calling, she spent several years saving money for her schooling. Yet at one point during this time, she had panicked and almost lost faith in her calling. "Had I made a horrible mistake? Was it foolishness for me to think that I could break the male monopoly on medicine?"

Turning to God for support, she had pleaded for assurance that the path she had chosen was the right one. God answered her prayer. To accurately describe the divine response, Dr. Blackwell turned to her own journal and read: "'Suddenly, overwhelmingly, an answer came. A glorious presence, as of brilliant light, flooded my soul. There was nothing visible to the physical sense; but a spiritual influence so joyful, gentle, but powerful, surrounded me that the despair which had overwhelmed me vanished. All doubt as to the future, all hesitation as to rightfulness of my purpose, left me, and never in after-life returned. I knew that, however insignificant my individual effort might be, it was in a right direction, and in accordance with the great providential ordering of our race's progress.'"

Elisabeth's heart pounded as she listened to Dr. Blackwell's answer to prayer, for it was so similar to the answer she had received when she had prayed about the divinity of the Book of Mormon and the truth of the restored gospel. Also, Miss Blackwell's experience expanded Elisabeth's understanding of God's love and concern for all of His children. To fulfill His divine plan, God inspired men and women throughout the world, regardless of their religion or national origin. Finally, Elisabeth's testimony of God's power to change men and women if they submit to Him was strengthened. Miss Blackwell had been repelled by the idea of studying medicine, but through submitting to God's will she overcame this revulsion and humbly followed her destiny. Similarly, Elisabeth's first reaction upon hearing from Maggie that Mormon missionaries had called was to reject them. But by humbling herself and praying for guidance, she was able to overcome her prejudices and eventually accept the restored gospel.

Dr. Blackwell went on to describe how she had eventually raised enough money for medical school and begun applying at various colleges, only to be rejected time after time. Although she was finally accepted at the Geneva College of Medicine in New York, she faced much opposition from professors, fellow students, and even towns-folk. The opposition did not end when she graduated. She found it almost impossible to establish a practice. Ironically, women were as opposed to her as men.

Elisabeth enjoyed all of Dr. Blackwell's presentation, but the high-light had been when the doctor had read her journal entry about her answer to prayer.

When she returned home that afternoon, Elisabeth entered the mansion with a flushed face and a happy smile. "You look like the cat that ate the canary," said Mrs. Kenny as she helped Elisabeth off with her coat.

"I had a most marvelous day. Classes were canceled and we were treated to a presentation by Dr. Elizabeth Blackwell—you remember, we talked about her when I was here first."

"I remember. Let's go into the drawing room and you can tell me all about it." When they were seated in the living room, Mrs. Kenny suggested that Rose might also like to hear about Elisabeth's day. Rose soon joined them and Elisabeth excitedly told the story of America's first female doctor

"I admire Dr. Blackwell immensely," Elisabeth said when she had finished her story. "She has sacrificed a great deal to tread her chosen path—even the loss of an eye."

"She on'y got one eye?" Rose asked, her mouth hanging open. "A docta lady?"

Elisabeth nodded. "She has a glass eye, but you wouldn't know it."

"How did that happen?" Mrs. Kenny asked.

"It was when she was studying in Paris. She was syringing the eye of a baby suffering from purulent ophthalmia from its syphilitic mother—"

"What big words!" Mrs. Kenny said.

Elisabeth flushed, embarrassed. She was so absorbed in her studies that it was easy to forget that not everyone spoke like doctors and medical students.

She tried again. "She was washing a sick baby's eye and some of the water splashed into her own eye. It became infected. The doctors tried everything to save the eye—bed rest, leeches applied to her temples, cold compresses, ointment of belladonna, hourly syringing, but all to no avail. To stop the infection from spreading, surgery was the only option. The loss of an eye ended Dr. Blackwell's hope to become a surgeon."

"How horrible," Mrs. Kenny said.

"Another sacrifice Dr. Blackwell made was that of marriage and children. She said that she considered the possibility of having a family but ruled it out in favor of medicine. She told us about another woman who has also devoted her life to medicine, Miss Florence Nightingale. On a trip home to England, Dr. Blackwell met Miss Nightingale and learned of her attempt to raise nursing to an honorable profession. I've followed Miss Nightingale's career in the newspapers."

Mrs. Kenny gazed at Elisabeth for a moment. "Tell me, dear. If you had to choose between medicine and a home and family, which would you choose?"

Elisabeth thought back to her experience with the young Indian mother and to how she felt with the baby in her arms. "A home and family," she said. "While I do feel that God has called me to spend this time studying medicine, my greatest desire is to have a loving husband and a house full of children. I admire Dr. Blackwell and Miss Nightingale enormously and have no doubt that God has called them to the paths they have chosen. But . . . but as for me, I have a longing in my soul that only motherhood can fulfill. Until that time comes—and I often despair of its coming—I'm content to study medicine, and I appreciate very much the opportunity you've given me to do so."

Mrs. Kenny seemed pleased at Elisabeth's response. "You're more than welcome, dear. It does my heart good to see you so excited. With Abby not coming around anymore and you missing your young man, I feared you would make yourself sick. But let's not talk about our worries now. We have a Christmas dinner to get ready for. And speaking of Abby, I hope she's still coming."

Elisabeth hoped so too. She also hoped that her friend would stop seeing Dr. Lester outside of classes, but she didn't say this aloud.

CHAPTER TWENTY-FOUR

"I was hoping to see you before I went home," Elisabeth said to Abby as they stood in the college corridor. It was December 24. "Are you still coming to Christmas dinner tomorrow night?"

Abby smiled. "We are. In fact, I have a surprise for you."

"A surprise?" Elisabeth waited to hear more, but Abby only gave her a mysterious smile.

"See you tomorrow night, then," Abby said and hurried away.

Elisabeth watched her friend almost skip down the corridor. *She seems completely carefree and happy. I wonder if Miss Morris and I are wrong about Dr. Lester?*

After supper that evening, Elisabeth was in her room writing a letter to Glynis Brenton when a knock sounded at her door. "Come."

Rose opened the door and smiled. "Somebody downstes fo' yo', Miss 'Lis'bet."

Elisabeth got up from the desk and walked briskly to the door. "Who?"

"Doan rightly know," Rose said, grinning from ear to ear.

Elisabeth hurried down to the foyer, her heart beating wildly in anticipation. Could it be Gren? It was! She wanted to throw herself into his arms but managed to restrain herself, settling for a long, tender handshake. "What a wonderful surprise," she said. "We weren't expecting you until tomorrow."

"I couldn't wait," Gren said, still holding her hands in both of his. "I can't believe I'm here. You don't know how I've missed you."

"Oh, I think I do. I've missed you too."

"Elder Taylor sends his greeting. He thanks you for your companionship to Sister Gilliam. She arrived safely at the home of her relatives and wanted to be remembered to you."

"That's good news," Elisabeth said, thinking of the pleasant conversations she had shared with Caroline. "Did Elder Taylor give you any . . . any restrictions for your visit? Since you are a missionary, I mean."

Gren shook his head. "He knows our situation. He only instructed me to act honorably—though he did say in jest for me not to go off and get married like Elder Willard Richards did when he was a missionary in England some years ago."

Chaperoned by Mrs. Kenny, they talked long into the night, their conversation only ending when Mrs. Kenny indicated that it was her bedtime and she wanted to show Gren to his room before she retired. Elisabeth accompanied them and stood at the door watching as Gren sat on the bed. "Compared to my bed of nails in New York, this is absolutely heaven."

The two women wished Gren a pleasant sleep, and Elisabeth followed Mrs. Kenny down the hall. At the door to Elisabeth's bedroom, Mrs. Kenny gave a knowing smile. "I approve of your young man. Sweet dreams, my dear."

Elisabeth went to her desk rather than her bed. She opened her journal and began to write: *Gren is here! Mary referred to him as "my young man." If only that were true. But things are as they are and I must be vigilant. I must not let him know how I really feel about him, although I think he already knows. Nevertheless, I must not bind him to me until I'm free. He must be free to choose another if he desires. And if he does?* She stopped writing and drove the thought from her mind. *Surely God will open up the way for us to be together if this is our destiny. Even Miss Blackwell had doubts about her destiny, doubts she overcame through prayer. Faith is the key. If I strive to live the gospel as best I can, things will work out for the best.* On this positive note, she closed her journal and prepared for bed.

On Christmas morning Elisabeth slept later than usual. When she finally did get up, the sun was streaming through the lace curtains. She quickly dressed and hurried downstairs. Gren was eating at the kitchen table. He arose and responded to Elisabeth's greeting with a broad smile and wished her a wonderful Christmas Day. "Mrs. Kenny and John just left on an errand," he said.

She felt a guilty pleasure in having him to herself. "So that's why you're all alone. A present from Becky and Jonathan addressed to both of us came a while back. Shall we open it now or wait till after our Christmas feast?"

Gren shrugged. "As you wish. But I'd like to give you my gift now. May I?"

Elisabeth's fingers trembled as she opened the slim, flat package. "A silk handkerchief! How exquisite."

"It's to wipe away your tears when we're apart," he said with a grin.

She smiled at him. "It will get lots of use, I'm sure. Now, your gift." She left the kitchen and quickly returned with a large brown paper package. Gren opened it to find a knitted object, which spilled onto the floor as he unfolded it. He stared at it nonplussed.

Elisabeth laughed. "Methinks I made it a mite long. It's a scarf. Try it on."

Gren stood up and wrapped it around his neck. The ends touched the floor. He grinned at her with raised eyebrows.

She laughed again. "Yes, I did get carried away. It's the first thing I've knitted in many years. Rose helped me. Perhaps if you wrap it around your neck a few more times." He did so, and she frowned. "That looks even worse. You look like a mummy."

He laughed. "Don't fret. It's a wonderful gift all the same. When I'm in my icy garret, I'll wrap it around my neck and use the excess to sit on!"

Elisabeth laughed. "I do have another little gift for you." She shyly handed him a small package.

He unwrapped it and his mouth fell open. "A pocket watch! How did you know? It's exactly what I need, the best gift I've ever gotten."

Elisabeth smiled. "When I slipped that gold guinea into your empty watch pocket, I determined to fill it. Please read the inscription."

Gren opened the cover and read, "Time rolls forward to freedom." His expression was tender as he looked at her. "Thank you, Elisabeth. This truly is a merry Christmas."

"Or happy Christmas, as we say in England."

For a moment their eyes met and spoke the words their lips dared not say. Reluctantly, they took their places across the kitchen table from each other. Then Elisabeth jumped up. "Your breakfast's cold. Let me warm it whilst I get my own."

Over breakfast, Elisabeth described the gifts she had sent to Jonathan and Becky: a precious little jacket that Rose had knitted for Elisabeth Rebecca, a blanket Elisabeth had knitted for the baby ("I assure you it was normal size," she told Gren), and a lovely cameo brooch for Becky. "I couldn't think what to get for Jonathan."

Gren's expression was wistful, and Elisabeth knew he was thinking of home. He finally expressed his thoughts. "I do miss everyone in the valley. It'll be wonderful when we're all together again. I get a letter from Becky every so often. The way she writes, you'd think she was living in the Garden of Eden, but I know things haven't been easy for the Saints in the valley."

Becky and Jonathan had joined the Deseret Dramatic Association, and Becky had been given roles in several plays. Elisabeth was sorry that she hadn't been there to see her and offer her support.

"Did you hear that an endowment house is under construction?" Gren asked. Elisabeth shook her head.

"It's to serve until a temple is ready," he explained.

Elisabeth felt Gren's eyes upon her and hoped that he was thinking the same thing she was. Would they ever be sealed together as man and wife for all eternity? Elisabeth couldn't bear to think of any other possibility, and she changed the subject. "Mrs. Kenny has agreed to chaperone us on a visit to Independence Hall and a concert at Christ Church Cathedral. Are you game?"

"I'd like that. Especially if we end up at the ice-cream parlor you wrote about."

"Parkinson's. It's definitely on the list."

It was almost ten thirty when John dropped them off in front of Independence Hall. It was a cold, bright day. They were staring up at the steeple when Mrs. Kenny said, "I wonder if Colonel Kane's in his office. Would you like to meet him, Mr. Sanderson?"

"I certainly would. I have an appointment to see him tomorrow on behalf of Elder Taylor. From all I've heard, he's a remarkable man."

A feeling of reverence enveloped Elisabeth as they entered the historic building. She paused just inside and took Mrs. Kenny's arm. "I confess it thrills me to know that in this building George Washington, Benjamin Franklin, and the other founding fathers forged this nation. In these rooms, the Declaration of Independence was adopted and the Constitution framed."

Gren looked about him. Then he smiled at Elisabeth. "I believe you appreciate America even more than I do."

Elisabeth was thoughtful. "Perhaps. Though I will always love England, this is my country now. Maggie often remarked on my fascination with America. I wouldn't be surprised if I knew more about its history than most Americans."

"I'm glad you feel that way," Gren said. "Despite its flaws, America is the best hope of the world."

Elisabeth turned to Mrs. Kenny. "It is a supreme irony that although the Saints were denied the protection of the Constitution and driven right out of the United States in 1847, there are no people who support the Constitution more fervently."

Mrs. Kenny nodded in interest as they began to talk, then the three of them wandered the halls in silence until they came to Colonel Kane's office. They knocked and were invited in by the genial philanthropist. After introducing Gren—Mrs. Kenny and the colonel already knew each other because of their mutual interest in the college—and being seated, Elisabeth apologized if their arrival was inconvenient. "We don't wish to intrude, Colonel Kane, especially on Christmas Day. Actually, I'm surprised to see you here today."

"It's no intrusion. There were a few things on my desk I had to tidy up." The colonel turned to Gren. "I received Elder Taylor's notification that you were coming, Elder Sanderson. It's fortuitous that you're here this morning. Would it be convenient for you to meet with me this morning rather than tomorrow? I will be occupied with family activities from this afternoon on."

Gren and Colonel Kane had their meeting, and they caught up with the ladies in the Declaration Chamber. This ended the tour, and they thanked the colonel for his kindness. Feeling well rewarded for their time in Independence Hall, the three of them emerged from the building to find John waiting for them.

"What o'clock is it, Mr. Sanderson?" Mrs. Kenny asked.

Gren proudly withdrew his watch. He smiled at Elisabeth. "According to my handsome, new gold watch, ten minutes before noon."

"Good," Mrs. Kenny said, "that will give us time to walk down Chestnut Street. I think my bunions will hold out till the end of the block. John, will you meet us at the end of the block?"

"Certainly, Mrs. Kenny," John bowed and climbed up to the driver's seat of the carriage.

"What is that wonderful smell?" Gren asked as they made their way along Chestnut Street past stores, offices, theaters, and public buildings.

"The Pie Man Shop," Mrs. Kenny replied. "Here it is." Mrs. Kenny took Elisabeth's arm and the three of them peered through the window and surveyed the many pastry delights displayed there. "They have some little tables in the corner of the shop. Shall we go in?"

Elisabeth and Gren needed no persuasion. They sat at a small table with a red-and-white checked tablecloth. A plump girl with a pretty face soon appeared with a three-tiered server loaded with pastries. Placing the server on the table, she left, then quickly returned with three small plates. "Please help yourselves," she said. "I'll tally up later."

"It's so hard to decide," Elisabeth said. "They all look so good." She finally chose a lemon tart, Gren chose a butter tart, and Mrs. Kenny settled on a jam tart. When they had finished eating, Mrs. Kenny placed a jam tart on Gren's plate. "Go ahead, my boy. They're delicious."

He thanked her. "Elisabeth and I will share it."

Elisabeth waved her hand. "Not me. I've had plenty. You're on your own, Gren."

Soon the serving girl returned. "Begging your pardon, but you two make a right handsome couple," she said to Elisabeth and Gren. "You should have your images took. Right next door, my beau's just opened a studio. Why don't you pay him a visit?"

Elisabeth almost said that they were not a "couple," but she let Gren speak for them.

"Thanks just the same," Gren said. "I understand daguerreotypes take some time, and we're in a bit of a hurry."

"Daguerreotypes do," the girl said. "But Sam's way takes only minutes. It's called tintype. Sam would like to set up a daguerreotype studio, but the equipment is too expensive. 'Course, daguerreotype portraits not only take quite a while, they're expensive—upwards o' five dollars. Sam can have you in and out in a few minutes and'll only charge you four bits."

"You really should have your pictures taken," Mrs. Kenny urged Elisabeth and Gren. "We have the time."

The young photographer was clearly delighted to see them. "I'm beholden to you, folks," he said. "My heart skips a beat every time I hear the doorbell ring. 'More customers!' I say to myself."

"Your young friend next door is very persuasive," Elisabeth said.

The photographer smiled. "She has reason to be. Her father says we can't marry until my studio's a success. So purchase freely. My future depends on it!"

"In that case," Mrs. Kenny said, "I'd like five tintypes of this young couple."

"None of yourself?"

"I'm too old for portraits."

"Nonsense. You have an ageless beauty."

Mrs. Kenny colored. "You flatter me, sir. Well, perhaps one picture."

It was almost 12:30 by the time they left the studio with the tintype portraits. They continued along Chestnut Street toward Christ Church Cathedral, stopping only to crane their necks in wonder as their eyes took in the eight-story Jayne Building. "I can't imagine we'll ever have a taller building than that," Gren said.

Elisabeth and Mrs. Kenny nodded their agreement. "Here's John," the older woman said. "And not a moment too soon. My bunions are aflame."

It was almost one o'clock when they reached the cathedral. The main floor was filled, so they were ushered up to the balcony. They eased into their seats, Elisabeth and Gren on either side of Mrs. Kenny, just in time for the program to start. Gazing around the building, Elisabeth admired the exquisite interior of the church. From the delicate wineglass pulpit to the slender organ pipes, all bespoke luxury and the finest workmanship. Soon the divine strains of the

Messiah filled the building. Elisabeth felt herself transported into another world as the choir's voices and the organ's silvery notes blended sublimely. For two hours she was in paradise.

Afterwards, as they rode in the carriage from the cathedral to Parkinson's Ice Cream Parlor, Gren said, "I don't know if it was the music or the beautiful surroundings, but I can understand why many people won't listen to the message of the restored gospel. If people who attend Christ Church each week feel the same feelings I did, I can see how they would feel close to God and not seek further spiritual guidance."

Elisabeth was thoughtful, contemplating Gren's words. "The Apostle Paul wrote to Timothy that in the last days people would have a 'form of godliness.' Perhaps that's what he meant. At the time of the Protestant Reformation, the reformers rejected the elaborate church ceremonies and exquisitely decorated buildings. Instead, they chose simply 'four walls and a sermon.' I think that beautiful buildings do aid in worship, but if it's all show and no substance, it is only a form of godliness."

Gren looked at her in admiration. "The ideal, then, is you."

"Me?" Elisabeth looked at him in surprise, wondering how he had made the unexpected transition from church buildings to herself.

"Beauty and substance in one lovely package."

Elisabeth was touched by his words. "Why, thank you, sir, though I'm not sure if I like being called a package!" Mrs. Kenny remained silent during this exchange, but she smiled at Elisabeth's response.

Their conversation was light and cheerful as they enjoyed their ice cream. John arrived with the carriage just as they were finishing the delicious treat. Stepping outside, they saw that the sky had clouded over. The brisk wind descending from the north carried moisture in it, and it had begun to sprinkle. John held a large umbrella above Mrs. Kenny and escorted her into the carriage. He was about to return for Elisabeth when she and Gren decided to brave the rain. Laughing like children, they reached the carriage just as the clouds burst. Tired but happy, they smiled at each other from opposite seats. Elisabeth couldn't remember when she had felt so happy. How thankful she was to share this time with Gren, even under the watchful eye of their chaperone.

They arrived at the mansion to find the preparations for Christmas dinner well under way. Thanking the cook and her staff, Mrs. Kenny sent them home to their families with generous allowances in their pockets. She then donned an apron and joined Rose in the kitchen. Rose was stirring the gravy pot. Elisabeth could see that the maid had been crying. She was about to speak to her when Mrs. Kenny gently pushed Elisabeth out of the kitchen, saying, "Rose and I will take care of everything. Just relax yourself. We'll eat about six."

"What's the matter with Rose?" Elisabeth asked with lowered voice.

"She's missing Thomas and Freddie," Mrs. Kenny whispered. "It being Christmas and all." Then she asked in a normal voice, "When will Abby be here?"

"About five thirty."

"And her doctor?"

Elisabeth sighed. "And her doctor."

Elisabeth went to her room and stretched out on the featherbed. She studied a tintype portrait. *We do make a handsome couple, if I do say so myself. I'm so glad we got them. I'll send one home to England and one to Becky and Jonathan. What a sublime day!* Sitting up, she eased off her walking boots and lay back down. She awoke to a knock at the door.

"Supper's mos' riddy, Miss 'Lis'bet."

"Thank you, Rose. I'll be right down." *I wonder if Abby is here yet?*

Rose, Gren, Mrs. Kenny, John, and Mr. Murphy surrounded the dining room table, which was laden with delectable dishes, dominated by a huge turkey. "We're all ready to eat," said Mrs. Kenny as Elisabeth took her place. "Should we wait for Abby?"

"We may as well go ahead." Elisabeth said. "I'd hate to see the food get cold. Abby has a tendency to be late."

Mrs. Kenny had no reservations about sharing her table with her staff, having been a servant herself most of her life. She asked John to say grace, and everyone gratefully began to eat. Ravenous from her outing, Elisabeth ate with gusto, though Abby's absence bothered her. Several times a noise pulled her eyes to the door, but it was only the wind and the rain.

"I'm worried about Abby," Elisabeth said when she had eaten her fill. "Maybe we should go to her lodgings and check on her."

"I'll be happy to take you, Miss Elisabeth," John said.

Elisabeth turned to Gren. He nodded. "Let's go. You'll not enjoy the evening till you know what's happened to her."

A biting wind and pouring rain greeted them as Elisabeth and Gren exited the house and hurried to the waiting carriage. The horses splashed their way through the deserted streets of the fashionable Spring Garden area, which had just been incorporated into the city that year. Their route took them south along the 113-foot-wide Broad Street and into Philadelphia proper, then west along Market Street toward the Schuylkill River in the seamier part of the city. The carriage halted in front of Abby's lodgings. Only one light showed through the windows of the grimy brownstone.

"Wait here," Gren said to Elisabeth. "I'll go."

He stepped around the puddles, ran up the stone steps, and banged on the front door. After a long wait, Mrs. Steinke opened the door a crack. Elisabeth, peering out the carriage window, couldn't hear what they were saying, but it was obvious that Gren wasn't having much success. When she could stand it no longer, Elisabeth leapt from the carriage and flung herself up the steps. "Where's Abby?" she demanded of the barely visible landlady.

"She says she went out walking a while ago," yelled Gren over the storm.

"Walking in this weather?" Completely baffled, Elisabeth looked at Gren. Then she turned back to Mrs. Steinke. "Which way did she go?"

"How should I know? Am I my boarder's keeper?"

"You *do* know," cried Elisabeth. "You're constantly spying through the curtains!"

"Well, I never!" Mrs. Steinke said, slamming the door. Fortunately, the toe of Gren's boot prevented the door from latching, and Gren pushed the door open again. Seeing that she had little choice, the landlady gave them the information they wanted. "If ye must know, her and her 'fancy man' had a fight. He takes off in his fancy carriage for Broad Street. Her went screamin' t'her room. Then she goes afoot t'wards the river. If that girl thinks . . ."

"Toward the river!" Elisabeth repeated, a horrible thought entering her mind.

Elisabeth didn't hear the rest of Mrs. Steinke's words. Grabbing Gren by the arm, she dragged him back to the carriage. "To the river, John," she yelled as she and Gren leapt into the carriage. Black thoughts filled her mind as the carriage careened along Market Street. It halted at the bridge over the Schuylkill River. On one side Elisabeth leaned out the door peering through the rain, while Gren did the same on the other side. Abby was nowhere in sight.

"Try the bridge?" John yelled from the driver's seat.

"Yes," Elisabeth cried as she pulled her head in the window.

Gren squeezed her arm. "We'll find her."

In the middle of the bridge, John abruptly halted the carriage and thumped on the roof with the whip handle. Elisabeth leaned out the window. A small, dark figure stood on the bridge railing, clinging with both hands to a vertical support wire.

Elisabeth leapt from the carriage with Gren right behind her. "Abby!" Abby whipped her head around and saw Elisabeth and Gren running toward her. She turned back and stared down into the dark waters of the Schuylkill. Fearing that Abby might jump before they reached her, Elisabeth and Gren sprinted. Abby's hands let go of the wire and her body went slack. She fell backward off the railing into Elisabeth and Gren's outstretched arms. Gren gathered Abby up and carried her to the vehicle, where Elisabeth wrapped her chilled body in several lap blankets.

"Home, John," Elisabeth called out.

Abby regained consciousness almost immediately but refused to talk during the ride to the mansion. Once inside, Elisabeth, Mrs. Kenny, and Rose worked to get Abby out of her wet clothes, into a nightdress, and under bed covers. Elisabeth was toweling Abby's long, dark hair when the girl finally spoke. "I've made a right mess of things, haven't I?"

Elisabeth gave her friend an encouraging smile. "You're safe now, dear; that's all that matters. Whatever the problem, we'll solve it together."

"Da missus, she sen' dis 'long," said Rose as she entered the room with a mug of hot milk on a tray.

"Thank you, Rose," Elisabeth said. Turning to Abby, she said, "Drink this. It'll do you good."

Abby obeyed without protest, then looked up. "Elisabeth—"

With a wave of her hand, Elisabeth said, "The morning's soon enough for explanations. You need to rest."

Abby nodded, finished the milk, and handed the mug to Elisabeth. "Good night, my dear, loyal friend."

Elisabeth left the room, closing the door quietly behind her. She went to her own room and changed into dry clothes. Downstairs, she joined Gren, Mrs. Kenny, and Rose in the small parlor. Gren, dressed in clothes three sizes too big for him, stood in front of the fire, and the two women were sitting on one of the couches. Mrs. Kenny had her arm around Rose. "I know it's hard," she was saying. "But the Lord knows your pain and He wants you to be with your loved ones again. He'll open the way for you. Perhaps now the best thing is for you to get a good night's sleep. Things always look better in the morning."

Bidding Elisabeth and Gren goodnight, Mrs. Kenny led a subdued Rose from the room. Elisabeth and Gren looked at each other from either side of the fireplace. Despite her somber mood, Elisabeth smiled. "You look like a clown I once saw at the Glastonbury Fair." She left the fireplace and sat on a couch.

Gren bowed to her. "John's clothes were too small for me, so I had to settle for the late Mr. Kenny's attire."

Neither of them spoke for a moment, and then Gren broke the silence. "We'll not soon forget this Christmas Day."

Elisabeth nodded in agreement. "'Tis strange," she said. "Rose and her family are separated by many miles. We are together in this room, but still a great gulf separates us."

"A gulf that the Lord will bridge." But then he sighed. "Now that your father has passed on, I guess any hope of an annulment died with him."

Elisabeth nodded. "I'm afraid so. Although, according to Lady Brideswell, there is still a chance. It would mean my returning to England, and it would cost a fortune. You wouldn't happen to have a fortune, would you?"

Gren smiled. "If I had, I'd give it all to you." He was silent for a moment. "Despite the gulf separating us, at this moment I would be nowhere else on earth. I'm well fed, in front of a warm fire, and out of the winter's blast. What more could a man ask for?"

Elisabeth could think of a few more things she'd ask for—freedom from Lord Claverley, a better life for her friends Abby and Rose, and above all, the freedom to be united with the man she had come to love, the man now gazing at her only a few feet away. These were her thoughts, but she said only, "We have been blessed. When I think of poor Rose and poor Abby crying themselves to sleep this Christmas night, I know that we are well enough off indeed."

CHAPTER TWENTY-FIVE

The next morning Elisabeth woke early. She lay awake for a long time thinking about Abby. What had driven her friend to attempt suicide? What could she do to help her? Finally, easing out of bed, she donned her robe and slippers and crept down the hall to Abby's room. Abby responded to Elisabeth's light knock. "Come in."

"Did I wake you?"

"No. I've been lying awake for hours. Oh, Elisabeth, what have I done?" Elisabeth sat on the bed and took Abby's hand. Tears came to Abby's eyes. "What drove me to the bridge hasn't gone away. But how could I end my life . . . and that of the little one I carry? Even though I betrayed you, and Miss Waldie, and my friends at home, I couldn't do it."

"You are with child?"

Abby nodded. "'Tis early, but I know. That was the surprise I was going to tell you. Before he knew about the baby, Sidney had promised to marry me. I was so excited to tell him. I thought he would be pleased. I hoped we could announce our betrothal at dinner. I was so happy . . . until I did tell him." Abby's face grew pale and she closed her eyes, remembering. Elisabeth squeezed her hand encouragingly. "He flew into a rage and demanded I go home to Pike's Point and never bother him again. He warned me that if I returned to the college he'd have me expelled as a . . . as a loose woman. I couldn't go back home in disgrace . . . not after all Miss Waldie and the people at home have done for me . . . not after I'd violated their trust and yours. All I could think of was ending it all." She broke into uncontrolled sobs.

Elisabeth put her arms around her friend and comforted her. When Abby finally got her tears under control and it was apparent that she had nothing more to say for the moment, Elisabeth said softly, "I can see how you might feel alone, but you do not need to face this by yourself. I will always be your friend and will do everything in my power to help you. And there is a greater power you can call upon. The Lord loves you and wants to help you, and there's no problem we cannot solve with His help. I can understand how you feel that you've betrayed the trust of Miss Waldie and the people of Pike's Point, but how do you think you've betrayed me?"

Through tearful eyes Abby looked into Elisabeth's face. "You told me not to tell anyone that you are married and from Utah Territory. I didn't want to tell Sidney, but he kept pestering me with questions about you. I tried to put him off, but he has a way of manipulating people. One day I finally told him all about you to make him stop asking. I'm so sorry, Elisabeth. I've never had a friend who cared for me as much as you have. Can you forgive me?"

Elisabeth's response was ready and sincere. "There is no harm done, Abby. Dr. Longshore and Miss Morris already know that I'm married and from Utah Territory. If Dr. Lester thinks he can use this information to hurt me, he will soon learn otherwise. As I lay awake this morning wondering what might have led you to the bridge, I was sure that Dr. Lester was the cause. Gren and I went first to your lodgings last night, and Mrs. Steinke told us that you had had a fight with your 'fancy man,' as she called him."

Abby nodded and looked hopeless. "I can't go back to the college with him there. What am I to do?"

"I've thought about that. Here's what I think we should do. You'll stay here. During the daytime you can do the reading assignments, and in the evenings I'll tutor you from my lecture notes. This way we can both prepare for the final exams, which will soon be upon us. What do you think?"

Abby agreed to the plan, but Elisabeth wondered about the strength of her friend's commitment. She appeared to have lost confidence in herself. Wiping her eyes, she sat back against the pillows and was silent for a moment. Then, leaning forward slightly, she took Elisabeth's hand in hers. "I appreciate your not condemning me for my part in this, Elisabeth. I'm well aware that this isn't all Sidney Lester's doing. Will . . . will God forgive me?"

Elisabeth gazed compassionately on her friend. There was a lot she wanted to say, but she didn't think that the time was right. She simply said, "Acknowledging your fault has put you on the path of forgiveness. The Lord loves us and is eager to forgive us when we repent."

Abby slowly nodded. For a moment she stared into space. "Oh, Elisabeth, Elisabeth, how could I have been so wicked!"

Elisabeth took her friend in her arms, and for a long time the two women let the tears flow unabated.

Abby was asleep when Elisabeth returned to her own room and dressed. Downstairs, she found Mrs. Kenny and Gren in the kitchen. "How is she?" Mrs. Kenny asked.

"As well as can be expected," Elisabeth said. "She's getting much-needed sleep."

"I'll visit her later," Mrs. Kenny said, "and let her know that she's welcome to stay here as long as she likes. For now I have some chores to attend to."

Elisabeth looked at Gren. "Happy Boxing Day, Elder Sanderson. Did you sleep well?"

Gren nodded. "And a merry Boxing Day to you. Yes, after all the excitement last night, I did get a good sleep."

"I see you've had breakfast."

"I have. Mrs. Kenny's been spoiling me. I'm sorry we didn't wait for you."

"That's all right. After that huge meal yesterday, I'm not really hungry. I know what we'll do. Let's open Becky's present. Don't get up, I'll get it."

Elisabeth peeled off the brown paper wrapper to reveal a handsomely decorated book with the words 'Christmas Annual' across the top in calligraphy. Her eyes lit up as she leafed through it. "How wonderful! Becky has gotten all our friends to write their favorite poems and stories."

Elisabeth and Gren sat at the table and reveled in each item in the Christmas Annual. Their thoughts wandered to their friends and family far away in the valleys of the western mountains. Mrs. Kenny soon joined them and also enjoyed the gift, even though she didn't know the givers. When the topic turned to past Christmases, Gren delighted in Mrs. Kenny's stories of Elisabeth's younger years. After a while Abby came downstairs. She approached the kitchen sheepishly. Mrs. Kenny arose and put her arms around her. Nothing was said of the previous night's escapade, and the rest of Boxing Day was passed in love and harmony.

The next day Elisabeth accompanied Gren to the railroad station. The pain of parting was as difficult to bear as it had been the first time. She thanked him for all his help in sharing the load of Abby's tragedy.

"I'm glad I was here," he said, holding her hands in his. "I shudder to think what would have happened to Abby had you not befriended her. I have confidence that with your help, she'll pull through this."

Elisabeth closed her eyes and his strength seemed to flow into her through their still-clasped hands. With all her heart, she wished for the day when she would never have to leave his side again. But she knew that although it was a lovely thought, it was only a thought. There was work to do this day if Abby were to gather up the pieces of her life and carry on—in spite of Dr. Lester and his selfish disregard for the lives of innocent people around him.

"Godspeed," called Elisabeth from the platform as the train slowly pulled away. Then a thought occurred to her and she called to Gren, "What did you and Colonel Kane meet about?"

Gren smiled. "I'll tell you in a letter," he replied as he waved good-bye.

After the train was out of sight, Elisabeth dabbed away her tears and instructed John to drive her to Mrs. Steinke's boarding house. Elisabeth rapped briskly on the door, and a few minutes later the landlady opened it. This was the first time Elisabeth had seen the landlady full face, in bright light. Always before it had been through a slit in the curtains or a crack in the dimly lit doorway. At first glance, Elisabeth was taken aback by Mrs. Steinke's appearance: two beady eyes above a hawk nose peered out from under hair that parted in the middle and sloped down each side like sheets of corrugated iron.

The landlady flatly rejected Elisabeth's request to collect Abby's things. Elisabeth smiled sweetly. "Very well, Mrs. Steinke, you force me to report your intransigence to Miss Morris at the college. No doubt your establishment will be taken off the college's list of approved accommodations."

The landlady relented.

"Your resourcefulness constantly amazes me, Miss Elisabeth," John said as they gathered up Abby's few belongings. "Most people would have gotten into a shouting match with that old battle-ax."

"Uncharacteristically, I had a shouting match with her the other night. But over the years I've tried to take Matthew 10:16 to heart." John looked at her quizzically until she quoted, "'Behold I send you forth as sheep in the midst of wolves: be ye therefore wise as serpents, and harmless as doves.'"

* * *

The next day, Abby stayed at the mansion and Elisabeth attended classes as usual—including Dr. Lester's anatomy lecture. As she was leaving, Dr. Lester called to her. "Did you have a good Christmas dinner, Miss Ashcroft?"

"Perfectly agreeable," she said.

"I'm sorry I missed it." His eyes watched her with a speculative gleam.

Elisabeth feigned friendliness. "Perhaps another time."

As she left the room, he stared after her with puzzlement on his face.

Seeing Miss Morris at her desk, Elisabeth stopped. "May I see you for a few minutes, Miss Morris?"

"Certainly, my dear." The elderly woman stuck a pencil into her haystack hair and arose. "Follow me."

Miss Morris listened intently as Elisabeth related all that had happened during the Christmas break. Elisabeth described her plan for helping Abby prepare for finals.

"I certainly hope that I have a friend like you if I ever get into such difficulties," Miss Morris said. Elisabeth raised her eyebrows at the thought. A little color came into the older woman's pale face, and she added quickly, "Not that I expect to get into such difficulties at my age! As for Dr. Lester, he must be disciplined. This definitely can't go on."

Elisabeth agreed and quickly outlined a plan she had devised to entrap the unscrupulous doctor. Miss Morris nodded from time to time as she listened.

When Elisabeth was done speaking, Miss Morris was quiet for a moment. Then she said, "If I understand you correctly, you'd like nothing to be done about Dr. Lester for the time being?"

"Exactly. At present, my first concern is helping Miss Smith."

* * *

As the week wore on, Abby sank into a state of depression. It became clear that her hope of attaining a medical career was slipping away. She did her assignments poorly and showed little evidence that she was preparing for the finals. As she descended further into despondency, Elisabeth became frustrated with herself for not being able to help and with Abby for not trying harder. On Saturday morning, Elisabeth awoke early and couldn't go back to sleep. She racked her brain for a way to pull her friend out of her hopeless state. From somewhere out of her reading past, the lyrics of a doleful song came into her mind:

> *When lovely woman stoops to folly*
> *And finds too late that men betray,*
> *What charm can soothe her melancholy,*
> *What art can wash her guilt away?*
>
> *The only art her guilt to cover,*
> *To hide her shame from every eye,*
> *To give repentance to her lover*
> *And wring his bosom—is to die.*

No! Elisabeth said to herself. *Death is not the only art.* A few minutes later she confronted her friend in the latter's room. "Abby, you've got to snap out of this lethargy. You'll lose the whole term if you don't marshal all your powers."

Abby stared at Elisabeth. Defiance flashed from her eyes. But it was only for a brief moment. Her face fell and she heaved a hopeless sigh. "I'm sorry, Elisabeth. Let's face it, there's no future for me or for my child. I cannot continue indefinitely here, and I cannot go back home. Perhaps I should have ended it at the river."

Elisabeth took Abby by the shoulders. "Enough of that talk. There is a future. May I be brutally frank with you?"

"Of course." This was accompanied with a forlorn shrug.

Elisabeth took a deep breath and slowly exhaled. "Abby, I love you like a sister, but it is time for me to speak my piece. Miss Morris and I both warned you about Lester and you ignored us. Like a foolish, wicked girl, you blindly let your passion rule you. You've relinquished that which is most precious to women, surrendered yourself to a man who is not worthy to lick your boots." Abby's eyes were like saucers, and tears began to course down her cheeks. Elisabeth wondered if she were being too hard on her friend, but she persevered. "All week you have been wallowing in self-pity. Well, my girl, you *should* feel sorrow for what you've done. Remorse is an important part of repentance. But remorse is one thing and self-pity is another. The Lord wants you to repent, but He doesn't want you to give up hope. You say that you can see no future for you and your child. Well, I can. I can see two ways. You could have your family raise the child, freeing you to resume your medical studies—if not here, then somewhere else. Now that Philadelphia has set the precedent, other medical schools for women will surely follow."

Elisabeth paused and gave Abby a handkerchief. She waited while Abby wiped her eyes. Abby took a deep breath and sat up a little straighter. A spark of interest showed in her eyes. "And what's the other way?"

"When we first met, you mentioned a man back home. Jerry, wasn't it?"

Abby nodded. "Jerry Potts. Dear, faithful Jerry. How could I have betrayed him so?" Tears welled up again and she dabbed at them.

"If this Jerry truly loves you, he'll forgive you. Would you marry him if he asked you?"

Abby answered immediately. "If . . . if he'd have me. I see now how wrong I was to think I was better than him and deserved someone like . . . " She didn't finish her sentence.

Elisabeth pretended not to notice. "Of course, it would be very wrong of you to marry Jerry if you do not have real feelings for him. But if you do, here's the second way. Go home to Pike's Point. Tell Jerry everything. If he's the man you say he is, he'll offer to marry you. Get married right away and both of you come back to Philadelphia."

Abby began shaking her head before Elisabeth had finished speaking. "I appreciate all the thought you've put into this scheme, Elisabeth, but you just don't know how things are back home."

"What do you mean?"

Abby became more animated as she explained. "Even though we've never been formally betrothed, Jerry thinks of me as his sweetheart. Once he finds out I'm in the family way, he'll take his gun and head for Philadelphia. He won't stop till Sidney's dead—or he is himself."

"What if you refuse to tell him who the father is?"

"It wouldn't matter. He'd hunt him down. Jerry may be uncultured, but he's not dumb. He'd find him soon enough. And even if he didn't go on a rampage, what would a man like Jerry do in Philadelphia? He'd be like a bull in a china shop."

Elisabeth grinned smugly. "I think I could find him work. Didn't you say he had a green thumb?"

Abby nodded and her eyes lit up. "You're thinking he might work for Mrs. Kenny?"

"Exactly. I'm sure we could find another job for Mr. Murphy—one to which he's suited. You and Jerry could live in the guest cottage. It would be perfect."

Abby was lost in thought for several minutes. Then she looked up sheepishly. "Supposing Jerry goes along with things, there's another problem—Miss Waldie. I owe her a great deal, and she's unalterably opposed to my marrying Jerry. I don't know if I could defy her."

"From what you've told me about Miss Waldie, she loves you very much. I'm sure that if you told her how important this is to you, she'd come around."

Abby gave Elisabeth a dubious look. "Perhaps you're right." Elisabeth could almost hear Abby's mind churning away as she considered the proposal. Finally, she nodded. "All right, Elisabeth.

I'll do it on one condition." Elisabeth waited. "That you go home to Pike's Point with me."

Elisabeth was startled. "Me? But I couldn't possibly—"

"How could I get married without my maid . . . I mean, my matron of honor? But more to the point, if anyone can talk Jerry out of gunning for Sidney Lester, it's you. I also want—no, I need—you with me when I confront Miss Waldie. Please come home with me, please!"

Elisabeth looked at Abby's expectant face. Taking a deep breath, she released it in a heavy sigh. "All right, Abby. I'll talk it over with Mrs. Kenny and Miss Morris."

"Oh, thank you," Abby cried, throwing her arms around Elisabeth's neck. "I know Mrs. Kenny will approve. She loves you to no end. And thanks for being so frank with me. I needed a good dose of honesty." She paused for a moment before adding, "It will be hard for you to believe this, but I really do love Jerry. I don't know what came over me with You Know Who."

Elisabeth smiled compassionately. "I'm sure it's not the first time nor the last that a naive girl is led astray by flattering words." She sighed. "Believe me, I know whereof I speak."

When Elisabeth spoke with Mrs. Kenny later that morning, she wanted to know what route the two women would travel. Elisabeth had already discussed this with Abby. They could take a steam train to Harrisburg and from there a stagecoach to Duncannon, up the Susquehanna River from Harrisburg. Duncannon was also accessible by boat. In either case, they would have to arrange local transportation from Duncannon to Pike's Point.

"I'd worry about you, dear," Mrs. Kenny said, "two young women traveling alone."

"You've forgotten—"

"I know, I know, you came all the way from England alone. But you weren't really alone. You had plenty of company."

"We'll be fine. Abby came to the city all by herself." She paused and became pensive before saying, "I'm sure there are worse predators in the city than there are in the hills."

Mrs. Kenny sighed. She knew that Elisabeth was not an easy person to sway from her position once she had made up her mind.

The next day Elisabeth explained her plan for saving Abby's reputation to Miss Morris, who was amenable to it. She readily agreed to arrange for their absence from the college. "I'll let the faculty know that you will be absent for about a week," Miss Morris said. "I'll say that you are accompanying Miss Smith to her home so that she can look after some urgent family matters."

"Thank you, Miss Morris. I realize that with the college term ending in a month, we have to resume classes as quickly as possible. It's important that Abby is back in time to write her exams and get credit for the full course of lectures."

"And you, dear?"

"I'd like to get some credit too, but as you know, Abby's working toward becoming a doctress. I'm just a listener."

"Very well, dear. Godspeed on your journey."

CHAPTER TWENTY-SIX

Three days later, Elisabeth and Abby, each with a carpetbag, got off a stagecoach at a crossroads on the Susquehanna Road a few miles short of Duncannon.

"Where is Pike's Point?" asked Elisabeth, not seeing anything that resembled a town.

Abby pointed up a long, dusty road that wound its way into the hills. "Up there, I'm afraid. We could have gone into Duncannon on the stagecoach and hired a cart and driver, but then we'd have had to retrace our way back to this point and it would have taken most of the day. This way, shank's mare can have us there in an hour or so."

"Shank's mare?"

Abby laughed. "On our own two feet. Almost home, and I'm already reverting to colloquialisms!"

Elisabeth picked up her bag and looked up the road. "A bit of a dander, as Mrs. Kenny would say. At least the sun's shining and it's warm for this time of year."

After walking for a few minutes, they heard a noise behind them. They turned to see a horse-drawn cart rumbling up the road and waited for it to catch up with them. "Why, Abby Smith, is it ye?" the driver said, pulling off his cap.

"It is, Mr. Montgomery. I'm home for a few days."

"I'm right glad t'see ye. Le'me help ye ladies into the back, an' I'll give ye a lift t'the Point."

Abby and Elisabeth exchanged glances. "I think we'd rather walk, Mr. Montgomery," Abby said. "But would you please take our bags up to the Waldie house?"

"Surely. Heft 'em up aside me." Having helped them to do that, Mr. Montgomery nodded and touched his whip handle to the rim of his hat in a salute. Then he cracked the whip, and the horse and cart started up the road.

"Pigs?" Elisabeth asked, wrinkling her nose.

Abby nodded. "Pigs. He must have hauled them down to market. I've heard that once you're accustomed to the smell of pigs you don't even notice it."

"I hope he wasn't offended by our refusal."

Abby laughed. "If we had accepted a ride, our clothes would be offending people all day—most of all us. No, I'm sure he wasn't offended."

Within an hour, Elisabeth and Abby, their faces glowing from the brisk jaunt, arrived at the home of Miss Emmeline Waldie. The two-story structure had seen better days, but it was by far the best house in the scattered village. As the women started up the driveway, they heard a shout from behind. A tall young man with coal-black hair came running toward them.

"Abby!" he shouted. "Abby!"

"Jerry?" Elisabeth asked.

"Jerry," Abby answered.

Jerry Potts swept Abby off her feet, hugged her, and swung her around. "I heered frum Monty ye wuz hyar," he said, kissing her and placing her back on her feet. "What a dandy su'prise."

Abby caught her breath and steadied herself before saying, "This is my friend, Miss Ashcroft."

Jerry pulled off his cap, smiled shyly, and put out his hand. Taking it firmly, Elisabeth could feel the rough calluses from his work. "Very pleased to meet you, Mr. Potts. Please call me Elisabeth. May I call you Jerry?"

"'Course, Miss Elisabeth," he said.

"Abigail! Abigail, my dear, come up here immediately," called a tall, stately woman from the front porch of the house. Her steel-gray hair was pulled back severely into a bun. "A *lady* doesn't stand talking in the road like a commoner."

Abby raised her eyebrows at Elisabeth and said a hurried good-bye to Jerry.

"When'll I see yuh?" Jerry asked. "Come fer vittles."

Abby flashed him a smile. "We will, Jerry."

Inside the house Abby introduced Elisabeth, and Miss Waldie invited them into the parlor, where they sat sipping lemonade.

"You shouldn't encourage that boy," Miss Waldie said.

From her place in an overstuffed chair, Abby shot Elisabeth a glance as if to say, "You see what I mean?" Miss Waldie, seated across from the two younger women on a once-fashionable settee, did not appear to see the look. A second glance passed between Elisabeth and Abby as if in silent agreement that this was as good a time as any to broach the difficult subject.

"Miss Waldie," Abby said, "you know, I hope, how much I appreciate all you've done for me. I'll be forever in your debt." She hesitated. "You're not going to like what I'm about to say, but say it I must. I've come home to marry Jeremiah Potts, if he'll have me."

Miss Waldie's hands went to her heart. Her face drained of the little color it had, and she fainted. Elisabeth and Abby hurriedly stretched her out on the settee and put a pillow under her head. Abby ran for smelling salts.

"She's subject to the vapors," Abby said as she uncorked the bottle and waved it under Miss Waldie's aristocratic nose.

The older woman slowly came around and with some help was able to return to an upright position. Her right hand clutched the settee's armrest as a modicum of color seeped into her cheeks and the blueness receded from her lips. Resuming her stately air, she said in a controlled voice, "Why would you possibly do that, my dear?"

"Do what, Miss Waldie?"

"Wed the Potts boy."

"Because . . . because I love him. I know you object to him—"

Miss Waldie cut her off. "Love is an insufficient reason for throwing away a promising career. Before you know it, you'll be living in a hovel with a score of offspring pulling at your skirts."

"I have no intentions of giving up medicine," Abby said evenly. "I'll only marry Jerry if he agrees to come to Philadelphia so that I can continue my studies."

Miss Waldie appeared slightly mollified. "Well, that's something." She was quiet as she digested this news. "There is nothing I can say to talk you out of this foolishness?"

"Nothing." Abby's voice was resolute.

"And what do you think of this, Miss Ashcroft?" Miss Waldie asked, turning to face Elisabeth.

Elisabeth chose her words carefully. "I think they will be very happy. And even though I am also attending the medical college, I would love to have some children pulling at my skirts—although a score does seem excessive."

A hint of a smile touched Miss Waldie's thin lips. She sighed deeply. "Of course, I would insist on having the nuptial here. The meeting house is not fit . . ." She stopped speaking, as if she had suddenly realized that she was agreeing to something she'd long opposed. Then, throwing caution to the wind, she opened her arms. Abby gave a joyful squeal and threw herself at the old woman. "Abigail Eugenia Smith, have I taught you not one iota of deport-ment?" At this, Elisabeth couldn't restrain a small smile, seeing how the love in Miss Waldie's eyes belied the severity of her tone.

Later, Elisabeth and Abby were walking to the Potts' home in silence. Elisabeth suddenly remembered something and smiled. "Eugenia?" she said.

Abby made a face at her but smiled also. "I was named after a great-aunt or something. It could have been worse. One of my sisters is called Drusilla. We call her Drusie."

With this, both girls began to giggle uncontrollably. With the first part of their mission accomplished, the release of tension allowed them to laugh like schoolgirls.

"By the way," Elisabeth said, when she'd regained her composure, "when do I get to meet your mother, and the rest of the brood—including Drusie?"

"Soon. We live quite a way out. I'd like to see how things go with Jerry before we go out there."

"I noticed that you didn't tell Miss Waldie the whole story."

"True. Fainting was bad enough. If I'd told everything, she'd probably have had apoplexy!"

"Apoplexy," Elisabeth quoted in monotone. "Inability to feel and move, caused by blockage or rupture of brain artery." She turned to Abby, expecting to see her smile, but Abby's face was somber. "Worried about how Jerry will react?"

Abby nodded and sighed. "Well, here we are."

Mrs. Potts was a neat little woman. Elisabeth wondered how her small frame had produced eight children. In stark contrast, Jeremiah Potts Sr. was a mountain of a man with an unruly mane of silver hair. As the Potts family sat around the rough table with their guests, the emphasis was on eating, not talking. After the meal, Abby and Jerry stole away while Jerry's sisters crowded Elisabeth, peppering her with questions about life in Philadelphia.

Some time later Abby finally rescued Elisabeth and led her into the hallway. "I've told him," Abby said. "He reacted about the way I expected. He's smoldering."

"How much did you tell him?"

"Everything except Dr. Lester's name. But he guessed that it was someone at the college, and I couldn't lie to him. He got pretty riled when I wouldn't give him the name, but he's calmed down a bit now. It's up to you, Elisabeth."

Abby led Elisabeth into Jerry's parents' bedroom, the only room in the house that offered any privacy. Jerry was sitting in a rocking chair, morosely cleaning a flintlock rifle. He didn't look up. Elisabeth looked at Abby, who wore an I-told-you-so look. The women sat on the bed across from Jerry, and for several minutes no one spoke.

"A handsome rifle," Elisabeth said, breaking the silence. "My father had a rook rifle."

Jerry looked up. "Rook rifle?"

Elisabeth nodded. "Yes, for shooting rooks."

Jerry looked puzzled. "Rooks?"

"They're birds over in England."

Jerry digested this information. "Good eatin'?"

"Oh, no! They're a kind of crow."

"Crow? Why d'ye waste powder and ball on'em fer if'n ye cain't eat 'em?"

"They're pests. They eat the farmers' grain and their rookeries are awfully noisy. Farmers shoot them and pay boys to climb up to their nests and smash their eggs."

Elisabeth was quiet, remembering a day when she was a little girl and had observed some boys up in a rookery throwing down eggs. An egg with a live bird in it had smashed near her. Picking up the naked little thing, she had run home with it. She had wept when it died.

Jerry had studiously avoided looking at Abby during his conversation with Elisabeth. He continued to ignore her. Stroking his rifle, he again addressed Elisabeth. "This here's a Kentucky long rifle." He leaned closer to the bed to offer Elisabeth a better look. "But it warn't made in Kentucky but hyar in Pennsylvany. It's fifty cal'ber and has a forty-six-inch barrel. The stock's made o' curly maple. The patchbox's made o' brass. It's a muzzle-loader. Wuz yer rook rifle a muzzle-loader?"

"I don't think so. I think it loaded up near the trigger."

"Breechloader. How accurit wuz it?"

"I don't really know." Elisabeth was happy to keep him talking.

"This here rifle kin clip the whiskers off a' gnat at two hunnerd paces!"

"So I've read," Elisabeth said. She had studied the War of 1812, during which the British had learned, to their chagrin, of the accuracy of American rifles, especially during the Battle of New Orleans. "Is there any reason that you're cleaning your rifle at this particular time, Jerry?"

Before answering Elisabeth's question, Jerry stared pointedly at Abby for a moment and then returned his gaze to Elisabeth. "Yep. I's agoin' after a skunk."

Elisabeth nodded. "I see. This skunk wouldn't happen to live in Philadelphia, would he?"

"Yep, he do." Jerry jumped up and placed the rifle in the corner. Opening the bedroom door, he yelled, "Ma, sack me some vittles. I's agoin' huntin' in Philadelphy!" He closed the door and returned to the rocker.

A minute later, Mrs. Potts stuck her head into the room. "There ain't nothin worth akillin' in Philadelphy, son." She quickly retreated.

"I'll go talk with Ma Potts," Abby said, rising. She closed the door behind her.

Several minutes passed in silence. Jerry glanced at the rifle in the corner. He appeared as if he again wanted to use it as a prop to keep his mind off the problem at hand.

"Your mother's right, you know," Elisabeth finally said. "There's nothing worth killing in Philadelphia. The man you seek isn't worth wasting powder and ball on."

Jerry looked up. "Ain't got no choice. A skunk's done wrong by my Abby an' needs akillin'."

"Why do you say you have no choice?"

"Thet's how things is. Allus wuz an' allus will be."

Elisabeth decided to take a different approach. "Do you believe in the Bible?"

"I guess."

"Well, in the Bible it says 'Vengeance is mine; I will repay, saith the Lord.'"

"Beggin' yer pardon, Miss Elisabeth, I don't wanna make no trouble. But what kind o' a man would I be if'n I didn't do sumthin' 'bout what thet varmi't did t' my Abby?"

Elisabeth looked thoughtful. "Ah, so you're doing this for your honor, not hers."

With furrowed brow, Jerry stared at Elisabeth. "Don't rightly know what y'mean." He dropped his head and seemed ashamed at his lack of understanding.

Elisabeth looked on him with compassion. "Jerry, I don't doubt that you love Abby, and I'm sure that given time you could hunt down and kill this man. But think of the consequences. The man in question comes from a very important family. They would make sure that the authorities hunted you down and hanged you. Even if they didn't find you right away, you'd be looking over your shoulder for the rest of your life. If you were executed for murder, where would that leave Abby and her child? First, her condition would become known, and she would be ruined. Second, with you dead, how would she support herself and child?"

He was quick with an answer. "Kinfolk'd look after her."

"Perhaps they would. But is that what you want? Do you want Abby to give up her chance of becoming a doctress and live off the charity of others?"

Jerry looked like a trapped animal. He gave a low, tormented wail. "What else kin I do? I don't know no other way!"

"Here's another way, Jerry. Do you truly love Abby?"

"'Course I do," he said, seemingly affronted.

"Then wed her at once and come to Philadelphia. Abby tells me you like to grow things. Is that right?"

He looked at her warily, wondering where she was going with this question. "Yep, I grow things."

"Well, there's an estate in Philadelphia crying out for your services. A nice little cottage goes with it. Abby could continue to attend college—"

"Attend coll'ge? Wi' thet skunk thar? Never!"

Elisabeth held up her hand. "Don't worry about that, Jerry. If my plan is successful, the college will be de-skunked before Abby resumes her studies. In the meantime, I'll tutor her from my lecture notes."

Jerry sat for a long time, his head in his hands and his elbows on his knees. "Ye've give me a powerful lot to study on, Miss Elisabeth. I don't rightly know what to do . . . has anyone else heered 'bout Abby's . . ."

"No one who'd wish her harm. Her secret is safe."

Jerry pondered Elisabeth's words for a long time before he finally looked up. "Let me study on it some."

Elisabeth was relieved. At least Jerry would consider her proposal. "Of course. Abby and I are staying at Miss Waldie's. We'll await your decision."

That night Elisabeth and Abby slept in Abby's old room. It was barely light when a rattling noise at the window awoke them. Elisabeth looked at Abby. The noise came again. Abby smiled. "It's Jerry. He's throwing pebbles at the window."

Abby quickly dressed and joined Jerry outside. She returned sometime later. Elisabeth didn't have to ask the outcome of her conference. Her beaming face said it all. The two friends squealed with delight and hugged. Suddenly, Miss Waldie was at the door.

"Sorry for waking you, Miss Waldie," Abby said. "Jerry has asked me to marry him."

The old woman gave a resigned smile. "I best get the preparations under way."

Later that day, Jerry drove Elisabeth and Abby out to Abby's home. While Abby was busy with her siblings, Jerry took Elisabeth aside. "Miss Elisabeth, how'd I go 'bout larnin' my letters proper?"

Elisabeth thought for a moment. "Once we get to Philadelphia, Abby and I could tutor you, and I'm sure that Mrs. Kenny would be happy to let you use her library."

He slowly nodded. "Good. I'd not want t'shame Abby in Philadelphy."

Tears sprang to Elisabeth's eyes. *Abby Smith, I hope you truly do repent of your folly and make yourself worthy of this good man!* She thought.

CHAPTER TWENTY-SEVEN

Three days later, Miss Waldie drove Elisabeth and Abby to the crossroads in her ancient carriage. Mr. Potts and Jerry followed in a cart with the luggage.

"Will you be coming home at the end of the term, Abigail?" Miss Waldie asked as they awaited the stagecoach.

Seeing the loneliness in the old woman's eyes, Abby gently explained that she could not. She and Elisabeth had accepted positions as junior residents at Blockley Hospital and Almshouse, a large facility for poor people in Philadelphia. It was a short appointment, but Dr. Longshore had assured them that the medical experience would be invaluable. Dr. Blackwell had worked there and had told of her experiences when she spoke at the college. Abby did not explain all this to Miss Waldie, only that she and Elisabeth would be working at a hospital for four months.

"You would finish there at the end of May. Perhaps you could home for a visit then?"

"We'll try," Abby promised. "But the spring will be a busy time for Jerry with his work on Mrs. Kenny's estate."

Elisabeth's heart went out to Miss Waldie. *Children may be a challenge, but spinsterhood is an even greater burden. I wonder what Miss Waldie's story is? Did she have an opportunity to wed, or did no man ever ask her? Here I am feeling sorry for Miss Waldie when I, too, am a spinster. But at least I have the Lord's promise that my singleness is temporary.*

"Hyar she come," Jerry said, looking down the road at the stagecoach lumbering toward them.

The women said their good-byes as Jerry and his father loaded the baggage onto the roof of the stagecoach. Picking up his bride, Jerry placed her in the vehicle, then he helped Elisabeth aboard. The three of them were the only occupants of the coach all the way to Harrisburg. Elisabeth couldn't help but be pleased at how well her plan had worked. Ironically, it had worked so well that it also caused her to feel a twinge of jealousy. *It doesn't seem fair that things have worked out so well for Abby and Jerry, while Gren and I . . .* Through strength of will, Elisabeth refused to go where her thoughts were taking her. Rather, she told herself that she should be happy for her friend and that comparing one's situation with that of another only led to unhappiness. She concluded her remonstration with the oft-quoted truism: "Comparisons are odious."

When the weary travelers finally reached the mansion, they found that Mrs. Kenny had fitted out a room for the newlyweds. "You can move into the cottage when we figure out how to evict Mr. Murphy," Mrs. Kenny said. "I've put the word out he's needing a job."

The next day, Elisabeth resumed classes at the college. She was not sorry when she learned that the last lecture of the day had been canceled. Since John was not expected until six o'clock, she went into the study room and began copying her lecture notes for Abby. She was busily occupied at this task when Dr. Lester entered the room. She pretended not to notice him as he quietly approached her.

"Miss Ashcroft," he said, "or should I say, Lady Claverley?"

Elisabeth looked up and then lowered her eyes. "I hope you will keep my secret, Dr. Lester," she whispered, adopting a tone of fear and desperation.

"Of course, my dear." Her new show of deference surprised him. "I am sure you have a good reason for going under your maiden name. You're secret's safe with me. Of course, it wouldn't do if our Quaker friend learned of it."

Elisabeth looked up innocently. "Quaker friend?"

"Dr. Longshore. I think he'd be rather shocked to learn that you've deserted a husband and that you're a member of a church that teaches polygamy. He and the members of the board guard the school's good name quite jealously. No doubt you'd be expelled immediately if they found out." Elisabeth flashed him a look of alarm, but she didn't speak. "Your husband is still in England, then?"

She nodded. "Although I do not miss him, I confess . . . I do find it very lonely here."

"I can imagine. It must be difficult for you to find suitable interests. After all, a woman of your intelligence . . ." He let the sentence hang in the air.

Elisabeth nodded her agreement. "Oh, yes. I often feel starved for educated conversation. I love discussing good literature, history, religion, and so forth."

"Indeed," he said, smoothing his right side-whisker. "I certainly understand. I, too, love to engage in enlightened conversation." For a moment he hesitated before tentatively adding, "Perhaps we might meet sometime . . . merely to discuss such things—history, philosophy, and so on. Now that I . . . understand your particular situation, you need have no fear that I would misunderstand our relationship."

Elisabeth feigned hesitancy. "Perhaps . . . of course, we'd have to be discreet. Mrs. Kenny knows my situation, and I doubt she'd approve."

He winked. "Discretion is my middle name. We'll talk again."

Elisabeth sat back in relief when Lester had gone. "So far so good," she said to herself.

"Ah, there you are, Miss Ashcroft," Miss Morris said as she entered the study room. "I understand that Mrs. Kenny is trying to find work for Mr. Murphy."

"She is. Do you know of anything?"

"I do. The gasworks requires a night watchman. From what I've heard, all that's required is to be there through the night. The former watchman passed away sitting in a rocking chair with a newspaper in his lap."

Elisabeth couldn't suppress a smile. "Mr. Murphy is eminently qualified for such a position. I'll make sure he gets down to apply right away."

That evening Elisabeth accompanied John to see Mr. Murphy. "Come in," called the Irishman from his chair by the fire. "Ah, Miss Elisabeth and Master John. Pardon fer not standin' but me lum-bay-go—"

"Enough about your lumbago, Murphy," John said. "We're here on business."

Mr. Murphy looked at John suspiciously. "And what kind o' business would tha' be?"

"They're needing a man of your abilities down at the gasworks. We have to move quickly to get you the position."

Mr. Murphy waved his hands in the air. "But I have a position." His eyes focused on Elisabeth. "Besides, if I takes another job, where would I live?"

"Don't worry, Mr. Murphy," she said. "We won't leave you homeless. We know of lodgings near the gasworks that would suit you to a T."

John raised his eyebrows. "We do?"

Elisabeth nodded. "Mrs. Steinke's boarding house."

John's face lit up. "Of course! The widow Steinke. You and she will get on like a house on fire, Murphy."

The Irishman resisted applying for the position, but Elisabeth and John were adamant. Within the week, he was the gasworks' night watchman and Mrs. Steinke's lodger. During that same week, Elisabeth forced herself to acknowledge Dr. Lester's increasing attentions. She was just finishing up her clinic duties on the following Saturday when he entered the room. He motioned for her to remain as the other students filed out. When they were alone, he said, "Would you like to come to my rooms for supper and some good conversation tonight, Miss Ashcroft? It would be all very proper. My housekeeper would prepare the meal, serve it, and be close at hand during the whole evening."

Elisabeth smiled at him. "Thank you, Dr. Lester. However, I think it would perhaps be . . . easier if you came to my home."

His eyebrows arched in surprise. "Your benefactress wouldn't object?"

Elisabeth lowered her voice and adopted a conspiratorial tone. "If you came late enough, she wouldn't need to know."

His eyes gleamed at her apparent willingness. "How late?"

"I think nine o'clock would be late enough. By that time the servants will be in their rooms and Mrs. Kenny will be asleep. There's a little parlor that opens onto the garden through French doors. I could leave the doors on the latch, and no one would be the wiser."

He looked askance at her. "You amaze me, Miss Ashcroft. I wouldn't have pegged you as one who'd conspire to slip a man into your house."

At this Elisabeth feigned anger. "If it bothers you, Dr. Lester, we need discuss a meeting no further." Picking up her books, she rushed out of the room.

He caught up with her in the hall. "I'm sorry I offended you," he said, his hand on her arm. "I'd be delighted to join you this evening. How do I get to the French doors?"

CHAPTER TWENTY-EIGHT

That evening Elisabeth sat on one of the two couches in the small parlor. The flames in the grate sent shadows dancing around the walls. She opened the book on her lap and tried to read. The clock on the mantel chimed nine times. Although the words in the book made absolutely no sense at all, she persisted. At two minutes past nine, the French doors opened and Dr. Lester slipped into the room. He looked around nervously. "A cozy place," he whispered.

Elisabeth looked up at him. "There is no need to whisper," she said, speaking in a normal voice. "Mrs. Kenny is asleep and the servants are in their rooms. We shall not be disturbed."

Lester surveyed the room. His eyes lingered for a moment on the painting over the mantelpiece and then continued around the parlor. "Where do those doors lead?" he asked, nodding at the carved pocket doors, which were slightly ajar.

"To the library." She arose and went to the doors, opening them a little wider. "Would you like to see it? The gaslight's already on."

He shook his head. "I didn't come to look at books. Might I ask for a drink?"

She walked toward him. "Certainly. What would you like? Water? Milk? Tea? Coffee? Lemonade?"

A frown crossed his face. "Have you anything stronger?"

"I'm afraid not. Temperance is the rule in this house."

"I thought as much." He withdrew a silver flask from the inside pocket of his fashionable coat and held it up. "Do you mind?"

"If you need it," Elisabeth said, sitting back on the couch. "You look rather nervous."

Lester took a swallow from his flask, then sat on the other couch across from her. "I just can't make you out. Before, you wouldn't give me the time of day. Now you arrange this tryst and slip me into your house. Are you playing me for a fool?"

Elisabeth gazed at him, wide-eyed and innocent. "It's hardly a tryst. The French doors are still on the latch. You can leave if you wish."

His eyes darted to the French doors and then back to Elisabeth. Leaning his head back, he took another swig from the flask. Then he studied Elisabeth as he slowly lowered the ornate container, corked it, and placed it on the side table adjacent to the couch. "You are the most beautiful and exciting woman I've met in a long time. Ever since I first saw you at the college, I haven't been able to get you out of my mind."

Elisabeth cocked her head. "Why, thank you, Dr. Lester." She then fixed him with her hazel eyes. "But I believe we are here to indulge in good conversation. If you've come after something else, you've come under false pretenses."

He laughed. "We both know I didn't come only for conversation." He got up and crossed to Elisabeth's sofa and sat beside her. She slid away from him. Draping his arm across the back of the couch, he said, "For one who arranged for me to be here, you're acting rather coy."

Elisabeth quickly stood up and went to the side of the fireplace, where a braided rope hung from the ceiling. She took the rope in her hand. "Shall I summon the servants, or will you desist?"

Lester smiled and shrugged. "You win. I'll behave."

"Thank you." She sat on the couch across from him.

Lester looked for his flask and realized it was on the table beside Elisabeth. He stood up, picked up the flask, and walked over to the fire. There he uncorked the flask and took a long swallow. Leaning one elbow on the mantel, he stared at Elisabeth. "Of what would you like to converse?"

"About you. What is your story?"

His eyes narrowed and he gazed at Elisabeth for a long moment. *He looks like a fox. No, more like a weasel,* she decided.

He gave a careless shrug. "I doubt you can want to know about me. Let's talk about polygamy. The notion fascinates me."

She shook her head. "Perhaps later. First, I want to hear about you."

For several seconds he stared at her, and Elisabeth could almost hear his mind calculating how much he should tell her. He shrugged again. "Well, if you really want to hear about my misspent youth. Except for me, the Lesters are upright citizens. One brother is a minister in the Episcopal church, like our father, and the other is a professor at Harvard College. I—" here he gave an exaggerated bow, "am the black sheep of the family."

Elisabeth feigned surprise. "A medical practice is hardly the profession of a black sheep."

Lester smiled and took another swallow from the flask. The liquor seemed to ease his suspicions and loosen his tongue. "Medicine was forced on me. For years I lived on an allowance from my family while I attended college. I was expelled from a dozen of them—Harvard, Yale, Princeton, Michigan, Pennsylvania . . . When I ran out of good American colleges, I went to Europe—"

"I know from your lectures that you're a very intelligent man," Elisabeth interjected, stroking his vanity. "Why were you constantly expelled?"

"Lack of effort. Complete indolence . . . and an unusual propensity for the opposite sex. If there had been a degree for seduction, I'd have graduated with honors." He paused to assess Elisabeth's reaction.

She felt the color rise in her cheeks. She'd expected that at some point he would catch her off guard and say something like this. It was a risk she was willing to take to see him punished and dismissed from the college. She took a deep breath.

"I've embarrassed you," he said, with pleasure rather than chagrin.

Elisabeth touched her cheek with her hand. "It's warm in here. Pray continue."

He smiled, obviously enjoying being in control of the situation. "As long as my family supported me, I led a merry social life. It's surprising how much society will overlook if one has money. I hobnobbed with the cream of university society on two continents. However, sooner or later I'd seduce the young wife of some old professor and out I'd go."

Elisabeth shook her head. "I'm surprised that some jealous husband hasn't shot you by now."

Lester laughed. "Because of their own vanity, most cuckolds cover up seduction. Only once have I been publicly challenged. It was in Paris, of all places. I'd thought that they were more sophisticated about such things there. A jealous husband challenged me to an *affaire d'honneur*."

Elisabeth's hand went to her mouth. "You fought a duel? You killed a man?"

Lester shrugged and shook his head. "No, only wounded him. But the unpleasant incident did end my time at the Sorbonne. From there I went to England. Ah, England, where having a mistress is a mere peccadillo—of course, you'd know all about that."

All too well, Elisabeth thought, but she refrained from commenting.

"In England I lived well on my family's money and soon became the darling of the upper crust. But after only three months, I got a most disturbing ultimatum from my illustrious father—get a profession or be cut off without a penny! I pondered my options. What profession would give me the most latitude to pursue my predilections? Religion was out for obvious reasons. The law is a bore. As for the military—well, despite my adroitness with a dueling pistol, I'm a lover, not a fighter. Academia had some appeal, but with an almost exclusive male student body, it would not have provided me with many opportunities beyond the wives of my colleagues."

Admitting this, Dr. Lester grinned at Elisabeth, who barely managed to restrain her disgust. After another swig from the flask, he went on. "Then it dawned on me. I would study medicine! In what other field could a man have better access to the female gender?"

Elisabeth could restrain herself no longer. "I am appalled to hear of such a misspent life," she gasped.

"Oh, there's much more," he said, delighting in the opportunity of shocking the vicar's daughter. The liquor had begun to cloud his reason, and it appeared that he could not see beyond the glory of the moment. Before going on, he drained the flask, recorked it, and returned it to his inside pocket. He stared at Elisabeth for a moment. "Where was I? Ah, yes. Through the good offices of my illustrious brother, Harvard once more opened its doors to me, and in the process of time I earned my degree. When the female medical college opened, an even greater opportunity presented itself." He leered at Elisabeth. "Could there be a better place for a man of my inclinations? The governors beseeched me to join the faculty. After keeping them dangling for a while, I finally gave in to their importunities. I must say it has been a very rewarding experience." He leered again. "Each orientation meeting I pick out my quarry. When the new college year began in October, I noted a few prospects. However, when you showed up late, my search was over. I immediately recognized your natural beauty, although I must say you do little to enhance it. A new dress and hairstyle would do wonders—"

Elisabeth ignored his criticism. "You mean to say that you purposefully accepted a position at the college so that you could seduce young women?" She deliberately raised her voice an octave. "How could you possibly think that you could get away with it?"

Lester smiled. "Have you not seen the adulation? But to answer your second question, my success as a seducer has rested with the principle of culpability."

"Culpability?" Elisabeth knew well what the word meant, but she wanted to draw him out further.

"Yes, culpability. If one becomes involved with another in some less than honorable practice, the key is to make sure that the other person is equally culpable. For example, if I seduce a man's wife, I make sure that she believes that it was her idea in the first place. If she is equally culpable, then she will not expose me. As for single women, society's disapprobation protects me. If an affair comes to light, a woman's reputation is destroyed, but a man's is enhanced."

"What's to keep me from exposing you?"

Lester's smile was indulgent. "The reason I am being so candid with you, Lady Claverley, is that I know how deeply the college administration fears scandal. If you expose me, I'll expose you. The revelation that you are masquerading under false pretenses could ruin you."

She shook her head in wonderment. "You say that as if you had absolutely no conscience."

"I don't," he said with a smug grin. "None whatsoever. I'm completely amoral."

"I can't believe that. You must believe in God. After all, your father and brother are ministers."

The question seemed to catch him off guard. He stared at Elisabeth for a long moment and then turned away from her. Placing both hands on the mantelpiece, he gazed into the fire. Almost imperceptibly, his shoulders sagged and some of the arrogance seemed to go out of him. "I once believed in God," he said in a low, reflective voice. "But that was a long time ago, when I was young and naïve." Pushing himself away from the mantelpiece, he gazed at the portrait over it.

Eager to know, Elisabeth asked, "What happened?"

He seemed not to hear the question and continued studying the painting. "Did you know that Pinkie was Elizabeth Barrett Browning's aunt?" He turned. "She died of consumption not long after Lawrence painted her."

Elisabeth nodded. "Yes. Sarah Barrett-Moulton."

He turned back to the painting. "I've only been in love once in my life." He nodded at the painting. "A girl much like her—beautiful, pure, even angelic . . ."

Elisabeth was surprised. His voice was soft, even reverent. She hadn't imagined that he had this side to his character. "What . . . what happened to her?" Elisabeth's voice was tender.

He spun around to face her, and his arrogance returned. In a voice of flint he said, "She died too."

"And you blame God for her death?"

He looked at her with contempt, and words came pouring out of him. "Of course not! How can I blame a being that doesn't exist? God is a myth. Moral restraints and divine punishment are nonsense. Life is to live—to live to the fullest. When you're dead, you're dead." He snapped his fingers. "Like that! There's no God, no judgment." His passion frightened Elisabeth. Had she taken on too much? Would he become violent like Claverley? "Karl Marx hit the nail on the head when he said that 'religion is the opiate of the masses.' Since time immemorial the ruling classes have been using religion to frighten people into docility. The scientific discoveries of the seventeenth century exposed religion for what it is. However, superstition was so deeply rooted that only the intelligentsia broke free. One day soon, religion will receive a deathblow. Have you heard of organic evolution?"

Elisabeth nodded, wondering where the conversation was going.

"Then you know that over the millennia man has evolved from lower forms of life. God didn't create man; man merely evolved."

Elisabeth drew herself erect. "I know no such thing. It's a silly notion. Let me say with Shakespeare's Malvolio, 'I think nobly of the soul, and no way approve this opinion.'"

His brows wrinkled and he pointed at her with an accusing finger. "Many brilliant men espouse evolution. The *coup de grace* will be when Erasmus Darwin's grandson, Charles, publishes the results of his studies."

Elisabeth tried to be patient as Lester rambled on about organic evolution. He maintained that once the younger Darwin's book was available, it would destroy belief in God for all but the truly ignorant and that religion would be consigned to the trash heap of history.

Elisabeth stared at him, shaking her head in disbelief. She tried to speak, but Lester wasn't finished.

He drew himself up and proclaimed, "In the way Hercules diverted two rivers to cleanse the Augean stables, the twin rivers of Marxism and Darwinism will wash away the accumulated superstition of past ages and usher in an era of science and reason."

He took a deep breath and Elisabeth used the pause to say, "Brave words, Dr. Lester. But they shall not come to pass. True religion will never die."

Lester looked around for his flask and then remembered it was empty and in his pocket. "You may scoff, but mark my words, the end of religion is near. More to the point, all those who have been bound down by religious scruples will realize that their restraint has been in vain . . . completely fruitless."

"So you live an immoral life—"

"Amoral."

"Call it what you will, as far as I can see you use these theories to quell your conscience so that you can satisfy your lusts. In the meantime you destroy the lives of impressionable young women such as Emily Pendergast and Abigail Smith."

Anger flashed across the doctor's handsome face. "What do you know about Emily Pendergast?"

"I know that you seduced her with your lies and left her with child as you did Abby Smith, forcing them both to withdraw from the college." Elisabeth leapt to her feet.

They glared at each other for a moment. Then Lester put up his hand, as if to fend off her verbal assault. "Calm down. I was invited here for rational discussion. Typical of your gender, you're being irrational."

It was all Elisabeth could do to restrain herself. But she was not yet ready to spring her trap, contenting herself by glaring at him. His lips twisted into an oily smile. "You say I lied to those girls. I am honest enough to admit it. We are all liars. That's how we get what we want."

Elisabeth's words were glacial. "Speak for yourself."

He ignored her. "Doctors lie all the time. 'Take this medicine and you'll be up in no time,' they say, when they know the patient is dying. Clergymen lie—'Open up your hearts and give to the poor' . . . then they use the money to build edifices to their own vanity and live in luxury while their parishioners live in squalor. Newspapermen lie to sell papers—'Utah Territory is filled with thieves and adulterers,' they say. Is it?" Elisabeth started to speak, but he cut her off. "You needn't answer. I'm sure people there are no worse than anywhere else. Politicians lie, oh, how they lie—'If you elect me, I promise . . .' once elected, their promises are forgotten. Are you familiar with the Cherokee Indians?"

Elisabeth glared at him. "I don't see—"

"No you don't see . . . but I do. 'Live like white men,' the government told them. 'We won't drive you across the Mississippi like the savage tribes.' So they lived like white men. They bought black slaves and established plantations, built schools and churches, established newspapers, Europeanized their names. And what did the government do? Drove them off their land and across the Mississippi anyway, killing thousands in the process. We say that Americans believe in the rule of law. Do we? The Cherokees pleaded their case before the Supreme Court and won. Did the government allow them to remain on their land? Of course not. The government lied."

When it seemed that Lester had run out of words, Elisabeth said, "Are you finished?"

He leaned toward her, his breath reeking of alcohol. "No, I'm not finished. I have yet to say that you, Miss Holier-Than-Thou, are a liar too. I know for a fact that you lied on your college application!"

Elisabeth slowly rose. Despite her wildly beating heart and flashing eyes, her voice was controlled. "Sidney Lester, like evil men throughout history, you justify your depredations and excuse your own evil because there is evil in the world. Well, sir, there is evil in the world. But there is also good. You have blinded yourself to the good to blot out your sins. Deep down in your soul, you know that your argument is false. It is true that we are all sinners. The scriptures make that plain. But our purpose in this life is to overcome sin, to overcome the natural man, to yield to the enticing of the Holy Spirit, to follow the example of the Savior. You, Dr. Lester, have thrown in with the adversary." She pointed an accusing finger at him. "You are an evil man, Sidney Lester, and a disgrace to your profession. I have never in my life seen such . . . such diabolical rascality! In your wicked presence, I find some comfort in saying that your nefarious ways are over." With this, she stalked over to the library doors and slid them open.

The color drained from Lester's face as Dr. Longshore and Colonel Kane emerged from the library. "You should be horse-whipped, Lester!" Colonel Kane said. "Horsewhipped within an inch of your life."

Recovering from the initial shock of knowing that the two men had heard all, Lester feigned nonchalance. He leaned on the mantelpiece as his cheeks changed from white to red. "It's your word against mine. Use what you've heard, and I'll bring down the college."

"Perhaps," Dr. Longshore said calmly. "Such a scandal could topple the college. Women's progress has many enemies, enemies who would delight in using this against us. So we are going to give thee a chance to redeem thyself. Earlier today, Miss Ashcroft suggested that we send thee to California. There thy medical skills could be put to good use. We suggest—"

Lester went on the offensive. "You suggest? You're in no position to suggest anything."

Dr. Longshore turned toward the library and called, "Miss Morris, please join us." The woman of many hats emerged from the library with a sheaf of paper in her hands. The college president turned back to Dr. Lester. "Miss Morris has made a shorthand transcription of all that has transpired here tonight. Tomorrow, she will set to work making longhand copies: one for thy father, one for the Medical Association of Pennsylvania, and one for our college records. If thee does not leave immediately for the West, we will be forced to deliver these transcripts."

Fear showed in Dr. Lester's eyes as he realized the implications of Dr. Longshore's words. "That's . . . that's blackmail."

Colonel Kane spoke. "Call it what you will, Lester. We see it as an opportunity for you to change your wasted life. Take it or leave it. If you don't take it, we may have to close the college, but your practice of medicine will be forfeit, and, I dare say, your worthy father would cut you off without a penny."

Lester glared defiantly at his accusers. He was not ready to concede defeat, nor were Dr. Longshore and Colonel Kane ready to compromise further.

Elisabeth saw a way to break the impasse. "Let me warn you, Dr. Lester, that you are only alive today through my good offices. Not a hundred feet from where you stand is a young man who would take your life if he knew that you were the one who . . . who offended his sweetheart, Abigail Smith. You may have bested some Frenchman, but I guarantee you'll come out second best against Jeremiah Potts. Agree to these generous terms, or I'll open those French doors and summon him."

Dr. Lester glowered at Elisabeth. Then his eyes darted around the room like those of a trapped animal. When he could see no escape, he shrugged and twisted his lips into a mirthless grin. With a hard look at Dr. Longshore, he conceded. "Check," he said. Turning to Elisabeth, he bowed and added, "Checkmate. Ironically, I've always wanted to see the West." With that, he left the way he had come.

Dr. Longshore breathed a sigh of relief. "I'm glad that's over." He turned to Elisabeth. "Miss Ashcroft, while I've never been to the theater, I cannot imagine anyone playing a greater role than thee tonight."

Colonel Kane agreed. "Hear, hear! An absolutely brilliant performance, Miss Ashcroft! When Lester inquired about the library doors, I thought we were done for. But you completely allayed his fears. While I hate to see that scoundrel slink off to pollute the West, I must agree that for all concerned, your plan worked admirably. My sincerest congratulations on a job well done."

Elisabeth blushed. "Thank you, gentlemen," she said. "Dr. Longshore, you may expect Miss Smith . . . Mrs. Potts, that is, and myself at the college on Monday morning to resume our studies."

CHAPTER TWENTY-NINE

Miss Morris rose from her desk to greet Elisabeth and Abby the following Monday morning. "Welcome back, Mrs. Potts," Miss Morris said. "I'm glad we were able to rid the college of . . . of encumbrances to your continuing."

"I'm happy to be back. Happy and so thankful to Miss Ashcroft."

Miss Morris nodded. "It's unfortunate you missed her performance on Saturday evening. It was a pip." To Elisabeth, she added, "I was writing up the transcript this morning and came across this wonderful phrase: 'diabolical rascality.' What an apt phrase to describe Sidney Lester's actions."

Elisabeth smiled. "I wish I could claim it. As it happens, I got it from our Doctrine and Covenants. It was used by the Prophet Joseph Smith to describe the actions of those who were persecuting the Mormon people."

"Ah, I see," Miss Morris said, seemingly unsure of how to respond. She quickly changed the subject and got onto firmer ground. "I've put an announcement on the college bulletin board stating that Dr. Sidney Lester has decamped for the West and has terminated his association with the college. Hopefully, that's an end to it."

The next month sped by quickly for Elisabeth. She and Abby continued to study together while Jerry saw to the grounds, which he had in spectacular shape in no time. Soon he was helping John with painting and other chores around the mansion. His spare time he spent in the library, poring over a *McGuffey's Reader* set. He flew through the primer, and books one through four by month's end. However, his pace through the *McGuffey's Speller* was a good deal slower.

"Abby certainly landed on her feet with that young man Jerry," Mrs. Kenny said to Elisabeth two weeks after he had begun work. "John thinks the world of him. He says he's a hard worker and as honest as the day is long."

Elisabeth agreed. "'An honest man's the noblest work of God.'"

"Franklin?"

"No. Pope."

"Which one?"

"Alexander."

"Pope Alexander?"

"No. Alexander Pope."

The two women laughed at their little game.

At the end of January, Elisabeth and Abby completed their classes, both doing well on final examinations. In fact, Elisabeth did so well that Dr. Longshore invited her to return in the fall as a graduate candidate rather than a listener. When Elisabeth and Abby attended graduation ceremonies to honor those who had completed their two years of study, they couldn't have been more excited if they were graduating themselves.

* * *

On the first Thursday in February, John dropped Elisabeth and Abby off at the Blockley Hospital and Almshouse for their interview with the matron. They entered the central building with some trepidation. Squalor greeted them on every side. Miss Morris's description of the hospital filled Elisabeth's head: *"Upwards of two thousand inmates inhabit the four buildings at Blockley. The buildings are run-down, overcrowded, under-heated, poorly ventilated, and under-staffed. A committee, known as the 'Guardians of the Poor,' oversees the hospital. The medical director is a Dr. Benedict, but the real ruler is the matron. No words can adequately describe Mrs. Urghart!"*

Putrid smells and pandemonium greeted Elisabeth and Abby as they tentatively made their way to the huge central room of Building Two. The fetid smell, Elisabeth and Abby were soon to learn, was a combination of sweating bodies, stale food, medicines, and mold. The odor penetrated everything, including the people who worked there. The pandemonium resulted from the hundreds of sick people demanding attention and not getting it because there were so few doctors and nurses. Elisabeth had an overwhelming desire to turn and run. She caught Abby's arm. "I'm not sure if I can go through with this."

Abby gave her an encouraging smile. "In for a penny, in for a pound."

Elisabeth felt her mouth fall open as they approached the matron, Mrs. Urghart. Ensconced in a huge armchair, swollen feet propped up on a purple velvet footstool, the three-hundred-pound matron barked orders at frightened nurses and terrified inmates. Elisabeth and Abby stood by as a frail old woman attempted to complain about the food.

"Paupers have no rights," Mrs. Urghart screamed. "Another word and it's the shower for you!" The old woman shuddered and shrank from the matron's presence.

Elisabeth and Abby fell under the matron's gaze. "What have we here?" The huge woman spoke loudly enough to be heard above the weeping and wailing.

"We're from the college," Abby said tremulously.

The matron studied the newcomers from under heavy gray eyebrows. "Prima donnas, no doubt. Names?"

"Elisabeth Ashcroft."

"Mrs. Jeremiah Potts."

The matron scrutinized Abby. "How far along?"

Abby's hand went to her barely rounded stomach. "How can you tell?"

The matron's eyes narrowed, but a hint of a smile touched her lips. "Nothing escapes me."

"Three or four months."

Mr. Urghart nodded. "Two months tops."

"Pardon?" Abby said.

Mrs. Urghart slowly mouthed the words as if Abby were an idiot: "You can only serve here for two months. After that you'd be useless. You," pointing at Elisabeth, "will work for four. Accommodations are in the attic with the nurses." Raising her voice even higher, she roared, "Wendell!"

"Oh, we're not nurses," Elisabeth said as an ancient, emaciated man limped forward. "We're training to be doctresses."

"I know what you're training for," the matron said. She turned to the old man, whose thin hair formed a ragged comb-over like a gray spider atop a yellowed cue ball. "Wendell, see they find the attic and get them bedclothes." Turning back to Elisabeth and Abby, she said, "Where's your baggage?"

Elisabeth and Abby exchanged glances. "We didn't know we had to stay here," Elisabeth said.

"New policy. You're on call twenty-four hours a day, five and a half days a week. You can go home on Saturday afternoons, but see you're back at eight sharp on Monday mornings. After Wendell shows you your room, go home and get what you need. Be back here tomorrow morning, eight sharp." She dismissed them with a wave of her pudgy hand.

Discouraged, the two junior residents trudged after Wendell as he limped his way up four flights of stairs to a huge attic dormitory.

"Man comin' in," called Wendell in a reedy voice as he entered the room, closely followed by Elisabeth and Abby.

The room was relatively clean, but stuffy. Only one of the dormer windows helped ventilate it. A row of wheeled, metal cots lined each wall.

"What man?" asked a freckled redhead from among a group of nurses. The nurses laughed and scrutinized the newcomers.

Ignoring the nurses, Wendell went to a large linen closet and opened the door. "Help yersels, ladies."

The two women withdrew frayed sheets that had once been white, as well as tattered blankets. They were following Wendell to the far end of the dormitory when one nurse yelled to another, "What did y'get?"

"Typhus! How about you?"

"Syphilis!"

Wendell smiled at Elisabeth and Abby's shocked expressions. Through toothless gums he said, "They's only talking 'bout what wards they's been assigned fer next week."

The orderly led Elisabeth and Abby to a room boxed into a corner of the dormitory. It contained two cots, identical to the ones in the main room, a small desk and chair, and a washstand. "Make yer beds, ladies. And see yersels out."

"At least we get our own room," Abby said to Elisabeth, trying to put a good face on things.

Elisabeth nodded. "I imagine we should be thankful for small blessings."

Elisabeth and Abby were making their beds when a knock sounded. Abby opened the door to a delegation of nurses. "We've come to welcome ye," said the freckle-faced one. "I'm Daphne. Blockley's a nightmare, so we try to look out fer each other." Daphne introduced the other nurses, who were mostly country girls—no strangers to hard work in appalling conditions. Elisabeth and Abby's cultured accents impressed the nurses, and their temerity at entering a field dominated by men brought out the nurses' sympathy.

"Watch out fer the male junior residents," warned Daphne, who remained after the other nurses had left. "They don't hold with women doctors. They deal mostly with the men inmates, but ye'll run into them in Maternity."

"Do they have to do nursing duties as we do?" Elisabeth asked.

"Heavens, no," Daphne said. "They think they're God's gift to the medical profession. They wouldn't soil their hands in bathing a patient or changing a chamber pot."

"What about the real doctors?" Abby asked.

"They're not bad—especially Dr. Benedict. He's a real sweetheart. All the girls are in love with him."

"And does he reciprocate?" Abby asked warily.

"Oh, no. He's happily married to some society gal."

"What about Mrs. Urghart?" Elisabeth asked.

"Don't worry about her. Her bark's worse than her bite. She—"

A cacophony of loud laughter and a metallic screeching inter-rupted Daphne.

"What in heaven's name is that?" Abby asked.

"Just the girls having a little fun," Daphne said as the three of them filed out of the room and into the dormitory, where they saw one nurse sitting on a cot and three others pushing it the length of the room. All four were screaming at the top of their lungs, while the metal wheels on the hardwood floor attempted to out-screech them.

Daphne looked on with a smile on her face. She shrugged. "It relieves the tension. Would you like a tour of the building?" Elisabeth and Abby nodded and apprehensively followed her.

When Elisabeth and Abby emerged from Blockley House later, Elisabeth took a huge breath of fresh air. She looked at Abby. "I'm still not sure if I can do this."

"Once we start working, the time will go by quickly. Anyone who can survive the trip from England in a crowded ship can survive Blockley!"

Elisabeth gave her friend a wry smile. "Perhaps. But I've been sentenced to four months. You only got two!"

* * *

"How was your first visit?" Mrs. Kenny asked when Elisabeth returned home. Elisabeth didn't try to hide her discouragement. "That bad? I have heard stories—"

"They're all true. It's a horrible place. Noise, putrid smells, and absolute squalor. It's much worse than I imagined—even worse than Dr. Blackwell and Miss Morris described it. What an absolutely depressing place! The floors and walls are cold and damp, except for those near the huge fireplaces that roast the people close to them and do nothing for those farther away. Sanitation is unheard of—buckets of slop and vomit everywhere, nurses and doctors wearing blood-spattered aprons. And huge jars of shiny black leeches. If I didn't already despise the practice of bloodletting, the sight of those clustered masses would utterly repel me. And the noises!"

Elisabeth didn't describe how the patients' incessant moaning and groaning was punctuated by the screams of those on the operating tables, denied the blessing of ether. Though some doctors used opium to anesthetize their patients, it had a tendency to wear off quickly, resulting in the patient waking up screaming in the middle of an operation.

"You don't have to go back," Mrs. Kenny said.

"I think I do, both for my own experience and to help Abby— although she seems to have taken it better than I. She did look a little gray, though, when we were climbing up the back stairs. Through a filthy window we saw a pile of dead bodies in the back courtyard. Wendell, the old orderly, explained that some cadavers are taken to the dissecting rooms. The others are stacked in the courtyard awaiting burial. It should be called Blockley Death House. There is little evidence of anyone being cured there. I think that the poor would be better to take their chances at home rather than go to that horrible place."

Her face pale at the imagined sight, Mrs. Kenny shook her head. "At least ye'll only be there for a few months." This was all the comfort she could give.

Next morning, Elisabeth and Abby found themselves in Dr. Benedict's office. Elisabeth thought he was young to have charge of such a huge enterprise. She was also impressed by how kindly he spoke to them. "Did you have a look around Building Two yesterday?" he asked.

"Yes, sir," Elisabeth said. "Nurse Daphne Miller showed us around."

The doctor nodded. "Then you know that the Maternity ward is on the first floor, Typhus on the second, Syphilis on the third, and the dormitory on the fourth. I apologize for the squalor. We're severely underfunded. The Guardians of the Poor try hard to raise money, but most rich people feel that the poor are responsible for their own lot. Helping them, they argue, only encourages pauperism. In the meantime, we carry on as best we can. Today you may accompany me on my rounds. Mrs. Urghart will assign you a floor."

Seeing the patients—or inmates, as they were called—as part of the whole was one thing; seeing them as individuals was another. Elisabeth's heart went out to each unfortunate as she and Abby accompanied Dr. Benedict on his rounds. The doctor warned the junior residents against emotional involvement, urging them to remain aloof. Each patient had a depressing life story, and it would not do for doctors or junior residents to take on the weight of each inmate's heavy burdens.

The Typhus ward housed mostly Irish immigrants who had contracted the often-fatal disease aboard the unsanitary and over-crowded immigrant ships. Fortunately, February was a low point of the disease. Dr. Blackwell, Elisabeth recalled, had spent the summer of 1848 at Blockley, a time when thousands of Irish immigrants were crowding the hospital, lying on blankets in corridor floors or stacked up like cordwood in the back courtyard awaiting burial.

"Well, tomorrow we begin," Abby said as she and Elisabeth sat in their room that evening. "I'm sorry you got the Syphilis."

"It's all one. Even the Maternity, where you'll be, is sickening. Dr. Blackwell said that she told the doctors when she was here about Doctors Semmelweis and Holmes' studies about puerperal fever, but I don't see any evidence that the doctors are following the sanitation rules that would stop the spread of that plague."

"Perhaps we can do a little—" Abby was drowned out by screaming from the nurses' quarters. She shook her head and raised her voice to be heard over the ruckus. "They're at it again."

Elisabeth nodded just as someone pounded on the door. Abby opened the door to find a panic-stricken Daphne. "Come quickly. Jenny and Flo's killing each other! Maybe they'll listen to you."

Elisabeth looked at Abby. "Why us?"

Nevertheless, they quickly followed Daphne. The crowd parted as Daphne pushed her way through the circle of screaming nurses. On the floor two girls kicked, scratched, and pulled each other's hair with wild abandon. Elisabeth took one look and promptly left the circle. She returned carrying a fire bucket and doused the brawling nurses with the icy water. They screamed and parted.

"Watch ye do that for?" Jenny said, sitting on the floor wiping the water from her eyes.

"Yeh," Flo added.

"Because you're acting like animals," Elisabeth said. She turned to Daphne. "Please get them towels."

The excitement over, the nurses began to disperse, but Elisabeth called them back. "Before you go, I'd like to talk to you." The nurses returned; some sat on the floor and others on the beds. "Have any of you heard of Miss Florence Nightingale?" No one responded. "She is a highborn lady from England, who, against her mother's strong objections, has given up her leisurely life to dedicate her days to making nursing an honorable profession. Several months ago she gave up her position as the superintendent of a women's hospital in England to go to the Crimea."

"Where's that?" Jenny asked.

"The Crimea is a place on the Black Sea where the English and French are fighting the Russians. Miss Nightingale and thirty-eight brave women are nursing the wounded and diseased British troops. In a recent newspaper article, it's reported that she and her nurses found the sick and wounded lying on dirty blankets on the floor of an old Turkish barracks. In defiance of most of the doctors and army officers, she brought about a miracle. She and her nurses, with some help from the less severely wounded, cleaned up the hospital, established a healthy diet, and set up round-the-clock care. She has demanded clean bedding, cots, bandages, and a host of other supplies from England. With Queen Victoria's support, her demands are being met. At the present moment, the newspapers report, she lies stricken with fever. When asked if she wanted to go home to England to regain her strength, she replied, 'I can stand out the war with any man.'

"I tell you all this because I want you to understand that we are on the cusp of a new age for nurses everywhere. You can anticipate these changes, and even help to bring them about, by acting like professionals—not scullery maids. Now, Jenny, why were you and Florence fighting like cats and dogs?"

Jenny and Flo hung their heads. Neither spoke. "They were fighting over a bed," Daphne said. "A bed beside that one window what actually opens. Before she left, Dacie Watson promised both of them the bed. Why don't you decide, Miss Ashcroft?"

Elisabeth thought for a moment. "How about this: Jenny, choose three of your friends. Flo, you do the same."

"Why?" Jenny asked.

"Just do it!" Daphne said.

Jenny and Flo picked their friends and Elisabeth explained her plan. "We'll have a bed race down to the end of the dormitory and back. Whoever wins gets to have the bed beneath the window. Agreed?"

"Agreed," Jenny and Flo said in enthusiastic unison.

Soon the two former combatants were sitting on their respective beds, clutching the metal back railings. Behind them, their friends, with expectant faces, clutched the same railings. Abby was at the far end of the dormitory to make sure that the beds touched the wall before reversing direction. Elisabeth stood at the start/finish line, which was made from two twisted sheets tied together and held at each end by a nurse. The other young women lined both sides of the racecourse. "Ready, steady, go!"

The nurse-powered beds hurtled down the hardwood racecourse while the spectators roared out encouragement. Abby jumped for her life as the beds reached the far wall. Quickly the pushers ran around to the rear of the beds and were off again. The roaring crowd and screeching wheels almost lifted the roof of the old building. Elisabeth stood well off to one side as the wheeled projectiles hit the twisted bed sheets at the very same moment. A hush fell over the room.

"I'm sorry," Elisabeth said, "but I must declare a tie." She turned to Abby. "Any suggestions?"

"We could move the beds so that they can both share the open window," Abby said practically.

"What a smart idea!" Elisabeth looked at Jenny and Florence to gauge their reaction. They smiled at the simplicity of the solution. One nodded shyly, and the other grinned.

It was decided. They would share the window.

CHAPTER THIRTY

The nurses were so satisfied with the outcome of the window controversy that Elisabeth and Abby became the arbitrators of the nurses' squabbles. In fact, the female junior residents were so respected by the nurses that the latter refused to let them do menial chores. The first time Elisabeth attempted to change a chamber pot Jenny was by her side. "I'll do that, Miss Ashcroft. Mrs. Trumper needs you."

Mrs. Trumper was dying. In the tertiary stage of syphilis, her nose had collapsed, and running sores covered her face. It was hard for Elisabeth to believe that Mrs. Trumper had once been a beautiful woman. Abandoned by her husband, she had turned to prostitution to support her children. She eventually contracted syphilis, a disease she had since been fighting for twenty years. Now she lay dying, abandoned by all, including her children.

"Write me a letter, Miss Ashcroft?" Mrs. Trumper pleaded.

"I'm not sure if we're . . ." Elisabeth began, and then abruptly changed her mind. "Of course, Mrs. Trumper. I'll return with pen and paper."

"Thank ye, dearie."

"Mrs. Urghart wants ye," Wendell said later to Elisabeth, who was finishing up a letter to Mrs. Trumper's youngest child.

Elisabeth looked up. "Presently, Wendell."

The old man nodded. "Don't be long, miss. She don't abide waitin'."

Elisabeth arose. "I'll make sure this is posted right away, Mrs. Trumper."

"Bless ye, dearie."

Elisabeth followed Wendell to Mrs. Urghart's throne.

The matron frowned. "What's this nonsense about letter writing?"

Elisabeth swallowed hard. "It's a service Miss Florence Nightingale has instituted among her nurses."

"Well, my girl, we don't have time for it here. There's slop buckets to be emptied and beds to be made. We'll have no prima donnas here. You'll do the work o' nurses, or you'll not work here."

Elisabeth had anticipated the matron's objection and was prepared. "As you like, Mrs. Urghart. Of course, letter writing has great advantages for you and this institution."

Mrs. Urghart was wary. "How so?"

"Most of the inmates have given up on life, and when people give up on life, they are hard to control. However, as I see it, letter writing, as a privilege, would be of great advantage to you. If inmates don't behave, you could take away that privilege."

Mrs. Urghart pondered Elisabeth's words. "You may have something there. All right, I'll permit it. But don't think this will get you out of your chores. You'll do the work o' nurses or you won't work here!"

Elisabeth nodded obediently. "Yes, Mrs. Urghart." As she returned to her duties, her heart sang. *Perhaps Abby and I can make a difference!* she exulted.

Despite the matron's manifesto, Elisabeth and Abby, when not accompanying doctors on their rounds, spent most of their time administering medicine, consoling the inconsolable, and writing letters. However, Elisabeth could not bring herself to administer the harsher medical treatments. She had never seen such suffering, the result not just of the maladies but even more so from the so-called cures. Like wanton warriors, the medical practitioners fought on the battleground of the poor patients' flesh. Bloodletting, blistering, and purging were the primary weapons in the war against disease. On her first day in the Syphilis ward, Elisabeth recalled Thomas Jefferson's words, "The lads in Philadelphia, with their calomel and arsenic, are vying with the sword of Napoleon for shedding the blood of man." Now, to Elisabeth's horror, she was forced to be a participant in the butchery. She was constantly torn between following the doctors' orders and following her own conscience.

On Saturday, Mrs. Kenny's carriage arrived at Blockley to pick up Elisabeth and Abby. Before it had come to a halt, Jerry jumped to the ground. He scooped his bride into his arms. In line with his desire to eradicate his Pike's Point dialect, he chose his words carefully. "I have missed you very much, my darling!"

Abby seemed a little embarrassed by his devotion. She glanced sheepishly at Elisabeth and then responded to her husband. "And I have missed you, Jerry. Thank you for coming with John to rescue us from this awful place."

"All right, you two," Elisabeth said. "Let's get into the carriage and away from this place. We reek like swine. I can't wait to get into a bathtub." After they were on their way, Elisabeth added, "Here's a scribbling that I got from a wall at Blockley:

'You may scrub, you may ventilate
The wards as you will,
But the stench of the almshouse
Will cling to you still.'"

"I'm surprised that anyone there was literate enough to write such graffiti," Abby said. "By the way, does graffiti have a singular—'graffitum,' maybe?"

Elisabeth smiled. "I think that the singular is 'graffito,' but I can't imagine when anyone would use it."

Jerry looked from Abby to Elisabeth and back to Abby and shook his head. "How'm I ever to learn all this stuff?"

Elisabeth sat back in the seat and closed her eyes. Although she was still a little jealous of Abby and Jerry's marriage, she nevertheless took satisfaction in knowing that she'd played a part in bringing them together. She thought back to that stormy evening on the Market Street Bridge. *It's strange how life can change so quickly from bad to good and vice versa.* Her mind turned to the inmates of Blockley House. Although she knew that some would recover, for the vast majority of them only death would bring an end to their suffering. *Why does life have to be so cruel?*

* * *

The following Monday morning, Elisabeth and Abby were called into Dr. Benedict's office. "I asked for you," the doctor said, "because a young patient in Maternity will soon be transferred to Syphilis. Her name is Amy Brown. She bore a syphilitic child recently that died shortly after birth. We didn't know Miss Brown had syphilis when she was admitted—often the first stage of the disease goes undetected, the painless chancre being . . . being internal. However, there's no doubt the child was syphilitic. It looked like a little old man—ill-developed, puny, wizened. Now Miss Brown is showing signs of the second stage of syphilis—skin rashes, lesions of mucous membranes of the mouth and throat. Also, she is suffering from aches, pains, and headaches, and her hair is falling out in patches. Unfortunately, she blames the hospital for everything, claiming she was in perfect health when her employer forcibly admitted her. We've had to strap her down to keep her from bolting."

"Can't she leave if she wants to?" Abby asked.

Dr. Benedict drew in a breath and slowly exhaled. He shook his head. "Unfortunately, she has nowhere to go. She was admitted by her employer, a Mrs. Taylor, who adamantly refuses to have anything more to do with her. A few days after the baby was born, Miss Brown stole some clothes and ran away. The night watch found her sheltering in an alley and returned her here. I've tried to convince her that once the second stage of syphilis runs its course, there's a good chance she can leave the hospital and seek out new employment. There's a lot we don't know about this disease, but for some reason many afflicted go into remission after the second stage and do not suffer tertiary disorders right away. The disease becomes latent and may not reemerge for many years."

"How can we help?' Elisabeth asked.

"I'd like you both to work with Miss Brown. Try to convince her that it's in her best interest to stay here until the second stage of the disease has run its course. We can't, of course, guarantee that she will not suffer long-term effects. Will you help?"

"Of course," Elisabeth said. Abby nodded her agreement.

The doctor was pleased. "Good. Perhaps you might visit her now and introduce yourselves."

Upon seeing the young woman, Elisabeth's heart went out to her. Despite a rash on her neck and a swelling around the mouth, she was still pretty. A scarf covered her head. "Would ye please take off these straps?" the girl asked politely.

Elisabeth and Abby exchanged glances. "Will you promise not to . . . run away?" Elisabeth asked.

"Aye," said the girl. When the straps were removed, she rubbed her wrists and sat up in bed. "Why cain't I leave?"

"Dr. Benedict says you've nowhere to go," Abby said.

"I do so! I'd go to my sweetheart, Dabney Taylor."

"And where is he?" Elisabeth asked.

Amy gave a rapid response. "Hampton Roads, Virginie. He's a sailor. If he knowed where I was, he'd be here double-quick. His evil mother's keepin' us apart."

When Elisabeth suggested that Amy tell them more about Dabney Taylor and how they met, the girl was pleased to do so. Readjusting the pillow behind her back, she made herself comfortable before beginning her tale of how she was brought up, an orphan, by Dabney's parents, and how they didn't approve of her and Dabney's love.

Finally Amy stopped talking and looked off into space. Then she said, "Dab an' me is gonna run away and wed. He don't know about the child. If'n I could only get outa here, I'd go to him."

"It's not that simple," Elisabeth said. "You have . . . you have a serious illness."

Amy's hand went to the rash on her neck. "I got it when I come here! If'n I don't get outa here, they'll kill me dead."

"How long has it been since you've seen Dab Taylor?" Abby asked.

"'Bout nine months."

"Have you written to him?" This from Elisabeth.

"Don't know where to write. Besides, I kin only write a little. If'n I can find out where to write, would ye write fer me?"

"Of course," Elisabeth said. "And Mrs. Potts and I will look into getting Dab's address. Since he's stationed at Hampton Roads, he's probably in the regular navy. Is that right?"

Amy stared blankly. "Regular navy?"

"Yes, rather than the merchant marine—don't worry, I have a friend who can find him." Abby gave Elisabeth a quizzical glance. "Colonel Kane," Elisabeth said. "If anyone can find him, he can."

Through the use of the amazing new telegraph system, Colonel Kane had Dab Taylor's address within the week, and a letter from Amy was soon on its way. The following week, Amy was transferred to Syphilis.

"Can I trust you not to run away?" Elisabeth asked as Amy was getting settled in the bed next to Mrs. Trumper's on the floor below Elisabeth and Abby's room.

"I promise."

"Good. Then we can dispense with the straps while we talk."

"But I ain't gonna take no more med'cine. It makes me puke an' foam at the mouth. Wendell says it's poison. That's why it makes teeth go black."

Elisabeth looked thoughtful. "I tend to agree with you and Wendell that calomel is not a good choice. But Dr. Benedict has prescribed it."

"I'll not take no more!"

"All right, dear. I won't make you do something I don't believe in myself. But I'll have to tell Dr. Benedict."

"Tell whoever ye like," said Amy, not unkindly. She wiped her brow with her hand. "It's stuffy in here. Cain't we open a window?"

Elisabeth sighed. "I'm afraid not. Most windows in this old building cannot be budged. In the nurses' quarters upstairs, there is only one window that opens. On the day Mrs. Potts and I moved in, two nurses fought over having their beds close to it." Amy smiled when Elisabeth told her about the bed race. "It's good to see you smile, Amy. Although mercury does darken teeth, yours are still nice and white."

"Thank ye, Miss Ashcroft—can I call ye by yer Christian name?"

Elisabeth thought back to Dr. Benedict's advice not to get too close to the patients. She hesitated before saying, "I guess it will be permissible. It's Elisabeth. But only use it in private conversation. When others are around, please call me Miss Ashcroft."

Amy nodded. "I will, Elisabeth. I like ye and Mrs. Potts. The nurses never have time to talk."

"They're overworked. That's why."

"How long will it take fer me to get a letter from Dab?"

"It's hard to tell. All we can do is wait. I must be going now. I'm sorry, but I must refasten your restraints."

"Never fear," said Amy, putting her wrists in position. "But ye can tell Dr. Benedict that I'll not run away till I get a letter from Dab." Motioning for Elisabeth to move closer, Amy nodded toward Mrs. Trumper. "What's she got?"

Elisabeth hesitated but felt it better to be honest. "Tertiary syphilis." The fear in Amy's eyes caused Elisabeth to quickly add, "But not all sufferers advance to the third stage. There's every chance that when your infection clears up, your health will return."

Amy looked at Elisabeth, then at Mrs. Trumper, and back at Elisabeth. She started to say something but fell silent.

That evening, Elisabeth happened to see Wendell on the stairway. "Oh, Wendell, may I speak with you?"

"'Course, Miss Ashcroft." His head went up and down like a small bird.

"Miss Brown tells me that you called Dr. Benedict's prescription poison. Is that true?"

"True," Wendell said, nodding even quicker.

"Although I tend to agree with you, don't you think saying such things hurts Dr. Benedict's relationship with his patients?"

"Don't know 'bout that, Miss Ashcroft," he said, his head pivoting the other way. "Do know calomel's poison! Ever heard the sayin', 'mad as a hatter'?"

The question surprised Elisabeth. "Why, yes, but I can't see—"

"Ever wonder why they's mad?"

Elisabeth shook her head. "I can't say that I have. I thought it was just a saying."

"Mercury fumes," Wendell said, looking around to make sure they were alone. "Thems that make beaver felt hats breathes 'em ev'ry day. Y'see, the beaver fur needs t'be treated with a solution o' mercury in order fer it to bond into felt. Breathin' them fumes every day goes to their brains and drives the hatters mad. Mark my words, Miss Ashcroft. Mercury's poison—pure and simple. Anything else, miss?"

Elisabeth could think of nothing else.

Later that evening, as the two of them retired, Elisabeth related to Abby her conversation with Wendell.

Abby stretched out on her bed. "Queer little man, Wendell. But I think he may be right about calomel. I wonder why the doctors insist on prescribing it?"

Elisabeth shook her head. "Who knows? I guess the medical profession won't accept anything else. Dr. Benedict says it does seem to help lessen the severity of attacks, but even he agrees that it's not a cure. If people would only live morally they would . . . oh, I'm sorry, Abby. I didn't mean . . ."

Abby smiled wanly. "Not your fault, Elisabeth. I'm the one who made the mistake. I confess I've worried about my baby. Who's to say the promiscuous Sidney Lester is not infected with something?"

Elisabeth strained to find something positive to say. "I don't think you have to worry. I'm sure he chose his victims well. He is certainly promiscuous, but he's also very clever."

"I hope you're right. I've also worried about . . ." Abby didn't finish her thought. Turning over on her side, she ended the conversation.

Elisabeth looked at her friend with compassion. She decided that she'd have to be more careful what she said around her. Jerry may have saved her from the shame of having an illegitimate child, but the memory of her folly would always be with her. True repentance resulted in Heavenly Father remembering sins no more, but unfortunately, His children continued to remember them, especially when physical reminders resulted.

These thoughts brought Amy to mind, and Elisabeth fervently hoped that Dab Taylor would do the right thing by her.

CHAPTER THIRTY-ONE

Over the next two weeks Elisabeth's heart ached for Amy, who lived for a letter from Dab Taylor. Each day the girl's hopes rose and fell. Elisabeth ran out of possible reasons for Dab not writing back. One bright spot was that Dr. Benedict had given permission for Amy's restraints to be removed on the promise that she wouldn't run away until a letter came from her sweetheart. On a Saturday morning, almost three weeks after posting the letter to Dab Taylor, Elisabeth was called to see Mrs. Urghart.

"This came for Miss Brown this morning," Mrs. Urghart said, handing Elisabeth a one-page letter, folded and sealed with wax. "I know you're in Maternity today, but you best deliver it."

Elisabeth's heart leapt the way it did when she received a letter from Gren. She hurried up the stairs to the third floor. Amy's face lit up when she saw the letter in Elisabeth's hand. Tears coursed down Amy's cheeks as the letter exchanged hands. "I'll leave you to read it alone," Elisabeth said. "I'm working downstairs today."

Elisabeth could hardly wait to hear the news, but it was late in the afternoon before she could get upstairs again. She found Amy glumly staring at the ceiling. Dab Taylor's letter lay beside her on the bed.

"Well? What does Dab say?"

Amy looked at Elisabeth without emotion. "He's comin' to see me on his next leave."

"I would think that is good news, but . . . but you don't seem very happy."

Amy sighed. "He don't say when he's coming."

"Were you able to read it all right? You said before that you only read a little. Would you like me—"

A frown crossed Amy's face and she snatched up the letter. "No. I understood it all." Her face softened. "Would ye do me a favor, Elisabeth?"

"If I can."

"I know I promised to put those straps back on when I got Dab's letter, but they chafe me something fierce. Can I keep them off fer good?"

Elisabeth thought for a moment, and then she nodded. "I'll have to clear it with Dr. Benedict, but in the meantime we'll leave them off."

Elisabeth asked if there was anything else she could do for her.

Amy slowly shook her head. "No, nothin' at all. I 'preciate all ye and Mrs. Potts've done fer me. Please don't be sad fer me. I'll sleep now."

Elisabeth stared down at her patient, perplexed by the haunted look in the girl's eyes. "All right, dear. Mrs. Potts and I will be going home for the weekend. I'll see you on Monday morning."

Amy closed her eyes and didn't answer.

At that moment Daphne Miller hurried toward Elisabeth. "Dr. Sharp wants to see you," the nurse said, alarm in her voice. "He's with Penny Quigley in Maternity." As Elisabeth and Daphne walked away from Amy's bed, Daphne whispered, "Dr. Sharp's one of the juniors what hates women doctors."

"Thanks, Daphne. Would you keep an eye on Amy Brown over the weekend? I'm worried about her."

Daphne looked back at Amy. "Of course, Miss Ashcroft."

Dr. Sharp glared at Elisabeth when she arrived at the foot of Penny Quigley's bed. "Quigley's chart says she's to have leeches on her temples. Why wasn't this done?"

"Miss Quigley refused treatment," Elisabeth said evenly.

"Refused treatment? Inmates don't have that right. You should know that by now, Ashcroft. Miller, bring a jar of leeches. Now!"

Daphne soon returned with the leeches. Dr. Sharp grabbed the jar out of her hands and plunked it down on a table in front of Elisabeth, who folded her arms and glowered at Sharp. "Just as I thought," Sharp crowed, "afraid to touch them. You are, aren't you? Another proof that women have no place in the medical profession. Go change some beds or empty some buckets—that's all you're good for."

Elisabeth fixed him with narrowed eyes. "How dare you talk to me that way? And how dare you belittle women doctors?"

Removing the lid of the leech jar, Elisabeth thrust in her hand, withdrew a handful of the slimy creatures, and flung them at Sharp. A collective gasp issued from Daphne, Penny Quigley, and the surrounding patients. Elisabeth turned on her heel and marched off.

"You hit him in the face with leeches!" Abby said, squealing with delight, as they rode home in the carriage. "I wish I'd been there."

"I did. I guess my career at Blockley is over. I'm actually glad you weren't there. Your time at Blockley is important to your becoming a doctress. As for me, my main concern is Amy Brown. I wish there were something else we could do for her. I know the letter contained bad news, but she wouldn't let me read it. I'm going to ask Mrs. Kenny if we can remove her to the mansion."

Abby didn't respond for a few moments. Then she said, "No doubt Dab Taylor abandoned her. We're so fortunate to have Jerry and Gren."

Elisabeth agreed, but she wondered if she would ever really have Gren. She wondered how many months or years would pass in this limbo before they could really be together.

The events of Elisabeth's day were quickly swept aside upon her finding a letter from Gren on the foyer table. Snatching it up, she dashed up to her room, broke the seal, and read:

Dear Sister Ashcroft,

> *We did it! The first issue of "The Mormon" came out today. Elder Taylor hired a bunch of newsboys to circulate it. There was almost a riot so many people wanted a copy. It would be nice to think that these people were interested in the Church. But Bro. T says that it's only curiosity. Anyway it feels good to have accomplished our goal. Emigration from Europe this year will be large. Bro. T is making preparations. Word has been sent to abandon the old route through New Orleans. As I'm sure you know, over 7,000 people died of yellow fever there two summers ago. The*

immigrants will be coming to Boston and New York instead—
maybe even Philadelphia. That's what I was meeting with
Colonel Kane about. Elder T could have got the information by
post but he knew how much I wanted to see you. Preparing and
looking after the immigrants will keep us busy this season. I am
tolerable well. Becky and family are well also. But you probably
know that. I live for the day we will be together again and in the
valleys of the mountains.

Yours ever,
Gren

With Gren's letter still in her hand, Elisabeth lay on her bed, closed her eyes, and tried to think of the good times. His letters usually brought her joy, but now she could not shake the image of Amy Brown floundering in a sea of sickness, the world's cares reflected in her young eyes.

All day Sunday Elisabeth worried about Amy. She thought about visiting her, but John had taken Mrs. Kenny to church and then to call on neighbors. On Monday morning, Elisabeth arrived early at Blockley and rushed up to the third floor. An empty bed confirmed her worst fear. She stared at the bed, willing Amy to appear. Mrs. Trumper was asleep or she would have asked her about Amy.

"Miss Ashcroft," said a voice from behind her.

Elisabeth turned. "Yes, Daphne?"

The nurse wasn't her usual ebullient self. "Dr. Benedict wanted to see you and Mrs. Potts as soon as you gets in."

"Where is Amy Brown?" Elisabeth asked, although she thought she already knew the answer.

Daphne lowered her eyes. "You best see Dr. Benedict." She quickly hurried away.

Elisabeth found Abby on the stairs.

"How is she?" Abby asked.

"She's not there," Elisabeth said, her heart sick with worry. "I think she's run off again. Dr. Benedict wants to see us."

The two women went down the three flights of stairs in silence. Dr. Benedict rose to greet them when they entered his office. "Ah, ladies, come in. Please be seated. I'm afraid I have some bad news. I'm not sure how to say this, so I'll just be out with it; Saturday night, Miss Brown slipped out of her restraints, climbed to the nurses' dormitory, and . . . jumped out of a window to . . . to her death. This note was clutched in her hand. I am sorry. I know you ladies worked with her."

Elisabeth felt her body grow cold and the blood drain from her face. Her last meeting with Amy flashed before her eyes. Elisabeth had made the decision not to fasten the straps. Also, it was Elisabeth who had told Amy about the open window in the dormitory.

Dr. Benedict held out the note to Elisabeth, but she could only stare at it. Abby took the note instead. When Elisabeth still didn't respond, Abby asked, "Would you like me to read it, Elisabeth?" Elisabeth slowly nodded, and Abby read Dab Taylor's note:

Amy

Im sorry your in hospitil. And you got the clap from me. If Id knowed I swear I wouldn't of got you with child. Ma told me about it. Jest as well it died. She made me promis never to see you agin. Im sorry.

Dab

Silence hung in the room. Suddenly, Elisabeth was on her feet. Clutching her mouth, she dashed from the room and fell to her knees over a slop bucket. Abby, who had followed her, knelt beside her. Gently wiping Elisabeth's face with her handkerchief, Abby helped her friend to stand. Dr. Benedict assisted in getting Elisabeth back to his office and seated.

"It's all my fault," Elisabeth finally whispered. "She didn't slip out of her restraints. I didn't fasten them. I'm the one who told her about the open window. I should have known by her demeanor that she was suicidal. I failed her in every way."

The doctor shook his head. "Don't blame yourself, Miss Ashcroft. Miss Brown knew what she was doing. You had no way of knowing her mind. She must have fastened her empty straps to protect you. I do not blame you in any way." He turned to Abby. "Please see that Miss Ashcroft gets home for a few days. I'll inform Mrs. Urghart."

Abby helped Elisabeth get up. As they exited the room, Elisabeth's legs crumpled beneath her. Despite Abby's supporting arm, Elisabeth slumped to the floor, hitting her head on the doorjamb before it all went dark.

CHAPTER THIRTY-TWO

When she regained consciousness, Elisabeth was in her own bed. Abby, Mrs. Kenny, and Rose hovered over her. "Thank goodness you're awake," Mrs. Kenny said. "Dr. Benedict wanted to keep you in the hospital, but Abby insisted that they bring you home. John's gone for Dr. Longshore."

Elisabeth's fingers went to the bump on her forehead. "How long have I been unconscious?"

"Quite awhile," Abby said. "How do you feel?"

Elisabeth smiled wanly. "Weak. I don't know what happened to me. I'm not usually the fainting type. The last time I fainted . . . it was a long time ago."

"You had quite a shock," Abby said. "I know how much you liked Amy. I did too. You must know that you have no responsibility in her death. The poor girl was distraught over her abandonment."

Elisabeth looked from Abby to Mrs. Kenny, who had suddenly grown pale. "You're as white as a sheet, Mary. Abby, please help Mrs. Kenny to her room to lie down."

Mrs. Kenny nodded. "I am ailing, right enough. Now that you're on the mend, I think I will have a lie-down. Rose, see to the front door, please."

A few minutes later, Rose showed Dr. Longshore into Elisabeth's room. "Good morning, Miss Ashcroft," Dr. Longshore said. "John filled me in on the happenings at Blockley. A tragedy. No wonder thee is distraught. Let me have a look at thee." He finished by examining her forehead. "A nasty bump, but not too serious. Thee will be up in no time."

"Thank you, Dr. Longshore. Please see to Mrs. Kenny. She's taken to her bed."

He nodded. "I will." He began to leave the room but stopped at the door. "Oh, by the way, Miss Ashcroft, being a Quaker and a man of peace, I cannot countenance thy behavior toward Dr. Sharp last week." Elisabeth looked up at him, embarrassed that he should have heard of the leech incident. With his eyes crinkling at the corners, he added, "But if anyone deserved it, he did!"

Elisabeth smiled sheepishly. "Thank you for your kindness, Dr. Longshore. However, you are quite right. My behavior merits censure."

After Dr. Longshore had gone, Abby sat on the edge of Elisabeth's bed. "I'm not going back to Blockley until you're completely well. Consider me your full-time nurse."

"Dr. Longshore said I'll be up soon, but I'm not so sure. I think I may have caught something at Blockley. And I'm worried about Mrs. Kenny. I've never seen her so poorly. I think you have two patients now."

"It will be my pleasure to look after you. I owe you both so much."

That night Elisabeth lay awake, going over and over in her mind what she could have done to prevent Amy's death. She was reminded of her father's death, and the old recriminations came back to assault her doubly. As the night wore on and sleep failed to rescue her, she sank deeper into depression, almost convincing herself that she had caught a disease and could end up like Amy or Mrs. Trumper.

By morning she felt drained of strength and confidence. Nevertheless, she determined to get up. She swung her legs over the side of the bed. As she began to stand up, a wave of nausea swept over her. She dropped to her knees and managed to get the chamber pot from under the bed just as she threw up. For a long time she remained in a kneeling position, leaning on the bed for support.

"Elisabeth!" Abby said. "What are you doing out of bed?"

Elisabeth smiled weakly. "Trying to figure out how to get back into bed."

Abby shook her head. "I'll have John find a bell for you. Next time you decide to get up, ring for me."

"Yes, Nurse Potts."

"Doctress-in-training to you, my girl."

Elisabeth leaned back on the pillows. "How's your other patient?"

"I'm worried about her. There's a gray cast to her skin, and she has no energy. Dr. Longshore sent a note to say that he had to go out of town. He's asked Dr. Preston to take a look at both of you. In the meantime, patient, I want you to stay in bed until further notice. Rose will be along with some breakfast."

"Thanks, Abby. But I couldn't eat a thing. Tell Mrs. Kenny I love her."

Next morning Elisabeth felt a little better—even hungry. Abby asked her if she would like breakfast. "Yes, please. I'll have the pan, as Mrs. Kenny would say—bacon and eggs, but hold the fried bread."

"You must be feeling better. Mrs. Kenny also looks like she's on the mend. I'll give Rose your order immediately."

"Here you is, Miss 'Lis'bet," Rose said a short time later. "Eggs 'n' bacon, jest wha' the docta order."

"Thank you, Rose."

"Yo' is welcome. I'll tidy up whilst yo' eat."

"Rose, the chamber pot!" Elisabeth clamped a napkin to her mouth.

* * *

"What happened?" Abby asked later.

"When my fork broke into the egg yolk, I got nauseated. Last night I worried that I may have caught some disease at Blockley. Now I'm sure of it. Something's awfully wrong with me—"

"Miss Abby, Miss 'Lis'bet'," cried Rose from Mrs. Kenny's room, "da missus, her need yo' he'p!"

Abby dashed to Mrs. Kenny's room. Elisabeth slowly eased out of bed and managed to stand on unsteady feet. By the time she got to Mrs. Kenny's room, Abby and Rose had gotten the old woman onto her bed. Rose then guided Elisabeth over to sit by Mrs. Kenny.

"She fell out of bed," Abby said. "She appears to have had apoplexy."

Shortly thereafter, Dr. Preston arrived. She confirmed that Mrs. Kenny indeed had had a stroke. After examining Mrs. Kenny, Dr. Preston visited Elisabeth. "I'm afraid it's serious. Considering her age,

I don't think that there's much hope. At the risk of sounding indelicate, do you know if she has a will?"

"I believe so," said Elisabeth, weakly. "Her lawyer is Mr. Dawes over in Independence Hall. His office is next to Colonel Kane's."

Dr. Preston nodded. "You don't look very well yourself. I understand you got that bump at Blockley."

"I did. I'm sick in more ways than one. I feel drained, and I get nauseated. Amy Brown's death haunts my nights. And now Mrs. Kenny . . ." Elisabeth said, distraught. "And I think I may have gotten a disease at Blockley."

"I very much doubt that you caught something from Blockley. Dr. Longshore and I have discussed your case, and we both agree that you are not seriously ill. But grief is a kind of sickness. It can lead to despair and even death. You have no blame in Miss Brown's death. Believe that and get well. When I return tomorrow, I'll give you a thorough examination."

Elisabeth followed Abby's instructions and stayed in bed all day. After supper, Abby and Jerry came to visit. Abby suggested that Gren be summoned, but Elisabeth refused. "No need worrying him," she had said. Their presence had cheered Elisabeth, but when they were gone, she again fell into despondency. She mourned Amy's death, worried about Mrs. Kenny, and missed Gren more than she could stand. The fear that she had been responsible for her father's death also returned to haunt her.

Despite Dr. Preston's assurance, Elisabeth couldn't shake the persistent thought that she'd picked up a disease at Blockley. *What if I've contracted syphilis or typhus or one of a myriad of diseases floating around that death house? Dr. Blackwell lost an eye from treating a syphilitic infant. There's no reason a bump on the head should make me so nauseated. I must have a disease.*

Elisabeth's mood darkened as the room grew dim. Self-pity caused the tears to flow, and she convinced herself that disease truly had invaded her body. Having slept so much throughout the day, she could not fall asleep now. Her mind teemed with dark thoughts and her tears would not abate.

At last she remembered another awful night, the one she had spent alone in the Nilsson cabin, convinced that everyone, even God, had abandoned her. Hope had eventually returned through fervent prayer and, without getting out of bed, she again sought relief in this way. Afterward she recalled Brother Nilsson's blessing that she would someday bear children. This buoyed her sagging spirits for a few moments. But then a frightful thought seized her: *What if I do have syphilis? What if my hair falls out and my face becomes hideous with sores? Could Gren love me?* The thought was too horrible for her to contemplate. Slipping out of bed, she fell to her knees and poured out her fears and desires to her Father in Heaven. So weak that she could hardly keep her body straight, she leaned against the bed, drained of physical strength. Her knees began to ache, but she didn't care. All she wanted was relief from these irrational fears. Gradually, her fears did abate, replaced by a calm strength and an assurance that there was nothing wrong with her that rest wouldn't cure. Marveling at the power of prayer, she climbed back into bed, and at last sleep claimed her.

A warm hand in hers awakened her. Her eyes blinked open to a sun-filled room. Gren was sitting beside the bed holding her hand, and Abby was standing behind him with a breakfast tray. "Gren!" Elisabeth said, wanting to throw her arms around him. "Oh, Gren." He leaned forward and pushed a blonde wisp from her eyes. Her hand went to her hair. "I must look a sight, my hair all frowsy and my face—"

Gren shook his head. "You look fine. I'm glad John telegraphed me. President Taylor sends his best and wishes you well."

Abby placed the tray on the bedside table. "I'll leave you two alone. I'm sure you have a lot to talk about."

"Thanks, Abby," Elisabeth said, and then turned back and gazed into Gren's smiling face. "Abby and Rose have been babying me. I asked that you not be bothered, but I'm glad they ignored me. It's so good to see you again. How did the telegraph people possibly find you in such a huge city?"

"John was smart enough to send it to *The Mormon* office. There's few people in New York who don't know where the Mormons are publishing their paper."

"I can't believe you're really here," Elisabeth said, and then in a subdued voice, "Have you heard about Mrs. Kenny?"

"Yes. And also about Amy Brown. Abby and John told me. It never rains but it pours. I looked in on you earlier and decided not to awaken you. Abby's bringing you breakfast gave me the excuse."

Elisabeth could feel the warmth coming into her cheeks, almost as if his presence caused health to flow into her body. She smiled. "You should never need an excuse to see me."

Gren nodded. "Speaking of breakfast, you'd better eat it before it gets cold. It's your favorite, porridge with brown sugar and cream."

She sat up in bed as he positioned the legged tray over her. "I don't really think I can eat anything, but I'll try."

He poured the cream and sugar for her and she took a few tentative bites.

"How long can you stay?" she asked.

"A few days. Elder Taylor asked me to meet with Colonel Kane again about European immigrants arriving here, so I guess you could say I'm also here on mission business."

After a few minutes she stopped eating and sighed. "I'm afraid that's the best I can do. Please thank Abby and Rose for breakfast and John for bringing you to me."

In the late afternoon, Elisabeth felt well enough to dress and go downstairs. She found Gren in the small parlor talking with Abby and Rose.

"Are you sure you should be up?" Abby asked.

Elisabeth smiled and nodded. "For a little while. Gren's presence is my most potent physic. I looked in on Mrs. Kenny before coming down. She's sleeping peacefully."

Later, Elisabeth and Gren visited Mrs. Kenny. Elisabeth had never seen her oldest friend so ill. The stroke had impeded her speech, and Elisabeth strained to understand her. At one point Mrs. Kenny mumbled something. Elisabeth leaned closer. Mrs. Kenny touched Elisabeth's eye and whispered, "Tears."

Elisabeth nodded and smiled wistfully. "Yes, Mary, I've been shedding many tears of late."

The old lady said something else. When it was obvious that neither Elisabeth nor Gren could understand her, Mrs. Kenny pointed to a pencil and paper on the nightstand. She scribbled something on the paper and handed it to Elisabeth, who glanced at it, smiled, and nodded. Mrs. Kenny mouthed the words "I love you." She then closed her eyes, and Elisabeth leaned over and kissed a wrinkled cheek.

"What does the note say?" asked Gren when he and Elisabeth were alone.

Elisabeth handed him the note. "All I can make out are a three, a zero, and a five. Perhaps you can decipher it."

Gren tried reading the spidery scrawl from every angle before shrugging his shoulders. "Except for the numbers, I can't make it out at all."

Elisabeth took the note and placed it in her Bible until she could study it further.

The next morning, Elisabeth woke before dawn. She got out of bed, donned her slippers and robe, and quietly made her way to Mrs. Kenny's room. The gaslight had been turned down, but it gave enough light for her to make her way to the old woman's bedside. The room was completely silent, and Elisabeth knew that her friend had passed beyond the veil. Kneeling by the bed, she took the old woman's cold, gnarled hand in hers and wept.

CHAPTER THIRTY-THREE

Later that day, John drove to Independence Hall to inform Mrs. Kenny's lawyer, Nathaniel Dawes, that his client had died. Mr. Dawes asked if he could have a meeting with Elisabeth, Gren, John, and Rose. Colonel Kane learned the sad news from Mr. Dawes and dropped over to pay his respects. Before leaving, he promised to inform Doctors Longshore and Preston.

Elisabeth didn't want to meet with the lawyer. She needed time to mourn her friend. However, the lawyer insisted that the meeting was necessary, as it had to do with Mrs. Kenny's burial arrangements. Elisabeth consented.

"I've called you together," Mr. Dawes said that evening, "because in her will Mrs. Kenny made an unusual request regarding her burial. She has asked for Mr. Sanderson to officiate at a brief graveside service."

Gren's face was full of surprise as he turned to Elisabeth. She smiled and squeezed his arm. Gren turned back and nodded to the lawyer, who continued, "I'm afraid this request has created a problem. Since Mrs. Kenny is a member of the Presbyterian Church, I took the liberty of visiting the minister on my way over here. He was very sympathetic—Mrs. Kenny has been generous to the church over the years. However, policy will not permit him to allow Mr. Sanderson to conduct the service if it is a Presbyterian one. Only an ordained minister can do so. Have you any suggestions?"

Elisabeth looked thoughtful and then nodded. "I think the Quakers might not have such strict rules. I'll ask Dr. Longshore. Perhaps we can have a Quaker service instead. Also, I would like Miss

Amy Brown, who died recently at Blockley, to be buried in a regular churchyard—not in potter's field. Perhaps we could have a joint service." She turned to John. "When this meeting is over, would you please go to Blockley and claim Miss Brown's body?"

John nodded his agreement.

"Good," Mr. Dawes said, looking at John. "Mrs. Kenny arranged for the undertakers Duffy and Gadsby to look after things. You can have them prepare Miss Brown's body as well." He turned to Elisabeth. "Please let me know what arrangements you can make about a burial site, Miss Ashcroft. Now, back to the will. Except for cash bequests to Rose and John, who has also inherited the carriage and horses, the entire estate goes to you, Miss Ashcroft. You have suddenly become a wealthy woman." The lawyer waited for Elisabeth's response.

She looked at him blankly. She might have expected this, knowing that Mrs. Kenny had no children or close family, but she hadn't yet fully accepted that her friend was dead and had difficulty comprehending that she had just inherited a fortune. She looked at Gren, and he gave her an encouraging nod. She then managed to say, "I shall endeavor to carry out my stewardship honorably, Mr. Dawes."

"I'm sure you will, Miss Ashcroft. I'm sure that Mrs. Kenny had great faith in you."

Before the attorney left, Elisabeth arranged with him to send a draft of one hundred pounds to Maggie Stowell in England. An accompanying note explained that Maggie could use the money for passage to America or for her dowry if she decided not to emigrate.

Not long after the lawyer's departure, Doctors Longshore and Preston arrived. Dr. Preston waited while Elisabeth spoke with Dr. Longshore, which took only a few minutes. When Elisabeth explained what was needed, he promised to look into finding a burial site for Mrs. Kenny and Amy Brown.

After he left, Dr. Preston listened to Elisabeth's lungs, checked her pulse, and carefully examined her eyes and throat. "Well, Miss Ashcroft, as Dr. Longshore and I supposed, you are not seriously ill, and I'm glad to see that you are in much better spirits today. Now I must be going. My condolences, again, regarding Mrs. Kenny."

Abby and Rose came into Elisabeth's room. "Well?" Abby asked. "What's the prognosis?"

Elisabeth smiled. "I'll live."

Abby smiled. "I had no doubt about it."

Rose nodded and her brow creased. "I wonda who de t'ird person be?"

"Third person?" Elisabeth asked.

Roses nodded again. "First, Miss Amy Brown, den deh missus. Death allus come in t'rees!"

On this somber note, Elisabeth excused herself to find Gren. She found him in the small parlor reading. He laid aside his book and smiled at her. After telling him about Dr. Preston's prognosis, she said, "I'm so glad you're here. And I'm glad Mrs. Kenny asked you to look after the service. Colonel Kane will no doubt attend the service, so you can arrange a meeting with him then."

Up to this time, Elisabeth had soldiered on, but now she broke down in uncontrollable sobs. Gren went to her and embraced her tenderly. For a long time she took comfort in the safe harbor of his arms. When the spell was over, she dabbed her tears with his handkerchief. "I'm so thankful you came here when you did. I couldn't have endured without you. Mrs. Kenny was the last link with my childhood. I already miss her more than I can say."

When Dr. Longshore returned to the mansion the next day, he was ushered into the drawing room. He complimented Elisabeth on her appearance. "Thee is looking well, Miss Ashcroft."

"Thank you, Dr. Longshore. I think my friend Mr. Sanderson had a lot to do with that. Oh, I don't think you've met."

Elisabeth introduced the two men, and the three of them sat down. The doctor reported that he had been successful in arranging for a burial site. It was at Longwood, south and west of Philadelphia, at the homestead of John and Hannah Cox. Until recently, the couple had belonged to the same Quaker congregation as Dr. Longshore. But the congregation had split over the Fugitive Slave Law, passed by Congress five years earlier.

"Even though we have different opinions on the best way to bring about abolition," Dr. Longshore said, "the Coxes are still my friends. They have not only consented to let you bury Mrs. Kenny and Miss

Brown at Longwood, but they have, on your behalf, engaged a man at a reasonable fee to dig the graves."

After Elisabeth had thanked him, Gren asked, "Is there anything I should know about how to conduct a funeral in a Quaker burial ground, Dr. Longshore? I wouldn't want to offend."

The doctor shook his head. "Not really. Quaker burials are very simple. Like our worship services, there is no set agenda. All are silent until the Holy Spirit moves one to speak. Thus it would be appropriate for thee and Miss Ashcroft to speak if you are moved to do so. The meeting ends when someone shakes hands with another. Since thee is nominally in charge, Friend Sanderson, thee can signal the end of the meeting by doing so."

The next day dawned cool and overcast, an apt setting for the burial service. At Longwood, a dozen people, including the Coxes, surrounded the open graves of Mrs. Kenny and Amy Brown. Gren said a few words about the surety of the resurrection and closed in the name of Jesus Christ. Elisabeth spoke of her love for Mrs. Kenny and her brief friendship with Amy Brown. For a long time silence reigned. Gren was about to shake hands with Dr. Longshore and signal the end of the ceremony when the doctor stepped forward and recited:

> "'And this is the comfort of the good,
> that the grave cannot hold them,
> and that they live as soon as they die.
> For death is no more than a turning of us over from time to eternity.
> Death, then, being the way and condition of life,
> we cannot love to live,
> if we cannot bear to die.
> They that love beyond the world cannot be separated by it.
> Death cannot kill what never dies.
> Nor can spirits ever be divided that love
> and live in the same divine principle,
> the root and record of their friendship.
> If absence be not death, neither is theirs.
> Death is but crossing the world, as friends do the seas . . .'"

Tears overflowed Elisabeth's eyes as she related these poetic words to her parents, Mrs. Kenny, Amy Brown, and all who had touched her life and had passed beyond the veil.

After another few minutes of silence, Gren was once more about to shake hands with Dr. Longshore when Rose, who had been quietly keening beside Elisabeth, suddenly shrieked, almost scaring Elisabeth to death. Flinging herself from the circle of mourners, Rose made for a man leaning on a shovel in the shadow of the meetinghouse. Instinctively, the man raised the shovel to defend himself. Then his face lit with recognition. Throwing aside the shovel, he fell into Rose's outstretched arms.

Fresh tears leapt into Elisabeth's eyes when she realized what had happened—Rose had found her Thomas! In death Mrs. Kenny had brought about the reunion that she had worked for in life.

Gren quickly shook Dr. Longshore's hand, ending the service. Without a word, Mrs. Cox ran toward the farmhouse, while her husband quickly piloted Rose and Thomas inside the meetinghouse, beckoning Elisabeth and Gren to follow.

The pleasant smell of newly worked wood permeated the building. Elisabeth approached Mr. Cox. "Is Freddie . . . ?" she started to ask, but afraid of what the response might be.

Mr. Cox beamed. "He's here. He and Thomas were on their way to Canada. God has intervened to unite them with wife and mother."

The meetinghouse door opened and a smiling Mrs. Cox led a ten-year-old boy into the room. Rose ran to her son. "Freddie, oh, my litta Freddie, how yo' growed!" She wrapped him in her arms. Thomas joined them. Elisabeth, Gren, and the Coxes looked on with bright faces, then turned to go. Rose looked up and said, "Doan go, please!" Tears streaming down her ebony cheeks, she introduced her husband and son to Elisabeth and Gren.

After the initial emotion of reunion had subsided, Elisabeth asked Thomas how he had been able to escape and rescue his son.

Thomas wiped his eyes on his sleeve before answering. "Wunst I larn he in Virginie, I pray aplenty. But prayin' w'out work hain't no good, so I plans fer muns my 'scape. Got sum he'p frum Missus Tubman's frens—"

"Harriet Tubman," interjected Mr. Cox in answer to Elisabeth's unspoken question. "She's known as 'Moses' among her people because she's helped so many of them escape on the Underground Railroad."

Thomas nodded and continued, "I hoofed it no'th, en when I got to whah Freddie wuz, I stole 'im by night 'n' brung 'im heah cuz I heered Rose might cud be in Philadelphy. I's done broke d'law, but we's all t'getter agin!"

"Will you stay in Philadelphia now that you're reunited?" Gren asked.

Thomas looked to Mr. Cox for guidance. "We'd love for thee to stay, Friend Thomas, but there's a price on thy head. If runaway hunters caught thee and Freddie, we'd all be incarcerated. No, I'm afraid the best thing for thee and thy family is to continue on to Canada as quickly as possible."

"In that case," Elisabeth said, "you can come home with us now, Rose, and pack. I'll arrange for Mr. Dawes to get you some traveling money from your inheritance. John can return you here tomorrow."

"Splendid," Mr. Cox said. "In the meantime, I'll arrange for three passengers on the Underground Railroad."

Later, some of those who had attended the burial service, including Dr. and Mrs. Longshore, Dr. Preston, Colonel and Mrs. Kane, and Miss Morris, made the trip back to Philadelphia. While Rose was packing, Elisabeth and Abby served light refreshments at the mansion.

"Oh, Miss Ashcroft," Miss Morris said as she and the Longshores were getting ready to leave, "a parcel came to the college for you. It's in the carriage. I'll get it."

"Thank you for all your help, Dr. Longshore," Elisabeth said as they waited for Miss Morris to return. "It was a lovely service, and that passage you recited was most appropriate."

"Thee is most welcome, Miss Ashcroft. It was the least I could do for Mrs. Kenny. She was a generous patron of the college and we held her in great esteem. The lines I quoted are those of William Penn. They are often recited at Friends' burials."

* * *

The next morning Elisabeth and Abby accompanied Rose to the waiting carriage. She had few belongings, which was just as well, as she and her family would have to travel light on their long journey to Canada, or "Canaan Land," as it was known among those escaping slavery. John loaded Rose's things into the carriage.

"We'll miss you so much, Rose," Elisabeth said. "To lose you and Mrs. Kenny is a double blow." Abby nodded her agreement.

"Yass'm," Rose said, fighting back tears. "I's gonna miss yo' all 'n' de missus sumthin' fierce."

Elisabeth handed Rose a drawstring purse of chamois leather. "Here's the traveling money from your inheritance. As soon as you get settled in Canada, send me a telegraph message, and I'll arrange for the rest of it to get to you. Also, here's payment for Thomas digging the graves. I'm afraid it was forgotten in the excitement of yesterday—"

Rose shook her head violently. "Oh, no, Miss 'Lis'bet', us cud neva take money fer doin' the missus a curtusy. Neva!"

"I understand," Elisabeth said, embracing the woman she had grown to love. "We'll miss you very much, but we're so happy that you are reunited with your family."

Abby also embraced Rose, and the latter got into the carriage. Elisabeth and Abby waved good-bye as the carriage moved off, conveying their friend to her family and ultimately to freedom.

When the carriage was out of sight, Elisabeth turned and looked up at the mansion. "Whatever am I to do with this big house? It will seem so empty without Mrs. Kenny and Rose. Which reminds me, Abby, do you think Jerry would mind if you stayed here with me and Gren bunked with him in the cottage until Gren leaves for New York?

Abby agreed to move into the mansion but she had no suggestion as to what Elisabeth should do with it.

Elisabeth awoke next morning to a knock on her bedroom door. "Come."

Abby opened the door and looked in. "Breakfast is ready, sleepy head."

Elisabeth yawned. "You didn't have to make it by yourself. I could have helped."

Abby grinned. "Well, I know how you wealthy people like to be pampered." Elisabeth threw a pillow at her.

Downstairs, Elisabeth found Gren, Jerry, and John around the breakfast table and Abby serving them. As Elisabeth took her place at the table, John was telling his plans of starting a carriage-for-hire business with the carriage and horses he had inherited. "Of course, I won't start it until you no longer need my services, Miss Elisabeth. Now, if you'll excuse me, I must go feed the horses."

Abby placed two griddlecakes on Elisabeth's plate. "Have you decided what to do with the house?"

Elisabeth nodded. "I'll keep it until after we graduate, and then I think I'll donate it to the college in Mrs. Kenny's name. What do you think of that?" They all agreed that it was a wonderful gesture and that Mrs. Kenny would have approved. Elisabeth turned to Gren. "Did I tell you that Dr. Longshore's invited me to return to school as a graduate rather than a listener?"

Gren smiled. "Congratulations. That's great that you and Abby will be able to graduate together. I'll move heaven and earth to be there. Of course, you ladies might not want to associate with Jerry and me once you become doctresses."

Abby smiled at her husband. "Oh, I think I'll keep Jerry around. He's the one who keeps my feet on the ground." Jerry smiled but didn't speak.

"Speaking of graduations," Elisabeth said, "we should have one for you, Jerry. I'm amazed at the progress you've made. When you go back to Pike's Point and speak to Miss Waldie, she'll be amazed too. Which brings me to something I was thinking about last night in bed. Your 'sentence' at Blockley will soon be up, Abby. Although I'd miss you terribly, how would you two like to go back home until you give birth? The baby should be old enough to travel by the time classes resume in the fall."

Abby and Jerry looked at each other and then at Elisabeth. Jerry spoke first. "With Mrs. Kenny and Rose gone, we'd feel we was . . . were deserting you, Elisabeth. It would not be right."

"I appreciate that, Jerry, but Miss Waldie needs you more than I. You've done such a wonderful job with the grounds and painting and all, this place can do without you for a while. On the other hand, Miss Waldie's house and grounds are in dire need of your services. Working your magic on the Waldie house would certainly dispel any latent dislike Miss Waldie might have for you. But that's not the main reason I'm suggesting it. I was touched when Miss Waldie asked when you would be coming home, Abby. She misses you so much. Also, it would be nice for you to have the baby with both of your families near."

Abby wiped a tear from her eye. "Oh, Elisabeth, what did we ever do to deserve your friendship? Only yesterday Jerry and I talked about going home for a visit, but we didn't want to desert you. Are you sure you'll be all right all alone in this big place?"

Elisabeth nodded. "Of course I will. I have a library full of good books to peruse and a city to explore. What more could I ask for?" Her glance fell on Gren, who gave her an impish grin. "Well, there is more I could ask for, but all in the Lord's own time."

Later, Gren entered the drawing room to find Elisabeth sitting on a couch lost in thought. "All packed," he said. "Soon I must leave you again."

Elisabeth looked up and sighed. "Please sit with me for a few minutes."

The two sat quietly, enjoying each other's company while they could, and in the silence Elisabeth suddenly remembered the package Miss Morris had given her. "I set it aside when I was saying good-bye to the Longshores. I think it's on the hall table."

Gren retrieved the package and handed it to her.

She read the return address. "It's from a lawyer's office in Boston. I can't imagine what it could be."

"Only one way of finding out." Gren removed a clasp knife from his pocket and cut through the string, then Elisabeth unwrapped the brown paper.

"Why, it's a doctor's bag! And there's a note." As she read the note, her face fell and she sighed. Already emotional from losing Mrs. Kenny, Amy, and her father, she handed Gren the note and again used his handkerchief to stem her tears. "That's the third," she said between sniffs. Gren's quizzical look prompted her to explain. "Rose said that death comes in threes, and consumption has finally claimed Dr. Osgood." Moments passed in which she only cried and Gren simply did his best to comfort her. "I thought I'd used up all my tears," she said when she'd regained her composure. Mechanically, she opened the black bag and began removing its contents, placing them on the table in front of the couch. As she took the forceps in her hand, her thoughts went back to the birth of Elisabeth Rebecca. "I'm glad I learned how to use these. I know they'll be of great use back home. In fact, all of these items will be useful."

Gren silently watched her. After a while he glanced at his watch again and sighed. "As much as I hate to go, I must. Are you sure you won't come to the train station?"

Elisabeth shook her head. "I'm sure. I couldn't stand another train-station parting." She removed a small pair of scissors from the bag and looked at them for a moment before turning to Gren. "May I have a lock of your hair?"

Gren smiled. "Cut away, Delilah."

Elisabeth did so and then cut a small lock of her own hair and gave it to him. After he had gone, she went upstairs and sat on her bed. Picking up the tintype portrait of her and Gren, she gazed at it for a long time, then put the lock of Gren's hair to her lips and bid his portrait farewell.

CHAPTER THIRTY-FOUR

That evening Elisabeth was in the library writing a letter to Becky when Abby came in. "I'm going to the cottage now. Is there anything I can do before I go?"

Elisabeth looked up and smiled. "No. Thanks for chaperoning. Are you off to Blockley in the morning?"

"I'm afraid so."

Elisabeth sighed. "Perhaps I should go with you."

Abby frowned and shook her head. "I wouldn't hear of it! You're still convalescing. You are well out of that awful place. I can't wait to be free of it."

Elisabeth's mind went back to the day she learned of Amy's death. She took a deep breath and sighed. "Perhaps you're right, Abby."

Abby quickly changed the subject. "Thanks for suggesting that Jerry and I go home for a while. We're really looking forward to it. Our only regret is leaving you here alone."

"I'll be fine. Go with my blessing."

After Abby had gone, Elisabeth sat lost in thought. *It's a long time from now until October. I'm not sure how to be a lady of leisure. What shall I do to fill my time? I suppose I should hire some servants. I wonder if Maggie has decided to emigrate? It would be wonderful to have her here. I'll write to her and invite her over. Mr. Dawes has already sent the passage money to her.*

Elisabeth cast her mind back to all the things that had happened to her since joining the Church. She could see a pattern of blessings and trials and wondered if the result of these twin forces had made her a better person. She finally decided that others would have to judge. For now, her job was to adjust to being a woman of wealth and to figure out how to fill the long months until October.

Kneeling beside her chair, she prayed for help. Afterwards, she resumed her letter writing. Partway through a letter to Maggie, something triggered a remembrance of her conversation with Lady Brideswell aboard the *Polar Star*. She stopped writing and went over the conversation in her mind. Lady Brideswell had said that an annulment might be possible but that it would take a lot of money to hire a barrister and buy the influence needed to be successful. "I have a lot of money!" she said aloud.

The idea of again pursuing an annulment fastened onto Elisabeth's mind. Lady Brideswell had said that the times were changing, that the threat of the government encroaching on church power had made the councils more amenable, that she and Sir Anthony would use their influence, that Elisabeth appearing personally before the council would be much more effective than a mere letter, that . . .

Exhilarated, Elisabeth ran from the library to find Lady Brideswell's card. She found it in her handbag and quickly returned to the library. Pushing Maggie's letter aside—perhaps she would see Maggie in person—she grabbed a new sheet of paper and began a letter to Lady Brideswell. The words seemed to flow unbidden. Suddenly, she stopped writing. *Papa told me that under no conditions should I return to England. Could Claverley sue me for desertion and the "theft" of the fifty pounds? Could he use the courts to take away my new fortune?*

For a moment she hesitated. Then, casting aside her doubts, she finished the letter and sealed it. This done, she went upstairs and prepared for bed. But sleep was not possible in her state of excitement. *I wonder how long it will take to get a reply? The new steamships make the crossing in as little as ten days. Twenty days plus a few days at either end would make a month. Could I really know in as soon as a month whether or not I'm going back to England? In the meantime, how can I prepare for a positive response from Lady Brideswell? I'll go see Mr. Dawes to arrange for the money. Perhaps he can also put me in touch with someone about the steamship schedules. What else need I do? Perhaps I should finish my letter to Maggie and tell her I might be coming . . . No, I'd better wait until I hear from Lady Brideswell. It will be so exciting to travel on a steamship and see England again. And if I do go, some of the long months between now and October will be filled. Should I return to Blockley while I'm waiting? No. The memory of Amy's death is still too fresh.*

"You're really considering going to England?" Abby asked next morning as the two breakfasted. "How exciting! Perhaps Jerry and I should postpone our trip home so that we can look after the place."

"Oh, no. I wouldn't hear of it. John can handle things here. Perhaps I'll hire some servants to help him. You and Jerry should go home as planned. Of course, it will be awhile before I hear from Lady Brideswell, and there is the possibility that she'll advise against my going. But the inspiration to write her came after prayer, so I anticipate a positive response."

Surprisingly, the next month went by quickly. On the hope that Lady Brideswell's letter would be positive, Elisabeth kept busy preparing for her trip to England. She found time to hire a part-time housekeeper, a Mrs. McCandless, a slightly plump widow in her early forties who had four children at home. Elisabeth engaged Mrs. McCandless not only because of her references but also because of her pleasant smile and gentle manner. John was especially pleased with Elisabeth's choice.

Shipping line brochures and schedules piled up on the library table as Elisabeth researched the best way to get to England. A company with a marathon name, British and North American Royal Mail and Steam Packet Company, that sent packages and cargo from New York to Liverpool, she discovered, had the fastest ships and best value for the money. Not that she had to worry about money, but she had never been extravagant and didn't intend to change.

"Are you sure you don't want us to stay until you hear from England, Elisabeth?" Abby asked one day at the beginning of April.

Elisabeth shook her head. "You need to go now before traveling becomes a worse chore. At six months on, it will be unpleasant enough for you on that long steam train and stagecoach ride. Or have you decided to take the boat from Harrisburg?"

Abby nodded. "Yes. We're going to take the boat to Duncannon and then hire a buggy to takes us the rest of the way. In my condition I'm afraid using shank's mare is no longer a possibility."

Elisabeth smiled. "Oh, how I'm going to miss you and Jerry."

Next morning, Elisabeth saw Abby and Jerry off. After the baggage was loaded in the carriage, Elisabeth hugged her two friends and handed Jerry a leather drawstring purse. "Here's a little something to make your journey more pleasant and to tide you over until I see you in September. Have a wonderful time at home. Remember me to everyone."

Abby looked at the purse. Tears moistened her eyes. "Elisabeth, you shouldn't spoil us. You've already been more than generous, paying for our journey and all."

"Think nothing of it. As Mrs. Kenny once said, what's the use of having money if you can't do some good with it? Now, you two go and God be with you. I look forward with great anticipation to seeing you and the baby in the fall. Thanks for all the work you've done on the house and grounds, Jerry."

Jerry nodded. "Thank you, Elisabeth, for all you've done for us. If it hadn't been for you . . . well, I would have made a great mistake."

Later that day Elisabeth sat alone in the small parlor feeling a little sorrow for herself. *It seems that everyone I love leaves me. Oh, well,* she forced herself to brighten, *I'll soon hear from Lady Brideswell and life's next challenge will present itself.*

The thought had no sooner flitted through her mind than Mrs. McCandless entered the room. She held up a letter and smiled. "I think you've been expecting this, Miss Elisabeth."

Elisabeth's heart leapt. She quickly opened the letter and read:

My Dear Elisabeth,

> *What a pleasant surprise to hear from you after all these months. I trust that you are well and that your term of medical studies was successful. Sir Anthony and I have enjoyed our time at home, although he is already planning another jaunt abroad. I think this time I shall let him go by himself.*
>
> *As to your request, I've consulted our family barrister, and although it is not a strictly legal matter, he is sanguine about an appeal. Because of his increasingly reprehensible behaviour, Lord Claverley's influence has diminished considerably of late. It is*

rumoured that he has run up huge debts for which he does not have the ability to pay. Since his mistress decamped, he has become even more addicted to liquid solace.

Mrs. Caroline Norton, whom we discussed on the boat, and her supporters are making great headway in changing public opinion in favour of the rights of married women. The social climate is even more amenable to your plight than it was when we talked.

So, my dear, please come ahead. You will, of course, stay with us at our home in the country and make use of our flat in London as needed.

The fastest way to England is the route via New York to Liverpool. If you do not have an alternate arrangement, please telegraph us when you land and we will arrange for you to get to us.

All best wishes,
Amelia

By the time she had finished the letter, Elisabeth's heart was racing. It was all that she had hoped for. She reread it and stared at Lady Brideswell's signature. *"Amelia." What a pretty name. How wonderful that she would go to all this trouble for one she hardly knows. The world is certainly full of good people. My mind is made up. Yes, Amelia, I'm coming to England!*

Elated, she hurried into the library and once again perused the steamship brochures. She was pleased to discover that the steamship *Franconia* was scheduled to sail from New York in only five days. Boarding time was 7:00 P.M. Checking a railroad schedule, she learned that the New York train left Philadelphia at noon and arrived at 4:00 P.M.

That evening she lay in bed and thought about her trip and about Gren. Should she go to New York a day early and visit him? Would she be able to leave America if she saw him again? Would her resolve weaken? After a long time she decided that she would forgo seeing him until she returned to America either a free woman or . . . or what? She didn't know. What she did know was that she couldn't stand another parting from the one she had come to love with all her heart. Rather, she would write to him and mail the letter before she embarked. By the time he got it, she would be on her way and it would be too late for her to change her mind. *How I wish that Mrs. Kenny and Abby were here to advise me!*

* * *

Elisabeth decided to go a day early anyway, and over the next three days she prepared to leave. First, she pressed Mr. Dawes into service to arrange her financial affairs and to book her passage on the *Franconia* via the telegraph system. Then, with the help of her new housekeeper, she packed. On the morning of the fourth day, Mrs. McCandless accompanied her to the train station in the carriage; they were driven by the ever-faithful John.

A little over four hours later, Elisabeth, carrying a purse and a small carpetbag, stepped onto the platform of the busy New York train station. Her other luggage would be transferred from the train to the ship. She stood on the platform for a moment to orient herself as a train puffed into the station and halted at the other side of the platform. Suddenly her heart fluttered and excitement swept through her. Were her eyes deceiving her? Was that Gren at the other end of the platform? *How did he know I was coming—Why is he going toward the other train?* Her unspoken question was quickly answered when a fashionably dressed young woman emerged from the train into Gren's arms. Elisabeth gasped and her hand went to her mouth. For a brief moment she hoped that she had been mistaken, that it was not Gren; but even from a distance she recognized the woman. She had seen her at the groundbreaking ceremony in Great Salt Lake City.

Elisabeth sank onto a bench as a knot in her stomach tightened. Uncontrollable tears wet her face.

"Are you not well, miss?" said a kindly voice. "May I be of service?"

She looked up to see a porter. Wiping her eyes with her handkerchief, she arose. "I'll be all right now, thank you," she said. "The spell has passed. I'll be catching a ship in the morning. Can you recommend a hotel for the night?"

"Yes, miss. the Phoenix. Would you like me to get you a carriage?"

Elisabeth nodded. Taking the carpetbag from her, the man escorted her out of the station. Numbly, she alighted from the carriage in front of a dress-and-millinery shop adjacent to the Hotel Phoenix. In the hotel room she threw herself onto the bed and again wept bitterly. When she could cry no more, she sat up, mechanically unlaced and removed her shoes, and, propping herself against the pillows, stared into space.

Once more, it seemed, she had made a colossal misjudgment regarding men. She had lost Jonathan Kimball to a younger, prettier woman, and now Gren had followed suit. *How could we enjoy such a wonderful relationship whilst all the while he had a relationship with this other woman?* She couldn't answer this question. As she thought about it, her practical side went to Gren's defense. *I can't lose what I never had. Why shouldn't he have a relationship with another woman? You've constantly said that you have no claim on him. You're the one who told him to find someone else. You're the one with a husband. Why shouldn't Gren pursue a younger woman who dresses attractively? What right do you have to judge him?*

Through force of will, she turned her thoughts to a world without Gren. What lay ahead for her in England? Was it possible that she could be thrown into jail for deserting Claverley and taking his money without his express permission? Could she be transported to Australia for her "crimes?" She smiled wryly when she recalled that Australia suffered from a shortage of women. Perhaps Brother Nilsson's blessing of her having a husband and children would come to pass in Australia, where a lonely sheepherder would find value in a thirty-one year-old spinster!

With a sigh, she finally got up, poured water from a China jug into a matching basin, and washed her face. Sitting down at a dresser, she stared at herself in the mirror. *Face it, Elisabeth, you've lost your prime. Your face is too pale from constantly having your nose in a book, your hair in a bun is anything but stylish, and your clothes are out of fashion.*

Her mind turned to the clothing she had packed for her trip. *Now that I have the money, the least I can do is buy some new clothes. I can't be seen with Lady Brideswell in a dress like this.*

Quickly pulling on and lacing her shoes, she went downstairs and out the door. For several minutes she stood on the pavement and studied the fashionable hats and dresses in the shop window. An elderly woman greeted her as she entered the shop. "And how can I be of service, miss?"

"Tomorrow I'm leaving for England. Please show me your most up-to-date frocks."

Three new dresses were only the beginning of her purchases. By the time she had finished shopping, she had purchased several pairs of white lisle stockings, two pairs of leather slip-on shoes, two poke bonnets, and a cream-colored summer coat. She returned to the hotel piled high with packages. Before going to her room, she asked the desk clerk about hairdressers.

"I can have one in your room within the hour," the desk clerk said. And he did.

"How would you like it, miss?" the young woman asked.

Elisabeth shook her head. "I have no idea. I am in your hands."

After the hairdresser had gone, Elisabeth studied her coiffure in the mirror from all angles. Ringlets framed her face, and a chignon graced the back of her head. She was pleased with her new look. The knot in her stomach was still there, but it had loosened somewhat. Later she wore a new outfit when she went down to the hotel restaurant, and the admiring stares helped boost her confidence. She would have to remember exactly how to do her hair in the morning, and take special care not to wrinkle her dress, she noted.

The next afternoon found her on a hard bench in the waiting room of the steamship company. In her hand was the letter she had written to Gren before leaving Philadelphia. *Should I still mail it?* She sighed and closed her eyes in thought.

"English paper, ma'am? Fresh off the boat yestiddy." Elisabeth's eyes blinked open. Before her stood a ragged newsboy, the stockingless toes of his left foot sticking out of his shoe. "Learn what's goin' on in London before you gets there, ma'am."

Elisabeth smiled at the boy. "I'll take one." She rummaged in her purse and handed him a dollar. "Keep the change."

His eyes lit up. "Thank you, ma'am. Thank you kindly."

Elisabeth was in the act of placing the *London Times* on the bench beside her when the word "Claverley" leapt from the front page. With trembling hands she read the headline: "Lord Claverley of Somerset Dead at Fifty-Seven." Round-eyed, she scanned the brief article. Claverley had been found shot to death in an alley in Soho near a notorious gambling house. The item went on to say that he had no survivors except for an estranged wife who had fled to America several years before, that he had died deeply in debt, and that his estate had been attached by creditors.

Stunned, Elisabeth closed her eyes, took a deep breath, and slowly exhaled. *It's over! At long last, it's over.* Tears pooled in her eyes. The irony that she was suddenly free and that Gren had found another was almost more than she could bear. But then her thoughts left Gren and, strangely, a feeling of compassion for Claverley flowed through her—compassion for this man who had died alone in an alley without anyone to mourn his passing. Suddenly she identified with his loneliness. Covering her eyes with her gloved hands, she wept.

"Y'okay, ma'am? Y'look a mite peaky."

Elisabeth opened her eyes and stared through her tears at the newsboy. "I'll be fine. Thank you for your concern. Will you do me a service?"

"Aye, ma'am."

"Please find me a carriage whilst I take care of some business."

He nodded and hurried off. By the time he returned, Elisabeth had canceled her ticket and had arranged for her luggage to be shipped back to Philadelphia. The boy led her to the waiting carriage.

She handed him a coin. "Thank you, young man. This is for you."

The boy's eyes bulged out of his head and his mouth fell open. "A eagle!"

Elisabeth nodded. "Ten dollars is little enough for the news you've brought me. Buy yourself some clothes, especially some new shoes." With the coin clutched in his fist, the boy thanked Elisabeth over and over before running off down the street.

"Where to, miss?" the driver asked.

She had missed the morning train to Philadelphia, so was about to have the driver take her back to the Phoenix Hotel when she found herself saying, "Please take me to where they're publishing the Mormon newspaper."

* * *

George Taylor looked up and leapt to his feet when Elisabeth entered the newspaper office. "Sister Ashcroft! How good to see you!" he said, wiping his ink-stained hands with a cloth. "You look wonderful." He glanced at the *London Times* under her arm and nodded. "You've seen the news. Gren found out yesterday when the *Franconia* got in."

"Where is he?"

George smiled. "Off to Philadelphia on the morning steam train, where else?"

Bewilderment clouded her face. "Why?"

"Why?" Bewilderment now showed on George's face. "To see you, of course. Don't you know he's madly in love with you?"

Elisabeth felt faint. "May I sit down?"

George grabbed a chair. "I'm sorry. How rude of me."

Elisabeth sat for a moment, unable to speak. When she finally found the words, she said. "George, I'm completely confused. Yesterday I saw Gren at the train station in the arms of another woman. Please explain to me what is going on."

George smiled, pulled up a chair, and sat across from Elisabeth. "Gren was at the train station to meet his favorite cousin, Flora Reynolds. She's been staying with relatives in Boston while waiting for her husband to return from his mission in England. He got in yesterday on the *Franconia*. Gren picked Flora up at the station and went with her to meet the ship. Flora and her husband were married just before he went on his mission, so they're spending a honeymoon hereabouts before returning home."

Elisabeth gave a relieved sigh. "What a silly goose I've been! I thought . . . well, never mind. When is the next train to Philadelphia?"

"Not until tomorrow morning—but I have more good news."

"More good news?"

"Yes. Did he write you that the New Orleans route has been abandoned in favor of the Atlantic ports?"

Elisabeth nodded. "He did. When he was in Philadelphia he met with Colonel Kane about some of the immigrants coming by way of Philadelphia."

"That's right. Gren's been appointed Church agent for the city. His job will be to help the immigrants get to Utah. When we heard the news about Lord Claverley last night, my father immediately released Gren from his mission and appointed him Church agent." He grinned impishly. "Now there's nothing stopping Gren from courting you!"

A soft rose color crept over her cheeks as she slowly shook her head. "I can't believe the long wait is over. Thank you, George. I'll stay at the Phoenix Hotel again tonight and catch the train in the morning. Please give my regards to your father."

The next morning she was in good time for the train. Admiring glances from fellow travelers assured her that she had done well in preparing to meet Gren as a free woman. She found a seat in the ladies' car and, filled with a delicious expectancy, settled in for the four-hour journey. When she finally stepped out of the car at the Philadelphia station, laden with her handbag, carpetbag, and packages, her heart beat rapidly and her breath came in short bursts. She started down the platform and suddenly froze. Gren was at the far end. Freeing a hand, she waved to him. He looked straight at her and then turned away. Immediately he turned back and, even at a distance, Elisabeth could see the wonder on his face. For a moment they both stood transfixed. Then, heedless of the others on the crowded platform, they began moving toward each other, slowly at first, but gradually increasing in speed. A few feet from him, she cast aside her belongings and threw herself into his outstretched arms. She could feel the beating of his heart . . . or was it her heart, or both hearts beating as one? For a long time they clung to each other, and then their lips came together. For the first time in her life, pure, unfettered joy pulsed through her being. When Gren finally released her, she was so weak she could hardly stand. It was as if her telestial body had experienced a sensation reserved only for celestial beings.

Full of love, Gren gazed into her eyes. "I . . . I didn't recognize you. You're even more lovely . . . are you all right, sweetheart?"

Elisabeth took a deep breath and nodded. "I've never been more all right in my life, but you've taken my breath away. May I sit down for a moment?"

He led her to a bench and then retrieved her abandoned belongings. Sitting beside her, he said, "I'm so glad you got the news before you boarded the ship. I was frantic until I got George's telegraph message."

"So that's why you're here. I couldn't imagine how you knew I was coming. Oh, Gren, I love you with all my heart."

"And I love you, Elisabeth, more than words can tell."

Arm in arm they left the train station and were soon heading home in John's carriage. Mrs. McCandless met them in the foyer and then excused herself to attend to lunch. Elisabeth took Gren's hand and led him into the small parlor. They sat together on one of the two sofas. Gren opened his arms and she cuddled up to him. She could have spent forever in the safety of his arms.

"I don't want you ever to leave me again," she said.

Gren sighed. "I'm afraid we'll have to part soon."

Elisabeth moved far enough away so that she could see his face. "Part soon? I thought you had been appointed Church agent for Philadelphia?"

He slowly nodded. "True. But my new calling is to escort the immigrants to Utah. I'll have to be going within the month. After organizing them here, we'll head west to a staging area at Hickory Grove in the new territory of Kansas. We'll form a wagon train, and I'll travel with it to the valley."

A crease crossed Elisabeth's brow as her mind digested this information. Finally, she pursed her lips and shook her head. "You're not going home without me, Gren Sanderson!"

Gren gazed into her face for a moment and seeing the determination there, said, "No. I don't believe I am. But what about medical school? Didn't Dr. Longshore invite you to return to the college in the fall as a graduate student? Would you give up such an opportunity?"

Elisabeth squeezed his arm. "To be with you, yes. Over these past months I've learned much that I can use back home. But now that I'm free, my dearest wish is to have a family." She paused and smiled. "That is, if I can find someone to marry me."

Gren smiled and got down on one knee. He took her hand in both of his. "Elisabeth, will you marry me immediately, if not sooner?"

The smile gradually left her face. She didn't want to extinguish the light in his eyes, but she knew she must, if only for a moment. Slowly, she shook her head. "No."

"No!" echoed John and Mrs. McCandless, who had been shamelessly eavesdropping at the open door. Elisabeth and Gren turned toward them. They quickly apologized and left.

Gren turned back and stared at Elisabeth in disbelief.

Elisabeth smiled wanly. "No, Gren, I will not marry you immediately—not until we're home in Zion, where we can be sealed for eternity. This time I want to do it right."

Gren breathed a huge sigh of relief. "Of course. As ever, you are right. Let me try this again." Once more he took her hand in his. "Sister Elisabeth Ashcroft, will you do me the honor of being sealed to me in the new and everlasting covenant of marriage in the new Endowment House in Great Salt Lake City, Utah Territory . . . at your earliest convenience?"

"I will," she said, tears coursing down her cheeks as she opened her arms to him. "I will gladly."

Their lips came together for a second time, and again Elisabeth relished the joy of long-awaited love.

CHAPTER THIRTY-FIVE

By early June, Gren and other Church leaders had shepherded a large party of immigrant Saints from Philadelphia to Hickory Grove, Kansas Territory. It had been a long haul: 350 miles from Philadelphia to Pittsburgh by rail; 1,200 from Pittsburgh to St. Louis by boat via the Ohio and Mississippi Rivers; 500 miles from St. Louis to Atchison by boat via the Missouri River; and 5 miles by wagon from Atchison to the staging grounds at Hickory Grove—2,055 miles in all. Now, the reinvigorated Saints were preparing for the last leg of their journey, 1,000 miles by wagon from Hickory Grove to the Valley of the Great Salt Lake.

"All is well in the camp," said Gren as he joined Elisabeth beside her campfire. "I thought you'd be asleep by now."

"I was reading until the light failed," she said, indicating the Bible that lay beside her. "I was hoping that you would stop over to see me after your inspection."

With a great deal of ceremony, Gren presented her with a walking stick.

"What's this?"

"It's a hickory cane to remind you of this place, Hickory Grove, although people are beginning to call it Mormon Grove. Well, sweetheart, how are you feeling? Are you ready to begin the last stage of our westward trek?"

"I couldn't be better. In part, thanks to this beautiful wagon. It couldn't be nicer. Thanks for commissioning it."

"Glad you like it. It was built by the best wainwright in the City of Kansas. Nothing but the best for you, my love."

Elisabeth smiled her thanks. "It will be good to be on our way tomorrow. Although I'm glad for our time in the East—I wouldn't have missed it for anything—all this turmoil over slavery scares me. It's threatening to ignite the civil war foretold by the Prophet Joseph. Did I tell you I discussed that prophecy with Mrs. Kenny?" Gren shook his head. "I told her that it would surely come to pass."

Gren nodded. "No doubt about it. Even though the Saints' being driven from Nauvoo was a terrible thing, it may be a blessing in disguise. When war eventually rages in the East, we will be safe in the valleys of the mountains."

Elisabeth agreed. "But I fear for Abby, Jerry, and the baby—and for all the friends we made in the East." She sighed deeply as she contemplated the future. Then she had a happier thought. "Perhaps the Potts will be with us in Utah someday."

After a pause, Gren asked, "Are you sure you're not sorry about returning west without a medical degree?"

"A little. I did consider accepting Dr. Longshore's offer. But being with you far outweighed my desire to be the first Mormon woman to get a medical degree. I'm happy to leave that distinction to a future Latter-day Saint sister. And you, love, are you sorry your mission was cut short?"

He shook his head. "Once we started publishing the newspaper, I felt the major goal of my mission was accomplished. Still, despite Elder Taylor's brilliant articles, the opposition to plural marriage is mounting. Who knows where it will end?"

Elisabeth sighed. "No doubt the coming years will be full of tears as well as joy for the Saints. The tears I shed over the deaths of Amy and Mrs. Kenny and Dr. Osgood were swallowed up in the joy of my being free to declare my love. I wonder what other trials and blessings await . . . I just thought of something." She picked up her Bible and quickly leafed through it. "Here it is," she said, taking a piece of paper from between the pages.

"What's that?"

"Mrs. Kenny's note. I think I finally discovered what it says. Yes, I'm sure of it. It's a scriptural reference. The squiggly lines in front of the numbers read 'Psalm.' See? It refers to Psalm thirty, verse five." She quickly turned to the passage, then, smiling through the tears that had sprung unbidden to her eyes, she read it aloud, 'For his anger endureth but a moment; in his favor is life: weeping may endure for a night, but joy cometh in the morning.'"

Gren moved closer to Elisabeth and wrapped her in his arms. "I'll be there to comfort you through all the weeping nights and delight with you in all the joyful mornings."

Elisabeth's faced glowed. As warm and protecting as Gren's arms were, the fire flowing through her was even greater. The Spirit whispered that soon they would be one for time and all eternity, and whatever tear-filled nights awaited them they would face together. She had no doubt that when the greatest of all mornings dawned, they would bask in its glory together and that their joy would be eternal.

Notes on Sources

As the name suggests, historical fiction blends fact and fiction. When a story finally gets into print, it is difficult for the reader to know which is which. In this and other novels, I've tried to be as true to history as possible. For example, when I mention gaslights, the telegraph system, Pitman shorthand, etc., the reader can be assured that these developments actually were in use in the 1850s. Similarly, the theory of organic evolution predated Darwin's publication of *The Origin of the Species* (1859), and Karl Marx's oft-quoted line "Religion is the opiate of the masses" was penned ten years before my fictional character uses it.

I won't attempt to list all of the sources for *Elisabeth: Passage of Promise,* but I would like to acknowledge my debt to two LDS sources: The *Diary of Jean Rio Griffiths Baker* and the *Journal of George Taylor.* Jean Baker's diary gave me the frame for Elisabeth's 1851 journey from Liverpool to New Orleans on the sailing ship *George W. Bourne* and the subsequent overland trek to the Salt Lake Valley. The Sister Brenton of the novel is loosely based on Sister Baker. Similarly, George Taylor's account of his journey from the Salt Lake Valley to New York City in 1854, with his father and fellow missionaries, provided me with the frame for Elisabeth and Gren's trip to the East. Caroline Gilliam actually was one of two women traveling with the missionary wagon train. Both journals are gold mines of historical information.

I also owe a debt to the writings of and about Dr. Elizabeth Blackwell, the first woman to receive a medical degree in the United States. Dr. Blackwell was a prolific writer. The information on Blockley Hospital and Almshouse came mainly from Dr. Blackwell's autobiography, *Pioneer Work in Opening the Medical Profession to Women.* The information on the Female Medical College of Pennsylvania (later the Woman's [sic] Medical College) came mostly from *History of the Woman's Medical College, Philadelphia, Pennsylvania, 1850–1950* by Gulielma Fell Alsop. To a lesser extent, I gleaned information from Latter-day Saint Dr. Ellis Shipp's account of her time at the Woman's Medical College in the 1870s, twenty years after the setting of this novel.

President Brigham Young's view of professional doctors as depicted in this novel is historically accurate; however, his views changed as the practice of medicine changed. Thus, by the early 1870s he was encouraging Latter-day Saints to go east for medical training. This encouragement extended to women, resulting in Romania B. Pratt, Ellis R. Shipp, and Martha Hughes Paul earning medical degrees in the East. The latter fact gave me the idea for sending my protagonist to do likewise. Not wishing to steal their thunder, however, I shaped the plot so that Elisabeth Ashcroft would not actually get a degree.

My three goals in writing LDS novels are to teach the principles of the restored gospel of Jesus Christ, to illuminate lesser-known, favorable elements of Church history, and to strengthen testimonies. If *Elisabeth: Passage of Promise* does this to any degree and in an entertaining way, my time will have been well spent.

About the Author

Tom Roulstone was born in Donegal, Ireland. With his parents and two brothers, he immigrated to Canada, landing at Halifax on his thirteenth birthday. He joined The Church of Jesus Christ of Latter-day Saints in Toronto when he was eighteen and served a mission in western Canada. He and his late wife Betsy have six children. He has a B.A. in history from Brigham Young University and an M.A. in history from Utah State University.

After teaching college history for almost a quarter of a century, Tom took early retirement in 2000 to pursue a writing career. *Passage of Promise* is his third LDS novel. He now resides in Parksville, B.C., on Vancouver Island.